The Sound of Sirens

An Inspector Walter Darriteau Murder Mystery

David Carter

TrackerDog Media

The Sound of Sirens

An Inspector Walter Darriteau Murder Mystery

© David Carter & TrackerDog Media 2017

ISBN: 978-1482307726
Updated and revised June 2021

The right of David Carter to be identified as the author of this work
has been asserted by him in accordance with the
Copyright, Designs and Patents Act of 1988
All rights reserved

This is a work of fiction. Any resemblance to real persons, living or
dead, is coincidental
Follow David on Twitter @TheBookBloke
Contact David via his website:
www.davidcarterbooks.co.uk

In Memoriam

Hazel Elsie Louisa Carter, nee Adshead
1924-1996

Much missed, never forgotten

Chapter One

The young man hid in the shadows, cigarette in hand. Moonless night, dry too, a hint of June balminess in the air. He thought he heard someone coming and peeked out from the disused shop entrance. He was right.

He had heard someone, but not the man he was waiting for. Pulled back into the shop doorway, took a drag on the fag. The stranger ambled by on the other side of the road, yanked along by a short-sighted Alsatian dog.

There was music in the air, soft rock, slipping from the Friday night pub across the way, drifting down the road, floating across the river, vibrating through the city.

Another man came round the corner. This time, the right man, an older guy wearing an expensive tweed cap, carrying a packet. He walked fast toward the doorway where the young man was taking one last suck on the ciggie, before tossing it to the ground and dancing it out. The older guy stopped in the doorway, right up close, peered through the darkness at the young guy. Said, 'You ready?'

The young bloke nodded. Didn't speak.

The older guy handed him the packet. It wasn't sealed, just folded over at the flap end, and said, 'It's the tall white guy, the guitarist, lead singer; you can't miss him.'

The young bloke grabbed the packet and nodded and said, 'When do I get paid?'

'When you deliver the goods.'

'Tomorrow?'

'OK, two o'clock, by the clock.'

'I'll be there.'

'Don't muck up!' the old guy said, and he turned around and walked smartly away.

1

The young guy opened the packet. Took out the handgun. Gleamed in the moonlight. Nice piece. Easy in the hand. Easy on the trigger. Not too large, not too small. Slipped it in the right blouson pocket. Stepped out of the shadows. Headed toward the pub.

The music was getting louder, reaching a climax, the end of the song, the end of the session, it had gone eleven and the live music licence expired at eleven o'clock.

Sissy Burke, the licensee nodded at the boys to stop. She'd already had one warning from the police about over-running, and she didn't want another. Her licence was at stake.

Sweat was pouring down the lead singer's face. Half a dozen pretty girls were hanging about, sipping the last of their drinks, glancing at the singer, seeking eye contact, looking for recognition, hoping to get lucky. His straight black hair was sticking together, plastered to his forehead. He was very sweaty, but still cool.

He needed a pee.

He needed a wash.

'Hey, Jeff,' he said, 'hold my guitar a mo, I'm going to the bog.'

Jeff jumped on the stage. It was more of a platform, set at one end of the lounge bar. He'd been angling to join ALL SOULS for weeks. Thought his big moment had arrived. Grabbed the guitar and stood at the mic and glanced at the other guys. Imagined himself on lead vocal. Imagined himself on lead guitar. Imagined the women staring at him in the way they looked at Neil. Jeff felt good; grinned and began strumming the guitar.

Sissy shot him a look. Glanced her displeasure at the others. They shrugged their shoulders and looked away. It was nothing to do with them. Jeff caught the mood and stopped strumming, began composing a silent song in his head.

The young guy walked into the pub. It was still pretty full. The music had stopped but the conversation was bubbling. Friday night and the weekend starts here, lots of smart guys hanging about, gaggles of pretty women in sophisticated weekend frocks, sexy summer shorts, tight jeans and tiny skirts, some drinking, some laughing, some joking, some planning on getting a burger, some planning on getting laid, some wanting to be sick, some holding empty glasses and discussing where they were going next, some checking on their remaining funds, some checking in their bags for their ciggies and tabs and lighters they would bring out the moment they were outside.

The young guy made his way through the bar toward the makeshift stage. All four ALL SOULS were there. The Asian guy on drums, packing his sticks away, the Chinese guy polishing his violin, the mean looking black guy holding his trumpet down by his side, trying to look cool, trying to connect with the women, not wanting to go home alone, and the long lanky piece of shit in the middle, the white guy, the lead singer and guitarist, with a distant look on his face, and a price on his head.

Pulled the gun from his pocket, pointed it at the white guy's torso, no second thoughts, let go four shots in quick succession, one, two, three, four, as if he was about to launch into a classic sixties rock song.

At the sound of the first shot a moment of stunned disbelief crashed through the bar. Someone was playing a joke, right? A second of silence. Then screaming and yelling broke out, and looks of disbelief at the sight of the guitarist blown on his back, bleeding, still clutching the guitar, not moving a muscle, eyes wide open, staring out in disbelief, not comprehending what had happened, hurting, shocked, and dying on his back like a beached and injured turtle.

The young guy turned round, waved the smoking gun at the crowded bar. Girls screamed, parted like the Red Sea. He grinned and walked through the valley of death and out into the balmy night, gaining speed as he went, hurrying round the corner, the hot gun back in his pocket, his neat new car just up the road. One minute later and he had vanished into the night, laughing as he went.

3

Neil had been washing his hands when he heard the first shot. Thought it was some kind of prank. Heard the second and third and fourth. Some racket, some joke. Shook his hands dry and ran outside.

The girls were still screaming; the boys looking shocked, dazed and confused. Some were calling the police on their mobiles, some calling their friends and family. Some idiots were taking pictures of dead Jeff, bloodied and on his back, couldn't wait to get them on their Bookface site before anyone else. Live murder in graphic colour, online and fresh. It's amazing what the modern world offered, you wouldn't believe it!

Neil ran to the stage. Couldn't comprehend what he saw. His guitar was ruined. Two slugs gone clean through it; right through dopey Jeff as well; and clean into the wall at the back.

'Who did it?' asked Neil.

'Never seen him before,' said the black guy, 'some young white piece of shit.'

Neil glanced at the other two. They pursed their lips and shook their heads and peered down at dead Jeff. What the hell was going on?

The sound of sirens floated in through the door. Police? Ambulance? Maybe both. Sissy was bent over the bar, crying. She'd lose her licence, she was certain of that, and she had big bills to pay, and bigger loans to service, and some from not so nice people.

Some guys who didn't want to be interviewed by the coppers were scurrying away. But too late.

The cops were already there, surrounding the place.

Two armed response units, plus four unarmed officers, rounding everybody up, setting up temporary barriers, tapes across the exits, keeping the nosey parkers out, keeping the witnesses in. No one would be allowed to leave until their details had been taken and checked, and until their initial witness statements had been heard.

One dizzy ginger girl said, 'I know that guy, he used to live on the estate.'

The bloke she was with said, 'Trust me, Sharon, you don't know him.'

4

'I bloody well do!'

The guy took her arm and squeezed it hard and said, 'He works for...' and he leant over and whispered the rest in ginger's ear.

Her brow furrowed and she said aloud, 'Yeah, you're right, Billy, I was mistaken, never seen the guy before.'

Chapter Two

Walter Darriteau had just finished his late meal. He hadn't been in the house long. Chicken chow mein. Ready meal job, one of the better ones. Ready meals were improving, and not before time, even if they were two to three times more fattening than your traditional meat and two veg.

He ambled back to the kitchen. Emptied the detritus, the cardboard cover, the plastic tray, the stained clear top, into the chrome kick bin. His cleaner was coming in the morning and he didn't want to be dirty and untidy for her.

Galina Unpronounceable was her name, Polish or Byelorussian, or Ukrainian, she was, something like that, one of those eastern European races where Europe thought about becoming Asia. Not an illegal, not our Galina, not working in Walter's house, no way. That would not have gone down well. He'd seen the proof. He'd seen the papers. Her real surname was full of w's and z's and c's and s's with nary a vowel in sight. Hopeless to him, he couldn't begin to say it.

She was a good kid though. Tall and slim and blonde and blue-eyed and hardworking. Did two straight hours every Saturday morning for a few pennies more than the minimum wage, worked like a maniac when she was in the house, never stopped once, even when Walter begged her to slow down and take a coffee with him.

Let herself in with the key under the stone if he didn't open the door. When she first came Walter left cash lying around as bait. Not a thing went missing, not a penny, and he felt guilty afterwards at trying to trap her, but the police officer in him would never go away.

She thought Walter was doing her a big favour, and she liked the man, and she liked his house. Couldn't believe he was a policeman.

Laughed her head off when she discovered that. Thought he was joking when he first told her.

'Really? A black detective, in England? How strange!'

He was thinking of watching a Spike Lee movie. He was thinking of going to bed. Couldn't decide which. He'd toss a coin. Heads bed, tails tales.

Walter glanced at his image reflecting back from the new window recently fitted in his kitchen. No one would ever get through that, bragged the salesman, dead locks and steel bolts that went straight into the wall. It had cost him an arm and a leg, but Walter didn't care about that, just so long as it kept the bloody burglars at bay.

He grabbed a damp cloth and began wiping down the worktops. Strange thing was his house was a lot cleaner than it had been for years, even before Galina came in the morning. Perhaps he was ashamed of inviting a foreigner into a dirty home; perhaps he was trying to impress her.

She was thirty, almost half his age; but he knew it would take more than a gleaming kitchen to impress Galina Unpronounceable.

The old phone in the hallway rang.

Who the hell was that at this hour?

An even money bet.

Had to be a wrong number... or work.

He hoped it would be work.

He always hoped it would be work.

It was indeed work.

Walter liked that, and smiled a smile that no one would ever see.

'Sorry to bother you,' said Karen, his sergeant.

'What are you doing working at this time of night?'

'Gibbons called me in. It's only a couple of minutes from my flat.'

'What's happened?'

'There's been an incident down by the river, The Ship Inn, some guy's been shot.'

'Is he on his way to hospital?'

'Too late for that, Guv. Morgue candidate.'

'Oh!' That surprised Walter, and he took a moment out.

She jumped into the vacuum and said, 'I'm going down there now. Do you want me to pick you up?'

'What do you think?'

'Thought so. I'll see you in five.'

Just enough time to swig mouthwash and find his shoes and cover the hole in his sock, and slip on a light jacket, and when he went to the front window and peered through the crack in the curtains, in the moonlight Karen was already there, pulling the unmarked BMW to a halt outside.

He went out and locked the front door and eased into the car. Karen pulled away and headed for the river.

'Know any more?' he asked.

'Not much, armed response are already there. Place packed apparently. Some guy came in and blew the singer away, member of the band, lead guitar or something.'

Walter resisted making a crack about the poor choice of music, or the crap playing, and stared ahead and already they could see pulsing blue light swirling around the roofs of the old buildings at the end of the narrow road.

He knew The Ship well, used to go there himself, but fell out of love with the place when it was taken over by the twenty somethings and their shouty louty music.

A minute later and Walter and Karen were walking through the bar. The uniforms were busy taking statements, kids huddled around tables, an older man who an hour before had been glad-eyeing the young things, looking guilty and eager to get home to his wife and kids. The woman licensee was still standing behind the bar.

She'd regained her composure and stood upright with her arms folded across her chest. She nodded at Walter as he came through the lounge. She'd seen him before, and you wouldn't forget Walter Darriteau in a hurry, though he hadn't been in for ages, and she wondered why.

The dead guy was still there where he'd landed on his back on the apology for a stage. The doctor was there too, staring down and pulling faces.

8

'There you are, Walter,' he said, 'I thought you might show up. This time you can ask me the time of death.'

'Thanks, doc. What was the time of death?'

'Six minutes past eleven, I know that because these guys tell me they had just finished playing at five past and death was pretty much instantaneous.'

Walter bobbed his head. Looked at the tall white guy standing to one side, the guy with his arms folded across his chest.

'What was the dead guy's name?'

'Jeff something or other.'

'Jeff what?' snapped Walter.

'Player,' said the Chinese guy. 'Jeff Player.'

'Appropriate name,' said Walter, glancing down at the holed guitar. 'Was he a good player?'

'He didn't play at all, he was hopeless, he wasn't even in the band, bit of a loner,' said the white guy.

'So what was he doing with the guitar?'

'I asked him to hold it for me, keep it safe, make sure it wasn't nicked while I went to the bog. He couldn't even do that right.'

'So you're the guitar player?'

The white guy grinned. 'Yeah sure. That's me.'

'What's your name?'

'Neil, Neil Swaythling.'

'And you didn't see the shooting?'

'Nope. Heard it though.'

'Did you see it?' Walter asked the Chinese guy.

'Couldn't miss it. Happened right next to me.'

'And your name is?'

'Ang Ung, spelt NG, my mates call me Nug.'

Ang Ung, smart name, thought Walter.

'Did you know the killer?'

'Nope. Never seen him before.'

'Did any of you know the killer?'

The Asian guy behind the drums shook his head. The black guy was putting his horn away in its case, didn't say anything, didn't shake his head one way or the other.

9

'You! What's your name?'

The black guy stared at Walter in that look he'd seen a million times. The I hate coppers look, and especially black coppers... like you.

'You talking to me?'

'We can do this here, or we can do it down the station, it could take all night, it's no problem for me.'

'Johnny,' he said.

'Johnny what?'

'Phillips.'

'And are you known to us, Johnny Phillips?'

'These days it's hard not to be.'

Maybe he had a point.

'Did you recognise the killer?'

'Course not. I'd have said if I had.'

That was a moot point.

'Thank you... Johnny.'

Karen came back to Walter's side. She'd been checking on how the interviews were progressing, looking for any ID on the assassin.

'Surprise surprise, no one knew him,' she whispered.

Walter bobbed his head and whispered back, 'Where have I heard the name Swaythling before?'

'There's the builder bloke,' she said, 'that's the only Swaythling I know.'

'Ah yes, Homes for the Discerning,' he whispered, parroting their advertising speak. Swaythling Homes built only a small number of properties, but they came individually designed and built, invariably on a huge plot, every one quite different, and every one with a huge price ticket attached, a price that began with seven figures and went upwards. Walter turned to the white guy and said, 'Could it have been meant for you?'

Neil shrugged his shoulders. 'The bullets?'

'What else?'

'Been wondering that meself.'

'I'm not surprised you thought about it. Can you think of any reason someone might want to kill you?'

10

'Nope. Definitely not!'

'Do you deal drugs?'

'Do me a favour, and even if I did, I'm hardly likely to tell you.'

'You might, if you were a dealer… if you valued your life.'

'I don't! Don't touch the stuff. Never have done. Don't deal, don't smoke. Don't approve of it! None of us do.'

Karen glanced round the band.

The black guy looked uncomfortable.

'It's an odd line up for a band,' Walter said, glancing at the logo on the base drum. ALL at the top and SOULS beneath. 'What kind of stuff do you play?'

'Mixture, everyone brings something to the table, fusion music,' said Neil.

'Fusion music is…' started Karen.

'I know what fusion is!' barked Walter, stopping her mid-sentence. 'And if I didn't there's a big clue in the phrase.'

'Sure, Guv, sorry.'

Walter glanced at the guy at the back. 'What's your name, drummer?'

'Shastri.'

'First name?'

'Patna.'

'Did you recognise him, Patna Shastri, did you know him?'

'I did not.'

'But you saw him, and you could give us an accurate description?'

'Course,' he said, nodding. 'And I've got an excellent memory.'

Walter bobbed his head, happy to hear something positive.

'And you all did… you all could?'

'Not me,' said Neil.

'Other than you,' said Walter.

No further disagreement.

'I want you down the station right now, all of you, while the killer's image is fresh in your minds. Make up photofits, we'll arrange the transport.'

'There's no point in me going,' said Neil.

'Oh yes there is,' said Walter. 'You might recognise the pictures, and you could be safer there too.'

Neil pulled a face. Perhaps the copper had a point, said, 'What about the instruments?'

Walter glanced across at Sissy, seeking help.

'They'll be safe here,' she said.

'They will, because police officers will stay here too.'

Out of the corner of his eye Walter noticed the doc covering the body. Made sense. Some people were disturbed by dead bodies, especially bloodied and holed ones.

'Get Neil out of here,' said Walter, wondering if there might be an accomplice secreted somewhere in the crowd, and Karen bundled him out through the back door and away to a car. Ordered the driver to take him straight to the station and hurried back to the crime scene.

'It's almost midnight,' moaned the Chinese.

'I don't care what time it is,' said Walter. 'There's a gunman out there who's partial to shooting people dead, and we need to find him. Your cooperation would be most appreciated.'

Ang Ung had promised his girlfriend a night to remember. She'd be disappointed and so would he. Ang sighed.

'Turn into a frog at midnight, or something, do we?' said Walter.

Nug pulled a face and shook his head and closed his violin case.

'What about Jeff?' asked Patna.

'He'll be looked after.'

'Bit late for that,' said Johnny Phillips, eyeing up a young uniformed policewoman. She was all right for a copper, pity about the job, but he'd still like to get to know her better.

'All the more reason to catch the culprit,' said Walter.

A striking woman appeared in front of Walter's face, not the usual young crowd from the Ship, more business-like. Glanced down at the covered body, looked back at Walter, straight in the eye and said, 'Inspector Darriteau, do you have any leads as to who was the assassin?'

Walter glanced down his nose at the newcomer. She knew his name. She was on the wrong side of forty, but not by much, auburn, wavy hair parked on her shoulders, pretty face, nice teeth, quality dark green suit. Walter glanced at Karen, as if to say, who let this woman in, and who the hell is she? Karen shrugged and turned away. Walter glanced back at the woman and said, 'And you are?'

'Gardenia Floem,' she said. 'Pleased to meet you, Inspector. Chester Observer, chief crime reporter,' and she held out a pink-nailed hand.

Walter ignored it.

'To answer your question I have been on this case for precisely ten minutes, so the answer is: No.'

'Is this a drugs related case?'

Walter shrugged as if to say, How the hell would I know? Said, 'We've nothing to say to the press at this time, now if you don't mind,' turned back to Karen and mumbled, 'Get her out of here.'

Karen stepped between them and tried to usher her away.

'The citizens have a right to be concerned when one of their sons is gunned down in a busy city centre pub,' the woman shouted, each word further away from Walter than the last.

'Goodnight, Miss Floem.'

'This is going to be big news, Inspector,' she squawked from further across the bar, as Karen continued to ease her toward the door and outside. 'Big news!'

Walter shook his head and tried to eradicate her words from his mind. Is this a drugs related case? Maybe it is, who knows? Walter whispered to himself, but I am not jumping to conclusions. He turned round and shouted, 'Come along now!' and glanced and winked at Sissy behind the bar. She was still standing in that same hard pose. He thought he might have detected a softening in her eyes, but he could have been mistaken. 'We haven't got all night.'

Karen came back and said, 'Sorry about that, Guv,' then turned to the remnants of the band and said, 'Where does Jeff Player live?'

'He used to live down by the canal, one of those new flats,' said Patna.

Karen noted the use of the past tense and nodded and took down the address. Someone would have the shitty job of telling Jeff's mother, delivering the death-o-gram, and she hoped to God it wouldn't be her.

Chapter Three

Luke Flowers was at the clock five minutes early. He leant on the railings on top of the ancient city walls and stared down at the frantic shoppers below, bustling around like bees in a blooming rapeseed field. He was waiting for Jimmy. He was waiting to get paid.

£25,000 for one night's work, one minute's work. You couldn't beat it. Luke enjoyed his method of making a living, and he was good at it too. Much preferred it to drug dealing or loan sharking or copying dodgy software. In his current line of business one night's work could keep him in treats for an entire year. Less hassle, less stress, less effort, less worry, more money, more free time, more travel, more cachet, more respect. It suited Luke just fine.

He was going to take his bird to Venice, two whole weeks with the lovely Melanie Kirton. Twenty-two, five five, long blonde hair, light brown eyes, figure to die for, the dentist's daughter with the incredible teeth and amazing tongue.

They thought, Melanie's parents, that their sweet child was far too good for the likes of Luke Flowers, and they might have had a point, but it didn't matter what the hell they thought, because Melanie was besotted with Luke. She adored her bit of rough off the estate, and couldn't get enough of him, and anyway, he was good looking in a boy band kind of way; a little on the short side it was true, but she could live with that. He drove a super silver sports car too, and was never short of money, and she was always thrilled to walk into a busy pub on his arm, to show him off to her mates, and besides all that, he was great in bed.

Luke planned to visit the travel agent as soon as he had been weighed in. He was taking her to the Royal Palace Hotel in Venice; Venezia, he liked to say the name in Italiano, brought it home to him how far he had come up in the world, a five-star place Luke

15

would once have felt uncomfortable in, but it was amazing how soon a working class boy could become used to luxury. You only had to look at footballers to see that. One minute a bit of rough, the next, hobnobbing with royalty and celebs. It was only a tiny step... providing you had the cash.

He thought of Melanie again, and the prospect of having her all to himself for two whole weeks, no whiney parents lurking in the background, no distractions, no work, no worries, just Melanie. He planned to give her a holiday to remember. He planned to give himself the holiday of a lifetime. When she returned to England she'd need a holiday to get over it. He sniffed a laugh and heard footsteps approaching.

He turned to see Jim'll fix it Mitchell striding toward him, that same tweed cap on his head, that same unhealthy look on his weaselly face. He wasn't carrying any packets and that was worrying. Maybe it was inside his short suede jacket. Jimmy joined him in leaning on the railings and stared down at a gaggle of giggling short-skirted girls. Didn't say a word.

'Got the dough?' asked Luke.

'Nope.'

'Don't play games with me, Jimmy.'

Jim sniffed and coughed and spat down on to the road below, narrowly missing a guy carrying a red placard bearing a quote from the gospel according to the book of Saint John.

'You whacked the wrong guy!'

'What!'

'You heard me. You whacked the wrong guy. The client is not happy.'

'I whacked the guy you told me to whack. The tall white guy, the guitarist, the guy in the middle. That's what you said.'

'You whacked the wrong guy. The right guy was in the bog.'

'Oh, geez. So who was the guy with the holes?'

'Some innocent local kid. But that's not the point. The client gave you a contract and you haven't delivered. They're most unhappy about it.'

16

'Well, they are not alone in that! You'll have to set up another hit, Jim, and bloody quick.'

'You're telling me. I'm working on it now.'

'When?'

'Maybe tomorrow, maybe the day after.'

'Sooner the better. I am going away on holiday.'

'You are going nowhere! Not until this mess is sorted.'

Luke pursed his lips and slowly bobbed his head. Melanie could wait, for a little while. Sometimes it was best to make them wait. Made it more exciting. Made them all the more eager.

'What kind of name for a band is All Souls? Sounds like arseholes to me,' said Jimmy, laughing a short, sharp laugh.

'I'll keep the gun,' said Luke.

'You will if you value your neck,' said Jim, giving Luke a hard stare.

'You phone me, yeah? When you've set it up.'

'Oh yes, Luke, I'll be phoning you. You can be sure of that.'

'Sooner the better.'

'Do you need more ordnance?'

'Need what?'

'Ammo, Luke, ammo.'

'Nah, I've enough for this baby.'

'Just make sure you use it on the right guy.'

'Just make sure you find him… and soon!'

Jimmy touched his cap; muttered, 'I'll be in touch,' and then, 'Keep your phone on,' and he ambled away.

Chapter Four

Walter had finally crept into bed at gone three. The completed makeup of the three photofits had been remarkably similar. A neat square headed guy, short brown hair, perfect unbroken nose in the dead centre of his pretty face.

They all placed the guy at around five, seven tall, slim, wiry build, but fit looking, like a cyclist or rower or a racing driver or even a slightly taller jockey.

Neil remained adamant that he didn't know the guy in the pictures, and neither could he come up with any explanation as to why he was the target for an assassin, and Walter believed him.

The last thing Walter thought of before falling asleep was the woman in green, standing before him, issuing questions; that come-on smirk on her fair face.

Do you have any leads as to who was the assassin?

Is this a drugs related case?

How the hell had she got there so quick?

She was an attractive thing; that was for sure, what was her name again? Gardenia Floem, that was it, not the kind of name you might expect, or ever forget. He wondered why he hadn't come across her before.

Walter dragged himself into the office at ten past eight. He felt wrecked, and it still hadn't been early enough to beat Karen. She was already there, poring over the photofit pics. She looked as if she'd had a full night's kip. How did she manage to do that, pondered Walter, though he knew the answer well enough. It was called youth, something that Walter hadn't visited for at least thirty-five years.

He ambled to the coffee machine, yelled over, 'Want one?'

'Nope,' said Karen, brandishing her bottle of cherry flavoured water in the air.

Walter shook his head and squeezed out the coffee and returned to his desk.

'What do you want to do today?' she asked.

'I'd like to go swimming at Barmouth, forecast is good, but that looks unlikely, don't you think?'

Karen stared at him in that way of hers, telling him to behave, didn't say a word.

Walter grinned. 'I want to go and see Swaythling senior.'

'He'll probably be at the office, that's cool; it's only five minutes from here.'

Walter nodded and said, 'And after that, I want to speak to Neil's mother.'

'Do you know where they live?'

'Not yet, daddy Swaythling can tell us all about that, can't he?'

'Is this drugs related, do you think?'

'Your guess is as good as mine. Neil didn't come across to me as a liar. If he was lying he was very good at it.'

'I agree. So if he's not into drugs, why is someone trying to kill him?'

'Million dollar question, Greenwood, million dollar question. Find the motive, find the killer, that's how it usually works.'

'I've an idea,' she said.

'Fire away.'

'He's very attractive to the ladies.'

'Really? I didn't see that, especially.'

'I think, Guv, I am in a far better position to judge than you. Trust me; he will have a string of girlfriends a mile long. Didn't you see the way his personal band of groupies were gawping at him?'

'Can't say as I did, but if you're right, what are you saying?'

'Crime of passion? Jealous girl wreaking her revenge on her former lover?'

'Is that what girls do in modern day Britain? Have their boyfriends gunned down dead for turning their backs on them?'

'They might, if they were wealthy enough, and angry enough; and well connected enough. It's nothing new.'

'It's a thought,' said Walter. 'Though not a happy one. Where would such a girl locate an assassin? You can't look in yellow pages, not even on the Internet either, not yet, God, I hope not.'

'Who knows? A casual word spoken in a pub or club, perhaps in jest, and some chancer says, I could do that, if the money was right, and the thing snowballs from there.'

'The sorry thing is, Karen, your theory is looking better the longer we examine it. This afternoon go and see Neil again and get a list of all his abandoned squeezes.'

'It'll be a long list.'

'So you said. And take Gibbons with you, just in case you can't withstand his charm.'

Karen giggled, and said, 'If I didn't know better, I'd say you were jealous.'

'What have I got to be jealous about?'

'Other than muscles, youth and looks, nothing at all, Guv,' she said, grinning again, and before Walter could say anything else, his phone burbled to life and he snatched it up.

It was half-past ten when they entered Swaythling Construction's offices. The whole place was luxurious. Deep pile blue carpet, sweeping semi circular light oak reception desk, blonde dolly girl behind the counter, large silver letters on the wall behind her announcing: *Swaythling Construction, Homes for Discerning People.*

Walter and Karen ambled to the desk.

Karen said, 'We've come to see Mr Swaythling.'

'Who shall I say is calling?'

Karen flashed ID and said, 'This is Inspector Walter Darriteau.'

The girl looked nervous. Pursed her lips and said, 'He is very busy today. Not to be disturbed. I may be able to fit you in at twelve.'

Walter turned about and set off down the corridor, said over his shoulder, 'This way, is it?'

Karen followed in a hurry.

The girl screamed, 'Oh, but you can't go in there.'

'Oh, but we can,' said Karen, as Walter came to the end of the corridor. Three sturdy light oak doors, one left, one right, one straight ahead.

Opened the straight-ahead and went right in.

Huge office, same thick carpet, same light oak furniture, big wide window looking out across the city, big-haired man, salt and pepper style, nudging fifty, sitting behind a heavy, impressive desk. Neil Swaythling in twenty-five year's time, Karen couldn't help but notice, still attractive though, heavy white shirt, perfectly knotted red silk tie, dark suit. The man stood up. He wasn't used to being interrupted. In the centre of the room was a square table and on the table was a detailed model of the latest creation Swaythling Construction was trying to flog. Brambury Heights, it was titled, and some map location in North Wales.

On the other side of the table were two well scrubbed people, man and wife by the look of them, well turned out for a Saturday morning, both around fifty, both slim and tanned, both greying, both light blue eyes, like two peas in a pod. House hunters, pound to a penny. They stared at the wild black man as if he were a bum.

Karen smiled down at them and the woman forced a smile back as if to say: Who he?

'Do you mind telling me what the hell you are doing in my office?' said Swaythling.

Walter flashed his ID. Introduced himself and his sergeant.

'We've come to talk to you about an attempted murder on your son, and the murder of one Jeffrey Player.'

'What!'

'You heard me.'

The palace buyers stood up and the bloke said, 'I think we'd better be going, darling, I'll call you in the week, Gerry.'

The woman stood too, looked uncomfortable, gathered her things together, smiled across at Gerry Swaythling, then at Karen, gave Walter another cursory glance as if he might smell, and followed her husband outside.

Gerry sighed and exhaled and stared at the strangers.

'You'd better sit down, and you'd better tell me what the hell is going on, and it had better be good. I'm a friend of Mr and Mrs West.'

Mrs West was Walter's boss, not that he cared one jot about that, or of who Gerry Swaythling happened to be friends with.

'Neil hasn't told you?'

'No, he has not! When did this happen?'

'Last night in The Ship.'

'Now that you mention it, I heard something on the radio. Didn't connect it with Neil. Is he all right?'

'He's fine, which is more than can be said for Jeffrey Player,' said Walter. 'Where were you last night? We tried to contact you.'

'In Cardiff. Sales visit.'

'And you can prove that?' asked Karen.

'Of course I can. Not that I would need to.'

'What we want to know is, are you aware of anyone who would want to kill Neil, or indeed Jeffrey Player?'

'I have never heard of this Jeffrey Player character. As for Neil, we don't see much of him these days. He has his own flat in town, and to be honest, he rubs me up the wrong way. We don't agree on anything, and he can be an irritating little turd sometimes. He seems to make enemies for fun, though I'd be surprised if anyone should treat him so seriously as to want to kill him.'

Hardly a ringing endorsement of the son and heir, thought Karen.

Walter was speaking again. 'We'd like a word with Mrs Swaythling too.'

'Oh, I don't think that's a good idea.'

'Be that as it may, I will want to talk to her,' insisted Walter.

'She's ill, Inspector, she's not a well woman.'

'What's the problem?' asked Karen, Walter thought coldly. But what the heck, he wanted to know too.

'Motor Neurone, early stages, though she doesn't get out of the wheelchair much.'

'Still like to talk to her,' said Walter.

'She needs to know that someone was gunning for her son, and we need to know if she knows why,' said Karen.

22

Gerry sighed and pursed his lips and said, 'All right, if you must. You can come tonight, say eight o'clock,' and he passed a card across the desk.

Karen stood and glanced at it, before pocketing it.

Walter said, 'How's business, Mr Swaythling?'

'Could be better, could be worse. We are never working on more than five projects at any one time.'

'How many at the moment?' asked Karen.

'Three, it might have been four if you hadn't interrupted.'

'I'm sure they will be back. They seemed to like you, Gerry,' said Walter, standing and examining the model of Brambury Heights. 'How much would this little pied-à-terre set me back?'

Gerry Swaythling pulled a face, said, 'It's hardly that,' and he stood up and moved toward his latest baby. Thought he'd humour the guy and answer his question. 'About eight, depending on finish and precise requirements.'

'Eight what?' asked Walter.

Gerry considered answering, thought better of it, and gave the black copper a look that said everything.

'So what do we get for the eight mill?' asked Karen, remembering that she hadn't checked her last four weeks' lottery tickets.

Gerry glanced at the girl. She was a decent piece of totty. He'd talk to her anytime. 'State of the art kitchen and bathrooms goes without saying, Italian marble, granite, whatever you want. Cinema, as big as you need, indoor pool, outdoor too if you're brave enough to have such a foolish thing in hilly, windy North Wales, and stables. Jacuzzi of course, hot tub, worldwide television, state of the art music in every room, individual climate control. It can even tan you while you are having your breakfast if that's what you want. You could enjoy sex on the carpet and top up your tan while you are doing it,' and he glanced at Karen to see if he'd shocked her. He hadn't. Swaythling shrugged and continued. 'Nuclear fallout shelter if you're of a nervous disposition, state of the art touch electronic controls, no switches in the place, not a one. As many garages as you can handle, solar heating, your own independent water and sewerage supply, your own independent electricity grid, the latest security sensors and

23

systems, no one would ever get in there without the CCTV telling you about it first. It would send real-time colour video to your mobile phone wherever you were in the world. You could live in a property like that while the rest of the world went extinct.'

'I'm impressed,' said Karen, holding eye contact.

A smile played around the corner of his mouth.

The guy was old enough to be her father, but he still thought he had a chance.

Maybe he did.

'Yeah, yeah, we'll have two of the buggers,' said Walter, becoming bored, 'where do we sign?' feeling left out.

'No one has ever bought two, Inspector.'

'There's a first time for everything,' said Karen.

'Oh, indeed there is, my dear, there is. And don't forget we can add anything else to the property you may desire?'

'Like what?' asked Walter.

'We are dealing with the super rich. Some of them have very discerning requirements, shall we say, not the normal run of the mill extras.'

'Like what?' repeated Walter.

'Could be something as simple as a detailed model railway running through all the rooms, delivering cups of tea, could be special state of the art quarters for weird pets like crocs, tigers, wolves and boas, or it could be something of a more personal nature.'

'Like what?' said Karen and Walter as one.

'Do I have to spell it out?'

'You do to me,' said Walter.

Gerry rolled his eyes and sighed.

'Let's just say dungeons and torture, get the pic, I am sure the young lady understands.'

Karen puffed out her cheeks and blew hard and said, 'Why me? Don't think so.'

'That's as may be, but I don't think you are as innocent as you look, my dear, but there we are. I must get on, I have another client arriving in ten minutes, so is there anything else I can do for you?'

'Not right now. We'll see you at eight,' said Walter, heading for the exit. 'And go easy on the babe on the doors.'

Gerry held up his hand. 'You have my word,' he said, smiling at Karen as he closed his office door behind them.

On the way out Walter waved at the doll and shouted across, 'Thank you, miss, no problem, Gerry's fine about it, bye-bye.'

The girl nodded and said a nervous 'bye,' and in the next minute they were outside on the pavement.

Walter said, 'What did you make of that?'

'He wasn't exactly devastated someone had tried to murder his son.'

'No, very casual, wasn't he?'

'You don't think he could be behind it?'

'Rule nothing out, Karen.'

'But why would he do such a thing?'

'No idea. Maybe his wife will shed some light.'

'Neil's mother?'

'If she is his mother.'

'You think she isn't?'

Karen watched Walter's lips forming and she knew what he was going to say, and beat him to it. 'I know, rule nothing out.'

Walter nodded and said, 'You're going off to see Neil, are you?'

'Might as well.'

'Come back and collect Gibbons before you go.'

'I don't need Gibbons.'

'You may not need him, but I want him with you. Come on; take me back to the station.'

Chapter Five

Jim'll fix it Mitchell had built his network more than a quarter of a century before. He'd lost his job as a twenty something working in a Chester department store, where he'd developed a profitable sideline of opening up the storeroom doors when no one was about.

Two friends he'd met in a sleazy city-centre pub grabbed whatever they could, threw it in the back of a white van, and made their escape.

Jimmy Mitchell failed to spot the cameras that had watched his every move. They were still a new thing back then, and Jimmy was arrested and convicted of conspiracy and theft, something he could hardly deny when he saw the pictures. The judge didn't believe his story that he barely knew his co-conspirators and added another year to his four-year sentence for insolence. Jimmy did not ID the men.

He enjoyed his break from society, tucked away in Shrewsbury prison on the banks of the sunny river Severn. He made new friends, learnt a great deal, and when he came out, using the contacts he'd made in Criminal College, he set up his own firm where he'd endeavour to supply any client with any product or service they required, no matter how outlandish or absurd it might be. So long as they could pay for it.

Any scruples he might have possessed were flushed from him as he'd festered in his cell. Society had made an example of him, and in turn, he would make an example of society.

His business model worked well. His clients never knew the identity of the agents Jimmy employed, while his agents never knew the identity of the person, persons, or businesses, for whom they were acting. Jimmy provided a safety buffer between the two, a broker dealing in skulduggery. Jimmy prospered, and his reputation grew. The police tried hard to identify his clients, but had little success.

From the outset the clients, some of whom Jimmy Mitchell had shared time with, fed him work, and in due course were impressed with his organisational skills and results. The agents in the field loved Jimmy because he was always thorough in everything he did. He would set up much of the plan and would set the agent running, and besides that, he paid them promptly, and he paid them well.

Jimmy understood there were only three things that ever changed matters. The first was money, backhanders, bribery, call it what you like; the second was threats, which were often enough by themselves, especially if the threats were directed at the loved ones of the target, rather than at the target himself, or herself.

Funny that, thought Jim, so many people were more afraid of violence against their family, lovers, or friends, than they ever were against themselves. He didn't think that way. Never had.

The third event altering factor; was violence.

Jimmy was not afraid to issue orders divvying up brutality, indeed in the early days he deemed it necessary to gain the kudos and respect he needed. He was proved correct. Cutting off the occasional body part and packing it in a gift box and delivering it to a target worked wonders, though some parts carried more effect than others.

Not many people could stomach that.

The clients came to respect Jimmy Mitchell, because they feared him. His business grew and prospered. Jimmy became a wealthy man who could do anything he wanted.

Eventually his tentacles stretched far and wide, covering the whole of Cheshire, spreading out across the map like black ink on a fresh blotter, throughout North Wales, the Wirral Peninsula, North Shropshire, and more recently into the heart of the twin squabbling cities of Liverpool and Manchester, where there was always a tense atmosphere, and considerable numbers of commissions to be gained. Specialists like Jimmy Mitchell were in high demand.

Following Luke's recent failure to eradicate the Swaythling kid, Jim had alerted his entire network that the real guitarist had to be found.

Top priority, five big ones in it for the spotter, and they only had to name the time and place, nothing more. Jimmy would deal with the rest.

It was easy money for someone, and the streetwalkers knew it and gave it their undivided attention. It didn't take long.

Bunny Almond came back with the news that Jimmy was desperate to hear, and it was as well he had, because Jimmy's client was more than a little miffed at Luke's failure to hit the target.

'Tell me what you know, cheapskate,' said Jimmy, pressing the mobile hard to his ear. He was addressing Bunny Almond, and cheapskate was Jim's nickname for the mixed race guy. Jimmy always used nicknames, especially when using mobile phones, because he worried about who might be listening.

He'd only use the same mobile for a maximum of two weeks and lob it in the canal and buy a newer, better one. It was a pain having to distribute a new number, but better that than run risks.

Bunny did not like the nickname, but he'd let that pass. Jimmy was a good employer and Bunny was desperate for cash, he needed a hit, and five big ones provided a great deal of happiness.

'He's in his flat right now. He's talking to two people, a blonde girl and a young fit bugger, think they could be filth, but he'll be going out soon. He often does in the late afternoon, he's got some older woman up on the Wirral, wealthy bitch, word is she pays him, couldn't comment on that. Lucky bastard, I say. He always wears a black leather jacket when he goes to plug her.'

'Where's the best place for action?'

'That's easy. Two rows of lockups at the back of the flats. One way in, one way out, very quiet there in the afternoons before the worker bees come home, an ideal place. The guitar player has to go there to collect his car, half an hour I'd say.'

'Well done, cheapo, and you'd better be right.'

'I am right. When do I get paid?'

'I'll ring you later.'

Jimmy rang off and rang Luke.

He was lounging in a packed bar down by the river with friends. The place was full of tourists and locally based Americans who worked in the American banks. Luke was drinking orange juice because he was expecting the call. Made his excuses and went outside and ambled along the riverbank to listen to the news.

'Wellington road flats, lockups behind, half an hour. Wearing a black leather jacket. Don't buy the wrong shoes!'

Jimmy rang off without another word. Luke pursed his lips and slipped the phone away. Went back into the pub, emptied his drink, said his goodbyes and left. The adrenalin kicked in. It was the best high imaginable, better than drugs, better than money, better than sex, better even than sex with Melanie Kirton, though that was a close-run thing.

He hurried across the city, smiled at a couple of neat female passers-by, apologised when he went to take the same slab of pavement as an oncoming pair of business type gents. He was in a good mood, no point in having conflict over pavement real estate. There was still time to fix that flight to Venice the following day, all he had to do was settle the score, and that was what he was about to do.

There was no one about at the lockups.

The place was deserted, and perfect for the job in hand.

Fourteen prefabricated garages on either side, metal up and over doors, fading coloured graffiti on three of them, featuring the names and logos of rock bands, some that Luke knew and liked, and breaking outfits that even he had never heard of. All that kind of youth crap design. All the garage doors were locked bar one. The open garage was empty, other than a dozing black cat hoping a rat might stumble by.

Between the garages was a dusty unmade road, compressed rough gravel, dry as a bone. At the far end was a solid high wall with ancient shattered green glass set in the cement on the top. Luke thought that was illegal. Damn well should be, someone might get hurt.

Perfect place for an ambush, perfect place for a killing; one way in, same way out, Luke understood that, retreated to the main road. Crossed over, propped himself up outside a bookmakers that was set next to the bus stop, and a big new orange wastepaper bin. He grabbed an old newspaper from the bin. Pretended to read the racing pages. He had a great view from where he was. Anyone coming out of the flats would have to pass by on the other side of the road, before cutting up the jigger toward the garages.

Five minutes passed, and nothing happened. Ten minutes, and Luke was sweating in his slacks. Fifteen and he was getting worried. Twenty, as he flicked his wrist again and glanced at the silver Rolex he had treated himself to on his last trip to Geneva.

On the other side of the road a tall guy came round the corner, black leather jacket, walking with a purpose toward the jigger, turned right, cut up toward the garages. Luke dumped the paper, dashed across the road between bad tempered traffic, cut up the alley, shadowing the target. Crept to the end where the lane turned left. There the pre-fabbed garages stretched out on either side, high glass-topped wall at the far end.

Slipped the gun from his pocket. Peered around the corner.

The guy was walking away down the centre of the lane, heading for his garage.

Luke followed. There was still no one about, just the rumble of traffic from the main road.

'Neil?' he called, friendly like, 'I think you forgot this.'

Neil turned round and saw the gunman; saw the gun in his hand. Didn't run. Didn't panic. Began walking back toward Luke, a cocky swagger about him.

'Why are you doing this?' he demanded.

Luke didn't answer.

'Who are you working for?'

Luke didn't answer.

'Bugger off out if it!'

Luke didn't move a muscle.

He wasn't lacking courage, this Neil character; Luke noted that. They weren't usually like him.

Neil ignored the gun, scowled, and kept on coming.

No skinny street punk was going to cow him.

Luke grinned and raised the gun; aimed and fired.

One, two, three, four!

The start of a rock number for the leader of the band. All Souls. Arseholes! All four striking home, thudding into Neil's torso and chest. His eyes carried that disbelieving look, as if no one ever believes they could be the one who was getting shot. It was something that only happened to other guys. It was something that only happened to losers on the telly, in the movies and in books, but not in real life, and certainly not in pretty Chester in the middle of a sunny summer afternoon. That would be impossible. Unthinkable.

Neil fell on his back, arms outstretched, surprised look still on his face. Didn't move, didn't utter a sound.

'One, two, three, four,' whispered Luke. 'Start singing your prayers, punk.'

Neil Swaythling didn't sing, didn't move, didn't bat an eyelid.

Luke heard kids coming up the jigger, maybe three, maybe four, sounded about eleven-years-old, and then a football being booted against a wall. It was as good a place to play footie as any, quiet and off the road. Time to leave. Luke turned round and hurried away, past the kids. One had a Chelsea shirt on, one a Manu, one Liverpool, one Everton, some mixture, some team, some arguments. The kids didn't notice him, so busy were they trapping and heading and shooting and shouting and chewing gum, and showing off.

Luke hurried back toward the city centre, the gun still hot in his pocket. Sat on a bench in the busy square, close to the statue of the baby elephant. Rang Jimmy.

'This time I've bought the correct shoes.'

'I bloody hope so.'

'When can you pay me?'

'Tomorrow, same time, same place.'

'I'll be there.'

Luke rang off, feeling good, headed down the hill toward the travel agents. Went inside, chatted up the smart, dark girl. She assured him he could still be on the following evening's flight from Manchester. Last late rooms available in the Royal Palace Hotel, Venice, so the computer said. Seven grand all in. Did he want it, or did he not?

'Hold on a sec, I'll give her a bell.'

Melanie answered on the third ring. She was taking a cigarette break from her job as an assessor in the Chester and Stafford Insurance Company. She was outside in the sunshine, sitting beneath the ornamental silver birches, watching the fishes swim round and round their modern rectangular pool.

'Are you still on for tomorrow?'

'Do you want me to be on for tomorrow?'

'Course, babe.'

'Where?'

'Venice, two whole weeks.'

'That depends.'

'On what?'

'On what you are going to do to me.'

Luke smirked at the girl behind the monitor. She was all ears. Smirked back.

'You know the answer to that.'

'Will I like it?'

'You'll love it.'

'All right,' she said, 'just this once.'

'I'm at the travel agent right now, I'll book it.'

'If you must, Luke-ee, if you must.'

Luke rang off; grinned at the girl. Paid a deposit, said he'd bring the rest of the cash in the next day. He was well known in Deeside Travel, a regular punter. They trusted Luke Flowers; he'd flown with them many times before.

'Bye,' said the travel agent girl when they'd finished their business, wondering why she couldn't find a handsome and respectable boyfriend like him, someone who'd splash seven gees on her without a second thought. Some girls were just born lucky. She probably didn't even appreciate what a fine man she had.

Chapter Six

Karen and Gibbons strolled back into the office. They'd been to see Neil.

'You've been ages,' moaned Walter.

'Hungry,' said Gibbons, 'picked up a burger.'

'How did you get on?'

'Much as I said,' said Karen.

'Go on.'

'He's got a woman friend up on the Wirral, an older woman,' said Gibbons.

'He's very protective of her,' said Karen. 'Seems she's worth a bundle of money.'

'Where did the money come from?'

'He wasn't keen to say,' said Karen.

'Doesn't this guy realise he's the target for a paid assassin? Doesn't it bother him?'

'He's writing a song about it,' said Gibbons.

'Oh, bully beef! That's going to keep the killer at bay!'

'He's confused,' said Karen.

'We are all freakin' confused! We are trying to help this guy... but he needs to help himself.'

'He doesn't think the gunman will try again,' said Karen.

'Oh yeah, and how does he work that out?'

'Says he'll move onto something else, says it was mistaken identity.'

'Do you believe that crap?'

'Nope,' said Karen.

'Me neither,' said Gibbons.

'Ah well, you can't help those who don't want to be helped. Did he have any fresh ideas as to why he should be a target?'

'Not that he told us.'

'The guy's an idiot!' muttered Walter.

'Or brave,' said Karen.

'Brave, my size ten brown boots! Well bugger it, bugger him, leave him to stew! We should be concentrating on finding the killer of Jeffrey Player, not worrying about someone who's acting like a prima donna.'

The phone before Walter burbled into action. Karen grabbed it. Results of the post-mortem on Jeffrey Player. Told them nothing they didn't already know. Four shots, four holes, two slugs lodged in the wall. Death by gunshot, one through the heart, stopped it dead, death instantaneous.

Across the city, Neil Swaythling opened his eyes. He felt as if he'd been kicked in the chest by the leading stallion in Michael Cowley's Cheshire yard. Neil felt dazed and dizzy. He felt sick. He tried to sit up.

Four kids came round the corner. They wore different coloured soccer shirts and were booting a football up against the garage doors. Kerrang, Kerrang!! as the heavy ball rebounded off the metalwork.

One of them saw the man half lying, half sitting on the ground, said, 'There's a fella there, look!'

They all turned to see, then ran towards him.

He looked shaken up. His cool leather jacket had neat holes in it. His face was pale and his hands trembled like a drunk's.

'Are you all right, mate?' said the Evertonian.

'Yeah,' managed Neil.

'Did a car run you down?' said the Liverpool.

'Yeah, a car ran me down.'

He glanced at the kids' shirts.

'Why don't you support City?'

'Moneybags City, you must be jokin'!' said the Manu.

'Not Manchester City. Chester City.'

They all looked at him as if he was touched. Deranged.

'Sod that! They're not even in the league!' said the Chelsea.

'You should support your hometown club.'

'Don't think so,' said Manu. 'Do you want us to fetch the bizzies?' he said, as Chelsea looked on, quite unconcerned, the heavy ball under his arm.

'Nah,' muttered Neil, 'I'll do it,' and he tugged his mobile from his pocket, relieved to see it still without a scratch. Searched in his slacks for the card the black copper had given him and poked in the number.

The phone in front of Walter burbled again.

He looked round for Karen. She'd gone to the Ladies. Gibbons was over the other side of the office haggling over some boxing tickets for the Friday night card at the Liverpool Arena.

Walter sniffed and picked up the phone.

A distant voice said, 'Can I speak to Inspector Darriteau.'

Walter thought he knew who it was, but didn't say. Said, 'Speaking.'

'It's Neil, Neil Swaythling, he's back, the killer, I've been hit.'

'Are you all right?'

'Dunno.'

'Where are you?'

'Between the lockups at the back of the flats in Wellington Road.'

'Has the guy gone?'

'Yeah, long since.'

'Did you know him?'

'Never seen him before.'

'And he thinks you're dead?'

'Guess so.'

'OK, stay where you are, I'll send someone down for you right now, a few minutes, that's all, it'll be Karen and Gibbons, the people you saw before.'

'OK, don't be long.'

'We won't.'

Karen was back, standing beside Walter. She'd picked up the end of the conversation. Walter filled her in. A moment later Karen and

35

Gibbons shot from the office and took the lift downstairs on the lookout for a good unmarked car.

Less than ten minutes later, the BMW pulled into the jigger and turned between the garages. The kids had vanished. Neil had staggered to his feet and was leaning against one of the dividing walls between two of the garages. Gibbons turned the car round. Karen jumped out and went to Neil.

'Are you all right?'

'I feel like I've been run over by a steamroller.'

'Here, take my arm,' and she helped him into the back of the car.

Neil collapsed into the back seat.

'Where did he get you?' asked Gibbons.

'Heart, chest, all over.'

'Those new Kevlar bullet proof vests are the business,' said Gibbons.

'Made from oil, weight for weight seven times stronger than steel,' said Karen, 'Good job you put it on.'

'Good job he didn't shoot you in the face,' said Gibbons.

'Good job he didn't shoot me in the balls,' muttered Neil.

'Yeah, that too,' said Gibbons.

Karen grinned as they cruised down the jigger, as the first of the evening worker bees was coming home from work.

Five minutes later, and they were back at the station.

Walter jumped from his chair and went toward the kid. Took his arm and eased him into his own chair.

'Take it easy,' he said. 'We'll have a quick chat, and then we'll get you to the hospital for a thorough checkup.'

Neil bobbed his head and managed a brave smile.

Walter clarified: 'You had definitely never seen the guy before?'

'No! Never.'

'Did he say anything?'

'Yeah, something like: Hey Neil, I think you forgot these.'

'And you turned round?'

'Yeah.'

'Local accent?'

'Pretty much.'

'Did he say anything else?'

'Not that I remember.'

'What was he wearing?'

'Grey slacks, white polo shirt, short lightweight jacket.'

'What colour?'

'Beige, I think.'

'And the photofits, how accurate are they?'

Neil glanced down at the pics that Walter had laid out on his desk. Neil pursed his lips and said, 'Pretty good, that's the best one, for sure,' he said, pointing at Nug's result.

Walter bobbed his head. 'We'll go with that one. Gibbons, get this pic out to all stations. Man wanted for murder. Airports as well, just in case he does a runner.'

Gibbons grabbed the pic and took it away for distribution.

'Do you want a coffee?' asked Karen.

Neil shook his head.

'Tell me about your lady friend?' asked Walter.

'I don't want her involved.'

'She might already be involved.'

'She isn't, I tell ya.'

'And she's loaded?'

'Yeah.'

'Where did she get the money?'

'Her husband had his own business. He was much older than her. They went on holiday to Miami; it was during a heat wave. He collapsed and died from a heart attack on the quayside. She inherited the business, plenty of cash in the bank, she says.'

'What kind of business?'

'No idea.'

'And now she's a lady of leisure?'

'Pretty much.'

'Where did you meet her?' asked Karen.

'At the Greenfield Country Club, in the disco. She came over to me and grabbed my hand and tugged me onto the dance floor. We just seemed to hit it off.'

'How old is she?' asked Gibbons.

'Age doesn't matter.'

'Maybe not,' said Walter, 'but what are we talking here?'

'Forty-three.'

'That's freaking old,' said Gibbons.

'Excuse me,' said Walter, 'but that's young!' and he shared a smile with Neil.

'Look!' Neil said, then stopped as if thinking of his words, as if pondering on whether to say any more, 'I've had dozens of girls, maybe hundreds.' Karen thought to herself, I told you that, Walter, but didn't say, as Neil continued, 'but I have never met anyone like Veronica. I love her to bits, and I want to marry her.'

Karen glanced across at him. He sure looked cut up about something. Gibbons thought him a stupid prat.

'And your parents don't like the idea?' said Walter.

'They hate the idea, hate her, threatened to disinherit me.'

'We'd still like to talk to her,' said Walter.

'Nope! I don't want her involved.'

'All right, we'll leave that for the moment, but I want you to do something else for me?' said Walter.

'If I'd done what you suggested before, I wouldn't be in this mess.'

'True, but forget about that. Will you do what we want this time?'

'Yeah, you name it, so long as it doesn't involve her, and on condition you nail the bastard.'

'That's the aim,' said Karen.

'OK,' said Walter. 'This is what I want you to do.'

Chapter Seven

The Swaythling's house was on a hill high above the river Dee. It was a striking new property set between the road and the escarpment that dropped away down toward the river. Built in traditional style, gables and tall chimney-stacks, but using every modern material and intelligence available.

Blackened windows like you see in people carriers to abolish the need for blinds and lace curtains, silver framed windows, self-cleaning glass, smooth Cotswold stone appearance, though it was not built of stone.

It wasn't on the grand scale of the palaces that Swaythling constructed for his clients, even Gerry Swaythling couldn't afford that, but it was a huge and striking property. Walter and Karen arrived outside at ten to eight. They drove past the house and turned round and came back.

'Pull in here,' he said, pointing to a disused paddock gateway on the other side of the road. From there they could see the house, protected by high and substantial black railings. In the centre of the railings was an electronic-controlled curved-topped set of metal gates. The tops were painted gold. The gates were closed. Walter and Karen could see the intercom and digital pad set next to them for the chosen few to punch in a password, and the gates would swing open.

There was a gleaming black Bentley parked on the brick paved driveway, presumably his, and a small BMW hatchback, maybe hers. Beyond that, slightly out of sight, was another vehicle, perhaps a coupé, silver by the look of it, though the evening sun was reflecting from it, making it hard to tell. Maybe Neil was at home.

'Eh up,' said Karen, and they both stared across the road, as a tall and slim young woman came out of the house. Tight blue jeans, short white top, flat stomach. She walked round the Bentley and the

BMW and jumped in the far car. Through their open car window they could hear the soft purr of the engine starting, as the coupé eased toward the gates that opened. In the next second, the silver Mercedes coupé swept out onto the road and flashed past them, the blonde's mane flowing behind her in the summer breeze. She didn't give them a second glance.

'I don't know who she was,' said Karen, 'but it wasn't Neil's mother.'

'Mmm,' said Walter. 'It wasn't Neil either. Interesting. About the same age as Neil. He doesn't have a sister, does he?'

'Not that we know of.'

'Come on, let's go and pay our respects.'

They jumped from the car, crossed the road, and in the next second Walter was buzzing the intercom.

A woman answered, a foreign lady, by the sound of things.

'Hello, who there?'

'Inspector Walter Darriteau, Chester Police, to see Mrs Swaythling.'

'Hold on. I check.'

They seemed to wait an age. Then the lady was back, 'You come in now.'

The gates swung back open, and they walked through to the front door and pressed the bell.

'Some house,' said Karen.

'I've seen better,' said Walter, as the front door pulled open. A slight young woman in a white blouse and black skirt smiled and said, 'Please come in. They will see you in a moment.'

Filipina, Walter guessed, the housekeeper by the look of her, about thirty, quite attractive, wondered if she was legal.

'I tell them you are here,' she said, and smiled and disappeared down a white marble floored corridor. Then she was back. 'They see you now. Please follow,' and they followed her along the same corridor that opened out to the left into the largest living room either of them had ever seen.

Mrs Swaythling was sitting in a winged back chair. She didn't look well. Grey hair, drawn face, very slight. Gerry was standing behind her, hands on her shoulders. Mrs Swaythling tried a smile.

'This is my wife,' he said, 'Holly.'

'Forgive me if I don't get up.'

'Of course,' said Walter, striding toward her, taking her delicate hand and gently squeezing it. 'Pleased to meet you. I'm Inspector Walter Darriteau and this is Sergeant Karen Greenwood.'

The two women exchanged glances and half smiles as Karen wandered toward the open window. It was floor to ceiling glass and swept back open, as if some giant had removed the entire wall.

'Mind if I have a look?' she asked.

'Be my guest,' said Gerry, leaving his wife's side and crossing the room and beckoning her out onto the terrace.

'Wow,' she said, 'some view.'

Far below on the river were a pair of rowing eights, chasing one another, and a couple of packed pleasure cruisers in line astern, working late and busy, and beyond that, the water meadows where beasts grazed, as the river wound away upstream, the setting sun lighting it up like liquid gold.

'What a view,' she repeated.

'We like it,' said Gerry, looking into her eyes.

'Take a seat, Inspector,' said Mrs Swaythling, and Walter slouched into one of the vast cream sofas.

'How are you?' he asked.

She pulled a face, didn't say anything, then she said, 'Good days, bad days,' as the other two came back inside, Gerry returning to his station behind his wife, Karen perching on the end of the sofa beside Walter.

'We want to talk to you about Neil.'

'Of course you do,' said Holly. 'Gerry said someone tried to kill him.'

'Yes, they did. Why do you think they did that?'

'I have no idea.'

'I told you that,' said Gerry, taking a moment to admire the seated sergeant.

41

'He has a lady friend, I believe?' suggested Walter.

'That bitch!' Holly Swaythling said.

'Veronica?' said Karen.

Holly sighed and nodded. 'Veronica Camberwell. Should be ashamed of herself, corrupting a young man half her age.'

Neil's words came back to Karen.

I've had dozens of girls, maybe hundreds.

Corrupted, he wasn't.

'Where does she live?' asked Walter.

'Up at Willaston, big ugly house, built in the 1800s, must cost a fortune in upkeep,' said Gerry.

'Neil says that you have threatened to cut off his inheritance,' said Karen, watching their faces for a response. She certainly got one.

'Did he?' shouted Gerry. 'Damned cheek!'

'The stupid boy!' said Holly.

'And did you?' asked Walter.

'We might have mentioned something,' said Gerry.

'Only in jest,' added Holly, 'more to bring him to his senses.'

'Do you have children, Inspector?' asked Gerry.

'Not that I know of,' said Walter.

'Well, if you did, you might understand,' said Holly.

'Could Veronica Camberwell have anything to do with this attempt on Neil's life?' asked Karen.

Gerry pursed his lips, pretended to think.

Holly said, 'Who knows? Someone must have done it. Nothing would surprise me.'

'You see,' said Walter, 'there has been another development.'

'What kind of development?' snapped Gerry.

'A big development,' said Karen, looking straight into Gerry's eyes.

Chapter Eight

'Well?' said Gerry, unaccustomed to being kept waiting. 'What kind of development?'

'There has been another attempt on Neil's life.'

Holly's mouth fell open. She balled her fist around the handkerchief and glanced around at her husband, then back at the police people.

'Where, when?' asked Gerry.

'Is he all right?' asked Holly.

'He's fine,' smiled Karen, 'we persuaded him to wear a bulletproof vest. It did the business.'

'Oh my God!' she said, close to tears.

'Where is he now?' asked Gerry.

'He's in a safe place. He's going to stay there until we sort this out.'

'I demand to know where my son is being held!' yelled Gerry.

'Neil wanted it this way,' said Karen. 'He said no one was to know, not even you.'

'The fewer people that know the better,' said Walter.

'But that shouldn't include us,' said Holly.

'For the moment it includes everyone,' said Walter.

'Ridiculous!' snapped Gerry.

'The thing is,' said Walter, 'we were wondering if you can think of anyone who might want to hurt Neil?'

'We've already told you the answer to that,' said Gerry.

Holly didn't say a word; just turned and stared up at her husband.

'Yes, you told us that,' said Karen, 'but we need more to go on. We can't find the culprit until we know the motive.'

'If we knew that we'd tell you,' said Gerry, growing increasingly irritated.

'Have you got any enemies?' asked Walter.

'No!' he answered, too quickly for the officers' liking.

'Tell me how it happened,' said Holly.

'The latest shooting?' said Karen.

Holly nodded and sniffed into the embroidery.

Karen glanced at Walter, who said, 'Earlier today, between the lockup garages at the back of the flats, one young man, here's his picture,' and he passed the latest photofit to them. 'Four shots, all struck Neil on the bulletproof vest. He was very lucky.'

'Oh my God,' wept Holly.

'You are upsetting my wife!' said Gerry.

'It's all right,' she said, glancing up at him again. 'We need to know what's happened; we need to help if we can.'

'Have either of you seen this man before?'

They both stared at the picture and shook their heads.

'Neil says it's a very close likeness,' said Karen. 'Are you certain?'

'Course we are!'

'And Neil doesn't know him either?' asked Holly.

'He says not.'

'This is drugs related, I'll bet!' said Gerry.

'Neil doesn't do drugs!' said Holly. 'You know that.'

'He insists he's not into drugs,' added Karen.

'That's what I said!' said Holly.

Neil's mother gazed down at the picture of the neat young man staring back.

'Why are you doing this?' she whispered. 'You evil, evil boy.'

'There is something else you need to know,' said Walter.

'Go on!' said Gerry.

'We have agreed with Neil that the press release will say that he was killed in the shooting.'

'What! Oh no!' grimaced Holly.

'That way we believe the killer will think he has done what he set out to do,' said Walter.

'Seems sensible to me,' said Gerry.

'But…' said Holly.

Walter interrupted. 'People are bound to ring for news. We don't want you to tell them he is alive and well.'

'Why ever not?' asked Holly, nearing the end of her tether.

Gerry answered the question. 'Because the police believe it might alert the killer, and he might try again.'

'Correct,' said Walter.

'But our friends wouldn't do anything like that!' she insisted.

'We don't know that,' said Gerry. 'Not for certain.'

'And you promise me he is well?' said Holly, turning back to Walter.

'Of course,' said Karen, 'he's fine, you can talk to him later on the phone.'

Walter clarified. 'He is a bit shaken up, anyone would be, badly bruised, and I'm sure he'll feel rotten for a few days, but he's been to hospital for a complete checkup and they don't need to keep him in. That's the main thing.'

Holly smiled nervously at the thought.

In the next instant, they all became aware of phones ringing through the house. The Filipina came running, 'Sorry to bother, but I getting calls, say Neil dead, what I say?'

Walter shared a look with Gerry. He nodded hard and said, 'I'll take the calls, Hilario, put them through to me.'

'Thank you,' said Walter, nodding, 'And don't forget, if you can think of anything, no matter how small, please ring me any time, and he reached forward and set a fresh card on the light oak coffee table.

'Thank you, Inspector,' she said, 'now if you don't mind I am exhausted,' and she closed her eyes and settled back into the winged back chair.

The meeting was over.

Gerry came back to the hall as they were on the way out.

'Condolence calls,' he said.

'First of many, I would think,' said Walter.

'And you'll get Neil to ring his mother?'

'We will, be later this evening,' said Karen.

'We'll let you know if there are any developments,' said Walter.

Gerry nodded and opened the front door, let them out, and watched the woman sergeant walk away toward the opening gates.

A minute later back in the car Karen said, 'Well, what did you make of that?'

'The mother knows something.'

'That's what I thought.'

'What do you make of him?'

'Flighty bugger, if you ask me,' said Karen.

'He liked you.'

'I think he likes women, full stop. Like father, like son.'

'We'll pay another visit tomorrow, when Gerry's at work.'

'OK, Guv.'

'In the meantime, find out everything you can about Veronica Camberwell. Where she lives, where the money came from, where and what her husband's business was, and see if you can find any link to Gerry Swaythling.'

'OK, Guv. So who was the glamorous blonde, do you think? I'm surprised you didn't ask about her.'

'I want to do that tomorrow, when he's not there.'

'Gotcha.'

'Come on; let's get back to the station. Time's marching on.'

They had only been back in the office a matter of minutes when Walter took a call. He glanced up at the clock. Half-past nine. He thought he was getting hungry. A woman's voice.

'Inspector Darriteau?'

'Yes. Who's this?'

'Gardenia Floem. Remember me?'

'How could I forget?'

'Would you like to make any comment on reports that Neil Swaythling was shot dead this afternoon?'

'Would you like to tell me where you received such information?'

Gardenia laughed girlishly, and said, 'You know us journalists, never reveal our sources.'

'Speak to the press office, they'll fill you in.'

'But is it true?'

'Speak to the press office.'

'Just a simple yes or no would do.'

'Ditto.'

She laughed again. She had a nice laugh.

'Are you any nearer to finding the killer?'

'Mizz Floem, I am very busy. The press office will give you everything we have.'

'Even I don't believe that.'

Karen came back and stood beside the desk. She'd freshened up. She touched his shoulder and softly said, 'Is it OK if I get off?'

Walter nodded and shouted after her, 'See you in the morning.'

'Do you mean me?' said Gardenia.

'No, I did not mean you, I really must go.'

'I'll ring you tomorrow.'

'I'd rather you didn't.'

'Funnily enough, lots of people say that,' she said, still giggling.

'I can believe that too. Goodnight, Mizz Floem,' and he put the phone down before she could say anything else.

Much later, after he'd climbed into bed, he was still thinking of the case. He knew he wouldn't get much sleep; he never did when a tough case was ongoing. He'd keep pulling all the facts apart and putting them back together in a different order, hoping something might look wrong.

It sometimes did.

It hadn't yet.

He thought of poor Jeffrey Player and wondered what the last thoughts were that gushed through his head before he was shot dead, the moment he saw the killer raise the gun, point at his heart, and fire. What had he been thinking of? Friends? Family? A girl? A boy? Becoming a rock star? Did he think it was a prank, or did he recognise his days were exhausted? And most important of all, did Jeffrey Player recognise his killer? Could this case yet be about Jeffrey, and not Neil? Maybe the killer meant to murder Jeff. It was possible. Rule nothing out.

Walter pondered on the expression on the killer's face at the precise moment of execution. Was he smiling, grinning, grimacing, what? Or maybe he showed a cold, indifferent face to the world as he went about his foul business. If Walter had to guess, he would go for that, the cold, indifferent look, though he would never know.

But of course he would. He could ask Neil, for he had witnessed the same pre-killing look the murderer adopted at the moment he was about to end someone's life. The key question was, why had the killer done it? Where was the motive? If Walter had to guess he would plump for personal gain, for money, pure greed, and if that were the case, he must have been working for someone else, and if that was right, then who, and just as importantly, why?

That was where they should concentrate their efforts.

Finding the client. Finding the brains behind the operation. Finding the person or persons responsible for winding up and letting go the boy band look-a-like squirt of a killer with a gun, the same person running riot on their patch, on his patch.

Bloody cheek!

Would you like to make any comment on reports that Neil Swaythling was shot dead this afternoon?

Gardenia's words came back to him. She seemed to have her finger on the pulse. Where had she dug up that little gem? She had a nice laugh though, and a sexy giggle, and long after that, the final thoughts that flickered through Walter's mind before he surrendered to sleep, were of Gardenia Floem, and her cute giggle.

Chapter Nine

Luke was at the clock at five to two. There was no sign of Jimmy. He leant on the railings and watched the young women below in their cute summer dresses going about their city business. They all looked so happy and carefree. He didn't hear Jimmy arrive. Sometimes he was like that, quiet and slippery.

'Well?' said Luke.

'The task appears to have been completed.'

'Of course it has been completed!'

'Did you actually see him dead?'

'I pumped four shots into him. I'm a good shot, I don't miss, not from that range. The guy walked towards me, he seemed to want it; he seemed to have a death wish. No one could have survived that.'

'You'd better be right.'

'I am right, now pay me!'

Jimmy shot him a look that told Luke not to be lippy.

'May I have my money now, please, Mr Mitchell?'

That was better.

Jimmy produced a packet from his jacket and slipped it across to Luke and said, 'It's not all there.'

'What do you mean, it's not all there?'

'I incurred additional expenses, after your earlier cock up.'

'What expenses? How much?'

'Eight grand, I had to pay out eight grand to fresh runners to locate the target.'

'Eight grand! Geez! Who did you employ? God?'

Jimmy laughed.

'It's your own fault, you shouldn't have screwed up.'

Luke harrumphed, then said, 'I'll have to go, I'm off on my holidays, taking the tart to Italy, gonna screw her senseless.'

49

Luke made to leave.

'Um, haven't you forgotten something?' said Jimmy.

'Oh yeah, sorry Jim,' and he reached inside his jacket and pulled out the envelope containing the gun. Passed it over. Jim peeked inside. Saw it was right, nodded his head. Said, 'When are you back?'

'Two weeks.'

'I might have something else for you.'

'Cool. You know my number, give me a ring.'

Jimmy nodded, didn't say a thing, and Luke nodded too and turned about and set off toward the travel agency.

Jimmy sniffed and took out his phone and rang Bunny Almond. Fixed a meet. Pay off his debts. He always paid his debts, even to a lowlife like Bunny Almond, though he wondered how he could reduce his cut. Couldn't think of an adequate reason. He'd pay him in full, this time. The guy would soon be off his head for a month, but that didn't matter because Jimmy didn't plan to use Bunny Almond again. He had too much to say for himself, and besides, changing runners was always good policy.

Ten minutes later, Luke bounced into the travel agents.

The same pretty girl was there.

'How are you today?' he asked, leaning against the desk and smiling.

'I'm great and I can see you are too.'

'There is no point in being miserable, is there, darling?'

'You're dead right there.'

'So how much do I owe ya?'

She glanced at her screen and pulled an invoice from her file and pointed to the figure.

She had nice nails, deep red and polished; the kind of nails that attracted a man. Luke pulled a fat roll of cash from his trouser pocket and began counting out the twenties. The girl couldn't look at anything other than the money. After he'd paid the balance, he peeled an extra one and rolled it up and slipped it down her blouse.

'What's that for?' she said, grinning.

'For being so helpful, you've been great.'

'Thanks, Luke. I hope you have a lovely holiday.'

'Oh, I intend to, you can be sure of that.'

He collected the tickets and papers and made his way to the door, turned round and smiled and winked and said, 'You behave yourself,' and in the way he said it, she imagined he was saying that one day he might come back for her.

She sure hoped so. She couldn't wait.

What a lovely and caring man he was.

Then he was gone, bouncing up the high street, tickets in hand, a smile fixed on his face. He popped into the bank and made a deposit, stopped off at Reg the Rag and bought an early evening newspaper, and headed across town toward the park where he could make his calls in peace.

The public park was at its best. There was a team of council workmen there, brandishing old green watering cans. Red pelargoniums, multi coloured dahlias, yellow pompom marigolds, blue alyssum, all jostling for space and sunshine in the crowded beds, pretty colours and aromas to attract the bees, not that Luke Flowers would have known that. He thought of it as a peaceful and pleasant place from where he could run his business and make his calls.

Two young women were sitting gossiping on the first bench, one rocking a tiny pram back and forth. They both looked well under twenty and they both smiled at Luke as he wandered by in his tight pants. Luke smiled back, and the girls giggled. On another day he'd join them and try his luck and attempt to lure them back to his flat for an afternoon threesome. It had worked before, but not right there because he had more important things on his mind.

He found an empty bench and rang Melanie. She had taken the day off to get ready. Her bag was packed; her passport was waiting on her dressing-table. She'd bathed and made-up, and brushed and combed her long blonde hair, and all she had to do was wait.

Luke often kept her waiting. He seemed to get off on it. That was cool, in small doses. She could handle the wait, and his mind games. Luke Flowers was worth waiting for. She went downstairs and sat on the sofa and explained to Pugsley that she would be away for two whole weeks and that he had better behave himself, or she wouldn't take him walkies when she returned.

The Springer spaniel coughed, he'd been eating something he shouldn't, and that was nothing new. He had a solid track record of eating non-food items. Mr Kirton's slippers, the plastic tiles on the utility room floor, the lavatory cleaner container in the upstairs bathroom, a sleeping hedgehog at the bottom of the garden, spines and all, the next door kid's football, not to mention Mrs Kirton's prize winning water lilies, all had succumbed to Pugsley's unusual diet.

She picked up her mobile and willed it to ring, and lo-and-behold, it did.

'You ready?' he said.

She could tell from the tone of his voice he was in a good mood, and he was a very moody man. But that was another reason she liked him so much. She could always tell when he was grinning.

'I might be,' she said.

'You'd better be.'

'Or what?'

'I can feel a spanking coming on.'

'Mr Flowers, don't be so horrible.'

'I'll pick you up at four.'

'I'll be ready.'

'You'd better be. Your parents won't be there, will they?'

'Course not. You know they don't get home till gone six.'

'Good! I don't want to meet them. Your dad's a right miserable git.'

'No, he isn't, not all the time.'

'Yes, he is!'

'Where are you now?'

'In the park.'

'What are you doing there?'

'Admiring the blooms.'

The two unmarried mothers came strolling by, glanced down and smiled at Luke. He was talking on the phone, to his girlfriend, they guessed, judging by the expectant look on his face, tight jeans on the pair of them, tight butts, and once past, the darker one glanced back over her shoulder, pouted her lips and blew him a Hollywood kiss, and the pair of them burst into fits of laughter and continued on toward the gates.

'Don't you think you should come and admire this bloom?'

'Sure, babe, I'm on my way home, quick shower and a change, and I'll be at yours for four.'

'Don't be late,' she said.

'Don't be cheeky.'

'Or what?'

'Torrid time for you, squeaker.'

'Don't call me that, you know I don't like it.'

'You shouldn't squeak so much, should you?'

Melanie flushed.

She couldn't help it if she squeaked when he aroused her.

Didn't all women squeak?

'Be ready!' he said, and he cut off and rang his mother.

She was at work, sitting at the bench, the sewing machines firing staccato thread into the blue denim. They weren't supposed to take calls at work, but the supervisor wouldn't hear above the din. She pressed the phone to one ear and her palm across the other.

'Luke?' she said. 'Are you there?'

'Yeah, mum, just to let you know I am going on holiday for two weeks. I'll send you a card.'

'Thanks, son.'

'And I've paid a grand into your bank account.'

'Oh, thanks, son! You didn't have to do that.'

'I know, but I did.'

'You're such a good boy.'

'Yeah mum, I am.'

'Have a wonderful time.'

'I intend to. Have to go,' and he rang off, just as the supervisor came back into the machine shop. His mother dropped the mobile into her lap and resumed firing.

One more call for Luke and then home.

He rang his little friend, Sahira; he couldn't forget her, must keep her sweet, promised to see her again soon.

She was pleased to hear from him, but whinged it had taken him so long to call, and then he was on his way back to the flat to wash and change.

Chapter Ten

Langley Wells resembled a hyena. Short and stocky with powerful cuffing forearms, and a weird head that started wide and narrowed down to a snout, a proboscis through which he regularly sniffed. His father had been short and stocky too, and his father before that; and all the male Wells inherited the same tapering face.

His mother was little and dumpy too, so as Langley grew, his final adult shape surprised no one.

He possessed a temper like a hyena, was fiercely territorial, quick to hatred, and never forgave. But he was also loyal to his friends and family, and generous with his cash when the situation merited it, albeit selectively.

His father was a baker, up at 2am every morning, sometimes waking the entire household as he banged around their council house looking for his boots.

As a boy, Langley Wells had no idea what he wanted to do with his life, but he knew that baking wasn't for him. He wanted a job that was clean and comfortable, where he could wear nice clothes, one where he could sleep in until at least 8am. It wasn't asking a lot, he reasoned, as he pondered on how he could attain his goals and dreams.

His father had been generous too, giving Langley more pocket money than any of his friends, and his mother topped it up, believing his father never gave the boy a thing.

Langley wasn't about to set her straight.

He wasn't interested in most of the things the other kids on the estate went crazy over. Expensive cards of footballers' ugly mugs stuck in albums, used and manky postage stamps. What was the point in spending good money on that? Trashy plastic toys that wouldn't see out the week. 45's you'd play a handful of times and become bored with, and any of the other faddish rubbish that everyone would be ashamed of buying two months down the line.

No, the young Langley valued his hard-earned money far more than that, and he wasn't about to squander it on worthless junk.

It was Willie Masefield who first asked Langley Wells for a loan. They were at school one morning just before lessons began. Langley and Willie shared a desk.

'I need ten bob,' Willie floated in the air, 'to buy a new tender for my engine. The old one's knackered. I could pay you back on Thursday, it's my birthday, Thursday is. Granddad always gives me cash for my birthday present.'

Langley pondered on the idea for a second.

'I might be able to help you,' he said, staring up at the ceiling as if thinking, another queer trait that all the male Wells family adopted.

'Could you?' said Willie, getting excited.

'Maybe. You certain you could pay me back on Thursday?'

Willie nodded, and gasped, 'Sure thing, pal.'

'I'd want fifteen shillings back.'

'What!'

'You heard me; I'd want fifteen shillings back.'

'Bit steep, ain't it?'

'Take it or leave it.'

Willie Masefield could comfortably afford fifteen shillings, after his birthday he could, and he so wanted that black coal tender with the yellow British Railways logo painted on the side.

'I'll take it!' he said, holding out his hand as if to shake on the deal.

That surprised Langley.

He had never shaken anyone's hand before, not to seal a deal, but he did so at that moment, though afterwards he wasn't sure he liked the idea. Willie's hand was fleshy and hot and sweaty. Not nice at all. It would put Langley Wells off shaking on deals forever.

'Well?' said Willie. 'When can I have the money?'

'Now,' said Langley, delving into his deep pockets where his mother's discarded maroon purse spent most of its time. It was a tiny purse, yet it bulged with coins, and to Willie's amazement, banknotes too. No other kid on the estate possessed money like that. Langley dragged out a shrivelled and torn rust coloured ten-shilling note. Laid it on the desk. Ironed it out with his wooden ruler. Picked it up and offered it across to his friend.

The temptation was too great. Willie grabbed it.

Langley did not let go.

'I'm giving you this on condition that you pay back fifteen shillings on Thursday.'

'I know. So you said.'

'Don't even think of letting me down.'

'I won't.'

Langley fixed Willie with his steel-grey eyes.

Said, 'I'll poke your eye out if you do.'

Willie glanced at Langley's muscular forearms and an horrific thought flashed into his mind of running round the playground with one eye; and one patch. He knew Langley meant every word.

Both boys were eleven.

The deal went well. Willie had his coal tender, and on the Thursday Langley was at school early, sitting at the desk, waiting. Willie joined him soon after, and pursed his lips. Langley imagined Willie was preparing an excuse. He couldn't wait to get down to business.

'Got it?' he said.

Langley was pleased to see Willie nodding.

Langley held out his hand.

Willie reached into his satchel, opened his plastic lunch box. There was an unsealed white envelope in there. Willie held it close to his face so that Langley couldn't see inside, pulled out a crisp new ten-shilling note, and slid it across the timber.

Birthday present from grandpa, by the look of it; imagined Langley. He picked it up and said, 'And the rest?'

'My mum says...'

'I don't care what your mum says! Pay up... or go blind!'

Willie peered into Langley's face. He didn't like what he saw, and he didn't want any hassle. Opened the envelope again and fished out two pristine and shiny silver half crowns, and reluctantly set them down on the desk.

'Thank you,' said Langley as he scooped them up. 'Nice to do business with you, Willie,' and he rammed the whole fifteen bob into the maroon purse, and snapped it shut.

The cash would stay there forever, until next time.

Willie was close to tears.

After that, word went round the school that if anyone ever needed cash, no matter how small the amount, no matter how soon the borrower needed it, no matter what they wanted it for, just don't tell your parents, Langley Wells could help. He began keeping a notebook, a small red card backed affair he'd bought in the post office for nine-pence, thin lined, all the better to cram more data into.

Business boomed, especially on Mondays, dinner money day, when some kids would often be short. In his specialised market, Langley had no competitors; and it wasn't long before he was expanding.

Mrs Buxton was her name, a skinny wastrel of a thing who was always complaining about something or other, four kids, no husband, always in and out of the bookies, dying for a fag and a pint and a hand out giro cheque. It wasn't hard to figure she would be short of cash before the week was out.

Sure enough, there came a day when she had no money to feed the kids. The pasta jar was empty. It was her daughter Denise who suggested the idea. Denise was hungry and so were the siblings.

'Why don't you try Langley?'

'Try Langley for what?'

'Money of course, mum, he's loaded.'

'And he'd lend me some?'

'Course he would. He lends to everyone.'

Mrs B pursed her lips and thought she'd try it.

'Look after the kids,' she said to the ten-year-old Denise, and she shot out of the house.

Lots of the estate kids hung around outside the red brick post office after school, where they bought crisps and cola and sweeties and comics. And even if Langley wasn't there, one of the others would know where he was.

He was usually to be found hanging about because it was a good place to do business. There would always be some kid willing to borrow a couple of bob to buy some chocolate or an ice cream and a bottle of Corona. Three bob back tomorrow. Not too bad. It suited both parties well. Most of the kids could find three bob later if they needed to, if they needed to pay back Langley Wells, even if they had to sneak it from their mother's purse, or the gas or electric meter money tin.

Mrs Buxton hustled over and saw him loitering there, leaning up against the side brick wall of the post office. The ugly little bugger was admiring the short skirt on Willie Masefield's younger sister, Rosie.

'Langley, love,' she called, 'can I have a word with you?'

Langley did not like being called Langley love, and he didn't like Mrs Buxton either, and wondered what the hell she wanted, as he wandered sulkily across to her.

'I need a little money, Langley love, just to tide me over.'

Langley switched on.

'How much do you want?'

She only wanted a fiver but thought she'd try it on; see what the queer little twerp was made of.

'I could do with twenty notes.'

Langley pulled a face, whistled through his teeth like they did in the old black and white movies. He could stump up the cash if need be, that wasn't a problem. Mrs Buxton was the problem. He didn't rate her, not one bit, and he wondered how and when he'd see his hard-earned money back.

'When will I get paid?'

'Thursday, Langley love, when my benefit comes in.'

Langley pulled a face and stared at the clouds. Then he said, 'Thirty quid back, Thursday without fail.'

'Bugger off!'

'Suit yourself,' and he turned on his heels. He wasn't that bothered, and headed back toward Rosie Masefield who was skipping on a big rope being swung by two friends, her pink skirt flicking up interestingly on the down jump.

'Oh, Langley love, wait a sec. You're all right, you're a good boy, I can do that, yeah, thirty quid back on Thursday. I can do that. I'll see you right.'

Langley paused and turned back and peered into her darting eyes. Against his better judgement, he agreed. There was something dangerous about it, something pioneering, with her being an adult, of sorts. It brought a feeling of excitement and exhilaration over him, and he liked that, he liked it a lot.

He took out his newer, larger, black leather purse, and yanked two tenners free. Held them screwed up in his balled hand. Offered them to her, palm down, so no one could see.

'Thirty back, Thursday night,' he reiterated through the side of his mouth, 'I'll call at five; make sure the money's ready.'

'You'll get your cash back, you little monkey, I'm trustworthy, me.'

She'd wanted to say little prick, not monkey, but guessed correctly that might have screwed up the deal.

Langley stared at her, and slowly opened his hand, and the hot balled tenners flopped into her grubby mitt.

'Ta, love,' she said, and she shot off toward the bookmakers, for she knew the evening meeting at Haydock was about to begin. The kids could wait a wee while yet.

It was the biggest loan he'd ever made, and it brought with it the biggest excitement, and the greatest worry.

Thursday night turned out a bright sunny evening. Langley was knocking on the Buxton's door at dead on five. He valued punctuality; he valued reliability, and if he expected his customers to be punctual and reliable, the least he could do was be the same. Young Denise came to the door.

'Hiya, Langley.'

'Hi, Denise. Is your mum in?'

'Yeah, sure. Come in.'

She was slumped on the sofa; staring at the telly, a mean look on her skinny face. She'd lost a bit of weight, and she didn't have much to lose. Maybe she wasn't eating well. The kids were dreadfully skinny too. Denise had legs like matchsticks.

'S'pose you've come for your money 'ave ya?'

'Yes, Mrs Buxton.'

'Don't you Mrs Buxton me!'

'We said five o'clock, Thursday. It is Thursday, it is five o'clock,' he said, glancing pointedly at the mantelpiece clock.

'I can't give you all of it; the best I can manage is a freaking fiver.'

'No good, Mrs Buxton. I don't do instalments. It's all or nothing.'

'Suit yourself, it's nothing then.'

Langley had planned for such an event. He reached into his pocket. Took out a box of matches. Struck a match. Denise's eyes lit up, stared into the flame. It reminded her of bonfire night. Langley presented the burning match toward the crammed newspaper rack.

'If you don't pay me right now, I'll burn the house down.'

'Watch what you are doin', you little bastard!'

'Pay me then!'

'Like hell! You can kiss my arse!'

Langley lit the corner of a section of the red-topped daily trash that was hanging out of the rack. Smoke filled the room. Flames licked up the side.

'Mum!' screamed Denise.

'All right, all right! I'll pay! Put that fire out!' she screamed as she leapt from the couch.

Langley grabbed a cushion and smothered the fire.

Mrs B went to the kitchen, came back a moment later, threw three tenners on the floor. Yelled, 'There's your money, you little prick! Now get out of my house before I throttle ya, you ugly little bastard!'

Langley stooped and collected his cash.

He was never too proud to get down and pick up money.

'Look at my beautiful cushion!' Mrs Buxton shrieked, smacking it, as Denise struggled to open the window.

Langley had his money and that was the only thing that mattered, for he understood what money meant: power. He would have the last laugh, as he usually did. On his way out Mrs B screamed after him, 'You have no idea what you are messing with! No idea!'

Back then, he didn't. Langley Wells had crossed the Rubicon. He had begun lending to adults. He had moved into a different league. From that day, he would face real and ferocious competition. He would soon find out how tough business could be, though he did have one small compensation.

Setting light to Mrs Buxton's house brought him a reputation. People gossiped about him, became wary of him, feared him even. He wasn't quite right in the head. Everyone knew that. Langley Wells was a psycho, a loony. He was almost twelve, a moneylender, and a known arsonist.

Chapter Eleven

Walter and Karen arrived outside the Swaythling home at two o'clock, rang the buzzer, and the Filipina let them in. Holly Swaythling was sitting in the same chair in the same room. 'Well, Inspector, I am surprised to see you back so soon.'

'There were one or two things we wanted to ask you, confidentially, while you were on your own.'

'Gerry would be furious if he knew you were here. You know that, don't you?'

'That's as maybe, but all we are concerned with is the safety of your son.'

'Yes, I understand.'

'Did you speak to Neil?' asked Karen.

'I did, thank you, and he said I was not to worry... but mothers always worry.'

'Yes, of course they do,' said Walter.

'So ask away, Inspector, before I fall asleep, as I always seem to do in the afternoons these days.'

'When we asked you yesterday if Gerry had any enemies he said no, but we thought you thought different.'

'I wouldn't have said enemies, exactly.'

'What then?' asked Karen.

Holly took a deep breath, as if that was an enormous effort.

'Ten, maybe fifteen years ago, Swaythling Construction wasn't anything like it is today.'

'Much smaller?' said Walter.

'Yes! Tiny in comparison, and delicate. We were going through one of the cyclical building slumps, as we always seem to do; it was a time when the banks would only lend to the people who didn't need the money.'

'Nothing much changes,' said Karen.

'True.'

'And Swaythling's did need money?' asked Walter.

'Very much so. The business was called Swaythling & Ford back then. Gerry had a partner.'

'A Mr Ford?' clarified Karen.

Holly nodded. 'Munro Ford to be specific.'

'What happened to him?' asked Walter.

'The business was in serious financial difficulty. They needed a hundred and sixty grand to survive. Eighty grand per partner. Munro had no connections; no money, nothing. His expertise was on the construction side. He needed to be led when it came to running and pushing a business forward. Pity really, he was a decent enough chap. But he had no influence, and not a lot of get up and go, and when it came to it, he couldn't raise a bean of finance, and there's no sentiment in business, Inspector. Gerry made it clear, he told him straight, if he couldn't help to save the outfit he would have to go.'

'And that's what happened?' asked Walter.

Holly nodded again.

'Munro took the huff and buggered off. He didn't get a penny for his share in the business; it must have rankled terribly, especially when you see what the organisation has grown into today.'

'It's profitable now?' asked Karen.

'Yes, very,' she said. 'You only have to look at this place to see that. Bought and paid for, this house is, not a penny owed on any mortgage. Neil will be a very wealthy young man one day, just so long as he sorts himself out, stops acting the goat, and dumps that fat cradle snatcher.'

'So what happened to Munro Ford?' asked Walter.

'Last I heard he was driving a taxi.'

'Ouch!' said Karen.

'Precisely,' said Holly.

'And Gerry raised the money?' asked Walter.

'Yes, he did.'

'All hundred and sixty K of it?' persisted Walter.

'He did.'

'From the banks?' asked Karen.

'No! Course not! They wouldn't touch him. Not back then.'

'So from where?' asked Walter.

'He wouldn't tell me for ages, years after.'

'But you know now?'

'Oh, yes.'

'So where did the cash come from?' asked Karen.

Holly paused for a few seconds, as if weighing up whether to reveal what she knew.

'The Lodge, of course.'

'The Masonic Lodge?' asked Karen.

Holly nodded.

There was a moment's silence as they all thought about that; before Walter said, 'There's something else I'd like to ask you.'

'You'd better be quick, I'm getting sleepy.'

'Yesterday, as we arrived, we saw a young woman leaving.'

'Ah, you mean Suzanne?'

'Do we?' asked Karen.

'The pretty blonde?' clarified Holly.

Walter nodded.

'I suppose you'd like to know who she is.'

'Yes,' said Karen. 'We would.'

'Well she... she's, Gerry's mistress.'

Another brief silence and Walter said, 'And you don't mind?'

'Course I mind! But there is nothing I can do about it, is there? He, Gerry that is, has, what shall we say, a very large libido, and, well, not to put too fine a point on it, I, with this condition,' and she glanced down at her failing body, 'can no longer fulfil his wishes. I suppose it's only fair. She's a decent enough kid, and to tell you the truth; we have become quite close. Crazy, isn't it? Best pals with my husband's bit on the side.'

'Where did he meet her?' asked Karen.

'The last holiday we went on, Portugal it was, Suzanne was one of the air hostesses. Gerry took a shine to her right off, as he often does, and she fell for his mature charm, hook line and sinker, stupid girl.'

65

'What's her surname?'

'Knight.'

'Where does she live?' asked Karen.

'Is that relevant?'

'Maybe.'

'She has a flat in town. Gerry pays her visits in the afternoon. Thinks I don't know about it, but I do. He stinks of her when he comes home, understated French perfume, and he's always in a good mood.'

'And what was she doing here yesterday?' asked Walter.

'Had some papers to sign.'

'What papers?'

'Something to do with her life insurance and Will. Gerry's organising it for her. They need a lot of life insurance in that line of work. Now I'm sorry, Inspector, but I will have to take my afternoon nap,' and she called for Hilario to show them out.

'Thank you so much for seeing us again,' said Walter, standing.

'If it helps find the maniac hunting my son, it will have been worthwhile.'

'Yes, of course, I am sure it will.'

A couple of minutes later they were outside in the car and Karen said, 'That was revealing.'

'Yes,' said Walter, seemingly miles away.

'Guv?'

'What?'

'Can I ask you something?'

'Sure.'

'Are you on the square?'

Walter guffawed, didn't say anything.

'Well?' she said, in that persistent way of hers. 'Are you?'

He still didn't reply, just pinched the flesh of his right cheek between his finger and thumb and shook it and said, 'What is this?'

'Your jowls.'

'Do you mind! I don't have jowls! What else?'

'Your cheek.'

'What else is it?'

'It's the side of your face.'

'What else!'

'It's your black skin.'

'Aha! At last! Correct!'

'And they don't accept black people?'

'They didn't back then.'

'And now?'

'Who knows? Don't care.'

'Would you have joined as a younger man, back then, if you'd had the opportunity?'

'That's a hypothetical question.'

'So what's the answer?'

'I don't do hypothetical questions. I want to talk about the here and now.'

'If you must.'

'When we get back to the station, find out where Munro Ford lives. I think we need to pay him a visit.'

'Sure, Guv,' but she was still thinking of the Lodge when she said, 'How come the Masons provided Gerry Swaythling with so much cash, when the banks wouldn't touch him?'

'I have no idea.'

'Don't you think we should look into that?'

'Where do you suggest we start? They are not going to talk to me, are they? I'm black, and I'm not a member, and they are not going to talk to you. You're female, and you're not a member either.'

Karen grinned and said, 'No, but Gibbo is.'

'Is he? I didn't know that.'

'I think so.'

'Well, even if he is, he's not going to help us out on this. They are sworn to secrecy, threatened with having their tongue ripped out at dawn if they spill the beans. You know the score.'

'Oh Gibbo won't mind about that.'

'I think you will find he does.'

'Leave Gibbo to me,' and she grinned wickedly and said, 'I still think we should put the frighteners on them.'

'I think you will find they are not easily frightened. Let's talk about something else.'

'Like what?'

'Suzanne Knight.'

'I am not surprised at all about that.'

'About her shacking up with Gerry?'

'Yeah, I knew he was that kind of man the moment I set eyes on him. He couldn't let a woman pass in the street without checking her out... and wondering.'

'He's fifty odd, for God's sake.'

'Doesn't matter, Guv, not with men like him. He'll never change.'

'Come on, take me back to work, we seem to be getting sidetracked, let's have an update meeting, everyone there, talk it through, see what ideas everyone has.'

'Sure, Guv,' she said, smiling to herself, for she still had clear ideas of pumping Darren Gibbons for information. She just might extract things where Walter couldn't, and that appealed to her.

Chapter Twelve

Langley Wells often thought about the old days. He liked to remember those tough but happy times. He liked to remember Rose too, as she was back then, Willie Masefield's kid sister, the same girl cum woman he had been married to for longer than he cared to remember.

He had celebrated his fifty-fifth birthday and was still running the same game, and business was still good. When had it not been? People always needed cash.

He still lived on the estate, and in the same house too, though they had long since bought the property under the right to buy scheme. It would have been foolish not to. He'd had an extension built on the side, another one jammed on the back, and another jemmied into the roof space, and they needed it too, with their three twenty-something sons, Lawrie, Lenny and Lewis, all still living at home, all enjoying on-off live-in girlfriends, and on-off grandkids that Langley liked to play with and spoil. The three boys, the L's, as they were known, all worked in the family businesses. Fact was, none of them had ever considered doing anything else.

There was a rumour going round the estate that Langley was a multimillionaire and possessed a sprawling villa on one of the Spanish Costas overlooking the Mediterranean.

That was ridiculous.

It was in Tuscany.

Or Tuscanshire, as the ever-growing band of expat Brits preferred to call it, as they roamed the countryside as if they owned the place, inspecting their vineyards in their dusty right-hand drive Range Rovers and Norton motorcycles.

It was a rambling building, the Wells Italian home, one that he'd added to over the years. It became something of a fortress, set on top of the perfect hill that looked out over the rolling Italian countryside, where heat-haze bobbled into the air like scent from a rose. Langley had acquired the run-down property years ago for a song during one of the regular property slumps, and had turned it into a wonder home.

He would disappear there twice a year to recharge his batteries, and would return with a deep tan, though he would never discuss it, and trained his family to do likewise. So far as anyone else was concerned, he had been on a cheap package holiday to Benidorm. What they didn't know, they couldn't become jealous about.

Outside the family no one knew of il Pratino Del Cielo, the adjoining lawn of heaven, in roughly translated English, though Langley much preferred the Italian version. He had learnt the language. It had taken him some time, but he'd managed it in the end. Il Pratino Del Cielo, the words rolled off his tongue, his Italian home, the epitome of his life's work.

He was happy there and one day he would retire there too, but not yet because he still had business to accomplish at home, for he could never lend money in Italia. That would have been beyond the pale.

He was sitting in the courtyard, straw hat on his head to keep off the worst of the midday sun, a half bottle of best Chianti before him, barely touched. He was not a glutton, never had been, preferred to savour the finer things of life in small quantities, figured that was the best way to gain true enjoyment, to take pleasure from everything, sparingly. Pigging out was for pigs, or porco, as he preferred to say in the local lingo.

He was still thinking of the early days.

He was thinking of his forthcoming marriage.

He was twenty and she almost eighteen.

He was thinking of the McIntyres, and bloody Bobby Watson.

Rose Masefield was Catholic and to keep her sweet, the wedding was held at Saint Mary's Roman Catholic Church. Langley's mind was not on the wedding. He still hadn't got dressed. He was thinking of Bobby Watson.

70

The freak had borrowed money from Langley, two hundred and fifty quid, and afterwards he had point blank refused to repay the loan. No one ever refused to repay Langley Wells because most of his customers knew full well they would need to visit the bank of Langley again next week, next month, next year, some time for sure, and they were desperate not to cut off his safe supply of ready cash.

If Bobby Watson could get away with it, and was seen and heard to be bragging in the Golden Bell about how he hadn't bothered to repay the strange Wells man, then anyone could. Langley grimaced at the thought, and tried hard not to see the total figure of unpaid loans he had outstanding. It was vast, stretching to more than two thousand individual transactions. The small red notebook had long since morphed into several vast maroon ledgers that could be screwed open and expanded, into which additional pages would often be added.

What would happen if they all decided not to pay?

He would be ruined.

All his hard work would have been for nothing.

Langley belched. The thought of it was giving him indigestion, and on his blessed wedding day too.

'Are you ready yet, Langley?' his mother called through. 'I swear that boy would be late for his own funeral,' she muttered.

'Don't speak of funerals today of all days, mother,' said Langley's father, 'not on the boy's wedding day.'

The problem was still in Langley's head when they piled into the car patiently waiting outside. Fact was, he was late for his own wedding, forcing Rose in her larger, smarter car to circumvent the block three times, as she grew more upset at the thought the crazy man had grown cold feet overnight. She would remind him of that countless times through the coming years. She imagined he experienced second thoughts when nothing was further from the truth, though he wasn't about to set her straight on that.

The thought of not turning up had never crossed Langley's mind. He loved Rose Masefield completely, loved her to bits, always had, and had never touched another woman, not in passion, and yet he still couldn't stop thinking about bloody Bobby Watson.

71

Carole and Norman McIntyre had been married for twenty-two years, coincidentally married in the same church. They lived on the far side of the estate and were irregular customers of Langley's. For once they didn't owe him anything and were mighty happy to be that way, and that was down to Carole Mac, as her friends called her, because she worked her rocks off.

Starting at seven cleaning at the local primary school, washing and polishing the brown square tiled floors. After that, she'd hurry to the kwik discount utilitarian supermarket on the out-of-town shopping estate, the place where they piled it high and sold it cheap, or at least told everyone they did, where Carole would spend the day working flat out on the tills, often serving many of her neighbours and friends who would smile at her embarrassingly.

She enjoyed her work there. It was interesting to see the rubbish everyone else bought, and the quality of the meals, or lack of it, some of them enjoyed. If Carole Mac had been forced to eat the sludge some of her neighbours took home, she would have emigrated.

At six o'clock she'd hurry home for a frantic tea, a quick wash and change, and scurry to the Golden Bell for half-past seven, where she'd turn on her smiley, bubbly head, and face many of the same people she had served earlier in the not-so-super supermarket. They would gaze into their pints, and check their lottery tickets, and moan about their lot in life, and throw some cash into the coin eating fruit machine, and wonder where it had all gone wrong.

By the time they had put the towels up and washed the glasses Carole would rarely get home before half-past eleven, in time to see her husband ensconced in front of the television set eating cheap crisps and watching football. For the most part, the McIntyres kept away from the tentacles of the eager moneylenders, and that was down to Carole Mac.

'Had a good night, love?' he'd say, the same thing every night.

Yeah, sure, wonderful, she would think, though she wouldn't say.

Norman hadn't been to work. He never did. He had a bad back. Collected a decent whack of disability allowance. That would do him.

He would struggle, grunting in pain, into their old hatchback, and drive to the Golden Bell and force down a few pints, yet when he was in the house alone he would race the dog up and down the stairs, laughing crazily, the dog barking mad, a game that he and the dog enjoyed. It kept them fit, and nary a twinge.

Carole Mac staggered to bed searching for sleep, for she had to be up again at six.

The following day when she came home for tea, he imagined he would make her happy because he'd bought an old goose in the Bell at lunchtime for three quid from Jackie Spenser. This time it had been plucked and gutted. God knows where it came from; probably from the canal.

You could always find something to eat on the canal if you were desperate enough, and especially where the smallholding ran down to the water, where chickens and ducks and geese would break free and make a run for it, out of the frying pan, and all that.

Norman McIntyre fancied himself as a cook.

He had taken to watching cookery programmes on the television when there was no football showing, and would copy the dishes and try them on his tired guinea pig of a wife.

He was experimenting that evening.

Intended to serve up roast goose with apples and prunes, and that was a first. He had been at it ages, and hoped his wife understood and appreciated how much hard work he had put into bringing the creature and creation to the table. Cutting and peeling and slicing the Cox's orange pippins, de-stoning the pound of no-soak prunes, messy job, as he squinted at his illegible handwriting, scribbled down, for those TV chefs spoke far too quick.

The old goose was roasting.

Smelling delightful, the aroma of sizzling fowl permeating every corner of their small home.

Needed a lot of emptying though, the fat did. Do all gooses, or was it geese, produce so much fat? He pondered, or was it because

73

this was an old beast caught on the hop? He had no idea, didn't much care either, so long as it tasted good, and his dear wife appreciated how much hard work he had put in, and all for her.

Still time for another run up those stairs with Daisy, though.

Up and down the stairs, up and down!

Deep breath!

Daisy was a cross bull something or other with a Doberman, Rottweiler cross, and an ugly bitch at that, and the thought occurred to him that his dog was almost as pig ugly as Langley Wells. He was getting married that same day, almost as ugly, but not quite. Norman laughed aloud.

Daisy worked herself into a state of excitement not seen since the last turkey roast the previous Christmas. The scent of roasting goose was too much for her, but there was still time to play, as Norman hurried to the stairs and yelled, 'Come on girl! Indoor walkies!' as he strode up the stairs one more time. He would try and complete fifteen runs that day. Twenty-two was his all time record, though he failed to match it.

Three times up and three times down, Norman laughing like crazy, the dog barking louder than ever, when Norman caught a whiff of burning goose.

Time to empty the bloody fat… again.

'Just a sec, Daisy,' he said, 'won't be a mo, you stay there, don't want your snout in the tray,' and he closed the hall door, shutting the dog out of the kitchen.

Went to the cooker. Saw the collected fat in the glass basin, three quarters full, sitting on the top of the cooker. Saw the electric ring beneath, glowing.

'Oh, shit!' he said. 'You're not supposed to be on!'

Reached across to the dials at the top of the back of the cooker, turned the front ring to zero, and breathed out. Glanced back at the smoking fat, knew he couldn't touch the glass for the heat. Considered reaching for the oven glove.

Too late.

Crack!!!

Crash!!!

74

Bang!!!

The toughened glass basin exploded.

Scolding fat blew into his face.

A chunk of jagged glass buried itself deep into his shoulder; another smaller piece removed his right eyebrow. Norman McIntyre collapsed to the floor. He couldn't see, he couldn't move. He entered a state of shock. Daisy barked, but no one paid any attention because Daisy was always barking.

Ten minutes later Carole arrived home.

Something smelled good, she thought, as she shrugged off her raincoat and let herself in by the back door. Duck by the smell of it, and Norman did a decent duck `a l'orange, even if he went a little heavy on the l'orange. The dog was barking, but the damn dog was always barking.

'Shut up, Daisy!' Carole yelled as she entered the kitchen.

Norman was lying on his back, moaning. His face covered in smoking goose fat and broken glass.

His shoulder bleeding fast.

There was a cut on his face, and a glutinous mixture of fat and fresh blood decorated her kitchen floor. Broken glass everywhere, ugly vindictive pieces that you wouldn't want to step on.

In the background, the aroma of burning old goose.

'Norman!' she shrieked, bending over him.

Norman moaned, nothing more.

In the hall, the dog barked again.

'Shut the hell up!' screamed Carole. She had never liked that hideous animal.

'Oh, God!' and she reached over and turned off the cooker, went to the hall door, pushed her way through without letting the dog into the kitchen. The dog wanted to play, the dog wanted to eat, the dog would have licked Norman's face clean, given the chance.

Carole hustled to the phone. Dialled triple nine.

'Ambulance quick, my husband is cooking! Quick as you can. I think he's dying!'

The ambulance set off five minutes later, the driver and his mate laughing at the tale they'd been told about a bloke roasting a dinner, set himself on fire, and now he was cooking too. You had to smile. You couldn't make it up. You heard such weird tales in the job. You'd better get your foot down before he gets cold!

Bobby Watson had been having trouble with his hearing. He was on the way to the evening surgery to have them syringed.

He was thinking of buying a new colour television, complete with the new revolutionary front-loading video recording machine. You could record dirty movies on them, and stop the picture still and replay the filthiest moments, and how clever was that? He still had most of the money he'd screwed out of the tight arse Langley Wells, and Langley wouldn't miss the money. Everyone knew he was loaded, though Bobby would have to borrow more. He would use one of Langley's competitors, and they would welcome the business too, because word was, they were struggling to compete with the ugly little git.

Bobby skipped across the road to jump the bus the three stops to the surgery. Thought he heard the bus coming. Probably not, with his ears. Glanced up to see the ambulance hurtling round the corner. Dashing toward the house of the roasting man, dashing toward Bobby Watson.

Bobby stood frozen, transfixed in the middle of the road.

'Look out!' yelled the paramedic, sitting alongside the driver.

Too late.

The aging, but chunky ambulance, smacked Bobby Watson full in the face, knocked him into the air, kicked him hard, bashed him again as he fell to earth, and ran him over for good measure. The ambulance skidded to a halt, half way on the grass verge. The paramedic jumped out and rushed back to inspect the carnage, as the driver slumped in his seat, shaking his head, cursing the day.

Langley Wells struggled to recover the money from Bobby Watson; and he never did.

Weird results spring from unexpected events, and they did from the sudden and violent death of Bobby Watson.

People began talking. Gossip was rife.

When Langley heard of Bobby's violent death, he was mortified. His business had never suffered such a loss. He would have to work doubly hard to recoup the damage.

But he need not have worried, for when he returned from his honeymoon in Corfu, the first time he had ever travelled to the sunny Med, he was surprised to discover that all his clients were up to date with their repayments, not one laggard among them. More than that, many of them adopted a more reverential air toward him. Spoke to him more politely too, asked him for advice, even, something no one had done before.

He made discrete enquiries to find out why.

The intelligence he received back amazed him.

Common wisdom had it that Langley Wells had ordered Bobby's execution. No one believed it had been an accident. Everyone knew Bobby Watson was in hock to Langley Wells for hundreds of pounds, and everyone knew Bobby had taken a stand and had reneged on the debt, and how it had cost him.

Langley Wells was putting matters straight; everyone believed that, it was obvious. It was only to be expected. It was a lesson to them all. Don't pay, don't live, an easy equation, the man had a history of it, setting fire to people's homes, bullying and intimidating them, it was no surprise. It was simple. If you borrowed money from Langley Wells you paid him back, whatever it took, and woe betide you if you didn't.

Langley smiled inwardly and remained silent.

Business boomed like never before.

Two of his thorny competitors melted away, frightened at what might happen to them. The aftermath of the peculiar death of Bobby Watson rumbled on for years.

Norman McIntyre was OK though, after a year or two, and several painful skin grafts, though his face never quite recovered.

He never laughed at ugly people again.

Carole Mac went back to work, determined more than ever to keep her family from the iron grip of Langley Wells, and his ilk. She'd heard there might be a few extra hours available at the school, maybe even weekends too. She'd take it if she could. Of course she would. She needed the money. The whole family did.

Chapter Thirteen

It was a couple of minutes to four when Luke pushed the doorbell at the Kirton's four bedroom detached family home. Melanie was in for a big surprise. He'd grown a thick moustache and was taller than before, Cuban heels, and most weirdly of all, he'd gone orange.

'What the hell?' she said, as she opened the front door, as Pugsley tried to dash out and race next door, to where the black poodle resided that Pugsley was sweet on.

'Oh no you don't!' she said, as she grabbed his collar and dragged him back to the kitchen.

'This it?' said Luke, glancing down at the single case.

'Yep, plus my hand luggage,' she said. 'I'll be with you in a tick.'

Luke turned about and hurried back to the car and rammed the case in the back of his silver sports. He was eager to get away, didn't want anything to do with either of the parents who were stuck up pricks, so far as he was concerned.

He sat in the car and watched her lock the front door. He wasn't sure he liked the primrose trouser suit, but the jacket was short and the pants were tight, and she had the most perfect backside, and the beige extra high heels were amusing.

Then she was in the car, glancing across at him.

'Are you going to tell me what this new image is about?'

'I felt like a change.'

'It's that all right. I'm not sure I like it. You look like a spiv.'

'You'll like it, squeaker,' he said.

'Don't call me that, I don't like it.'

'I'll call you what I like.'

79

'I thought the point of going to Italy was to get a tan, not to go there caked in a false one.'

'The point of going to Italy, doll, is for us to spend some quality time together, get my meaning? Are we going to enjoy this holiday, or are we going to bicker?'

She glanced at him again and into his blue eyes and realised she might spoil things, and remembered how much he excited her, and said, 'Oh sorry, darling,' and she reached across and kissed him, depositing pink lipstick on his lips, and muzzy.

The moustache tickled, and she didn't know whether she liked that either. It wasn't even his, it couldn't have been; it wasn't there when she last saw him. What was the complete wazzock playing at? He was always doing crazy things, though she didn't say, for she didn't want to upset him again.

In the next second he'd started the car and they were away, heading toward Manchester airport and glorious Italy beyond.

They had been on the flight twenty minutes when he ambled to the lavatories and removed the moustache and slipped it into the slim plastic cover and then in his wallet. He didn't think it possible the police were looking for him, but it was always best not to take chances, and he liked the excitement of disguise.

He hadn't yet decided whether to wear it on the return journey. He washed his face, but the tan was not for turning, so he winked at himself in the mirror and returned to Mel.

'That's some improvement,' she said, staring up at him and linking his arm as he sat beside her, and maybe she could get used to the additional height too. It had never bothered her before, his slightness, but this new taller Luke could grow on her. 'Come here,' she said, and she pulled him close and kissed him properly, a promise of things to come, he imagined.

Honeymooners thought the older couple across the aisle, stuck out a mile, lucky things. Make the most of it, for it will only be a fleeting moment.

The hotel was beyond fabulous, their suite luxury beyond compare, the views to die for, the food incredible, the wine as good as she had ever tasted, and the sex beyond measure, and so much of it. The guy was like a buck rabbit on rechargeable batteries. He could not get enough of her, something she put down to her innate ability to attract men, something she had recognised since she was twelve, and something she felt very comfortable with, and grateful for.

True, he could go over the top, become a little rough, more than a little sometimes. But she could live with that, especially if it pleased him, because that was what she wanted to do. Please Luke Edward Flowers totally and utterly, and she would do whatever it took to accomplish it, almost anything.

She was sitting in the salon, Luigi's this time. It had become something of a ritual whenever they went to Italy, or anywhere else. She would have her hair done in the best local salon, and that meant the most expensive place, and expensive in Venice was expensive indeed.

She needed it too, after the torrid night he'd put her through. Her hairstyle was wrecked and ruined and needed all of Luigi's skills to set it right.

'Signorina,' he pleaded, 'what-a you do with this fine-a blond-a hair? Mamma Mia!'

She smiled at the handsome man in the mirror and shrugged her shoulders, tried hard not to blush, too embarrassed to say a word, for she imagined Luigi could guess if he tried.

Luke sat outside on a crowded bench, as a bunch of middle-aged Americans hiding under straw hats, threw corn for the pigeons. One of the birds thanked the visitors by squirting poop at them as it dashed for the barley.

Luke saw it coming, swayed to his left out of the way, and it landed on the corn thrower's left forearm.

'It's lucky, you know,' the guy grinned, beaming round and staring stupidly at the others, and Luke, and anyone else who saw it, as the

American's wife handed him a tissue and said, 'Wipe yourself, Wilbur.'

Lucky my backside, thought Luke, as he took out his phone and rang Sahira.

'Where are you?' she whispered.

'Venice,' he said. He could tell she was whispering, but he heard her OK. If she was whispering, it could mean she was at home and didn't want to be overheard.

'What are you doing there?'

'On holiday, what do you think?'

'With her again, I suppose.'

'Don't start that again. Where are you?'

'In my bedroom. I was just thinking about you. When are you coming home?'

'Week on Friday.'

'That long! When are you going to see me again?'

'Don't know yet, we'll have to fix something later.'

'You do want to see me again, Luke, don't you?'

'Yeah, course I do, doll. You know that.'

'Sometimes I wonder.'

'Look, I'll bell you as soon as I get home. I'll have to go, the battery's going.'

'OK, make sure you do, and Luke…'

'What?'

'I love you very much.'

'Course you do, doll.'

Then she said in a rush, 'Sorry I'll have to go, dad's coming!' and she cut off, leaving Luke staring at his silent latest design handset.

Silly bitch, he said aloud, but it didn't matter, for the Americans had gone, to be replaced by a gang of nouveau riche Russians who smiled down at him, but couldn't speak or understand a word of English.

Ten minutes later Melanie came out of the hairdressers and stood before him and said, 'Well, what do you think?'

Luke's eyes widened, and he jumped up and grabbed her and kissed her lips and blonde hair and whispered, 'You look fantastic.

Come on!' and he grabbed her hand and tugged her back toward the hotel.

'I thought we were going for a trip on the lagoon.'

'Bugger the lagoon!'

'Luke!' she protested, 'I was looking forward to that.'

'I have something far more important you can look forward to, come on!' and he dragged her back to their suite, and the amazing big bed.

Chapter Fourteen

Walter stood up and called across the room, 'Listen up everyone!' The hum of conversation died away. and they all turned and stared at Darriteau. 'Better! Time to focus. Jeffrey Player, murdered, shot dead in the Ship pub, Friday night.' Walter nodded at Karen, who was standing by the info board.

She nodded back and smiled at the gang and pointed at the smiling picture of Jeff Player, the photograph supplied that morning by his sniffling mother.

Walter began again. 'The attempted murder of Neil Swaythling between the lockups,' Karen pointed to Neil's pic. 'We believe the killing of Player was a mistake, an accident. We think the killer was gunning for Neil. The unfortunate Player got in the way.'

No one disagreed.

'Neil is housed in a safe place,' Walter's deep and lugubrious voice filled the room. He kept the young Swaythling's whereabouts secret to three people, himself, Karen, and the boss, Mrs West. He'd done that because he was worried there could be a mole in the house, some idiot prepared to sell info to the press, or anyone else who waved a bunch of banknotes. It had happened before, and Walter wasn't taking any risks. 'He will remain out of sight until the killer is caught. As you know, the murderer believes his last strike was successful, that's what the press believes too, so let's keep it that way. Anyone found releasing anything different will be disciplined, and if I have my way, fired,' and he glanced at Mrs West, as if seeking support. Most of those present did so too. She sensed her moment.

'Make no mistake about it,' she said. 'Anyone releasing information on this sensitive matter could be endangering Neil

Swaythling's life. In the event of Neil being murdered, anyone doing so could be charged as an accessory to murder.'

In her strident and unattractive voice, she'd made her point.

Walter bobbed his head and said, 'Thank you, ma'am.'

Mrs West stared out at her charges. She found it hard to imagine any of them had sold intelligence for cash, but Walter believed it, and that was enough for her to take it seriously. Walter was talking again.

'This is an accurate picture of the killer.'

Karen pointed at the pic and smiled at her audience, much like a porter might at an art auction.

'Neil Swaythling saw the killer up close and personal, and he says this is a good likeness, so we know it to be true. We believe the killer is local, Neil said his accent was definitely local, so he shouldn't be that hard to find.'

'Maybe he's fled the area,' said Hector Browne.

Detective Constable Hector Browne was the newcomer on the team. He had been fast-tracked from university and made no secret he was aiming for big things in crime detection. He was six feet tall, thin as a rake; boasted wavy dark reddish hair, side parted, and wore heavy spectacles that he said he didn't need. Everyone was wary of Hector Browne; but they always were with strangers.

Walter bobbed his head and pressed on.

'Yes, that's possible, though we have been watching ports and airports, but even if he has, it's maybe temporary. If he's local, it's likely he'll soon be back. There are three big questions here. One, why was he trying to kill Neil Swaythling, what is the motive? Two, who is he, and three, where is he now?' Walter motioned to Karen and she took up the story.

'Neil Swaythling's father is Gerry Swaythling, the owner of Swaythling Construction. For those of you that don't know, Swaythling Construction is a successful builder of super-luxury homes. We are talking of dealing with the mega rich here. Some years ago Swaythling had a partner called Munro Ford, but they fell out big time and Munro was ruined. I am expecting to trace his address later today and when we do we shall pay him a visit.'

85

'So what are you saying?' interrupted Hector. 'That Munro is trying to kill the son to get back at the father?'

'Could be,' said Karen. 'We don't have anything better.'

'So this killer guy is a hired gun doing it for money?'

'That's possible,' said Walter.

'Geez, it sounds more like Chicago than Chester,' said Hector. 'Are you sure you guys are not getting carried away?'

Walter glared at Hector, as did everyone else. Didn't appreciate his bumptious tone. Perhaps he needed bringing down a peg or two.

'If you don't think it's possible, wonderboy,' muttered Gibbons, 'have you got anything better?'

'Could be any number of things,' said Hector, aware he was basking in the not altogether unwanted spotlight.

'Such as?' said Karen.

'Maybe Neil stole the killer's girlfriend. Neil's a handsome guy, maybe the killer got annoyed and tried to kill him.'

'So why did he shoot the wrong man?' asked Walter.

'Ah yes, hadn't thought of that.'

'Geez,' said Gibbons. 'We are wasting our time here, Guv.'

Walter nodded at the crowd and began again, as Hector faded into the background.

'Ten, maybe fifteen years ago, when the bust up at Swaythling occurred, the business almost went bankrupt. They needed a big loan to climb out of the black hole. There was a recession on at the time...'

'When isn't there?' muttered Gibbons, and one or two tittered at that.

Walter continued. 'The company survived by introducing finance from an outside source.'

'Like where?' said Hector, unable to keep out of things for long.

'We don't know exactly where,' said Karen, 'but it would seem it came from someone within the Lodge.'

'The Masons?' clarified Hector, eyes wide and interested, and Walter wasn't alone in wondering if Hector Browne was a member of the Lodge.

Walter nodded, and checked out Gibbons. He'd gone quiet, Karen watched him too. He may have been silent but she would ask him about it one-to-one when the opportunity arose.

'What is the significance of that?' persisted Hector.

'We don't know,' said Karen, 'but if there was any trouble repaying the loan, or if the lender and the lendee fell out, there could be something there.'

'Also,' said Walter, 'bear in mind if the bank wouldn't lend, the eventual lender would demand hard terms, a big interest rate; maybe more than that, maybe additional difficult terms and conditions, and that could have placed more stress and pressure on the business.'

'What does Swaythling say about that?' asked Hector.

'We haven't asked him yet.'

'Why the hell not?'

Karen pulled a face and glanced at Walter. He jumped in.

'Sometimes it's best not to leap in like a blind bullock, especially when we are not sure of our facts. We are throwing ideas around here, nothing more at this stage. We are looking for constructive comments and anything that might push the inquiry forward,' and Walter nodded at Hector to see if the penny had dropped.

Hector scowled and looked away.

'There is another thing,' said Karen.

'Like what?' said Gibbons.

Karen continued, 'Relationships between Neil and his parents are strained. Neil said his parents threatened to disinherit him. Gerry admitted the two men didn't get along and rarely spoke. Neil doesn't live at home anymore, he's dating a woman in her forties and the parents are aghast at that.'

'Probably looking out for grandkids,' said Walter. 'Neil's an only child and this Veronica Camberwell woman ain't gonna provide that.'

Hector again, 'Are you suggesting the father might be targeting his only son because he hasn't given him grandkids? Killing him isn't going to do it, is it?'

'We are not suggesting anything, Hector; we are merely looking at all possibilities, examining the known facts. We know the

87

relationship between them is strained, we can't ignore that, and until we know different, we keep an open mind. Gerry Swaythling is someone who could be behind this. No more, no less.'

'Geez, a bit of a long shot.'

'Sometimes long shots come up,' muttered Gibbons, glaring across at Browne and mouthing, 'knobhead!'

'Rule nothing out,' said Karen, echoing Walter's words, 'until we know different.'

WPC Jenny Thompson had been quiet to date, though she didn't miss much. In a moment's silence she asked, 'This Veronica Camberwell woman, what do we know about her?'

'I am coming to that,' said Karen.

'She's hardly likely to order Neil's killing if they are lovers, is she?' said Hector, sighing aloud.

'I'm not saying she is,' said Jenny, fighting her corner. 'But if we know something of her background, it might lead us somewhere.'

'Quite right, Jenny,' said Walter, nodding at Karen who he knew had been working on Camberwell's CV.

Karen took up the thread and said, 'She lives in a big rambling house near Willaston village on the Wirral, a former Baronial manor; built yonks ago. She was left it by her husband when he died of a heart attack when they were on holiday in the States. He was twenty years older than her. There's no mortgage on the property and she's got pots of cash in the bank. Seems she likes to spend it by going out clubbing where she has met a succession of attractive young men. Neil is the latest model.'

'Lucky her,' said Jenny, and the two women shared a knowing glance.

Karen continued, 'Her husband invested in a sleepy Mersey based freight forwarding business in the seventies, bought out the partners, changed its name to Camberwell Freight, and built it into one of the biggest businesses of its type operating out of Liverpool. They have offices in...' and Karen glanced down at her notes, 'Tower Buildings, that's the one, fifth floor. A conservative value for the business is put between four and five mill; and Veronica has recently placed it on the market.'

'For sale?' clarified Walter.

'Yes, with Jones and Sons in Hamilton Square, Birkenhead.'

'How the other half live, eh?' muttered Gibbons, thinking of his burgeoning overdraft, and the frequent hoity toity letters from his bank manageress.

'You're just miffed she didn't make eyes at you,' smirked Jenny, and they all laughed at that, and Gibbons said, 'Too bloody right.'

'Is there any connection between Camberwell and Swaythling?' asked Walter.

'Not that I can find, other than Neil,' said Karen.

'Keep looking. Just because we haven't found it, doesn't mean it isn't there.'

'So where do we go from here?' asked Mrs West, who had been silent for some time, content to watch her charges, allocating each one a five-minute slot, for staff assessment purposes. Those individual reports would soon be due again. It was a good question, and Walter was eager to answer.

'We are going to interview Munro as soon as his whereabouts are known. Gibbons, I want you to keep looking into Veronica Camberwell's background, and Browne and Thompson, you concentrate on Swaythling. The rest of you, take a good look at this ugly mug,' and he pointed at the killer's photofit face, 'and get out there and find him!'

Chapter Fifteen

Walter called Karen into the private office. She sat by the desk and wondered what was on his mind. He sighed and eased back in his chair and said, 'This Masonic business, I'm loath to do it, but I think we need to pay them some attention.'

'My thoughts all along.'

'Thought we might ask Gibbons in, see what he thinks.'

'Doubt he'll say a word.'

'We don't need him to say anything,' and he winked at her and picked up the phone and dialled Darren's extension.

'Supercop!' said Gibbons, expecting it to be the switchboard girl.

'Yes, well, thank you for that, Gibbons; would the supercop care to join us, room four?'

'Sorry, Guv, be with you in a tick.'

Karen budged over and set out another chair close to the desk. Gibbons knocked, Walter yelled him in, and in the next moment he sat at the desk, wondering what was going down.

Walter said, 'We need to look more closely into the affairs at the Lodge, we need to look at any big loans that came Gerry Swaythling's way; who they were from, and on what terms.'

Gibbons shifted in his seat.

'Can't talk about that, Guv, you know how it is, sworn to secrecy, and all that.'

'One man has been murdered,' said Karen, 'and another is in the crosshairs; you can't ignore that, Gibbo.'

'I know that! But I am not involved, and I can't say anything about it.'

Walter leant across the desk.

'I don't want you to say anything about it, Gibbons; I don't want you to betray any solemn oaths into which you may have entered.'

90

'Thanks Guv; knew you'd understand.'

'I don't want you to utter a word, and I won't ask you anything about the Lodge. I just want you to give an indication, say strum your fingers on the desk, to one simple question. You don't need to speak, you don't even need to think about it, no one will ever know.'

'I don't know about that, Guv.'

'This is important, Darren, for you, for us, and for Neil Swaythling. Think carefully about it,' and Walter stared into the vulnerable young man's eyes.

Gibbons stared back, didn't say a thing, didn't blink; didn't move a muscle.

Walter paused as if thinking of his question and then said, 'Are we wasting our time, or do we need to look further into Swaythling's financial affairs?'

They stared at Gibbons, glanced down at his hand on the desk. It didn't move, not a flicker. Muscular arm, big firm hand, rock solid, neatly clipped and clean fingernails, fingers still. Walter sighed, said nothing; still looked. The middle finger, right hand, flipped up and down in an instant, just the once. If you hadn't been concentrating, you'd have missed it. Nothing else. Gibbons turned and glanced out of the window. Sat perfectly still and said, 'Is that everything, Guv?'

'It is, thank you, Darren, you can get off now.'

Gibbons jumped up and shot outside.

'What did you make of that?' asked Karen.

'Definite affirmative, I'd say.'

'Not a nervous twitch?'

'Nah! No chance. Does he look like a man with a nervous disposition?'

He didn't. Karen shook her head.

'The local Lodge meets at 8pm on Tuesday,' said Walter.

'How do you know that?'

'I overheard two traffic guys talking about it in the bog. They shut up like nervous clams when I came bumbling out of the stalls to wash my hands.'

Karen couldn't stifle a laugh.

Walter was talking again. 'You know the friendly fire solicitor?'

91

'Which one?'

'Wilkes and Partners.'

'What about them?'

'Their office overlooks the Lodge.'

'So?'

'I thought you could go down there and sweet talk Mr Wilkes into letting us use his premises to monitor who goes in and who comes out, on Lodge night. You don't need to tell him that. Say we are monitoring street violence at night, something like that. We'll have to send a couple of the rookies down there to do it, otherwise he might get suspicious.'

'What if he's a Mason?'

'He isn't.'

'How do you know?'

'He's Jewish.'

'And Jews are not admitted either?'

'Not often.'

'Wilkes doesn't sound like a Jewish name to me.'

'It isn't. The family name was Wilkenberg; they came from Germany, years ago, long before the Nazi scum oozed from the slime. Around 1900 I think.'

'Why did they change their name?'

'Expediency. It's a common thing, immigrants fiddling with their names to fit in with the locals, been going on for centuries. Muller becomes Miller, Rainsberg becomes Rainsbury, that kind of thing. You don't think those guys in Buckingham Palace were always called Windsor, do you?'

Karen giggled, then pulled a thoughtful face and said, 'Don't tell me, your name isn't really Darriteau?'

'Oh, shut up!'

'When do you want me to see Wilkes?'

'No time like the present, Sergeant, and take Jenny with you. Mr Wilkes likes the ladies. I'd have gone myself otherwise.'

'How do you know all this?'

'Retentive memory, all good policemen have a retentive memory.'

'And women, Guv, and women.'

'Yeah, that too, I'll see you later.'

After she'd gone, he went and had a chat with Mrs West. Fixed up for Gibbons to attend a five-day course on dealing with hostage situations, it was a local thing up at Bromborough, and it started the next day, he didn't even have to leave home, and it would get him out of the way, just in case DC Darren Gibbons was the mole.

Gibbons wasn't best pleased about it, thought he smelt a rat, but Mrs West insisted it was something he must do, and ten minutes after that he was on his way home to get ready to listen to five dull days of hostage speak.

Karen came back an hour later and called Walter into a private room.

'We're in luck.'

'Oh yeah?'

'The room that's overlooking the street has a great view across the road to the Lodge entrance and it's being redecorated, the room that is. They haven't started yet, but all the furniture has been taken out. It's perfect.'

'And Mr Wilkes?'

'Sent his regards, said we could have it for the week.'

'We only need it for the one night.'

'Told him that, he seemed happy enough.'

'Do you think he knew what we are after?'

'He'd have to be pretty thick if he didn't.'

'I don't care what he thinks, so long as we get what we want.'

'Course. We need to have our people in there in situ before seven.'

'Shouldn't be a problem.'

'Who are you thinking of using?'

'Jenny and the new guy.'

'Hector Browne?' she said. 'Is that wise?'

'I think so, he's a bright kid. Any reason why not?'

'No reason at all, just so long as he isn't a Mason.'

93

'He isn't, I've checked.'

'How did you do that?'

Walter tapped his nose, and she knew he wouldn't say anymore more about that.

'He's young, he's keen, and he's capable.'

'He's also bumptious, big-headed, unlikeable… and a moron.'

Walter grinned, didn't say a word.

'You were right about Wilkes, by the way,' she said.

'Oh?'

'He asked Jenny for a date.'

'The fool. He must be fifty if he's a day. What did Jenny say?'

'Said she was engaged.'

Walter laughed. 'Is she?'

'First I've heard of it.'

'What a pillock.'

The following morning, Walter and Karen called Jenny and Hector into the private office.

'We have an important job for you,' Karen explained.

'Great,' said Jenny.

'What kind of job? asked Hector.

'Reconnaissance. Observation and photography,' said Karen.

Hector exhaled and sat back in his chair. Long boring hours doing nothing, trying to keep the eyes open. It wasn't his idea of detection in the twenty-first century.

'Where?' asked Jenny.

'Across from the Masonic Lodge,' said Karen.

'When?' said Hector.

'Tuesday night.'

'It's an important job that has to be done well. Are you up for it?' said Walter.

'Course,' said Jenny.

Hector nodded.

'Don't nod, Hector, speak,' said Walter.

'Sure, Guv, if that's what you want.'

'Good. We want you to photograph everyone going in, and everyone coming out. We've arranged a room for you in Wilkes & Partners, solicitors, they have an office opposite, Jenny has already seen the room, it's perfect, isn't it, Jen?'

'Sure, Guv, great view, first floor, right across the street.'

'We want video and stills, you'll need to be there by half-past six, and you won't get away until the early hours, so get plenty of sleep the day before, and don't come in till lunchtime. Understand?'

They nodded, and both said, 'Sure, Guv.'

'On the Wednesday morning at nine we'll go through everything you take.'

Hector was already wondering how much kip he'd get on Tuesday night.

Walter said, 'Go and see Bob Smith, he'll show you the equipment we want you to use. He'll kit you out with everything you need, ask him to fill you in on anything you don't understand. Make sure you know what you are doing, and don't muck up.'

'Sure, Guv,' said Jenny.

'Off you go,' said Walter, and Jenny and Hector left the room.

'Do you think they are capable?' asked Karen.

'They'd better be,' said Walter. 'Anyway, how hard is it to take a few pictures?'

There was a knock on the door.

'Yeah!' shouted Walter.

Debby Wilson opened and looked around the side of the door.

'Thought you'd like to know we've found an address for Munro Ford.'

'Good girl, where?' said Walter.

'Marnon Heights.'

'Number?' said Karen.

'Fifteen.'

'Is he in now?' asked Walter.

'Don't know, Guv.'

'Thanks, Debby,' said Walter, and the girl smiled and closed the door. 'She's a bright kid.'

95

'She is,' said Karen, and she's easy to work with, which is more than can be said for…'

Walter interrupted. Stood up and said, 'Yes, I know. Come on; let's see if Mr Ford is at home.'

Chapter Sixteen

Marnon Heights was an eight-story council owned block a couple of minutes from the railway station. Not many of the occupiers had taken up the option to buy their flats, and it was easy to see why. The properties were hard to sell; the tenants forever coming and going, and the police were regularly called to the block to sort out domestics and worse cases.

Karen pulled the car to a halt in the small car park. There were three or four tired vehicles there; one had a flat tyre, and another a broken rear window. A large dog came running toward the BMW as the car rolled to a standstill. Karen didn't much like dogs; she'd faced more than her fair share of wild beasts, and this one looked real mean.

'After you,' she said, glancing across at her boss.

Walter looked out and smiled at the brown and black mixed up creature.

'She's a pussy,' said Walter, as he opened the door and got out and faced the sniffing, growling, and nervous animal. Walter's hand went to his pocket, pulled out a digestive biscuit, and tossed it to one side. The dog leapt on it as if it hadn't eaten for a week.

'Come on, Karen,' he said, smiling back at her, and she jumped out and scuttled round behind her boss, ensuring he was always between her and the dog.

'I told you, a pussy.'

Number fifteen was on the third floor. The lift was off. It could have been worse. Walter cursed.

Karen sprinted up the cold stone steps, shouted back, 'Keep you fit, Guv, come on!'

She was standing outside the door of number fifteen, looking bored and relaxed by the time he arrived, panting and unhappy. She went to knock.

'Give me a minute,' he said, struggling for breath.

She pursed her lips and waited for him to knock.

They could hear music, though whether it was coming from number fifteen, or somewhere else they couldn't be sure.

Walter knocked; three heavy bangs.

Muffled sounds came from within; and the door opened.

White guy, maybe forty-five, looked tired and world-weary, wiry build, curly hair, going grey, grubby white tee shirt, hundred times washed jeans, cheap worn out trainers.

'Munro Ford?' asked Karen.

'Who wants to know?'

'This is Inspector Darriteau.'

Munro blew out through his nose. Said, 'Cops! Geez! What have I done now? Failed to buy a TV licence, mucked up my council tax, forgotten to tax the car?'

'None of those things,' said Walter. 'Not today.'

'So what do you want?'

'We want to talk to you about Gerry Swaythling.'

'Well, I don't,' he said, and he went to close the door.

Walter's big boot put a stop to that.

'We can do it here, or we can do it at the station.'

Munro scowled and said, 'You'd better come in.'

There didn't appear to be anyone else in the flat. The place was untidy, but not dirty. The furniture and fittings were all past their best, but Walter and Karen had been in hundreds of worse places. There was a white clothes-horse set up to one side of the living room with freshly ironed clothes onboard, as if he'd had a busy morning. The radio was on and he turned it off.

'Take a seat,' the guy said. 'How can I help?'

'Someone shot Gerry Swaythling's son.'

'Neil, yeah, read about it in the paper.'

'Did you know Neil?' asked Karen.

'Met him a few times when he was young, haven't seen him in years.'

'Why would anyone want to kill Neil?' asked Walter.

'How the hell would I know? Drugs probably, that's the thing behind most street violence these days.'

'Neil wasn't into drugs,' said Karen.

'Then I have no idea,' Munro said, plopping into a small armchair in the corner.

Walter studied the guy and raised an eyebrow. Didn't say a thing. It was enough.

'Wait a minute; you don't think I had anything to do with it, do you?'

'Did you?' asked Karen.

'Don't be ridiculous!'

'You had the motive,' said Walter.

'Who's been telling tales?'

'No one,' said Karen. 'It's public knowledge you fell out with Gerry Swaythling. He ruined you, didn't he?'

'Yes, he did, the creep, but that doesn't mean I'd take it out on Neil.'

'Tell us what happened between you and Gerry?' asked Walter.

Munro scratched his nose, thinking about it. Took a big breath, decided to talk.

'There was a recession on, we'd had two terrible years. Things were getting worse. Most builders can't hack it after two lean years. The bank wouldn't extend the overdraft, worse than that, they began calling in loans. We needed to find cash to survive, and fast.'

'How much cash?'

'About a hundred and fifty K.'

That stacked up, thought Walter, 'Go on.'

'He was in the club, wasn't he? And I wasn't.'

'You mean the Lodge?'

'The very same.'

'Who lent him the money?'

'No idea, I never found out. Gerry wouldn't tell me; perhaps he worried I might go to the same source to raise my half.'

'Did you try to raise the cash?' asked Karen.

'Course I did; got nowhere, I was a builder, a former brickie; people didn't take me seriously, especially in the economic climate back at the time. I think Gerry liked that, figured out it would be easier to get rid of me, him and his scheming wife, Holly. They couldn't wait to see the back of me.'

'She's ill,' said Walter.

'Yeah, I know. Doesn't change things.'

'So what happened?'

'Somehow he raised the cash, God knows how he did it, the banks wouldn't touch him or the company by then, but give Gerry credit, he found it, and made the most of it by firing me.'

'Any compensation?'

'You have to be kidding!'

'When did you last see Gerry?' asked Karen.

'Bumped into him four or five years ago in town. He blanked me, him and his stuck up wife, blanked me as if I was a dead man. Can't say as I was surprised. They are both stuck up berks, the pair of them, imagining they are better than they are. They think that money makes a gentleman, but it sure as hell doesn't.'

Walter could empathise with that, took a moment out, then said, 'How do you make a living, Mr Ford?'

'Drive a taxi. Do you need a lift? I'm on in an hour.'

'We're OK,' said Karen.

Walter pulled the photofit from his pocket. Set it on the coffee table. 'Ever seen this guy?'

Munro picked up the picture. Studied it a second, and said, 'Tell you the truth; you can see dozens of kids like him any Friday and Saturday night in the pubs in the city, dozens of them.'

He had a point; the guy sure was ordinary looking, typical twenty-first century boy next door.

'You must have had a burning desire to get even,' suggested Walter.

'Maybe I did, but I've never done anything about it; if that's what you think. Life's too short to go round bearing grudges like a mean pit bull. I've moved on. I have a new girlfriend and we hope to get

100

married. Gerry and Holly Swaythling can go fuck themselves for all I care. I'm sorry for Neil, but there we are. There is nothing I can do about that. It had nothing to do with me.'

Walter bobbed his head and stood up. Karen followed suit, and a minute later they were back outside, staring down at the same dog. It licked its lips and looked hopeful, its docked tail doing its best. Walter glanced down and pulled another bicky from his pocket and set it before the dog. The animal barked a gentle and appreciative thank you, and the coppers jumped in the car.

'Where did you learn that little trick?' said Karen.

'What, that dogs get hungry, ooh God, let me think,' and he pulled a face and glanced at the roof.

'Don't be sarky.'

'Don't ask silly questions.'

'What did you make of Munro Ford?'

'Pretty grounded individual, I'd say,' said Walter. 'You?'

'I believed him.'

'So did I, doesn't mean to say we should rule him out. He's still got a good motive. Find out where he drinks; find out who he talks to, find out who his fiancée is, and it would be interesting if we could connect him to the killer.'

'Maybe he doesn't drink.'

'He does, for sure, didn't you smell his breath?'

Chapter Seventeen

Hector Browne and Jenny Thompson arrived at Wilkes & Partners offices at half-past six. There was an office manager there who had been expecting them. He invited them up to the room, and they began setting up the tripods and cameras that would be pointed across the road.

The manager showed them the kitchen and told them to make whatever they wanted, coffee, tea et cetera, bade them a good night, and left them to it, leaving last-minute instructions to make sure they pulled the front door closed on their way out.

Jenny made two mugs of coffee as Hector fiddled with the equipment until it was just so. She came back and set the mugs on the bare floorboards and settled down into one of the old office chairs they had taken back in there. There was a whiff of white gloss paint in the office, but nothing they couldn't cope with.

'You'd better turn off the lights,' he said, and she jumped up and switched off as they sat in the evening light.

'How many do you think will come?' she asked.

'I asked the sarge that, she said between forty and ninety depending on holidays and sickness, and how many could be bothered. I'll look after the live video, you do the stills.'

Jenny was cool with that. The camera was ace, almost new, Japanese, superb zoom lens, and easy to operate.

'It won't get dark till ten,' she said, 'plenty of light.'

'The streetlights will go on long before that,' he said, pointing at the glass globe antique-style triple lamp standard ten yards to the left.

'Should have no problem picking them out,' she said, glancing through the viewfinder again, before double-checking on the mini screen on the rear of the camera.

The Pythagoras Lodge 888 had met in that same Chester building for more than a century. It was a prosperous and popular Lodge where admission was reserved for men who fulfilled the Lodge's exacting criteria.

As the Worshipful Brother Harry Quirke always said: Be very cautious who you recommend as a candidate for initiation. One false step on this point may prove fatal. If you introduce a disputatious person confusion will be produced which may end in the dissolution of the Lodge itself. Where you have a good Lodge, keep it select, great numbers are not always beneficial.

The officers of the Pythagoras Lodge 888 took great heed on those words and remained strict, and far more potential candidates were blackballed than not, even in difficult times.

The first visitors arrived at 7.29 pm.

'Hey up,' said Hector, swivelling the camera. 'Here come the early birds.'

Two men aged about forty, evening suits, dicky bow ties, white gloves. Hector pressed the record button and the camera silently whirred. He could hear the noise of the still camera beside him, clicking and clacking, as Jenny went to work.

The officers watched the men ring the bell, the door open, two similarly dressed guys inside, younger, burly, fit looking, come to the step, smile at the early arrivals, step to one side, and the visitors were ushered into the building and the door closed behind them.

'Get them?' asked Hector. He was surprised at how much he was enjoying the evening shift.

'Yep. You?'

'Oh yeah, sure.'

Five minutes flew by, then two more, and another one running behind to keep up. Same set up. Evening suit, white gloves, exchange greetings, and in they went.

The next guy was by himself.

'It's Gibbons!' whispered Jenny, her eyes widening. 'Wonder what he'd say if he knew he was on camera. Smile Gibbo!' and the cameras clicked and whirred.

After he'd gone in, Jenny asked, 'Why do they all wear white gloves?'

'Dunno. Think it's something to do with keeping clean hands.'

'Clean hands, from what? Physically or metaphorically?'

'Everything, both, I guess.'

'Does that include giving dodgy loans?'

Hector laughed.

'We don't know if anyone gave any loans, and neither do we know if they were dodgy.'

Jenny didn't answer. She was too busy. Another three guys had arrived, one in his fifties, two in their twenties, short and stocky, all looking alike. Click, click, click, and then they were gone. Then two more.

'Look who we have here,' said Jenny, grinning.

'Who?' said Hector, going to work on the movies again.

'Hoskins and Hooper, Traffic Division, pair of tossers, the both of them.'

'I'll take your word for that.'

Click, click, click, click.

By eight o'clock they had counted and recorded fifty-two evening suited gentlemen into the building, all of them white, most of them aged between thirty and sixty, a sprinkling either side of the great divide. Three more came late, they'd be for the high jump; everyone knew what sticklers the Lodge was for punctuality. A big cash fine and a public rebuke heading their way. Jenny's mobile burped. It was Walter.

'How's it going, Jen?'

He was sitting in front of the telly, steaming chicken Madras balanced on his lap.

'OK, Guv. Fifty-five happy souls gone into the happy house, including Gibbons, Hoskins and Hooper.'

'And you've filmed them all?'

'Oh yes.'

104

'Good girl.'

'And you want us to stay until they come out?'

'Yeah, 'fraid so, I want to see if any different ones come out, maybe some of the higher officers who could have been in there all along.'

'Got you, Guv. We'll stay till the lights go off and the place is locked up.'

'Well done. I'll see you in the morning.'

'Night, Guv.'

Hector and Jenny shared a look. Now for the long, dull, and boring part. Three, four, maybe even five hours, while those inside got up to heavens knows what, before they all started coming out again.

'Do you want another coffee?' he asked.

'Please,' said Jenny, and Hector went off to have a good snoop round the offices. Solicitors were like everyone else. In a busy office someone would always leave some interesting papers lying around, and perhaps forget, under pressure of work, to lock confidential documents in the huge safe. Hector was optimistic. It wasn't an opportunity he was going to miss.

The next morning, Walter arrived at the station at twenty past eight. Karen was already there, looking pleased with herself; and surprisingly, so were Jenny and Hector.

'Get much sleep?' asked Walter.

Jenny stopped at Walter's desk and grinned and said, 'About six hours, not too bad.'

'Did you get what we wanted?'

'Yep, spot on, Heck's just getting the stills printed, should be ready in five.'

'Well done, room four when you're ready.'

Walter went and fetched coffee and took his place in room four. Karen came in and sat down and said, 'It's looking good.'

Hector arrived and slipped the CD into the play machine. Turned on the big screen fixed to the wall, as Walter said, 'I'd like to see the stills first, and then the movie.'

'Sure, Guv,' said Hector, looking happy with himself, as Jenny came in and closed the doors and set her fat file down on the desk.

Walter glanced round the team and nodded, and they all nodded back.

'Stills first,' he said. 'Can we do it in chronological order?'

'Sure,' said Jenny, setting the first twelve by nine photo on the desk. Black and white images, good resolution, clear picture, white time and date impressed in the bottom left corner, 7.29 yesterday evening. Two middle-aged guys. The officers stared down and then at each other.

'Anyone know either of them?'

'Nope.'

They all agreed on that. Strangers.

The next set of pics were of three men. Same thing. All unknown. So far, so bad.

The next one, a couple of minutes later, was Gibbons.

'He looks so serious,' said Karen.

'Maybe he's thinking about us, thinking about him,' said Jenny.

'Maybe he is,' said Walter, recalling that single strumming finger.

The next shots were of three guys, two young and one old. There were numerous images of them, including one of the younger ones approaching the door, ringing the bell, the other two standing back, conversing about something, none of them smiling, none of them smoking.

'Well, look who we have here,' said Walter, grinning at the others.

'Who?' said Hector and Jenny as one.

'Langley Wells, isn't it?' said Karen.

'The same,' said Walter. 'And, if I am not mistaken, two of his fine sons as well. I can never tell them apart.'

'Who's Langley Wells?' asked Hector.

'Loan shark,' said Karen.

'Loan shark?' said Jenny. 'Could he have financed Swaythling?'

'Good question,' said Walter.

106

'I wouldn't have thought back then they were that big,' said Karen.

'Wouldn't you?' said Walter. 'You'd be surprised. I think we'd better pay Mr Wells and his fine family a visit.'

They laughed at Hoskins and Hooper going in next, looking serious and uppity. Walter reminded Hector, Jenny, and Karen not to discuss the inquiry with anyone else, and no one was to be ribbed or teased about the pictures. They were all strictly secret, and that meant from anyone.

Two more middle-aged men, one of them known, one not. The known guy was none other than Gerry Swaythling.

'Still a member, then,' said Karen.

'Never a doubt,' said Walter.

Then a couple of dozen blanks; faceless white guys that none of them knew. Then another single guy, strolling fast toward the door, flamboyant white scarf around his neck, tall and confident in his own skin.

'Well, well, well,' said Walter, grinning down.

'Who he?' asked Karen.

'Don't any of you know?'

No one did.

'That's Donald West.'

'Who's Donald West?' asked Hector.

'Don't you know?' said Walter. 'Penny still not dropped? That, ladies and gentlemen, is Mrs West's husband, your boss's better half.'

'Oh cripes,' said Jenny, taking a closer look at the picture, for there was always something fascinating about other people's partners.

'Did you know he was in the Lodge?' asked Karen.

'I did not,' said Walter.

'Does she know about this surveillance op?' persisted Karen.

'Not yet.'

'Oops!'

At Walter's request, Hector started the film show, and they watched the same comings and goings on live video. It didn't show anything more than Jenny's stills. They moved on to the departures, picture quality so good after the daylight had vanished.

There were nine people on the leaving shots that hadn't appeared on the going in pics, perhaps committee members, bar staff, and security people, but none of the nine were identifiable.

Walter thanked Jenny and Hector and sent them on their way and after they'd gone Karen said, 'When are you going to tell Mrs West?'

'Soon. After we've been to see Langley Wells.'

'When do you want to do that?'

Walter's stomach rumbled.

Karen jerked her head back and grinned.

'I'm going to grab a bite to eat, pie and a pint, fancy it?'

'No,' she said, 'I've brought tuna on brown.'

'OK, be back in an hour; get a car organised, and we'll go then.'

Chapter Eighteen

Langley Wells' home was in the centre of the biggest housing estate in Chester. He had lived there all his life. The house looked in fine fettle, as Karen pulled the blue unmarked BMW to a standstill behind a pair of black four by fours parked on the road outside.

Walter stepped out. It was thinking of drizzling; he thought he saw lace curtains rustling in the downstairs front room, though he might have been mistaken. Karen joined him, and they walked up the path and rang the bell.

Rose Wells came to the door. She looked tired and weary.

Karen said, 'I'm Sergeant Greenwood, and this is...'

'I know who he is,' she said. 'What do you want?'

'We'd like a quick word with Langley, Rose,' said Walter.

'What about?'

'Just a little business.'

'Have you got an appointment?' she asked, unable to keep a smirk from her wan face.

Karen glanced up and down the road, as if surprised anyone would need to make an appointment to see anyone on the estate.

'Come on, Rose, it would be much easier if we do it here,' said Walter. 'We don't want to take him to the station.'

'I'll see if he's in,' she said, and she closed the door.

They weren't kept waiting long.

Rose came back and sniffed and said, 'You'd better come in, and wipe your flippin' feet!' and she beckoned at the new copra doormat.

They were shown through to a rear sitting room set in a section of one extension. There was a modern desk there, nothing much on the desk surface, a pocket calculator, a tub of pens, little else.

Langley Wells sat relaxed behind the desk; and behind him were three younger, fitter looking copies of the man himself.

'Hello Langley,' said Walter. 'Long time, no see.'

Wells bobbed his head and said, 'Darriteau.'

'This is Sergeant Karen Greenwood.'

Langley nodded at her. Said nothing.

She thought they all looked a little strange.

The three standing men couldn't keep their eyes off her, and they were all thinking the same thing. What would father say if I dated a copper? This copper? Karen smiled at them nervously. They disconcerted her; didn't smile back, didn't speak; just stared.

'Are these your sons?' asked Walter.

'They are unless Rose has been keeping things from me.'

'They look like you.'

'They should be so lucky.'

Walter nodded at the boys. They didn't nod back.

Langley thought he'd better introduce them.

'Lawrie, Lenny and Lewis,' he muttered.

Three peas in a pod, thought Karen, and that idea made her smile. The guys all imagined she was smiling at them, and them alone.

'Take a seat,' said Langley, pointing to the two chairs placed before the desk for the purpose.

Walter made himself comfortable.

Karen did too, crossed her legs, her long grey skirt riding up a fraction, attracting the attention of see no evil, speak no evil, hear no evil, who stared down at her, as if they were one pig ugly three-headed-being.

'So, what can I do for you?' asked Langley, picking up a pen and tapping it on the polished desk.

'Some years ago,' said Walter, 'you lent a considerable amount of money to the builder Gerry Swaythling.'

'Who says I did?'

'Do you deny it?'

'If the coppers ask, we deny everything,' and he grinned and turned round and smiled at his sons. 'Isn't that right, lads?' They grinned too. Nodded like dogs in the back of a car. Focused back on the girl.

'What I'd like to know is, was the loan repaid?'

Langley sniffed.

'I can't comment on a financial transaction I know nothing about.'

'Let me fill in the details,' said Walter. 'The amount was around 150K.'

Langley blew a rush of air from his puffed-out cheeks.

'Really, Inspector, do you imagine I could afford to lend that kind of money, and years ago at that, you say? I wouldn't be living here, would I? I think you must be mixing me up with someone else.'

'A few days ago Gerry Swaythling's son, Neil, was gunned down in broad daylight.'

'I read about that in the paper. Terrible business. How is he?'

'He's dead.'

'Really? I heard he was holed up somewhere.'

'Where did you hear that?' asked Karen.

'Little birdies twitter, little bird, that's where I hear everything.'

'You know Gerry Swaythling well, don't you?' asked Walter.

'Do I?'

'Oh yes, you met him as recently as yesterday.'

'You do your homework. I'll give you that, Darriteau; own a spy in the Lodge, do you?'

Walter didn't answer, said, 'How is the money lending business doing these days?'

'Don't do it anymore, you know that, Mr Darriteau, hundred percent legit these days.'

'Doing what?' asked Karen.

'I am sure your boss knows.'

'Tell me,' she said.

'I don't have to answer your questions, you know that, but I will, because I'll humour you, and I have nothing to hide. Lawrie looks after Wells Motors, nice garage on the Greyhound Industrial Estate, you must know it, pop in next time you want a good car, hope to land a Ford franchise next year, make our fortune it will, won't it boys, if we get it.'

111

The boys muttered, 'Sure thing, dad.'

Langley took a breath and sailed on. 'Lenny looks after our property letting business, Well-Lets, we rent out property all over the area, find a tenant or full management, do you a good deal if you want to find somewhere nice to live, or if you have a property you want to rent out. Property letting, that's the future, people will always need somewhere to live, better than any pension plan, solid as lead. We have a few of our own hooses these days, buy-to-let jobs, you know how it works, it's doing well, I'm proud of it, and I'm proud of the boys, all three of them. Lewis looks after our finance business, investing some of our hard-earned money here and there, could be in anything, wine, stamps, pictures, sculpture, even ostriches, we've tried most things. Some pay a big dividend; some give us a good kick up the backside.'

'But you still lend money?' said Walter.

'Can't do that, Mr Darriteau, can't get a consumer credit licence, you know how it is.'

'Why can't you get a licence?' asked Karen.

'Because in my misspent youth I had one or two minor transgressions, that's why, and the authorities never forget these things, and if you add that to the small fact I live on a council estate, there are your reasons.'

'Why don't you move?' persisted Karen.

Langley laughed. 'We can't afford to, and even if we could, we like living here, don't we boys?'

The three monkeys nodded and the middle one said, 'That's right, pa. We like being amongst our own kind. People round here are reliable, straight and honest,' and they all nodded at that weird notion.

'What gets my goat,' said Langley, 'is these companies advertising short-term loans on daytime TV. They are charging more than I ever did! 3680% APR, as clear as day, up on the screen for all to see, for God's sake. How does that work? I'm portrayed as a heinous criminal for providing a public service people want, when I used to do it, that is. While they are held up as paragons of blinking virtue, members of the establishment, robbing the public senseless. I

112

couldn't believe my eyes when I saw that interest rate on the TV the other day. How brazen can they be? Something should be done about it. Shouldn't be allowed, leeches on the backs of the common people. That's what they are.'

'Ridiculous!' said one son, and they all nodded like hungry hyenas, and licked their lips and tut-tutted and re-focussed on the delicious blonde, as if they could surround her and eat her.

'Let's get back to Gerry Swaythling,' said Walter.

'If you must.'

'There's a young killer walking round out there who has shot dead two young men at least, and he needs catching. Don't you agree?'

'Couldn't agree more, Mr Darriteau. Naughty boys always need disciplining. There's nothing wrong with a good smack.'

'Do you know who the killer is?'

'Ooh Mr Darriteau, even if we did, which we don't, we have never been grasses, as you well know, sorry and all that, but we can't help you there.'

'It's not grassing, it's a public duty,' said Karen.

Langley didn't comment. The sons looked angry.

The cheek of the little bitch to correct their father in front of them.

Walter spoke again.

'There is a line of thinking that says you could have a big grudge against Gerry Swaythling, that you might want to hurt him, and his business, or his family.'

'If somebody would care to utter those thoughts in public, I would take great pleasure in suing the backside off them.'

'Did you pay the young man to shoot Neil Swaythling?' persisted Walter.

'Oh, come on, Darriteau, that is pathetic. If I did such a thing, which I did not, I am hardly likely to admit it to you, am I?'

'Conspiracy to murder carries a very long sentence,' said Karen. 'At your age, you'd probably never get out alive.'

Langley pointed the pen across the desk. The blonde bird was annoying him.

113

'That, missy prissy policewoman, sounds too close to a threat for my liking. I'd be careful if I were you.'

'We are trying to stop anyone else getting hurt,' said Walter.

'So you say, though I can't say as I like how you are going about it.'

'All I am saying, Langley, is that if you are not involved, and I take your word on that, maybe you might get to know who is. All we need is a name.'

'I could give you many names of people I don't like, and you could go out and hassle them, and, I'll be honest with you, that would amuse us.'

'You could do that, Langley, but that's not your style.'

Langley nodded his agreement.

'Then I am sorry, but I can't help.'

'Does Gerry Swaythling still owe you money, still paying off the debt?'

'We seem to be going round in circles, Inspector. I have no comment to make on that.'

'We will find out in the end, Langley.'

Langley sat back in his chair and sighed.

Didn't say a thing.

Karen and Walter glanced at one another. It seemed the meeting was done.

Walter said, 'Thank you, you know where I am if you hear anything.'

'Good day,' said Langley, and one of the boys showed them out, patting Karen's backside as she went through the front door. She spun round to remonstrate but he closed the door in her face.

'What did you make of that?' she said back in the car.

'Not here,' he said. 'Drive down by the canal.'

She drove to Telford's Quay and parked and switched off the engine and repeated her question.

'Much as I expected. I didn't imagine he'd tell us much.'

'Do you think he lent Swaythling the money?'

114

'Oh, yes. There wouldn't be many candidates who could manage that back then. He would have been one of them, either in whole or in part.'

'Do you think he's been repaid?'

'That's the old thing with illegal lenders. The debt is rarely, if ever, paid off. The interest piles up, and the lender doesn't want it to end. It's possible Swaythling is still paying, it's possible he'll always be paying.'

'Do you think Wells has an interest in the Swaythling Construction business?'

'If there are still payments being made, then one way or another, he does. The question is, has Swaythling fallen behind with the payments, or maybe stopped making them altogether, and is that the reason why Wells, or one of his agents, has taken a pot-shot at Neil?'

'It was interesting that Wells said that Neil was holed up somewhere. Was that a guess?'

'Flying a kite, I'd say,' and Walter reminded Karen of the possibility of a mole. It had happened before, and he asked her if she thought it might be Gibbons.

'I wouldn't have thought so, Guv, but who knows?'

'Precisely.'

'Come on; let's get back to the station. I have that awkward meeting with Mrs West to look forward to, and after that, maybe we should review everything to date.'

'Sure, Guv,' and she started the car and headed for base.

Chapter Nineteen

Jimmy Mitchell tried Luke's mobile again. He'd been trying to get hold of him for a few days. This time the call was answered. 'Hey up, my man,' said Luke. 'I've been thinking about you.'

'Thought you were never coming back. I've been trying to reach you for a while. How did the holiday go?'

'Brilliant, gave that blonde wench a holiday she will never forget. Polished the old fella senseless, you know how it is.'

'Good for you. Now forget about her and what's in your trousers, and let's talk business, assuming you still are in business?'

'Could be. Have you had any hassle?'

'None at all, things have gone very quiet.'

'That's what I like to hear. Do we need to meet?'

'Yes, we do. Can you be at the usual place at two tomorrow?'

'Don't see why not.'

'I'll see you there.'

Jimmy rang off while across the city, Luke punched in Sahira's number.

'Hi, Luke,' she cooed.

'How are you, my darling?'

'I'm good. Been thinking about you. Thought you must be due back.'

'Oh yes, honey, I'm back, and I'm so looking forward to seeing you.'

'That's good to know. When?'

'I've booked a room at the Red Rose Motel, same name as usual, same room as before. I've a short business meet at two tomorrow, and I'll see you there at three.'

116

'Oh, Luke, I don't think I can make it, family ties and all that, you know how it is.'

'No, no, no! I'm not having that! You get your black arse down there! I'll expect to see you naked and waiting, understand?'

Sahira sighed and took a beat. 'I'll do my best, Luke.'

'You'd better!'

Luke rang off and grinned. He liked the foreign birds; there was something exotic about them. True, Melanie Kirton had been an exciting girl to spend a whole fortnight with, but he wouldn't want to marry her, no way. He wouldn't want to marry anyone. He wouldn't want to wake up every morning and find her there. He'd lose interest within a month. The foreign birds offered something different.

There was that Chinese bint from last year, Lee Pung was her name, she was the same, a real thrill. They seemed more submissive somehow, more grateful for the attention, whereas the English birds took it for granted they were wonderful, and deserved to be courted and bedded, if they wanted.

The foreign birds took nothing for granted and tried harder. Looked after their figures better too. Lee Pung tried hard, and Luke would still have been seeing her, but for the annoying fact her boyfriend jetted in from Hong Kong, gave her a sound thrashing, and took her back east on the first available flight. No sweat, no worries, for there were plenty more exotic creatures in the sea, so far as Luke Flowers was concerned. Sahira Khan slotted into the unexpected vacancy perfectly.

She'd served him his late night curry in The State of Kerala takeaway restaurant close to the railway station, and the way she looked at him, unsmiling, but wanting, through those deep and dark eyes, as her father fussed about behind her, chasing up a bad tempered backlog of aromatic dinners. That look told Luke everything he needed to know.

He knew she would fit the bill; and take the place of the departed Pung; and be overjoyed to do so. He'd rung the restaurant three

117

times over the following twenty-four hours under the auspices of placing an order until she was the one who picked up the phone.

'I saw you last night,' he said.

'I know,' she whispered, knowing it was pointless in denying she remembered him.

He gave her the time; he gave her the place, and he looked forward to spending time alone with her, and after that they enjoyed frequent afternoon liaisons at the Red Rose Motel when the feeling took him, when he wasn't busy elsewhere. The following day he intended giving her a sharp reminder of what he was about.

Luke arrived at the clock at dead on two. Jimmy turned up a few seconds later. They leant on the rails and gazed down, then waited for a party of German school kids to pass by behind them, and Luke said, 'Some business in the air, I believe? Economy picking up, is it?' and he laughed aloud.

Jimmy took out a cigarette and stuck it in his thin-lipped mouth. Silver lighter, cupped his hands, lit and sucked.

'Shouldn't smoke, it's bad for you.'

'That's rich, coming from you.'

'So? Do you have some business for me, Jimmy, or don't you?'

'Could be, Luke-ee boy, could be.'

'Worth my while getting out of bed?'

'Oh, yes.'

'So? Don't keep me waiting and sweating, Jimmy boy, spill the beans.'

'It'll pay a lot more than usual, because it's more risky than usual.'

'I'm still listening.'

'There's a guy, hasn't been paying his bills, upset important people.'

'It's a common thing in twenty-first century Britain. Not coughing up. Long may it continue; I say, keeps us all in business.'

Jimmy didn't comment on that. The sad economy might keep an irritating little slug like Luke Flowers in business, but Jimmy had fingers in countless commercial pies, legit and otherwise, and he could take it or leave it. When anything became too risky, he'd junk it; and he knew the current proposition could do that.

'The guy in question is famous.'

Luke smiled. He liked the sound of that. He adored glamour in all forms. A bit of celebrity never did anyone any harm.

'How famous?'

'Very famous.'

'In what field?'

'Can't tell you that yet.'

'So what's the deal?'

'100K. All payable on completion. Not a bean up front.'

'Reliable paymaster?'

'Very.'

'What's your cut of the 100K?'

'Nil, nothing, nada, I've negotiated my slice on the side.'

'Sweet Jimmy, sweet. That's why I like dealing with you.'

'The thing is, after the deed is done the heat will be tremendous. The Met will get involved. It wouldn't just be the local plod on your tail, or mine. You'd have to go abroad, maybe for six months, lie low; keep schtum. Disappear. Understand? Could you do that, Luke?'

Luke pursed his lips. He could use another long holiday, he'd been home three days, and already the travel bug had bitten again. Jimmy seemed nervous. Maybe he was on to something big.

Jimmy was speaking in that mumbling, quiet way of his, as if he thought he was being overheard.

'You'd need to have everything in place beforehand, all booked and paid for, get out of the country before the curtains came down. If you didn't leave within a matter of hours, you wouldn't make it. It would involve detailed planning.'

'You're the planning maestro, Jimmy.'

'I'll help you all I can.'

'I've always fancied doing the cross America drive thing. It might be a good time to arrange that.'

'That should be OK, though I suggest it would be a good idea to cross the border into deepest Meckico, lie low for a while, hunker

119

down with a couple of senoritas, and stay away for as long as possible.'

Luke liked the sound of that. He'd grown to adore the sunshine; and he knew he'd love the senoritas.

'By the sound of it, this guy must half be famous.'

'He is.'

'And you're not going to tell me who it is?'

'No! All I need from you is confirmation that you are up for this, now you understand the risks.'

'You want an answer now?'

'Not necessarily.'

'But soon?'

'Yes.'

'I can give you an answer now.'

'Go on.'

Luke smiled that charming smile of his, the one he flashed at the girl in the travel agency, and the sexy piece in the unisex cutters who clipped his hair, and the common girl with the big lashes and huge jugs who served his petrol, and the girl in the Indian restaurant, the same bit of skirt he would soon be on his way to see, that crushing smile that few women seemed able to resist.

'Course I'm up for it, Jimmy, you know me. I'm mister reliable.'

'Good boy! I'll be in touch as soon as I get the green light.'

Jimmy tossed the dying cigarette to one side, kicked it into the wall, and walked away without looking back. Luke hurried back to the car, a zesty spring in his step. His mind was working overtime, pondering on who the target might be, as he headed south for the Red Rose Motel.

There was a dark and dusky maiden on the reception desk at the Red Rose. Luke smiled and winked at her. She played the ice maiden and looked away, as if it happened ten times a day, which it probably did. Luke grabbed the key and made his way through to the ground floor bedrooms. Found room fifty, his favourite place on earth.

Sahira was there, just as expected, naked on the king-size bed, her hands clasped behind her head, her body language one of longing. She stared up at him, that same deep unsmiling look she had given him the first time they'd met. There was something desperate about that look, something Luke found irresistible.

He hurried to the side of the bed and sat down and said, 'How much have I been looking forward to seeing you! I've missed you,' as he clasped his hands around her head and stooped and kissed her on her ample lips.

A second later, his whole demeanour changed.

She wasn't surprised at that.

That was Luke all over.

He was such a moody guy; it was one of the reasons she liked him so much, as all the books on the subject confirmed. Sometimes you had to put up with the moodiness of a man to enjoy the passionate times he produced when the feeling took him. With a man like Luke Flowers sometimes you had to accept the friction that came with it. Sahira could do that, for she thought he was the most exciting individual who had ever cast eyes upon her. Fact was, she'd put up with almost anything to be alone with Luke. She couldn't help herself.

He grasped her long, dark hair and dragged her from the bed into the centre of the room. Hands on her shoulders, and forced her to her knees.

Chapter Twenty

Walter tapped on Mrs West's door. 'Come!' she said, peering over the top of her slim-line designer specs. Walter shuffled in and tried a smile. 'Take a seat, Walter. I can see there is something on your mind.' Walter huffed and puffed and sat down. 'Well?' she said. 'Is it the Swaythling case?'

'In a way, ma'am, yes.'

'Fire away, I'm all ears,' and she set her fountain pen down.

'We've been carrying out a surveillance operation.'

'Oh yes, where?'

'Across the street from the Masonic Lodge.'

She sat back in her seat, removed her pink specs and folded her arms.

'Did you not think to keep me posted about this?'

'You were busy, ma'am, and you said I was not to bother you with day-to-day matters.'

'I'd hardly call that day-to-day, but I'll let it pass. And what did you discover?'

'That Langley Wells and his sons are members.'

'The loan shark family?'

'The same.'

'And? What else?'

'Gerry Swaythling is a member too.'

'So? Are you surprised by that?'

'No, ma'am, not at all. The thing is, we think it was Wells who baled Swaythling out when his firm was in trouble, enabling him to dump his partner, Munro, and gain control of the business. If that was the case, it is possible Swaythling is still paying off the debt. Maybe he was getting peed off by that, maybe he stopped paying, or imagined the debt had been paid in full. Perhaps the pot-shots at

Neil were a gentle reminder that their business had not been concluded.'

'All possible scenarios, Walter, I grant you, but can you prove any of this?'

'Not yet.'

'Could one of the sons have carried out the shooting?'

'No, ma'am, the description doesn't fit, and it's not Langley's style.'

'So you think the Wells outfit hired an assassin?'

'Maybe, yes. There are lots of desperate people out there who will do anything for a good payday.'

'What does Swaythling have to say about it?'

'Haven't asked him yet.'

She gave him that schoolmarm look, as if to say, why come telling me half a story, crack on and finish it, and come and see me.

'He's the next call on the list, ma'am.'

'Good. Anything else?'

'One little thing. Your husband is a member of the Lodge.'

Mrs West smiled her cold smile.

'Is that a statement or a question?'

'It's a fact, ma'am, he was photographed going in and coming out.'

'It's not a criminal offence, so far as I know.'

'Course not, ma'am, just wondered if he ever said anything about the gentlemen in question.'

'No, Walter, he hasn't, and before you say anything else, I'm not asking him either.'

'No, course not, ma'am, I was just keeping you informed.'

She slipped her glasses back on, picked up her pen, and began reading and correcting some long report, and then she mumbled, 'Anything else I can do for you?'

'Nothing right now, ma'am.'

'Good. On your way then.'

Chapter Twenty-One

Wazir Khan was born in the 1920s in a small village ten miles from the city of Calicut, the ancient capital of the state of Kerala, on the southern tip of India. He came from a good middle class family who took their Islamic religion seriously, but kept it to themselves.

Wazir's parents had always enjoyed good relations with their Hindu neighbours, and as a boy, Wazir played cricket with them on the public field behind the Christian hospital.

He delighted his parents. He was a capable boy, eager to learn, keen to better himself and would cram in three part-time jobs, aside from his school work, that he completed under pain of the punishment the disappointment his parents would portray if he failed them.

When he was fourteen, his father arranged for him to take an apprenticeship in his uncle's locksmith's shop in Calicut. Wazir rose at six every morning to walk barefoot the ten miles to work. As in everything, he worked hard and pleased his master, who increased his tiny pay packet, as Wazir learnt everything there was to know about making, dismantling, and servicing locks of every size and shape.

Most of the locks came from England and the best ones too. MADE in ENGLAND, they had stamped on the reverse, or the underside, and Wazir would imagine what that great land might be like.

When he was twenty, he disappointed his parents.

He became involved in politics, and everyone knew that politics brought trouble, and being a good Muslim, he wasn't a follower of the mad Mahatma Ghandi. Like so many young men, he wanted a lot more than that. He wanted direct action, and he wanted it now.

He wanted change and recognition. He wanted independence, and he wanted power. The country was going through a period of enormous turmoil.

The British were sidetracked with their own silly wars against Japan and Germany. Little wonder magnificent India was low on their list of priorities. Wazir Khan and his friends sensed their moment approaching.

Yet when it came, after so much longing, the twenty-something Wazir felt crushing disappointment. True, the country was heading for the yearned for independence, but not as one united country, but as three: India, West Pakistan, and East Pakistan.

Muslims were encouraged to pack up and move to one of the Pakistans. Wazir's parents were too old and frail to contemplate such a hazardous journey. Both Pakistans were some 1400 miles from their southern Indian home, and none of the family wanted to leave Kerala, the place of their birthright, the place of their ancestors, stretching back for as long as anyone could remember, or trace.

The Khan family stayed put, avoiding the mass migration of some twenty million people, both ways across the borders, avoiding the inevitable slaughterings and destruction that followed, violence and mayhem that would account for the lives of a million human beings.

Soon afterwards, when Wazir was at work, an out-of-control Hindu mob attacked and burnt the Khan family home to the ground. Both of his frail parents died in the inferno, embraced together in the corner of their home, clutching metal photograph frames to their chests, the glass and the pictures long gone, the frames bent and buckled and ruined in the ashes.

It was only by luck that Wazir's wife, Nadirah, and their young son Ahmed escaped. They were attending the Christian hospital where the nuns were concerned about a cut to Ahmed's foot, an injury caused by a rampant mule stamping on the child. When Wazir heard the news, he was distraught and angry.

He gave up his job in Calicut, and drew his paltry life savings from the bank, and retrieved the ancient ceremonial sword, the same family heirloom handed down from father to son for over four

126

hundred years. Sensing upheaval, Wazir had buried it in a shallow grave at the back of the house. During his noon meal break at the locksmiths, when no one was watching, he secreted it in the centre of a large hollowed out cricket bat.

He worried that rioting street gangs would steal it if they ever set eyes on it. The crazy hooligans had taken his parents; they had destroyed his home, but they would not set their filthy hands on the family's ancient artefact. Aside from his savings and what remained of his family, it was the only thing of value he possessed.

The family treasure with the mythical past was sound asleep inside the largest cricket bat Wazir could find. He'd halved the bat from top to bottom, hollowed it out, and once the sword was in place, had stuck it together as meticulously as he did the locks he worked on all day, the deadly tip running up into the bat handle, the be-jewelled ivory sword handle safe and sound within the blade of the bat. The cracks where the two halves joined were barely visible, and the moment he applied a fresh coat of varnish and a smudge of Kerala mud, they disappeared.

Wazir decided he would move what remained of his family, but not to either of the Pakistans, for that seemed so far away. Two days later they began the shorter four hundred mile journey to Colombo in Ceylon.

It took them five days, some by mule, some on foot, then a short distance on an old single-decker bus that was stoned by angry Hindus, then two hundred miles on the cranking and clunking British built railway, and a sea crossing on an overloaded ferry, that heaved and yowled in protest at the weight it was expected to carry across the stormy Gulf of Mannar.

Wazir, Nadirah, and Ahmed arrived in Colombo, found a small and inexpensive guesthouse by the docks where resting sailors stayed. The Khan family would stay there for three days, as Wazir sought accommodation and work. He wasn't alone. Thousands of displaced persons had the same idea, for Colombo was thought to be a safe haven. Wazir trudged the docks seeking inspiration, and it was there, one afternoon he found it.

The steamship, The City of Cairo, a City Lines boat from Liverpool, was busy unloading tractors, cars, and machinery from Britain. It would take back cotton, cottonseed, and a small quantity of jute. It would sail in three days. Just enough time for Wazir to obtain the necessary documentation from the back street forgers who could produce anything, for a price.

The British had concocted the mess that was partition, reasoned Wazir, they should be held accountable. The family would travel to Liverpool, England, on the big ship, where the Khan family would live in peace and harmony, amongst the English. That was the plan.

When she first heard the idea fall from Wazir's lips, Nadirah thought her husband crazy, imagined the sun and losing his parents had turned his mind. But she was a good Muslim wife, and good Muslim wives do their husband's bidding, no matter how ridiculous the idea might seem, and besides, Wazir was set on the plan. He had already spent money on the necessary papers and she would do as he commanded. The boy Ahmed thought the prospect of a long trip on the big ship incredibly exciting. His foot was on the mend, and he couldn't wait to board and set sail.

They suffered terrible seasickness as the steamship lurched across the Arabian Sea, heading for the Red Sea, and the Suez Canal beyond. On through the Med, a cursory nod at Malta and Gibraltar, and into the fearsome Atlantic Ocean. The Khan family had never experienced cold like it, and were eternally grateful when on one bright spring morning in 1948, the steamship the City of Cairo slipped toward the mouth of the placid Mersey river, where one hour later, she was nudged home by Rea tugs, as she edged into the King's Dock.

The Khan family collected their meagre belongings and staggered down the gangplank and stood confused on the quayside, glancing up at the grey and rusting hulk of the steamship that had delivered them to this strange, cold, and windy land.

Wazir, wielding the cricket bat, took out the wallet his wife had bought for his birthday, and removed the small scrawled note from within, taking care to hold it tight, lest the biting wind rip it from his fingers. He glanced at the untidy writing his great uncle had written for him. Four words that would determine the destiny of the Khan family: 99a Upper Parliament Street.

Chapter Twenty-Two

The sound of the front door bell at Walter's house burst through the hallway. Walter was in the kitchen glancing at the weekly freebie newspaper, while running an electric shaver over his face. He switched off and ambled to the front door, pulled it open. Galina Unpronounceable smiled in. He'd forgotten it was her day.

'I come in?' she said, her big blue eyes sparkling in the summer sunshine.

'Sure, course,' said Walter, standing to one side as she swept in and down the hall toward the kitchen.

She didn't wait a moment. Filled the kettle, switched it on. She would always need a good supply of boiling water to clean, didn't seem to understand it came out of the tap that way.

Walter followed her into the kitchen.

'Want a coffee?' he asked.

'No, not now, maybe later,' she said, as she unwrapped a fresh pair of yellow rubber gloves and slipped them on her long, dainty hands.

'How have you been keeping?' asked Walter, making small talk, taking advantage of having another human being in the house, in his house, and a mighty attractive one at that.

'I good, I busy, I must get on, and you, Mr Darto, how you keeping?'

She always called him Mr Darto, couldn't seem to cope with Darriteau, though Walter hadn't given up on that.

'Yeah, I'm good, very busy at the moment.'

'You have important case?'

'Yes, I have an important case.'

'Chasing naughty men?'

130

'Yes, you could say that, though girls and women can be naughty too.'

The kettle boiled and she tipped the contents into the sink, a cloud of steam rising in her face.

'Women not naughty like men, never,' and she half turned and smiled at him, standing there leaning against the worktops.

'Maybe you're right.'

'What these naughty men do?'

'Murder.'

'Killed someone?'

'Yes.'

'How?'

'Gunshot.'

'Terrible. What happen when you catch them?'

'They will be tried and if found guilty, they will be sent to prison for a very long time.'

Galina scoffed. 'Not enough! They take someone, they should go,' and she turned again and swept her index finger across her porcelain-like throat.

'Mmm,' said Walter. Fact was, he didn't have a view on that, just so long as they were off the street, away from society, unable to repeat their crimes; that was all that concerned him.

'You good policeman?' she asked.

'I have my moments.'

'Your moments?' she said, not understanding what he meant.

'Sometimes good, sometimes bad.'

'We all like that,' she said, 'sometimes good, sometimes bad.'

He found it hard to believe she could ever be bad, but he knew well enough that anyone could, in the right circumstances, become as bad as it was possible to be.

'Why you not married?' she asked.

That took him aback. Said the usual thing.

'No one would have me.'

'Bull-shit!' she said, two separate words, surprising Walter with the language.

'Are you married, Galina?'

131

'Oh yes, husband back in Ukraine, he work on railway, two children, two boys, Dimitri and Alexander.'

'You must miss them.'

'Yes, sometimes, but they enjoy the money I send.'

'I'm sure they do.'

She was busy washing the breakfast things that Walter had left in the sink. She did everything in a hurry, and she did everything with great purpose. Walter wondered what her husband was like; and why he had let his pretty wife travel to Britain and skivvy around people like him for a few pennies above the minimum wage. If she were his wife, but that was a pointless line of thinking, because she wasn't and never would be, and already she had grabbed the cleaning things and was heading down the hall.

'I clean bath,' she shrilled, and hustled up the stairs, muttering. 'Sure to be filth!'

Walter took the newspaper and went and sat in the front room, but though he glanced at the type he didn't take it in, 'Sure to be filth!' he said aloud and guffawed. Yes, that was probably right, and then he thought of the Jeff Player murder again, and the attempted murder of Neil Swaythling, and wondered why he couldn't figure out what it was about.

Twenty minutes later, Galina breezed into the sitting room carrying the old Hoover. Set it down. Walter resisted asking her if she had found ample filth.

'I make coffee before I start, Mr Darto?' she said, staring down at the big man hunched in the armchair.

'Dar-ri-teau,' he clarified again. 'Good idea,' he said, 'have one yourself; there are chocolate biscuits in the tin.'

She came back with a tray bearing two mugs of steaming instant coffee and set them on the low table. Handed him the red tin of biscuits.

'I not eat, bad for you, bad for figure,' and she set her palm on her flat stomach and patted and said, 'You think I have good figure, Mr Darto?'

132

'You have a fine figure.'

That seemed to please her, judging by the satisfied smile that swept over her fair face as she shook her head, and her blonde tied back hair waggled like a horse's tail.

'You like me come and cook you dinner one night?'

That was new.

'Maybe, after the case is over.'

'When will that be?'

'Who knows?'

'Who knows what?' she said, not understanding him again.

'I don't know when the case will be closed.'

'Yes, I see.'

'You a good cook, Galina?'

'I think so, but you decide.'

'Maybe I will.'

'Good Ukrainian food, that what you need, Mr Darto, from Kiev. I cook you food from Kiev.'

Did she mean chicken Kiev? He hated bleeding chicken Kiev.

'I must get on, I won't get finish,' and she plugged in the cleaner and looked ready to go.

'Sit down for a second, drink your coffee, take a break; everyone is entitled to a break.'

She exhaled a big breath and cupped the mug in her hands, and sat down in the chair opposite, crossing her blue-jeaned legs.

'Tell me about murder?'

He knew he shouldn't discuss the case with this immigrant worker he barely knew, but he did precisely that, leaving out names and places, and other details she didn't need to know.

'You have very exciting job.'

'You think so?'

'For sure.'

'It doesn't seem very exciting to me at the moment, I'm stuck.'

'Drugs!' she said.

'Don't think so, there's no evidence of it.'

'Jealousy!' she said.

133

Walter smiled. 'Maybe,' but who was jealous of whom, and more to the point, about what, that was the question.

'I know why he did it,' she said.

'Why?'

'For money, for sure, bad men only ever do anything for money.'

'Or women?'

'No! Bad men, bad money, find the money, find the bad man.'

That seemed simple enough.

Made sense too.

A couple of minutes later and she was on the move again, grabbing the cleaner, turning it on, running around the living room, swishing his legs and feet aside as she flashed by. She didn't once stop again that day until her hand was out, and he was placing the notes into her grateful paw. Then she gathered her things together and made her way toward the front door.

'You not forget,' she said, 'I cook you dinner when case closed.'

Walter nodded and mumbled, 'See you next week,' and then she was out through the door, leaving him with one parting comment, 'Bad man, bad money, Bob's your uncle, as you English say,' and she giggled, and set off down the road without looking back, leaving Walter to mutter to himself, 'I'm not English... I'm Jamaican, and British,' as he closed the door, and went upstairs to get dressed and ready to go back to work.

Chapter Twenty-Three

Luke Flowers rolled out of bed. He was alone in the flat, though he didn't plan to be alone later that night. He strolled to the kitchen and dumped cereal in a bowl, and splashed milk over it. In the sitting room, his mobile called. Luke set his spoon down and went into the other room. Picked up the phone. A number he didn't recognise.

'Hel-lo?'

'There has been a development.'

It was Jimmy on another new phone, and Luke's heart beat faster. Jimmy Mitchell had that effect on men like Luke.

'Can you be at the usual place at 2pm?'

'Sure.'

'See you later.'

Both men arrived at the same time, a couple of minutes past the hour. Jimmy was carrying a padded packet. There was a gaggle of Japanese tourists laughing and joking beside the clock, having their picture taken, and when they saw the two local men, they fell silent and respectful, and Jimmy and Luke liked that, and acted as if they were important.

'Come on,' said Jim, 'I'm not talking here. Let's go for a stroll.'

'So long as it's worth my while.'

'It is Luke-ee, it is.'

Luke jammed his hands in his slacks' pocket, and the two men followed the city walls down toward the river. At the riverbank they walked upstream past the multi coloured pleasure boats, busy loading up tourists.

'So,' said Luke, 'Are you going to tell me what's on your mind?'

'Not here, too many people about,' said Jimmy. 'We'll find somewhere quiet.'

They took the old pedestrian suspension bridge and headed across the river. A group of young men had ignored the warning signs and were taking turns to leap from the bridge. One fell close to a passing cruise boat packed with camera waving visitors. The dregs of the splash squirted over the nearest passengers, and everyone thought that hilarious.

'Daft git!' muttered Jimmy.

'I used to do that,' said Luke, 'when I was younger.'

The men shared a look and Jimmy said: 'Why am I not surprised?'

Once over the river, they turned right and followed the bank downstream towards the weir, seeking a vacant seat. They didn't have to go far. The third bench was empty, and well away from its neighbours. Jimmy sat down, and Luke followed suit.

A young woman in tight pink leisure pants came jogging by, her black and white spaniel panting alongside. She half smiled at Luke sitting on the seat and headed down toward the old road bridge.

'Shouldn't be allowed,' whispered Luke, following her taut figure with his eyes as she trotted away, half expecting her to turn round.

She didn't.

'Don't you ever think of anything else?'

Luke smirked. 'Nope, not often. What else is there?'

'Business, that's what,' said Jimmy. 'Now pay attention!'

'I'm all yours,' said Luke. 'All ears.'

Jimmy glanced about again. No one coming, no one behind them on the bank, no one on the nearside of the river, just the subdued hum of people at play in the distance, and the gentle flowing water on an ordinary sunny summer's day in the old city, down by the river.

'I've firmed up the contract,' whispered Jimmy through the side of his mouth.

'Glad to hear it.'

'Terms as discussed. 100K, all payable on completion.'

'I can live with that, so long as you assure me the paymaster is kosher, and you personally will make the payment.'

'I can do that. Everything's in order.'

'Then I don't see a problem.'

Jimmy glanced around again. He seemed uncharacteristically nervous. Maybe the big deal he was talking about was getting the better of him.

'I've organised a false passport for you.'

'My, you are looking after me, Jim.'

'I'm honouring my side of the deal, but once the deed is done, you are on your own.'

'You are making me nervous now.'

Jimmy fished in his shirt pocket and took out a packet of cigarettes and a gold lighter.

'Want one?'

Luke shook his head. 'I am trying to cut down.'

Jimmy took a heavy draw on the cigarette and said, 'Your name is Jason Mondale; you are booked on the four o'clock flight to Florida on Sunday afternoon from Manchester. You can hire a car and travel to Mexico from there.'

'So soon?'

'Is that a problem?'

'Nope, just interested. So when's the hit?'

'Sunday, late morning.'

'Where?'

'Ness gardens.'

'Where the hell's that?'

Jimmy took another drag, and grinned and said, 'Funnily enough, Luke, it's in a place called Ness.'

Luke danced his head left and right and said, 'OK, funny-funny, I deserved that, but where the hell is Ness?'

'Up Wirral way; just before Neston and Parkgate. Maybe fifteen minutes' drive, tops. Study your map, use your satnav, or whatever crap you use these days. I don't give a toss. Just make sure you know where you are going, and when you need to be there. Go and recce it out beforehand. That would seem sensible.'

'Sounds OK to me. Is there a big do going on there, or something?'

'Yeah, a charity bash, the main man's presenting some prizes, and then there's a walkabout planned, and a chance for people to have their pictures taken with him, and an autograph session after that. He'll be signing his new book, encouraging the kiddies, all kinds of shit like that.'

'And his autograph will be in big demand?'

'Oh yeah, big time, lots of press, and maybe TV, too, but none of that will happen. You understand? He'll be gone by then. You'll hit him the moment he first enters the car park and gets out of the car.'

'You've got it all planned.'

'That's what I do, Luke, I plan things – and you DO things. Understand? I plan – you do!'

Luke nodded three times like a horse looking out of a stable, and said, 'So are you going to tell me who the target is?'

'Haven't you guessed yet?'

'I have no idea.'

'The big black git!'

Luke shook his head. Still none the wiser.

Had no idea who Jimmy was talking about.

'Which big black git? There's a lot of them about.'

'The footballer of course, the main man, the centre forward.'

There was a brief silence.

Jimmy imagined he could see and hear Luke's brain ticking over. Recognition at last.

'The England centre forward?'

Jimmy's turn to nod.

'As I said, he's made a lot of enemies. His time's up, he's run out of credit.'

Luke whistled through his teeth, said: 'Good job I'm not a Liverpool City supporter.'

'Don't give a toss about football, me,' said Jimmy, dragging on the cigarette one last time and hurling what remained of it down the bank and into the water. 'It's business, that's all you need to think about. Business. Good… paying… business.'

'Can see now why you said there will be a lot of heat.'

138

'It'll be massive. The authorities won't take kindly to the England centre forward being blown away.'

'Has anything like this ever happened before?'

Jimmy thought about that for a second.

'Not that I can think of, not in this country anyway. Maybe in Colombia, or some other filthy hole of a place, but not here.'

'Jermaine Keating,' said Luke savouring the name, 'Jermaine Keating.'

'That's the fella. I don't think you'll whack the wrong guy this time, do you?'

Luke stifled a laugh. 'No, Jim, not this time. So what time does this bash at Ness gardens kick off?'

'Half-past ten. I want you in the car park by ten o'clock. All the details are in here,' and he waggled the brown packet. 'Park the car where I've indicated, and when the guy arrives, and by the way, he drives a huge black Audi, blacked-out windows, the works, private plate KEAT1, all the usual rubbish, you can't miss it. He'll probably show up with his mistress, a white bitch. Miss Birkenhead, something like that, big tits and thick as pig-shit, but don't be sidetracked by the tight skirt.'

'You know me, Jimmy.'

'Yeah, that's what worries me.'

'You worry too much, Jimmy, that's your trouble.'

'If the girl gets in the way, tough tits Tallulah, but make sure you hit the target, usual thing, four hits, all in the chest. You'll only be feet away, you won't miss. You won't bugger it up!'

'Oh no, Jim, I won't miss.'

'Any questions?'

'Yeah. Loads of them. How and when do I get paid?'

'I was coming to that.'

'Good for you.'

'I'll meet you in Thornton Hough, in the car park by the cricket ground. After it's over, you'll come straight to me. It's only a ten minute drive, max, there's a map in the pack; you can't go wrong. I'll weigh you in there and send you on your way.'

'How will you know I've completed the job?'

'I'll know, my watchers will tell me.'

'I wouldn't have expected anything less.'

'You know me, Luke-ee, I'm an organiser.'

'I take it you've got the piece in the bag?'

Jimmy nodded, didn't say a word, set the padded packet on the bench between them.

'And afterwards?'

'You can return it when you get paid.'

Luke frowned and visualised the scene.

The tall black guy, super fit, radiating health and vitality, perfect teeth, big smile, diamonds in his ears, razor short hair, slashed eyebrows, big busty blonde at his side in a tight dress, with an inner city voice that could kill cuckoos, maybe a security guy or two in attendance as well. What about them?

'What happens if there's security?'

'Shoot them dead!'

'Just like that?'

'Yes! If you have to.'

'You don't mess about, do you?'

'Never compromise your own safety. Listen, the weather forecast is fantastic, everyone will be relaxed and in a good frame of mind. It'll be the perfect Sunday morning. No one would ever imagine that some lunatic in the car park is about to blow away the England and Liverpool City centre forward. Trust me, it'll be a doddle, it'll come as a complete surprise. But if any hurray heroes get in the way, do as I say: Shoot them dead!'

'You are not asking much.'

'It's what you're being paid for!'

There was a short silence as they envisaged the scene; and the inevitable chaos afterwards. It would become one of those landmark days that everyone always remembered. Where were you the day the England centre forward was gunned down and killed? No one would ever forget that.

'How long before I can come back?'

'Six months, not before.'

'How can I contact you?'

'There's a secure email address in the pack. Make sure you talk in abstracts and never use a name.'

'I am not stupid, Jimmy.'

'I know that, but you can't be too careful.'

'Can I ask you something?'

'May as well. It'll be the last chance you get, at least for the foreseeable future.'

'What has Jermaine Keating done to deserve this?'

'I told you, he's made a lot of enemies. He hasn't been paying his bills, he hasn't been paying his debts, thinks he's gone above everyone else, forgotten where he came from, forgotten who he owes. It's more to knock him down a peg or two, than anything else.'

'Blowing him away is not knocking him down a peg or two!'

'Yes, it is. It's a warning to his cronies. One or two of his mates are treading the same disrespectful path. You do the job and they will know how dangerous the path is.'

'You are marking their card.'

'Of course! Big time. In future they would rather step on an IED.'

Luke pulled a face. Guessed there was more to it than met the eye. More to it than he would ever know. Didn't care less.

Didn't want to know.

There was always more to it.

Everything seemed clear enough.

Ten seconds work.

Big payday.

One hundred grand!

Simple as that.

Dozens of people would kill to be in his killing shoes.

That was a gimme.

Luke was already counting his blessings.

He had three days to wind down his affairs, literally in some cases.

He'd have to make some final assignations to give himself fresh memories to take away. He'd have to concoct a story they would believe, and an idea germed in his mind. A new job in Australia, six month's trial so he couldn't take them with him, maybe later when

141

he saw how the job panned out. Yeah, that had some mileage in it. It would be interesting to see which of them took his impending departure the hardest.

Luke giggled like a kid. Sometimes life was sweet.

'Any more questions?' asked Jimmy.

'Nope. None.'

'Good, see you on Sunday at the cricket ground in Thornton Hough.'

'You will Jimmy, you will.'

The pink jogger returned. Luke smiled at the girl, and she smiled back. Then she was past and gone.

Somewhere close by, a gaggle of geese were kicking up a racket.

Luke peered up the path.

Jimmy had gone too.

Luke Flowers was alone with his padded envelope, and his instructions that would change English football forever.

Chapter Twenty-Four

1948, and Wazir Khan and his family were still standing on the quayside. He approached three dock workers who were taking a break, leaning against a brick wall, brown paper packs of cheese sandwiches in their filthy hands. 'Please,' said Wazir, 'Please, where I find?' and he showed them the old piece of paper.

The men stared at the scruffy strangers, the foreigners invading their homeland, glanced disdainfully at the oft-folded note, as if it contained vital words of an illegal proposition.

'Upper Pearli?' said one.

'They all live up that way,' said another.

'Sod off!' said the third. 'Fuck off back to where you came from! We don't want youse lot round here!'

There was beer on their breath. Wazir peered into their hateful, bloodshot eyes. It wasn't as he had imagined. It wasn't as he'd hoped. He turned and beckoned his family away from the men, away from the quay. They picked up their tiny bags and headed down the dock road toward the big buildings they could see in the distance. It began to rain. Ahmed the boy shivered. Above them, the overhead dock railway clattered along. They took shelter beneath, out of the rain, out of the wind, as the Khan family hurried on toward the big buildings.

Wazir noticed two policemen coming toward them. He guessed they were policemen, he had seen pictures in books of English policemen; indeed some police in India wore similar, if lighter weight uniforms. It was the strange hats that were so familiar.

Wazir approached and stood before them. Adopted his best English accent, pronunciation he had heard on the radio, and said,

143

'Excuse me, gentlemen, but I am seeking this address. Could you possibly help me? Can you set us on the right road? Please, sirs.'

'Please, sirs, is it?' said one to the other, grinning.

Wazir nodded and added, 'Yes sir, please.'

The first policeman nodded across the dock road and said, 'See that tram, the green tram,' he was speaking loud as if Wazir was deaf, or an idiot, 'THE GREEN TRAM!'

Wazir glanced at the old tram as it clanked along the road. 'I see the tram.'

The policeman nodded and grinned at his colleague as if he were making headway. 'That tram goes to Upper Parliament Street; all you have to do is follow it.'

Wazir glanced back at the green and cream tram, gaining speed and clanking and heading away.

'But we can't follow it, it goes too fast, we have child,' glancing down at Ahmed.

The policemen peered down at Ahmed, too. He was a cute kid, and the boy looked worried.

The officer was talking again, 'That's OK, the trams run every fifteen minutes, just follow each one as they come along, you can't go wrong.'

Wazir beamed. 'Oh I see, thank you so very much.'

'You're all right, pal,' said the policeman.

The second one spotted the cricket bat.

'YOU LIKE CRICKET?'

Wazir glanced at the bat; thought of the bejewelled sword sleeping within.

'Oh yes, I like cricket, we all like cricket in India.'

'MIND IF I HAVE A GO?' said the policeman, reaching down and easing the bat from Wazir's grasp. Nadirah looked alarmed. The boy still looked worried.

The policeman didn't notice. He grabbed the bat and was practising his batting stance, grinning at the others. Playing a classic cover drive, an aggressive cut through the slips, a hook over his left shoulder, high in the air, over the ropes. 'SIX!' he yelled, and looked pleased with himself.

The officer stood up and handed the bat to Wazir.

'IT'S A HEAVY BAT!'

'Yes,' said Wazir, 'heavy bat,' confused and unsure of what to say.

'YOU MUST SUPPORT LANCASHIRE,' said the show-off batsman, 'LANC-A-SHIRE!'

'Lanc-a-shire,' repeated Wazir. 'From now on I support Lanc-a-shire.'

The policemen shared a look, one nodded and said, 'That's the ticket.'

Wazir turned around. He thought he heard another tram coming. The policemen smiled at one another, grinned at the strangers, and pointed across the road to the approaching tram.

'YOU FOLLOW TRAM!' said one of them. 'YOU'LL BE ALL RIGHT.'

'Yes, we follow tram,' said Wazir, and he beckoned his family across the busy road, to be closer to the clanking beast banging toward them.

After they had gone, one policeman said to his mate, 'See! They are not all thick. I have always been able to communicate with foreigners.'

'Yeah, Harry, course you have, let's grab a cuppa tea.'

99 Upper Parliament Street was a four-story mid Victorian property. Its best days were long behind it. One window on the second floor was smashed. The front door was cracked and bowed and needed a paint, and up above, some of the Welsh slates on the roof had come loose and slipped down, several balancing on the edge, as if a puff of wind would send them hurtling to the street below, but to the Khan family, it looked like a palace.

They were tired and cold and hungry, and needed to get inside out of the drizzle. There were four white bell pushes lined up beside the door, and after studying them for a second, Wazir pushed A. He could hear the long continuous sound of a bell ringing inside. They all could.

145

A moment later the door opened and a handsome face peered down at them, a friendly face, an Indian face, who glanced at the little boy, and the pleasing-on-the-eye woman, and the upright gentleman… and the impressive cricket bat he was holding.

Had they come all this way from the State of Kerala, carrying a blessed cricket bat? What did the man imagine he was going to do? Play cricket all day? In this climate? Ignorance is bliss. What a fool! The handsome man scoffed and said the most welcoming words he could have uttered.

'You'd better come in, you look tired and hungry. We have been expecting you.'

The following morning, Wazir was set to work in the laundry. Worked twelve hours a day, seven days a week, but the work wasn't overtaxing, and his family was safe and fed, and at the end of the month Wazir received two crisp green one-pound notes. Nadirah worked in the kitchen, and when she wasn't doing that, was told to clean and polish the house. She received nothing and was happy to do that, for a while. Ahmed would be instructed in prayer, while discrete enquiries were made as to where he could attend a suitable school.

The Khan family shared one small room at the top of the house, set in the attic where water would drip in whenever it rained.

Wazir volunteered to climb up and fix the roof; and everyone stood outside in the street on the morning he did it. The roof wouldn't leak again, and Wazir's determination, skill, and courage were noted.

He spent part of the money he received on a good lock, MADE in ENGLAND, it said, like the ones at home, and fitted it to a cupboard that was set in the eaves in their little room.

Inside the cupboard the cricket bat soundly slept, safe and secure, out of sight, out of mind, and inside the bat, the bejewelled ceremonial sword slumbered on.

No one outside the Khan family knew it was there.

It would remain incarcerated for years.

Chapter Twenty-Five

Walter and Karen were back in Swaythling's office, sipping best Robusta coffee. Swaythling insisted, and even Karen tired some. The same model palace was on display, and Gerry Swaythling had topped up his tan. His new white teeth stood out against his face, and that was the way he liked it.

Walter and Karen sat a little way back, on the visitor's side of the desk. Gerry eyed the black bloke hunched over his coffee like a grizzly bear, the girl relaxed in the chair, her legs crossed, displaying a little leg. She was easy on the eye; that was undeniable, though Gerry guessed she would have a score of admirers lurking in the undergrowth.

She had a way of smirking as she spoke some men might find irritating, disconcerting even, but Gerry didn't. He liked it, for he imagined it sent out come-and-get-me signals. He saw such signals, real or imaginary, every day of the week. She was giving another positive signal too. Her right leg, the top one was drifting back and forth, the foot thrusting in and out, rhythmically, a sure-fire sign in Gerry's eyes she was interested in him. He'd seen that telltale movement many times before, and it was a big plus point.

Walter guzzled the rest of his coffee and set the china cup and saucer on the low glass table.

'So, Mr Swaythling, why didn't you tell us you are a member of the Pythagoras Lodge?'

'Call me Gerry, please, fact is, you didn't ask,' and he exchanged eye contact with Karen. His eyebrows twitched, hers were as still as Stonehenge. 'And anyway, unless the law has changed, there is nothing wrong with being a member of the Masons. Why don't you join? Do you want me to propose you? You should see the charity work we do...'

Walter had heard it all a thousand times before, and didn't want to hear it again, and he didn't want to join either, and said, 'It might have helped.'

'I don't see how.'

'Because, Mr Swaythling, you borrowed a significant amount of money from someone in the Lodge to enable you to buy out Munro Ford, and save the business.'

'Oh yes, and who have you been talking to?'

'That is irrelevant, the question is, who did you borrow the money from? Has it been paid back? And did the arrangement end amicably?'

'I can't see the relevance of all that.'

Karen jumped in, 'The relevance, Mr Swaythling, is that if the loan was not repaid, and if the arrangement turned sour, the lender might have put pressure on you by targeting your son, and murdered, perhaps accidentally, Jeffrey Player.'

Gerry Swaythling uttered a nervous laugh.

'You're barking up the wrong tree, young woman. The arrangement has not turned sour. It's a ridiculous idea. You are wasting your time with this line of enquiry.'

Walter noted the use of the present tense. Has not, not did not. The arrangement was ongoing; the loan had not been repaid.

'So the loan has never been repaid in full?'

Swaythling shifted in his chair and muttered, 'The loan is being satisfactorily serviced.'

'Oh, come on, Mr Swaythling, that won't do, it isn't a straight answer. How much of the loan is outstanding, and how much is being repaid?'

'This has nothing to do with the attacks on Neil! And if I may say so, it has nothing to do with you either.'

'We will decide that,' said Walter. 'How much are you paying?'

There was a momentarily silence as if Gerry was weighing up his options before he said, 'Three grand a month.'

'And how long has this been going on?' asked Walter.

'For longer than I care to remember.'

'And how long will it go on for?' asked Karen.

148

Another pause for thought, another short silence, then he let slip from the side of his mouth, 'In perpetuity.'

'You are repaying three thousand pounds a month forever?' clarified Walter.

Swaythling looked uncomfortable. He glanced at Karen as if for sympathy. She thought he looked like a chastised boy at an upper class prep school, and he didn't seem far from tears. Pathetic.

Swaythling bobbed his head and looked away.

'So you are now paying £36,000 a year to service the debt?' said Walter.

Again Swaythling nodded as if he couldn't bear to hear it spoken aloud.

'And how long has this been going on for?'

'Fourteen years.'

Walter pursed his lips and stared at the false grey ceiling. Walter's own grey matter churned over, albeit slowly.

'That's over half a million.'

'Yes!' said Swaythling, one short sharp single abrupt word. 'So what?'

'With no sign of it ever ending?' clarified Karen.

He didn't look at her this time, just nodded again, and glanced nervously at his watch.

'And you are happy to pay this forever?' asked Walter.

Swaythling shrugged his shoulders as if to say, what choice do I have?

'Is Langley Wells happy with the arrangement?' asked Walter.

'I suppose... What has it got to do with him?'

'I think we both know he is the lender,' said Karen.

'I'm not confirming that, and regardless of who it is, it is not illegal. We have done nothing wrong.'

'It is illegal,' said Walter, 'if you have borrowed money from Langley Wells, and are paying excessive interest, because he does not have a credit licence to lend. In fact he has been banned from obtaining one by the Office of Fair Trading.'

'Be that as it may, it makes no difference to me; this is a private arrangement between friends. It is legal and above board.'

'That's debatable,' said Karen.

Walter again. 'In effect you are being blackmailed by Langley Wells to hand him £3,000 a month, every month, forever. Why bother?'

'Blackmail is an emotive word.'

'Why don't you stop paying? Tell him enough is enough is enough. You have more than repaid the loan,' said Walter. 'Several times over.'

'I think we both know that would not be advisable, and anyway, I can afford it, it's chicken feed.'

'That's not the point,' said Walter.

'What hold does he have over you, Mr Swaythling?' asked Karen.

'He doesn't have any hold over me, little miss know it all!' his voice rising to a crescendo, sufficient to alert the staff outside their boss was being given a tough time by the local police. 'You are missing the bloody point!'

'What is your point?' asked Walter.

'The point is that if I hadn't been paying, then the Wells gang, or whoever it might be, might have had cause to give my family grief, but I have. I can show you the bank transfers, if you are that interested! I have never missed a single payment, not once!'

'Quite! But if your son was out of the way, Wells couldn't threaten to harm him, could he?' said Karen.

'Don't be ridiculous!'

Swaythling was on his feet, pacing up and down behind where Walter and Karen sat.

'So who is trying to kill your son, Mr Swaythling?' asked Walter.

'How the hell should I know? That's your job! But one thing I can tell you, it isn't me, and it isn't Wells either! Now do you mind?' and he opened the office door and said aloud, 'Show these gentlemen out!'

Walter and Karen shared a look, Karen smirked, and they left the room. Walter first, Karen following, and as she passed him, holding the door she whispered, 'I am not a gentleman.'

'You could have fooled me!'

In the car outside Karen said, 'Where does that take us.'

Walter shuffled his thoughts into some kind of order.

'We now know it's definitely Wells who lent the money. We have a better idea what he is capable of, how much clout he possesses, for want of a better phrase, and, that he is still receiving illegal payments. We could prove it too if the bank records back it up.'

'So why don't we build a case against Wells?'

'That will come, though it will be difficult to prove. Swaythling will deny it, concoct some story the payments were for something else, perhaps something to do with the Wells property outfit. Wells will deny it too, and they'll both employ the best weaselly solicitor available, probably that Herringbone gentleman, or whatever his name is.'

'Robertson Herring-Shone,' said Karen.

'That's the joker.'

'Is Wells capable of murdering someone?' asked Karen.

'Course he is,' said Walter. 'We all are, but I don't think he has, not in this case. As Swaythling said, why hassle someone who is paying you £3,000 a month. You don't murder the golden goose.'

'So if it's not Wells, is it Gerry Swaythling?'

'He didn't pull the trigger, we know that, but if you are asking me, did he order it, then the answer is, he could have done. The question is, why would he?'

'We know Gerry and Neil don't get on,' said Karen.

'We do, but it's a hell of a big step from arguing with your son, to ordering his murder.'

'So, if it is Swaythling senior, there must be some terrible hidden skeleton in the cupboard we are unaware of.'

'True, I wonder what that could be? Maybe we should have another go at Neil.'

'And if it's nothing to do with Gerry, the only others in the frame are Munro Ford... and Veronica Camberwell.'

'Yes,' said Walter. 'Or someone else. I think it's high time we paid a visit to Willaston, and Mrs Camberwell. I wonder what she's like.'

'Makes no difference,' said Karen, starting the car, 'You're far too old.'

151

'Cheeky!'

They didn't get far with Veronica; they didn't see her at all. A neighbour said she had gone to stay with her cousin in Leeds; she'd taken Neil's death badly and couldn't bear to live in the big house alone. At some point Veronica Camberwell was in for a big surprise.

They hadn't been back in the office more than ten minutes when Karen took a call for Walter.

'It's that newspaper woman again for you, Gardenia Floem.'

'Oh, OK,' said Walter and he grabbed the phone.

'Hello, Inspector.'

'Hello, Mizz Floem.'

'It's a quiet day here on the news desk so I thought I'd give you a quick ring to see if there's any news, more specifically any progress on the Player murder, and the attack on Neil Swaythling.'

'Am I missing something?' asked Walter.

'How do you mean?'

'Was Neil Swaythling not murdered too?'

'I don't know, Inspector, you tell me.'

'I don't know what you mean.'

'Rumours are circulating.'

'What kind of rumours?'

'I suspect you know well enough.'

'Come on Mizz Floem, do your duty, tell me what you have heard.'

Karen was engrossed. She couldn't hear all the conversation, but had a good idea what Ms Floem was saying.

The interesting thing was Walter had adopted the chatty-up soft voice he used whenever he was talking to a woman he fancied. He fancied Ms Floem, didn't he, the dirty old dog. No wonder he had employed a new cleaner to smarten up his house. Maybe he was hoping to lure the reporter back there. Karen could imagine that, she could almost hear his words, why don't you come round to mine and we can swap notes, you help me, I'll help you, you scratch my back, I'll scratch yours, et cetera et cetera, and who knows where that might lead? Geez! They might even have children. Imagine that! Little Darriteaus running round the office creating havoc. Karen smirked again.

'Not to put too fine a point on it,' Mizz Floem continued, 'word on the street has it that you have Neil Swaythling holed up somewhere as you tempt to lure the killer into the open.'

'Don't be silly, Mizz Floem.'

'Come on Inspector, help me here. I am feeding you intelligence; surely you can give me something that might interest my readers. My paper can be very useful to you, we both know that, but sometimes we like a little gem in return. What have you got hidden in that office of yours I can use?'

'You should speak to the Press Office, Mizz Floem, Bernie Porter is the man.'

'Useless dog turd, if you don't mind me saying.'

'Mizz Floem, I am surprised at you.'

'Walter,' she said, and she had never called him that before, 'Is there nothing you can tell me?'

'Not today, Mizz Floem.'

'Pity, you disappoint me.'

'Keep in touch, Mizz Floem.'

'Oh, I will… ciao,' and then she was gone.

'Ciao,' Walter repeated. 'Who the hell ends their conversations with "ciao"?'

'You like that woman, don't you?' said Karen.

'Don't know the woman,' said Walter, keeping a straight face.

'No, but you'd like to, eh?'

Walter harrumphed.

The phone rang again.

Karen snatched it up. Turned serious.

Walter watched her face. She wasn't smirking any longer.

'Yes, he's here, I'll put you through.'

'Who is it?'

'Langley Wells.'

153

Chapter Twenty-Six

Walter shared a look with Karen and rippled his eyebrows and grabbed the phone. What could have made Langley Wells swallow his pride and ring the police? Walter sniffed and grunted, 'Hello.'

'Inspector Darriteau?'

'That's me.'

'It's Langley Wells.'

'Mr Wells, what can I do for you?'

'I have been thinking about our chat.'

'Oh, yes?'

'I'd like another meet, just you and me.'

'Why don't you come into the station and we can talk here?'

'Don't be ridiculous!'

'So what do you suggest?'

'I want you to come here, alone, leave that smart arsed girl behind, she got my boys into all kinds of a tither.'

Walter and Karen shared another look.

She couldn't hear the conversation, but guessed they were talking about her.

'What about Pierre's restaurant in town?'

'No! Too public. I want you to come here.'

'I'm not happy with that.'

'Suit yourself! What's the matter? Are you afraid? Look, I'll personally guarantee your safety. You know me, Darriteau, if nothing else I am a man of my word.'

For a lowlife, Walter knew Wells had some vague notions of standards, though they were not values Walter could share.

'When did you have in mind?'

'Come at three o'clock, the boys will be out. They'll be just you, me, and Rose.'

'All right, I can do that.'

'Come alone, Darriteau. If there's more than one of you, we won't open the door.'

'I get the picture.'

'Good!' said Wells, and he cut the line dead.

'What did he want?' asked Karen.

'I don't know; must have taken a lot for him to call; wants to see me at three, just me.'

Karen pulled a face and tried to hide her disappointment.

'Do you want me to drive you?'

'No, but you can organise an unmarked car.'

'OK, Guv,' and there was a short pause before she said, 'Go wired up, and I'd take a gun if I were you.'

Walter sniffed a laugh and said, 'I don't think that will be necessary.'

He left the station at a quarter to three. Karen had fixed him up with a dark green Ford saloon that had seen better days. It stank of cigarette smoke and stale coffee, but it was the only unmarked vehicle available.

Walter started the car and headed onto the inner ring road. It was roasting inside. He made to buzz down the windows. Couldn't find the buttons, no surprise, the car didn't run to electric windows. He grabbed the handle and began turning, and hot air rushed in.

He remembered the weather forecast predicted one of the hottest days of the year. He blew out hard and pulled the car to a standstill at the lights at the fountains roundabout. Wished he hadn't bothered with the jacket, and that was a first for the year.

The house looked the same, the neighbourhood quiet, grassy unkempt lawns turning brown, an abandoned kid's trike on the pavement; the kids not home from school. The four by fours were missing. Walter guessed the sons were busy at their property and second-hand car businesses, and whatever mischief they were up to.

The drapes were open, but no one could see into the house through the doubled up lace curtains. Most of the locals knew better than to try. He imagined he saw the curtains shivering, though he might have been wrong.

Pulled on the handbrake, wound up the windows, and hauled himself out of the car. He took out his handkerchief and wiped his forehead. Blew out hard and wished he'd double deodorised that morning, but it was too late now. Eased open the gate, limped up the path and rang the bell.

A moment later, Rose came to the door and opened up.

'Right on time,' she said. 'Guess I shouldn't be surprised.'

Unless he was mistaken she half smiled at him, and that was a first.

'Well, don't just stand there; come in before the rats get in.'

Same copra mat, same wiping of the feet, same performance, shown through to the room at the back, the sitting room cum office. Langley wasn't there. No one was.

'Wanna cup of tea?' she asked.

'No thanks, though a glass of water would be nice.'

'Might run to that, you look hot, make yourself at home,' and she turned and left him alone in Langley's private office.

He glanced down at the desk. Same tub of pens, same calculator, no papers visible; one wood effect filing cabinet to one side. He hadn't noticed that before, maybe it hadn't been there last time, locked by the look of it. No obvious key. Walter wondered what secrets lay within, details of all of Langley's transactions maybe, going back years and years, perhaps including the Swaythling business.

Walter pondered on the half warm welcome, and why he had been left alone. It couldn't be an accident; the Wells family weren't stupid, they were up to something. Maybe he was being monitored, his every move filmed. Were they hoping he might attempt to enter the filing cabinet, or the desk drawers? Maybe they hoped it might produce some juicy blackmail material. Who knows what went through the minds of the Wells gang?

There were several family photographs on the wall, some with young children, looked like recent pics, probably the boys' kids, but there was another larger black-and-white photograph, not of the family.

It featured a large gathering, perhaps fifty or sixty people, taken a few years before, not ancient, but not recent either, and there in the middle were Langley and Rose, looking pleased with themselves, while a few heads along the row was another familiar face, Gerry Swaythling, a little younger, but not much, looking mischievous and happy with his arms around an attractive girl on either side, a brunette and a blonde, no surprise there, and no sign of the wife anywhere.

The men were dressed in evening suits and bow ties, the girls in dresses to die for that must have cost a month's wages for some people. Beneath the smiling faces was an inscription: Imperial Hotel, Valletta, Malta, and a date from ten years before.

It was a Masonic meeting, had to be, holiday bash in the sunshine, took along the girls so they didn't feel left out, and Malta had a long history of freemasonry, Walter knew that because reading up on the subject was a passion of his, along with native American Indian chiefs, Geronimo being his particular favourite, and cricket of course. Wisden was essential reading and a must buy at Christmas, even if he had to buy the newest edition for himself. No one else would. It would be his little treat.

'1730,' he said aloud, recalling his history, as Rose came back into the room carrying a large glass of water, clinking ice cubes as she walked, a slice of lemon floating like a tropical fish.

'What?' she said, setting the glass on the coaster on the desk.

'Oh nothing, just talking to myself.'

'You can get done for that.'

Walter grinned. 'Thanks for the water, Rose.'

She almost smiled, but thought better of it.

'Langley will be with you in a minute. Sit down and take a drink. You look whacked.'

'Yeah,' said Walter, 'good idea,' and he grabbed the glass and sank most of the content, and dropped into the chair.

157

'No charge for the water, and no interest either,' and this time she did smile, before she disappeared.

1730 he mused again. The year the French first took freemasonry to Malta, if his memory was still intact. It had probably been there longer, and there would be active branches still, willing to host UK parties, especially the wealthier visitors who were going to stay in the best hotels, and spend a great deal of money. The door opened again and Langley Wells came in and shut the door behind him.

'Sorry to keep you waiting, Darriteau, had my accountant on the phone, awful windbag, he is,' and he hurried around the desk and sat down. Walter glanced at Langley and thought he looked more hyena-like than ever. He emptied the glass and set it on the coaster.

'Want another?' asked Langley.

'No, I'm fine,' and Walter folded his arms, an obvious invitation for Langley to begin.

'It's taken an awful lot for me to invite you here.'

'Really?'

'Yes, it has. No one must know of this meeting. Does anyone know you are here?'

'Only my sergeant.'

'Ah yes, the sex bomb.'

'You think so?'

'Not me, the boys!'

'Can't say as I have noticed.'

'Liar!'

There was a short pause, as if Langley was debating whether he should say anything further. Walter waited.

'No one else knows you are here?' said a nervous Langley.

'Rose does,' said Walter.

'Ah well, she doesn't count, she's my right arm, Darriteau, trust her with my life, I would, and there are few people I could say that about.'

Walter rolled his eyebrows; he was becoming bored with small talk.

'You're not wired, are you?' said Langley, rippling his nose.

'Course not, give me some credit.'

158

'Didn't think you would be, just checking. The thing is, Darriteau, I have been thinking about our last little chat.'

'So you said on the phone.'

'Yes, well, this isn't easy for me. We, the people on this estate, are brought up to be wary of the police, and not without cause, and the idea of grassing someone up, it just isn't done.'

'What are you trying to tell me, Langley?'

'I abhor violence, Darriteau, always have.'

Walter raised his eyebrows. Didn't say a word.

'Don't look like that! I do, and that's the God's honest truth. Yes, I may have clipped the odd out-of-liner over the ear once or twice when they were misbehaving, just knocking them back into line, that kind of thing, the sort of thing your lot used to do before you got so paranoid about it, and damned scared of the lawyers.'

'Things change, Langley. None of us can carry on like we did thirty, forty years ago.'

Langley picked up a pen and began fiddling with it.

'Yes, well, what I am trying to say is that I cannot do with guns. Young men, not much more than youths, in short kecks only ten years since, running round toting weapons as if they are in the O.K. Corral. I can't be doing with it, and neither can my family, and you have my word that we do all we can to put a stop to it, and that's the truth. But these days sometimes, and it is most unfortunate, things can and do get out of hand. Out of control.'

'You are referring to the Jeffrey Player killing?'

Langley nodded. Didn't say a word.

'Do you know who did it?'

There was another pause and Langley said, 'I have heard a few things, whispers, things I don't like.'

'If you put someone in the frame for murder for your own ends, I am duty bound to warn you that you could be prosecuted for perverting the course of justice, and that offence carries a hefty sentence.'

'God give me strength, Darriteau! Don't threaten me! I am trying to help you here.'

159

Walter held up his hands; palms facing Wells and said, 'Just so long as we understand one another. I am not anyone's fool.'

Wells shifted in his seat as if the ordeal of speaking to a police officer was the worst torture imaginable.

'I know that! I wouldn't have invited you here if I thought you were.'

Walter bobbed his head.

Hoped Wells would start speaking again, and he did.

'Do you want my information or not?'

'Of course I do, Langley. All information from the public is gratefully received, and will be investigated. You can be sure of that.'

Wells didn't look convinced. His bottom lip came out. He looked from side to side for comfort and support, as if he half expected to see his sons standing there, but the room was silent and empty.

'This information is anonymous.'

'If you want.'

'I do!'

Langley Wells took a big breath.

'The prick's name is Luke Flowers.'

It meant nothing to Walter, but that wasn't important. A name had spilled from Wells' lips and that meant something, though Walter was unclear why Wells was talking to him.

'Does he live on the estate?'

'I have no idea, and I don't want to know either!'

That came out in a rush and carried a hint of spite, and then as if Wells had thought better of it, he said, 'Not any more, but I'm sure you won't have any trouble in finding him.'

'Why did he do it?'

'No idea!'

'Drugs?'

'Told you… no idea!'

'This Luke Flowers character, was he working for himself, or for someone else?'

'Don't know that either! But it was nothing to do with me, you can be sure of that. Gerry Swaythling is a friend of mine, and I don't care whether you believe that or not.'

160

'Gerry Swaythling is paying you a great deal of money. You can afford to be friends.'

'Don't start that again!'

'Is there anything else you can tell me?'

'No! There isn't. I've said far too much already.'

One benefit of wearing a considerable pair of trousers was small objects could be concealed in deep pockets. Walter stopped the car in a private road of fifties detached houses less than five minutes drive away, each home protected by a high hedge. That protection worked two ways. He couldn't see in, but no one in the houses could see Walter sitting in the car. He fished out the state-of-the-art mini recorder and played the conversation back.

You are referring to the Jeff Player killing?

Do you know who did it?

I have heard a few things, things I don't like.

He hadn't been trying to entrap Langley Wells. He knew the evidence wouldn't be admissible. He'd done it for the sheer hell of it, and if Langley confessed to crimes, it would encourage the investigation.

As it was, Wells had fingered the killer. Walter wondered who Luke Flowers was, and where he was at that moment, and, if he hadn't done it off his own bat, then who was the young man working for? But most of all, Walter pondered on why Wells had told him at all.

He rang Karen at the office.

'We have a name in the frame.'

'For the Player killing?'

'The same.'

161

'Did Wells tell you that?'

'Maybe.'

'So? Who is it?'

'Luke Flowers.'

'Means nothing to me,' she said.

'Me neither; and it's a name I would remember.'

'I'll run it through the computer.'

'Do that, I'll be back soon.'

Six minutes later and Walter was ducking the car into the underground car park. A minute after that he was in the private office playing the tape to Karen.

Does anyone know you are here?

Only my sergeant.

Ah yes, the sex bomb.

You think so?

Not me, the boys!

Can't say as I have noticed.

Liar!

'Skip that bit,' said Walter.

Karen laughed and fast-forwarded.

'How did you get on?' asked Walter, slumping in his chair.

'We have one Luke Flowers in the system. Luke Edward Flowers.'

'And?'

Karen opened her diary and slipped a printout containing a photo across the desk. It was unmistakable, the likeness to the photofit and artist impressions, though the official photograph had been taken some years before.

'Why didn't you say?'

Karen smiled. 'I wanted to hear what you had first.'

'Cheeky! Where does he live?'

'The address we have is Moorcroft Avenue on the same estate, about a quarter of a mile from Langley's place.'

'I don't think he lives there now,' said Walter.

'What makes you say that?'

'Just a feeling.'

'He's not on the voters' roll,' said Karen.

Walter sniffed. 'Voters' roll, be damned, when did people like him ever vote?'

'I think he might still live there.'

'I'll bet he doesn't,' said Walter.

'Wanna bet?'

'How much?'

'A tenner?'

'Done! Organise an arrest warrant, fix a car; and get some backup too, and make sure you wear a vest.'

'Your concern is touching, Guv.'

'It's not you I am worrying about. It's my hide that gets kicked black and blue if my sergeant is mashed.'

'I am not planning on that happening.'

'Good! And take a gun.'

'You can rely on that.'

'By the way, what was he done for?'

'Copying and selling CDs at car boot sales. Seventeen he was at the time.'

'Big time?'

'Oh yes, had 5,000 items in the car when he was arrested, must have made a lot of money, got six months' youth detention.'

'Obviously didn't cure him.'

'Course not! What do you expect?'

Chapter Twenty-Seven

1950's Liverpool: and Wazir Khan landed a decent job. Everyone told him the English would never employ an Indian Muslim, but Wazir took no notice of that. He was determined to find employment, and did. In his spare time he had been pounding the streets, and his wanderings took him to the Skelhorne Street city centre bus station.

Wazir knocked on the office door, entered when commanded, and stood before a broad man sipping a mug of the sweetest stewed tea imaginable. Jimmy McTavish was his name, and Jimmy McTavish interviewed Wazzie, as he was to become known, in ten minutes, and employed him in another ten.

Wazir Khan was pleased and amazed in equal measure. He would become a bus conductor employed by the Liverpool City Council, when all the double-decker buses ran a crew of two, or three, when the Inspector hopped aboard.

He would start training the following morning, and would be let loose on the old green AEC Regent III double-decker bus, on the city centre to Crosby run the following week.

Wazir thanked Jimmy Mac and hurried home to share the momentous news with his wife. He would earn six pounds ten shillings a week before stoppages, whatever they were. Jimmy Mac grinned and returned to sipping tea.

Despite his name, Jimmy Mac was black, and proud of it. Came from one of the oldest black families in Liverpool. Could trace his roots back five generations to slavery and Jamaica, where his ancestor was known as Reego. He, like so many others, took his owner's name as his own as soon as he could. He received the amazing news of his freedom on arrival in Liverpool, where he was working on a sugar trader, took one look round, and stayed. Jimmy

164

Mac never considered living anywhere else, and was more scouse than most of the locals.

He shared a two-bedroom flat in Toxteth with his wife Norah, who was almost as black as Jimmy Mac, and three eating and sleeping machines, his sons, Reego, Daniel, and James Junior. All the menfolk in the McTavish family were avid Liverpool City Football Club followers, though they were far too clever and cute to consider attending a match in the flesh. No one was stupid enough to do that, not in their community, for in the fifties blacks weren't welcome in the stadium. Times were a-changing, but they weren't there yet.

The football club employed a new manager, a man the McTavishes had never heard of. The new guy had a huge job on his hands, for Liverpool City were languishing in the second division, living in the shadow of the big clubs in the city. Like many others in the area, the McTavishes hoped for the best, and feared the worst.

Wazir enjoyed his job. He'd brush off the racist remarks; he'd laugh them away, and grew to enjoy the banter with the office girls commuting to and from the city, morning and night.

Some of them were fascinated by his smooth, dark skin, and thick and shiny, neat parted hair he wore longer than the fashion, and the sparkle that flashed from his brooding dark eyes, even if his English was difficult to the local ear. Wazir thought the same of them, but didn't say.

He wasn't short of offers, from the women, he could see that in their English eyes, but would never entertain such a stupid thought, for Nadirah was the love of his life, and always would be. She had been chosen especially for him by his parents when he was seventeen, and surely that was the correct way of doing things. A man was given a pure wife, and a woman was married to a decent man. Both families had seen to that.

Three months after he began work on the buses he began doing something that would concern him for the rest of his days. Things were not going well at home. His hosts were unhappy he had taken

165

independent employment. They demanded more and more money from Wazir and his wife, and made suggestions they would be kicked out onto the street if it wasn't forthcoming.

Nadirah had secured two additional cleaning jobs that paid a little cash, and the Khan family were determined to save every penny, for England had fired unimaginable dreams and targets within them, and they wanted them soon, this year, not next.

Wazir worked out a way to supplement his wages.

When a passenger left the bus, he would go to their empty seat and look for the spent ticket. If he could find it, and if it was in perfect condition, he would rescue it and slip it into a small wallet he kept for the purpose.

If a new passenger required the same fare the recently departed soul had paid, Wazir would turn around on some spurious mission, as if to help an old lady toward her seat, or to the jumping off platform, or to help someone with luggage, he would recover the used ticket and hand it to the new traveller. No one suspected a thing.

The paid fare would not go into his corporation leather satchel, but into his deep trouser pocket. Wazir had perfected a way of doubling his wages; and tax-free at that, trebling even, at busy times like Christmas.

It worried him and affected his sleep. He told his wife he was working all the overtime he could find, never mentioned his deceitful scheme to her, for he knew she would be aghast. He felt guilty at deceiving her, but he could not stop himself. He could barely look Jimmy McTavish in the eye, and lived in dread of discovery, of an inspector jumping on his bus, and especially one particular inspector, known to the men as Ged the Gestapo.

Gerrard Fox lived on the Wirral peninsula in a semi-detached house in Prenton, a residential area that Gerrard portrayed to his city bound colleagues as akin to Beverly Hills.

Wazir decided he would go there and see for himself. In his mind, one day Wazir Khan would possess a house in Prenton too, but for now, he was more concerned in balancing the books whenever the inspector appeared.

The old bus was standing at the Pier Head, coughing and wheezing filthy black smoke that anointed its passengers, before they boarded for the four o'clock run to Crosby where it would turn around at Endbutt Lane, and trundle back down to the city.

'Move along the bus, please, plenty of seats upstairs,' Wazir called out, as the bus filled.

Ding! Ding! He pressed the bell, and the bus heaved and shook and eased away from the stop.

At the last second, Ged the Gestapo flew through the air, caught hold of the vertical bar, and heaved himself on board with a glare at Wazir, and a smile and a wink at the pretty young wife with the podgy toddler on her lap, on the bench seat just inside the bus.

'And how's my Paki-Lackey?' Ged yelled down the cabin, as Wazir went about collecting fares.

Ged always addressed Wazir in that way, and many of his workmates did too, including his own driver. Not many thought it odd; it was the norm, it was only in jest. Foreigners had to learn to have a sense of humour.

Jimmy Mac never used the phrase.

'I am not a Pakistani,' Wazir protested, on first hearing the expression, 'I am a Muslim from India, I am Indian.'

'India, Pakistan, there's no difference to me,' Ged sneered, smirking at some passengers, some of whom stared at Wazir with a mixture of curiosity and sympathy, though they would look away when Wazir caught their eye. 'All the same hellhole to me,' continued Ged. 'I served in Ceylon in the war; I know what I am talking about.'

Wazir would bite his tongue and grin his way through the tense times that Ged the Gestapo spent on Wazir's bus.

Ged didn't like Wazir Khan.

Didn't agree with it at all, the policy of letting in the natives, as he referred to Wazir, and anyone else with a less than pristine white skin, come to that. Ged was determined to get rid of Wazir Khan, he had no business working on the buses, on his buses. Come to think of it, he couldn't imagine why the hell Jimmy Mac had employed him in the first place. But then again, it was Jimmy Mac,

167

and natives always looked after their own. It was just the same in Colombo. Lazy fookers they were, the lot of them, Ged would tell his pals in the Bus Staff Club at the back of Paradise Street, where you could get a pint of sour local Higsons ale for a penny less than anywhere else.

Ged would air his views in public when Jimmy Mac wasn't present, because for some godforsaken reason Jimmy Mac was well thought of by the powers that be, and was senior to all the inspectors, including Gerrard Fox.

'Show me your papers!' snapped Ged.

Wazir presented the records of his journeys that day. It was only the start of the shift and the standard cash float was accurate and intact. Wazir was a meticulous bookkeeper and would always pay his overspend fund, as he referred to it in his mind, into the Post Office in India Buildings, indeed he had done so that lunchtime, in case he was checked and searched. Good job he had.

Ged wasn't convinced.

'Takings are down, Khan. Can you explain that?'

'How do you mean, Inspector?'

'It's plain English, oh I forgot, your English isn't great, is it? I'll spell it out for you, lah! Four buses are out on the Crosby run, and your takings are the lowest. How do you explain that, my subcontinental chum?'

Wazir pulled a puzzled face and shook his head. He couldn't explain it at all, and had no intention of trying.

'Someone has to take the lowest,' suggested Wazir, after a few seconds thought.

'Yeah, but it's funny how it's always you, Paki-lack!'

'Maybe they don't like me.'

'I can understand that!'

'I'll try to sell more tickets, Mr Fox.'

'Inspector, to you! Have you got any money on you?'

'I have four shilling and thrupence in my pocket.'

'Show me!'

Wazir took out the change.

'Is that all you've got?'

168

'It is, Inspector, I tell you.'

'Well, let's have a little look, shall we,' and Ged Fox began tapping Wazir's pockets for evidence of stolen money.

Nothing there. Clean as a whistle.

Ged grimaced and rammed his hands deep into his dark raincoat pockets. He leant toward Wazir and whispered, 'I'm watching you, Khan, you're up to something, one slip from you and you're out,' and he turned and heaved himself up the stairs.

'I not slip up,' shouted Wazir, after Gestapo Ged, 'I honest man,' but Gerrard Fox was already on the top deck sitting on the back seat sucking hard on his pipe, and wondering how the hell the native was getting away with it.

Saturday, and Wazir was late home. Nadirah fretted. Wazir had jumped on the ferry across the Mersey, a pleasant enough ten minutes and the river was busy, but soon across, where he strode up the gangplank after everyone else. The tide was out and the climb substantial, and the air thick with the stench of oily mud and filthy seawater. At the top at the exit Wazir took in the view.

To the left was Birkenhead Woodside railway station. The London train was about to depart and was letting everyone know about it. Black loco and tender spitting smoke and steam, ten rapidly filling maroon carriages, as latecomers raced from taxis and buses to board. Ahead, and to the right, were a sprinkling of blue and cream Birkenhead Corporation buses, the same old work horses that Wazir crewed every day, as an old green Crosville single decker came bumping down the hill, its journey done, an F27 from Frankby, wherever that was.

Wazir hurried past the bus shelters, glancing at timetables and journeys, until he found one that went to Prenton, the number 77. He'd remember that, and he jumped aboard. He asked an old guy to tell him when they arrived and the old bloke dressed in filthy work clothes said, 'Sure, kiddo,' before taking a second glance at the dark stranger, and then back at his Liverpool Echo.

Prenton was pleasant. Three story Edwardian properties stretched along the main street, shops and banks and a post office on the ground floors, what looked liked spacious apartments above. Across the road were garages and petrol stations and smaller shops that sold wine and flowers and stationery, and all the things needed in suburbia.

Everywhere gaggles of sallow people gathered in groups, dressed in old and worn dark coats smelling of mothballs, brown and green and blue, though it wasn't cold, and Wazir should know about that, because England was bitter. Folks gossiping and sharing news, and they would stop talking and stare at Wazir as he approached, as if he was the first dark skinned man they had ever seen, which for many of them, he was.

He glanced in the window of an estate agent. Looked at the houses, and the prices, and beyond that to two bored looking staff, a man and a woman, the woman almost falling off her chair when she focussed on the dark and threatening looking stranger with the big bright eyes gawping through the glass, staring menacingly, she imagined, at her.

Wazir turned and set off down a side street. A long straight road crammed with almost identical semi-detached houses. Why did the English like to live attached to their neighbours so much? He wondered, and pondered on which of these houses could be Gerrard Fox's. In truth, it wasn't as Gerrard had portrayed his hometown.

It wasn't what he expected of Prenton either, on the much-praised Wirral peninsula. There must be better areas than this, he imagined. It was pleasant enough, but it sure as heck wasn't Beverly Hills, and Wazir Khan had set his sights higher.

He returned to the main street and jumped a bus back down toward the river. He wouldn't come that way again. In the future, he'd find somewhere else to live.

Somewhere nice.

Somewhere better.

Somewhere more exciting.

Somewhere with prospects.
Somewhere to build his empire.
Somewhere to spend the rest of his life.

Chapter Twenty-Eight

18 Moorcroft Road, Chester. Coming up teatime. The curtains were drawn, but that wasn't unusual on the estate. Some residents were mighty protective of their precious possessions, and the fewer people that knew they existed, or could see them from the street; the more chance they would remain unmolested. Some curtains were never opened, some lights were never switched off.

Karen pulled the nondescript Ford to a gentle standstill on the far side of the road and glanced at her boss. Gibbons and Hector Browne were in the back. Three toddlers were playing with a big yellow toy dumper truck on the grass verge outside the house.

The old fashioned radio crackled to life.

'In position, Guv.'

It was the back-up crew covering the road at the rear. Four men, all in civvies, another unmarked car; two of them unarmed, two of them armed, all with sweating palms. The local watchers had clocked both cars had long since, and phones were ringing all over the estate.

'Wait for orders,' purred Darriteau.

'Got you, Guv.'

'We are going in now, stay in the car, stay alert, keep the weapons out of sight.'

'Got you, Guv.'

'Come along, children,' said Darriteau, and he heaved himself out of the car. Karen, Gibbons and Browne jumped out and followed Walter across the road.

The toddlers glanced up from their play. Karen smiled at one boy and he smiled back. The little girl looked worried, been listening to mummy and didn't trust strangers. The third one, another boy, jumped up and down and ran down the road, an anguished look on his face, shouting nonsense.

Walter and his team were outside the front door. Exchanged a look. Walter's hand relaxed in his right trouser pocket, caressing the trusted Glock pistol. He prayed he wouldn't have to use it. Karen's left hand in her light blouson pocket, hot and sweaty, wrapped around the handle.

Walter nodded Gibbons to the door. He glanced at Browne, bobbed his head, and stepped forward and pressed the bell.

No sound, no big barking dog, always a relief, no man shouting, then the distinct sound of footsteps inside approaching the door, heavy feet on a wooden surface.

The door opened and a hefty middle-aged woman peered out, stared at the four of them, coppers, obvious as hell. She recognised the big black bastard. He had something of a reputation, been in the papers and on the TV, and you couldn't miss him.

Walter could see the guy's photofit picture written in her face, fatter and older, but distinctly Luke. It was all over her. This was the mother.

'Mrs Flowers, we have a warrant for the arrest of Luke Flowers,' said Walter, as Gibbons and Browne pushed past her and headed down the hall.

'What the hell! You can't go down there,' she screamed, and hurried after them. Walter followed too, saying, 'Is Luke in, Mrs Flowers? It would save an awful lot of time. It's for the best.'

She swivelled round and came back to him.

'No, he is not! Hasn't lived here for years! Now get these morons out of my house before I lose my temper!'

'Where is he, Mrs Flowers?'

'I have no idea!'

'He's wanted for a very serious offence, Mrs Flowers,' said Karen. 'Murder and attempted murder.'

The woman's mouth fell open. A brief silence and then she yelled, 'Don't be ridiculous!' and as if a tiny hint of recognition seeped into her brain, she added, 'Not my Luke! Surely not. He's a good boy!'

'Where is he?' asked Walter.

'I told you, I have no idea, and even if I had…'

The hall phone rang.

Mrs Flowers snatched it up. 'What!'

Then she calmed down and said, 'Yeah, they are here now, thanks for ringing, Ronnie, thanks for letting me know,' and she put the phone down.

'Upstairs clear!' yelled Gibbons.

'Kitchen clear!' shouted Hector.

'There is no sign of him here,' said Karen, coming back to the hall.

'Aiding a man wanted for murder carries severe penalties,' said Walter. 'Even if he is your own son.'

'Listen to yourselves! My son could no more kill next door's cat as murder a human being,' yet even as she spoke the words she recalled the regular thousand pounds that dumped into her bank account. Where had that come from? She had always known he was involved in something shady. But who wasn't? She assumed it was dodgy DVDs and CDs and knock off phones and computer software. He had always been a whiz at that stuff.

'Someone is going to get hurt, Mrs Flowers. You could help stop that,' said Walter.

'Tell that to the fairies, you're away with the mixer, man!'

'When did you last see him?' asked Karen.

'I'm telling you nottin'.'

'Fair enough,' said Walter. 'Your choice. Cuff her Gibbons and take her down the station, we've got all day.'

Gibbons produced a pair of steel cuffs, shiny, strong, new and cold.

'Oh eh, there's no need for that,' she protested.

'You can help us here, or you can help us there; it's up to you,' said Walter, attempting a smile.

'Why don't we go into the front room and sit down,' suggested Karen, beckoning them all into the Flowers' lounge as if she owned the place, and she took Mrs Flowers by the arm and led her inside and sat her on the sofa. Karen balanced on the arm, as Walter sat in the comfy armchair opposite.

'When did you last see him?' asked Walter.

174

Mrs Flowers sighed and glanced round the room, at her own house filled with coppers, the two young blokes were in the hall, leaning on the lounge doorframe, looking in. She'd brain Luke for bringing trouble to her door the next time she saw him.

'Before he went to Venice.'

'When was that?' asked Karen.

'Three, maybe four weeks ago.'

'Why did he go to Venice?' asked Walter.

'Holiday. Took his girlfriend. Posh bit of stuff. Far too good to be introduced to me.'

'Do you know who she is, and where she lives?' asked Karen.

Mrs Flowers shook her head. Sighed hard. 'Think he's ashamed of me, doesn't like me meeting his girls. Father's a dentist, think that's what he said.'

'Where does Luke live now?' asked Walter.

Mrs Flowers knew that question was coming, and she didn't want to answer it. She didn't want desperate coppers on her son's tail. Said the first thing that came into her head.

'He's got a caravan or summat, no, maybe it's a chalet, on the coast up near Rhyl.'

'Come on, Mrs Flowers, you can do better than that, you must know where your son lives.'

'I don't!' she snapped. 'He's at that stage when he likes his independence, doesn't want me dropping in on him every five minutes. Cramps his style, he says. Rings me now and again, and that's about it.'

The look in her eyes told Walter that was at least partly true. The woman had been abandoned by her husband, and by her children. She'd been left alone to grow old by herself; to face old age alone, sitting on that comfy sofa, with nothing more for company than a 65" television. The kid had probably bought that as some kind of compensation, as if he were fulfilling his family duties, or maybe salving his conscience. Walter had seen it a thousand times before. People grow slow, fat and old, and sometimes the relatives don't want to know.

Then she said, 'You won't hurt him, will you? He's all I've got.'

175

'We don't want to hurt him, please believe me on that,' said Walter. 'But we need to speak to him; and he needs to come forward. He will be safe with us; you have my word on that.'

She stared across the room at the black man and into his still and determined eyes, and she believed the policeman, and that was a first.

'I'll see what I can do,' she said, and out of nowhere a tear formed in the corner of her eye and stuttered over her ample cheek.

Karen spotted it and put her hand on Mrs Flowers' shoulder, gave her a squeeze and said, 'Can we make you a cup of tea?'

'No!' she snapped regaining her composure. 'The only thing I want is for you to get out of my house.'

'Have you got an up-to-date photo?' asked Walter.

'No!' she said again, only school ones, 'he was most particular about that, never wanted his photo taken, hated it, said it would bring him terrible bad luck.'

'I wonder why,' said Karen under her breath.

Walter bobbed his head and took a card from his wallet and set it on the tile-topped coffee table.

'That's my number, call me any time.'

Mrs Flowers said nothing.

The officers let themselves out. They hadn't expected to make an arrest, but it would have been nice.

Chapter Twenty-Nine

The first time Wazir Khan visited Chester he knew it was the place for him. He couldn't explain it, but he felt at home there. He had been scouting out various towns with a view to relocating his family, Southport, Frodsham, Prestatyn, Formby, he had visited them all, considered them all, but it was the city of Chester that captured his heart.

Jimmy Mac gave Wazzie a glowing reference, and the Chester City Bus Company could hardly refuse him a position, and because their accounting and reporting of cash taken was more stringent, Wazir could no longer supplement his income, though he didn't mind. It didn't worry him for he was happy to be away from the deceit and shame of stealing money from the public purse.

He found a small first-floor flat in Brook Street just around the corner from Chester General Railway Station. The flat was damp and cold, partly because the shop downstairs had been abandoned and was semi derelict. It wasn't unusual to wake in the morning to find a drunk there, sleeping off a heavy night, curled up in the muck and rubbish that gathered in the empty shop.

In his spare time Wazir set about painting and decorating the flat until it was the best home the Khan family had ever enjoyed. It was 1964; the height of Beatlemania, and their son Ahmed had just turned twenty. Ahmed boasted the haircut, the clothes, all the records, and the girls too, one in particular, a local kid by the name of Gloria Barnes who worshipped the ground that Ahmed trod. George Harrison with a tan, she called him, my gorgeous Georgie, with a tan.

Despite that, Ahmed was a conscientious boy. He continued to work hard; studied mechanical engineering at Chester Technical College, and was working on innovatory lock designs, an interest that impressed his father. He worked hard in the expanding local mosque too, and was well thought of in the community, even if he was consorting with a Christian girl.

Wazir had confided in Nadirah that perhaps they could take over the shop downstairs and open a new locksmith business, and all the family were in favour of that.

They were to be surprised and disappointed.

Wazir took a lease on the shop, and came home beaming, to announce his latest bright idea.

'We will open a restaurant, an Indian restaurant,' he said. 'We will serve curries and make our fortune.'

'But you know nothing about cooking!' protested Nadirah.

'No, but you do,' countered Wazir, and your Aunty Husna in Calicut does. Write to her. Get her to send her best fifty recipes. Ask her to send us a new recipe every month. Send her a two-pound postal order. She'll help the family, of course she will! For two pounds she will.'

'Do you want to know a secret? I ain't being no waiter,' chipped in Ahmed.

'And everyone knows the English don't like curry! You're wasting your time,' protested Nadirah.

'They do, they will! You'll see! Once they get the taste, they'll love it,' insisted Wazir.

'Slow down!' shouted Ahmed, glancing at his excited parents. 'I feel fine about it; but don't expect me to wait on table.'

'Shut up, boy,' said his mother, 'and stop talking gibberish.'

'Oh, please me!' said Wazir, joining in the fun, as Ahmed and Nadirah shared another smile.

'Just don't expect me to hold your hand,' said Ahmed, grinning.

'I am not cooking curries all hours of the day and night. It'll be a total disaster!' said Nadirah, and she stormed out, leaving Ahmed to share a knowing masculine look with his father.

The State of Kerala Restaurant opened for business on the fifth of October 1964. It was the first authentic Indian Restaurant in the city. Wazir took a small display advertisement in the Chester Observer; even invited the newspaper's food writer to attend the big opening night.

The writer arrived with his wife, as did fourteen other curious souls. The writer cleared his plates, the wife barely touched a thing; and her constant grimacing worried Wazir, for he imagined a crucifying review would follow, a report that could kill the new enterprise stone dead.

The subsequent write up was substantial. It even carried a picture of the Khan family outside the front door, pointing up at the sign, Ahmed smirking, wearing his pressed high collared Beatles' jacket and well groomed Harrison-esque hair.

The newspaper text included the phrase: While this will not be to everyone's cup of tea, the State of Kerala is a welcome addition to the city's eateries. Whether it will catch on, only time will tell, but in the meantime, make sure you pay a visit, in case you miss it.

The Khan family portrayed it as being a great success, which it was not. But they were open for business, and taking money, and backed up by Aunty Husna's unique recipes that flowed in once a month, as reliable as one of Ahmed's lock designs, the menu grew, as did the clientele, and in time, the reputation of Wazir's weird culinary establishment.

'If you want something different for your tea, or your dinner, get down to the State of Kerala,' was a comment that began to be uttered in hushed tones in the city's bars and clubs, and slowly, very slowly, people did just that. 'It's hot!'

And it was, in more ways than one.

The years rolled by and the State of Kerala prospered. Wazir hated paying tax and reinvested as much of the profit in improving the business as he could. He bought the freehold of the building they rented; and the one next door too; and expanded the restaurant into there.

179

He was forever improving the fixtures and fittings in the parts of the restaurant you could see, and the parts you could not, the kitchen, and the living quarters, and the one thing that remained the same, untouched and unrivalled, was the prized menu, for it was the foundation stone of the business.

No one else possessed a menu like it, and no one knew the recipes either, and they were jealously guarded. Cheapskate copycats came and went leaving the State to prosper. The Khans began importing ingredients, rare and exotic spices that could not be obtained in Britain.

Lying in his bath one evening, Wazir imagined the bare main wall behind the bar needed a focal point. He thought a picture of rural India would do the trick, but the three pictures he commissioned were disappointing, and to put it bluntly, were not up to the job. Not substantial enough or eye catching.

It was Ahmed who suggested the answer.

'Use the sword,' he said. 'Use the sword! It was what it was meant for!'

Despite his initial misgivings Wazir warmed to the idea, and the following Saturday the cricket bat was retrieved and opened. It was a defining moment in the history of the Khan family. Everyone was there. Wazir, who had glued that bat together all those years before, Nadirah, who had helped to bury it in Calicut in the yard at the back of their house to save it from Hindu looting, Ahmed, his hair now lank and thinning, and his fattening English wife Gloria, with their fast growing son, Mohammed. They stared in wonder as the bat was split, and the magical sword revealed.

It looked as if it had been made yesterday, as if it had been cleaned that morning, as if it had been sharpened an hour before. It was hundreds of years old, yet a thing of unique beauty, as those gathered there staring down at the flashing jewels set within the ancient ivory handle would forever testify.

What warrior had first held it?

What tales could it tell?

How many people had fallen under its spell?
How many foes had perished to its blade?
It was high time the sword saw the light of day again.
Time indeed for the precious artefact to regain its glory.

The Khan family commissioned a special display case that would house the family weapon that had taken on mythical status. The box resembled the cases English fishermen used to display prize catches. But this box was different. The glass was toughened, unbreakable, bullet proof, cost a fortune, but the taxman was paying, anything to reduce the tax liability on the business. It would go through the books as essential fittings for the restaurant.

The wood was solid mahogany, hundreds of years in the growing, nurtured in the tropics, like the sword itself, tough as nails, virtually unbreakable, while the case was fastened shut utilising a special heavy duty lock that Ahmed had designed and built himself.

There were only two keys.

One for Wazir, and one for Ahmed.

It was fitted to the wall behind the bar, and floodlit, enabling the jewels to shimmer and sparkle, mesmerising passers-by. The case was draped in best Calico cloth, made in, and imported from, Calicut in the State of Kerala, especially for the occasion.

The sword would be unveiled on the Sunday evening, where Wazir, always with an eye for free publicity, invited the same aging food writer from the Chester Observer to attend the ceremony, and the special dinner that followed. In the next edition the writer wrote a fabulous review, and afterwards the crowds flocked to the ever-expanding State of Kerala like never before.

Next, Wazir set his eyes on another adjacent empty unit that had come available. Many people wanted food in a hurry, they didn't always want to come in and sit down and be waited on. A take-away was the answer, and like everything else he touched, it became a great success. Wazir Khan and his family were on a roll.

Wazir woke up. He had been dozing and was alone, sitting in the luxurious lounge above the main restaurant. He'd been thinking about the old days, about how he first thought of opening a restaurant, and all the things that had happened since. He thought about the old days a great deal, though he strived hard to think of the future too. The doctor said he should retire, take it easy, he deserved it, but he won't. He's in his late eighties. Frail but sharp, and as full of plans as ever. Nadirah potters around, oversees the menus and cooking, and worries that quality standards might slip, though they never do. She's eighty-four.

Ahmed is in charge, or at least he thinks he is, though Wazir might disagree. Gloria has long gone. Christian, and flighty. Only to be expected. Ahmed doesn't miss her. None of the Khans do.

It took him a long time to fall in love with catering and the restaurant business, but he did. He was proud of the perfect State, as he called it, and proud of his parents for all they had achieved; through the hardships they had endured.

He's sixty-seven, that cute boy the two policemen stared at on that drizzly day on the Liverpool dock road, as one officer wafted the cricket bat high in the air.

Mohammed, Ahmed's son, was forty-four, and in his prime. He boasted a pretty wife in Akleema, and two fine children who both work in the business. Sahira, his beautiful daughter, and Maaz, the son and heir, who one day would carry the flag for the Khan dynasty.

Recipes and ingredients still arrive from India once a month, though not from Aunty Husna, she has long gone. But from her niece, and payments still flow to the subcontinent in exchange. They are not as good as they once were, but that is to be expected. The late Aunty Husna was something special.

The State of Kerala prospered like it never had before, and Wazir was a contented man. He'd enjoyed a good life, aside from the terrible demise of his parents. God had been kind to him, and to the family.

The phone in the private quarters rang.

Ahmed answered.

182

It is the local Imam.

He wants to speak with Ahmed and Mohammed and Wazir too, if the old man is up to it.

He wants to see them in the morning, first thing. Can they come before eight o'clock? It's a delicate matter that cannot be discussed over the telephone.

Ahmed agreed and goes off to find his father. He is watching cricket, the ubiquitous Indian Premier League.

'It'll be something and nothing, the summons,' mutters Wazir. 'They probably need more funds for some project in Pakistan. Take your chequebook.'

That was the usual cause of excitement at the mosque.

'Watch the cricket,' implored his father. 'Watch the Indian batsmen; they know how to play the game.'

Ahmed's cricket watching days were long behind him.

He was a worried man.

He saw black clouds everywhere.

Chapter Thirty

The Incident Room was packed. Still before 8am, and the aroma of bacon butties filled the air. Jenny Thompson rushed round with cups of coffee. She didn't need to do that, but Walter was happy she had. Karen declined. Gibbo happily seizing the unwanted cup.

'Listen up,' said Walter, getting to his feet, the polystyrene cup steaming in his hand. 'Thanks to all who came in early; and thanks for those who came in on their day off, and so to business. Luke Flowers,' and everyone glanced at the photofit on the wall they believed accurate. 'He is not living with his mother. She says he's got a caravan or chalet on the North Wales' coast. Rhyl, somewhere like that. I think Mrs Flowers is being protective. We know he likes travelling, just come back from Venice, according to his mother. He doesn't sound like a caravan type of guy to me. I think he has a flat in the city. He's not on the electoral roll, but it shouldn't be difficult to trace his address. Gibbons and Jenny, I want you round the local travel agents. He must have booked that holiday somewhere, and they will have his address. If he does have a flat, he should be paying council tax. Hector, that's your job. Find him on the council tax roll, and we are in business.'

Hector nodded and appreciated being given a job to himself. Said, 'Sure, Guv, that makes sense.'

'You two,' Walter continued, pointing to two junior officers he was ashamed to say he couldn't name. 'Get on to the local health centres and libraries. You might have some joy there. Don't take any flannel from the health centres. They can be an awkward bunch of lilies on those helpdesks. We don't want to know about medical records, we just want an address. Tell them it's a matter of life and death, and maybe they'll understand, and check out the dentists too,'

184

he shouted to no one in particular. 'Find one with a pretty daughter with a boyfriend called Luke, and you could find his address that way.'

'Sure, Guv,' they said in unison.

'And remember this, this guy has killed one person, and thinks he's killed another. He's armed and dangerous and not to be messed with. He won't hesitate to shoot again. I don't want any dead heroes. I don't want to tell someone's mother their faultless offspring has stopped a slug. As soon as you find an address, you tell me, got that?'

Walter scanned the room and everyone nodded and muttered, 'Sure thing, boss,' and even his boss, Mrs West, who was standing observing proceedings, propped up in her office doorway, nodded her assent.

She did a lot of that, nodding and staff observation. It was as if the bi-annual officer appraisal reports were never far from her mind, as she took five minutes to watch each officer in turn. They all knew she was doing it because she always did. They felt her steely eyes settling on them; usually when they had something to say. They'd answer Walter, and glance nervously at John, as she was known, to gauge how they were doing.

It unnerved them. It sure as hell unnerved Walter.

'Questions?' asked Walter.

'Where did he get the gun?' asked Hector, unable to pass up an opportunity to speak.

'God knows,' said Walter. 'There are suppliers of such things. Hopefully when we find Luke it will lead us to the gunsmith. Anything else?'

No one had.

'Right, get on with it! I want to make an arrest before teatime; drinks on me if we do.'

'That's more like it!' said Gibbons. 'Mine's a double vodka.'

'Come along, children! Be on your way,' yelled Walter, beckoning those that were going out through the door.

The Khans pulled their black BMW 5 Series into the mosque car park. Ahmed was driving, he often did. His son Mohammed sat beside him, and the old man, Wazir, was in the back, his eyes closed, his breathing heavy.

'Just before we go in,' said Ahmed, 'does anyone have any late thoughts on why we are here?'

Wazir opened his eyes and said, 'Pound to a penny they want money. Famine and flood. The same old stories.'

'Famine and flood are not to be ridiculed,' said Mohammed, from the front seat, turning round and fixing his eyes on the grandfather Mohammed thought was getting more out of touch with each passing week.

'I know that!' snapped Wazir, fighting to keep the irritation from his voice. 'I was only saying…'

'For what it's worth,' said Ahmed, 'I think it's something more serious.'

'Like what?' asked Mohammed.

'I wish I knew.'

'There's only one way to find out,' said Wazir. 'Let's go in and see,' and he opened the car door and dragged himself out onto the tarmac.

Mohammed and his father shared a look and joined him and headed for the front entrance of the refurbished mosque.

Luke Flowers enjoyed an early breakfast. He had a busy day because the next day he would leave for Mexico. He had a lot to do. Melanie was arriving in an hour and that would enable him to say his goodbyes properly. He intended giving her something to remember him by. She'd be surprised he was going to Australia at short notice, but absence makes the heart grow fonder. He was a great believer in the maxim, so long as it wasn't out of sight, out of mind.

After he'd seen her off, he'd still have time for Sahira. There would always be time for that, and though he wouldn't have time to see anyone else, there were several others that kept infiltrating into his busy brain.

186

The Imam Sabir was waiting in his office for the Khan family. He was wearing his best robes; made from the cloth his proud grandfather had bought for Sabir's birthday, robes he would only wear on solemn occasions.

The Imam had adopted the name Sabir, for it meant patience, for he was astute enough to realise it was one attribute he did not possess. He hoped that through taking the name it might seep into his consciousness. So far, it hadn't worked.

The Khan men were shown to his room. The Imam sat behind his polished mahogany desk. He would not get up. It wasn't for him to stand. Three generations of Khans entered the room and glanced nervously down. It had never happened before, being summoned at an early hour. Something important was happening, and none of them could guess what.

The assistant Imam, an older man named Hujjat, was standing to one side of Imam Sabir. Hujjat was also fully robed, but unlike Sabir, he was happy to take a backseat, less ambitious, content to defer to Sabir. He didn't make eye contact with his superior, nor with the summoned ones. Hujjat hailed from the Punjab; was pious, gentle and even-tempered, a man Wazir liked and respected.

Wazir said, 'Hello Hujjat,' barely breaking the silence.

Hujjat didn't reply, didn't smile, just pursed his lips and nodded slightly.

There were three plain chairs set out before the desk.

The Khans were not invited to sit.

Wazir was becoming irritable.

Imam Sabir glanced up from his laptop computer, as if surprised. Saw three men standing there, as if they had come into his domain uninvited, as if he, Sabir, had been impolite to them.

'Oh, gentleman, please sit,' beckoning toward the seats.

Ahmed said, 'Thank you, Imam Sabir,' and sat in the centre chair, Wazir to the left, Mohammed to his right.

The Imam looked upwards, as if to heaven, as if seeking inspiration, as if calling on all the patience God might grant him. He closed the laptop with a click, and began.

'Thank you for coming at short notice, and thank you for coming at such an early hour.'

'It matters not what time you call, Imam,' said Ahmed. 'We would come at any time for you. You know that.'

'For sure!' said Mohammed, not wishing to be left out of any burgeoning conversation.

Wazir glanced across the room through his tired eyes. He had been wrong. Whatever the Imams wanted, it wasn't funds for food and famine, and he felt ashamed he thought such a thing. Something important was about to be revealed.

The bell to the door at Luke's flat rang. One long ring. Luke finished his coffee and jumped to his feet. Ran to the door, a spring in his step. Opened up.

She looked fabulous.

Two items of clothing only.

Short-sleeved white blouse, tight fitting stone-washed jeans.

First thing Saturday morning or not, she'd spent a great deal of time on her makeup, and had washed her blonde hair, and that was as Luke would have expected.

He reached out onto the landing, grasped her left wrist and dragged her inside, cooing: 'How's my darling Melanie?'

A big smile cracked across her face.

He'd shaved and applied best aftershave, over applied, but over application was always better than under, gelled his perfect hair too, and he looked cute in a red jockey shirt and black trousers. What was it about him that excited her so, that brought butterflies to her entire being? That was something that mystified her, but it always had.

They kissed hungrily and when they came apart she said, 'What's all this about, Lukee, baby?'

'I've got something to tell you.'

188

'Like what, Lukee?' whispering her reply into his ear, and dreaming that maybe, just maybe, he might propose. It was about time he did. Most of her lovers managed that after a few weeks. It sure wasn't as she imagined he might do it, but so long as he did, that was all that mattered.

'I've got something to show you.'

Melanie smirked. 'Like what, Lukee?'

'Get in that bedroom and get your kit off!'

'But Luke, it's not yet nine o'clock.'

'Don't care. Do as you are told!'

Chapter Thirty-One

The Imam Sabir sniffed and rubbed his nose before beginning. 'This is a matter of great delicacy.'

'So we understand,' said Ahmed.

The Imam held up his hand, as if to tell the middle Khan not to interrupt. Ahmed sat back in his chair. He could recognise a reprimand when he saw it.

'This matter concerns a member of your family.'

'It's bound to be Maaz again,' muttered Wazir. 'What's the crazy boy done this time?'

Imam Hujjat fixed Wazir with his eyes and growled: 'It has nothing to do with Maaz! He is a decent, God fearing boy, and a man we have high hopes for.'

Wazir looked duly rebuked, shifted in his seat, and glanced at the others, but no one looked back.

Ahmed and Mohammed were one step ahead.

It only left the women. It had to be Sahira.

The Imam fixed Mohammed with his gaze and spoke the words, 'Your daughter, our sister, has shamed us all. She is fornicating with a kaffir.'

Stunned silence.

Mohammed broke the spell.

'But... but, that cannot be right, Imam. She is never left unattended in the house, she is not permitted to have boys, men, to the house unless we are present, and she has never brought a kaffir to our property, never, not once.'

The Imam brought his hand to his mouth and scratched his scrawny grey whiskers. Glanced up at Hujjat, and back at the stunned Khan clan. The Khans had been negotiating a good marriage for Sahira, and filthy rumours could scupper everything.

190

'She is fornicating with a kaffir!' repeated the Imam, 'letting herself be abused by a Christian youth, the scummiest Christian yob you could ever meet. A man of terrible repute, a lecher, sinner, criminal, and fornicator!'

Mohammed clasped his hands together and squirmed in his seat. Beads of sweat popped from his forehead like mini-sprouting cabbages.

His father Ahmed glanced as his anguished son.

Mohammed went to speak but Ahmed interrupted, 'Let us hear what the good Imam has to say, Mohammed. We need to know more about these dreadful accusations.'

Sabir glanced to his left and looked up at Hujjat, and bobbed his head once in as pious a manner he could muster.

Hujjat was on the move, making for the side wall where dark drawn curtains obscured part of the wall as if there was a window there. He drew back the curtains, but there was no window, just a large flat screen television fixed flush to the wall. Giant size, top ticket price, donation no doubt from Javed Grewal's electrical shop. Hujjat glanced back at Sabir, as if for instruction. Sabir nodded, and Hujjat slipped the DVD into the player.

DC Hector Browne had been brought back to earth. He had no idea how hard it was to trace someone through the local council tax records. He could not find a Luke Flowers, nor a Luke Edward Flowers, nor an L Flowers, or L E Flowers, or a Luca Flowers, or Lucan Flowers, or Look Flowers, or any similar name.

If this guy Luke Flowers had a flat in the city of Chester, he wasn't registered to pay council tax. So either he had registered in another name, possible, though Hector thought unlikely, or he hadn't registered at all, in the hope of avoiding paying. The council would catch up with that. They always did. Browne pondered on it and wondered where he should go next.

DC Darren Gibbons had visited five travel agents with his oppo, Jenny Thompson, with no luck. There were still another five to do, including the one on the high street, where the pretty girl always smiled at fit young men like Darren Gibbons.

The other teams were finding out how difficult and busy receptionists could be on health centre counters. It wasn't that they didn't want to help, but essential health matters took priority, and some of the officers had some sympathy with that.

Libraries had proved equally useless. Luke Flowers was not a library kind of guy, or if he was, he was into the book reader devices that were revolutionising the whole publishing and reading business.

Karen owned one, adored the thing, given to her by an ardent admirer who had long since been binned, though she kept the electronic reader after he'd gone. She had to have some decent memories of David Gardner, for there weren't many others, and she would squint at that grey slab at every opportunity.

Walter sat back in his chair, his hands behind his head, and gazed unblinking at the ceiling. He often did when he was reviewing a case in his mind. Karen had seen that semi-trancelike state many times, and when he visited planet Darriteau, she knew better than to interrupt.

Mrs West had been to the Ladies to freshen up and was coming back when she spotted him, sitting there, unmoving and silent.

She didn't accept the deep thinking scenario that Walter portrayed. In fact, she often wondered if he had perfected the art of falling asleep with his eyes open. She wouldn't put it past the strange man under her command.

Joan West was concerned.

She had a violent unsolved murder on her desk, and the buck would stop with her. She was thinking Walter Darriteau's best days might be behind him. She'd give him another forty-eight hours. If there were no developments by then, she would consider calling in outside help. She had to be seen to be proactive. No one liked a leader who sat alone in their office and did nothing. Leaders had to lead, and had to be seen to lead, even if she led everyone up the garden path. Being seen to be doing something was important in the service, and far more important than staring into space. Walter's sloth-like manoeuvres irritated some, and had sometimes resulted in a lack of promotion.

Walter was still thinking. Didn't care less what other people thought. Why had Luke Flowers tried to kill Neil Swaythling?

He was no nearer a satisfactory answer. Indeed, the question seemed to be getting lost in the headlong pursuit to arrest the cretin.

Imam Hujjat drew the curtains across the actual window on the other side of the room. The glass was frosted to keep out prying eyes, but the summer morning light was excluded too.

A colour picture filled the big screen.

Shivering images, a humming sound, nothing spoken. Then a clear image.

There was a long corridor, bland cream walls, bland beige carpet, bright blue doors, as if to point out to worse-for-wear travellers where the doors actually were.

A figure came down the corridor and opened one of the doors and went inside. It was a maid, white skin; some might consider quite pretty, early twenties, tied back dark hair, going about her duties.

Everyone stared at the screen.

No one spoke.

Another minute passed.

The time and date appeared at the bottom left corner of the screen, flickering unobtrusive transparent letters and numbers. The tape was made ten days before.

Wazir tried to remember what he was doing ten days ago. Trouble was, he could barely remember yesterday. Mohammed and Ahmed were pondering on the same thing. What and where and who?

Another person came down the corridor. A young woman, a pretty young woman, long dark hair, brushed western style, black suit, the skirt a little shorter than usual, as if it had been taken up, or folded up, pretty legs, as if to attract the eye, flaunting red lipstick.

The woman was Mohammed's daughter, Sahira.

She had no luggage, other than her handbag, a present from her mother. All the Khans recognised it. She produced a key, glanced around, opened up and disappeared into the room, the next room to where the maid had gone in.

193

The Khan men shared an anxious look.

Still, no one spoke.

The film rolled on.

Nothing happened.

The door next to Sahira's room opened, and the maid came out. She was carrying a large red plastic box of cleaning materials and bustled into another opposite room.

Another break, a period of nothingness, just shaking film of a bland, empty, and still corridor.

The Khans shared another look as if to say, 'Is that it?'

In their hearts, they hoped it would be.

In their heads, they knew it would not.

A man came down the corridor, short, young, slight, boy band good looking, a spring in his step, a clear smirk on his face. He was swinging the key around in his hand as if he didn't have a care in the world, as if it was his birthday, and he was about to receive the best possible present.

He stopped and opened a door and went inside.

He had gone into Sahira's room.

Back in the present, in another part of town, Luke patted Melanie's backside and pushed her out through the door of his flat. He hadn't been altogether honest with her. He had told her he was going to Australia for three weeks to attend a computer software conference. He had attended similar things before, but only in the UK.

It wouldn't be three weeks at all, more like three months, more likely still, six months; in fact the real truth was he didn't know when he'd be back.

It depended on how exciting Mexico was, and how alluring the senoritas, who he knew would adore him, and his newfound wealth.

He took a shower, and a soak in the bath for a short while, and then arrange another going away meeting while he still had time.

The pretty girl in the travel agent was real helpful.

Of course she knew Luke Flowers.

He was one of their best customers.

194

Always going away somewhere or other, a real jetsetter, though she did not know he was leaving for Mexico. No one did, because that jaunt had been arranged by Jimmy Mitchell under a false name.

She spoke of Luke in glowing terms, and it was obvious to Darren and Jenny she had a crush on the guy. Probably hoped he would take her with him next time. She didn't know how lucky she was.

'And you have an address?' asked an excited Jenny.

'Course we do. Here it is. 28 Glanford House. It's a new building, only ten minutes from here, on the way to the station, just beyond the city walls.'

Darren rang base and spoke to Walter.

'Guv? Got an address! 28 Glanford House, new build flats, near the railway station.'

'Good boy! Well done! I know the place. Make your way there. Meet you there in ten. Don't go in till we arrive. Don't do anything stupid. Be careful!'

'Got you, Guv, see you soon.'

Imam Hujjat fast-forwarded the DVD. Explained that nothing much else happened, then stopped and started it again.

The door to the room opened, and the man came out. His short hair dishevelled, as he walked jauntily away down the corridor and disappeared.

Two more minutes and the door opened again.

Sahira came out. She paused and touched her hair.

Her father, Mohammed, thought she looked guilty.

He stared at his feet.

Ahmed frowned and glanced at his father as if for support.

Wazir stared straight ahead as if he couldn't see a thing.

They all watched her hurry down the corridor and disappear.

They were all thinking the same thing.

How could she betray them in such a way?

Ahmed asked: 'How long was she in there?'

'Two hours and twelve minutes,' said Imam Hujjat without a moment's hesitation.

'There must be an innocent explanation,' said Wazir.

195

'There is no innocent explanation!' said Imam Sabir, his patience deserting him. 'She has been regularly fornicating with this kaffir!'

'You don't know what she has been doing,' suggested Ahmed.

'What do you think she was doing in there, playing marbles? Take the scales from your eyes, Mr Khan,' said an exasperated Sabir.

'What do you mean... a regular basis?' asked Ahmed.

'This is the fifth time, same man, same place!' said Hujjat. 'We do not know how many other times there have been, in other places, with other men.'

'Oh, no,' said Mohammed, his hand going to his forehead. 'You mean?'

'We don't know for sure,' said Sabir. 'It is up to you to find out. She is your daughter, and she is disgracing herself, she is disgracing the Khan family, and she is disgracing this mosque. You must do something about it... and you must do it soon.'

'You can rest assured we will act today,' said Ahmed, keen to bring the disgusting business to an end.

'How did you get this video?' asked Wazir.

'That is none of your business!' said Sabir, patience finally exhausted.

Hujjat said, 'We have a spy in the hotel, Wazir. It was only by God's good fortune we discovered the matter. If it had been anywhere else, then...' and he wafted his hand through the air, and let that thought die on his lips.

'You should leave us now,' said Sabir. 'Come again on Tuesday morning and explain what actions have been taken. Ring me if there is any news.'

The Khans stood as one. They did not need telling twice, Wazir taking longer to get to his feet. They bowed to the Imam and left the room.

In the car going home Wazir said, 'Times are changing, things are changing, try not to be too hard on her.'

Mohammed almost choked.

'Wazir, you are becoming senile in your old age! I cannot be too hard on her for the sins she has committed!'

Ahmed didn't think his father senile, but he didn't agree with him either. The girl had behaved abominably, beyond abominably, and he wondered how he could show his face at the mosque again. He would be a laughing-stock. The entire family would be a laughing-stock; people would stop and stare at them in the street, raise their hands to their mouths and gossip behind their backs about the dreadful Khans whose womenfolk had gone astray, shaming the community.

Chapter Thirty-Two

Luke dressed in a hurry. He fancied a farewell drink. He left the flat and hurried to the Laughing Cavalier that was set overlooking green lawns by the river. He often went to the LC, as it was known.

It was a trendy place, one of those new pubs that opened at 7am and filled the void, before alcohol could be dispensed, by serving coffees and breakfasts. He might jump on a poached egg on toast. Saying girly goodbyes was a hungry business.

Janice was there, the boss's wife, getting on a wee bit, but still attracting the eye, her of the tight blouse and amazing chest. None of the young men missed that, nor the old ones either.

'How are you, Luke?'

'I'm great, going to Australia tomorrow. Can't wait.'

'Lucky you. What can I get you?'

'Just a coffee, ta, maybe have some eggs later,' and he took a seat on a corner pew and found his mobile and pondered who to call next.

Walter and Karen arrived at the flat by car. Glanford House, three stories high, red brick, white windows, gabled roof, like a million other blocks that had shot up across the kingdom in the past ten years.

On seeing their car, Darren and Jenny came out from behind some camellia bushes. Hector Browne arrived panting, saying, 'Thought you might need some extra help.'

Walter nodded at them in turn and slipped his hand in his jacket pocket to where the Glock was sleeping.

'Come on, team,' he said, 'time to earn your corn,' and they strode up the path.

The outside door was security locked. Inside, they could see a tall guy in full multi coloured cycling gear. He had brought his racing cycle out from the storeroom and was busy fitting his helmet. He was taller than Luke and older than he looked. He came to the door; saw the five strangers hanging about outside, thought they were perhaps Jehovah's Witnesses, or some other weird bunch. He pushed the bike to the door and opened up. Walter held the door open for him and the guy said: 'Can I help you?'

Walter flashed ID. 'What's your name?'

'Colin Cresswell.'

'And you live here?'

'Yes.'

'Which flat?' asked Karen.

'24. Look, what's this all about?'

'Do you know Luke Flowers?' asked Walter.

'Lukee, yeah course, he's a neighbour of mine.'

'Is he in the flat now?' asked Karen, her hand caressing the weapon in her pocket.

'No, you've just missed him, went out about fifteen minutes ago.'

'Do you know where he went?' asked Walter.

'No idea, but he was all dressed up. Hot date, I'd say. He's got a fancy girlfriend; father's a dentist, so he says.'

Walter bobbed his head. Thanked the neighbour. Told him to have a good ride, and Walter said, 'If you see him, tell him his mother's looking for him.'

'What about?' asked Cresswell, straddling the bike.

'Tell him his dog's died.'

'Didn't know he had a dog.'

Walter grinned, and the guy shook his head; a puzzled expression on his face, and rode away.

Gibbons had set his boot in the outside door to stop it closing. It had a strong spring. It would have snapped shut in seconds. They went inside and sprinted up the stairs, Walter puffing behind, knowing he should have used the vacant and standing lift.

Gathered outside the flat, Walter, breathing hard, said, 'I'm getting fed up with this. Just missing things. Either we are getting slow, or criminals are getting cuter.'

No one said a word. Just glanced at the dark brown door, and the brass figure 28.

'Kick it down!' said Walter.

Hector and Gibbons approached the door, drew back their right foot in unison, and kicked hard in perfect symmetry, like a pair of marching fascist soldiers on parade. Straight legged, thrusting, decisive, and forward.

The door crumbled under the impact and surrendered, shaking and collapsing in a noisy and showy heap into the tiled hallway beyond. Walter stepped into the void and his troops followed him in.

The admonished Khan men arrived back at the State of Kerala. Hurried up the stairs, even Wazir, for ancient adrenalin had woken up his old body. They found Nadirah and Akleema in the private kitchen, baking cakes.

'Where is Sahira?' demanded Mohammed.

The women turned and saw the blazing looks on the men's faces.

'She's taking a bath. What is the matter?'

'Get her out of the bath and get her in the sitting room!' said Mohammed.

'Why? What's going on, Mohammed? Tell me what is happening.'

'Do as your husband says!' snapped Ahmed. 'And do it now!'

Maaz came running, alerted by the raised voices.

'What's up, peeps?' he grinned, as he unplugged his iPod from his ear.

'I'll tell you later,' said Mohammed. 'Turn that bloody thing off and put it away!'

'Of course, father,' said Maaz, eager to know what was going down.

Wazir was sitting in his favourite armchair in the sitting room. Ahmed came in and stood in front of the window. Mohammed arrived and stood beside him. Maaz ran in and sat beside Wazir, and said from the side of his mouth, 'What's happening here, old man?'

Wazir scowled and said, 'You'll know soon enough.'

Nadirah and Akleema came to the door, and Akleema said, 'Here she is, the naughty girl, whatever she has been up to.'

Sahira breezed in, still not understanding the seriousness of the situation. She had finished bathing, and had dressed in grey slacks and a Hamas Tee shirt. The Khan men were all there, one in his twenties, one in his forties, one in his sixties, one in his eighties, four generations of misery, judging by the look on their sour faces.

'What's the matter, folks?' she said, but by the time she had finished her question, those same looks told her everything she needed to know. She was in big trouble, and she could guess why.

Mohammed, her father, stepped forward three paces and slapped her hard across the left cheek.

Sahira yelped and held her face, tried hard not to cry. Her cheek was on fire. Stinging hot. She flicked her tongue over the teeth on that side. Felt blood, and tasted it, and thought a tooth had come loose.

'What is happening?' screeched Akleema.

'Get the women out of here!' yelled Mohammed, and Maaz leapt to his feet and ushered Nadirah, who was staring at Wazir; and Akleema out of the room. Maaz closed the door in their faces and retreated to the sofa.

'Do you dare deny it?' yelled Mohammed.

'Deny what?' said Sahira, regaining a little composure as a trickle of blood spilt from her lips.

'That you have become a common prostitute! That you are sleeping with kaffirs, and God alone knows what else you have been up to.'

Maaz's mouth fell open.

He grinned and glanced at Wazir, as if for confirmation.

Wazir stared at the door as if he could see through the timber, to his wife and Akleema, waiting and listening on the far side.

201

'I am not a prostitute!' insisted Sahira. 'I love Luke, if that's who you mean. We hope to get married.'

Mohammed had heard enough.

He slapped her again, and yelled: 'You have brought disgrace to this door, to this family, disgrace to the mosque, disgrace to your religion, disgrace to me, your father. You will never be allowed out unaccompanied again!'

'But father...'

'Don't but father me! From now on you will only eat one day in three. If I catch you stealing food, I will cut off your right hand!'

'But father, I...'

'I can't tell you how much you disappoint me. You are nothing but a common whore!'

In the Laughing Cavalier, Luke finished his coffee. He had decided on his next assignation and he would make it a good one. It would be his last meet in England for a long time and it had to be special. He made a quick phone call, and after that he began to text. When he'd finished, he ordered an early light lunch. An active man had to keep up his strength.

In the sitting room above the State of Kerala, the text dumped into Sahira's mobile with a tinkly sound, alerting the recipient it had arrived.

Everyone heard it.

Sahira pulled her mobile from her slacks' pocket.

Tried to delete the text.

Too late.

Mohammed jumped forward and jerked the device from her hand.

He had always been against her possessing a mobile phone. It was a ridiculous idea. Wazir had bought it for the girl for her birthday, to curry favour, so Mohammed imagined, but Wazir was losing touch with reality. His day-to-day decisions were becoming more questionable.

Mohammed glanced at the incoming text.
Raised his eyebrows.
Shook his head.
For one moment it looked like he might cry.
He read it aloud so they could all hear.

Going away for 3 mths. Need to see you before I go, this aft. 1pm, same pad. Get yr black arse down there. B naked + waiting. Thrashing awaits. L.

Sahira burst into tears.
Maaz looked disgusted, confused, and dumbfounded.
Wazir scratched his chin.
Ahmed tried to feel pity for the misguided girl, but could not.
Mohammed felt murderous; then said, 'Where is the "same pad"?'
Sahira thought a moment, and said: 'The Red Rose Motel, room fifty.'
Mohammed bobbed his head, deep in thought, aware all eyes were on him.
'You are not to use the telephone, you are not to use the Internet, you are not to leave the building, you are not to eat or drink until I say, you are not to play music, turn on the radio or television, and you are not to discuss this matter with a living soul. Not with your mother, not with your great grandmother. You are not to open your mouth to speak at all. You are to remain silent. Do I make myself clear?'
'Yes, father.'
'Maaz, take her to her bedroom, shut her in, make sure she does not come out, and no one speaks to her.'
'Yes, father,' said the twenty-one-year-old Maaz, and he jumped up and grabbed the twenty-two-year-old girl's arm, and dragged her from the room. As far as he was concerned, she was no longer his sister. She was a sinner, a reprobate, an outcast, and he wasn't in the least bit surprised.

203

Walter's team searched Luke's flat. Found something interesting. A loaded gun wrapped in an American sweatshirt. It was a British made Webley Scott automatic pistol, 9 millimetre, an ugly, dated looking thing. Walter had seen one like it before, years ago, when he was attached to Scotland Yard.

There had been an anti-apartheid rally and riot going on outside the South African embassy. Windows were broken, and a main door damaged. Things had turned nasty. An in house security guard, a BOSS South African secret service agent, had been knocked over in the melee. A similar gun had tumbled from his pocket and had been kicked away by a rioter. The young Darriteau had gained a mention in reports by dashing in and recovering the weapon before it fell into the wrong hands. Just as well he had, for it was loaded.

This one was loaded too, six rounds, way more than enough to kill someone. Walter pondered on whether Luke Flowers was looking to kill someone else, and if so, who, and where, and when. One thing was certain, Luke would have to come back to the flat to retrieve the gun, unless he had another one stashed away somewhere else.

'Hector?'

'Yes, Guv.'

'Go downstairs and man the front door. Keep an eye out for Luke and keep out of sight.'

'Sure, Guv.'

But Luke didn't return to Glanford House, and time was marching on, and the team was growing hungry, and that included Walter, and that was nothing new.

Chapter Thirty-Three

Luke finished his early lunch of poached eggs on toast with lots of brown sauce, and set down the complimentary newspaper the Laughing Cavalier provided. He went outside to walk the meal off before he'd head for the Red Rose Motel.

He hurried along the riverbank, across the pedestrian bridge, and back along the opposite bank, past the bench where he sat with Jimmy Mitchell, admiring the joggers.

There was no one sitting there, and no joggers either, and then on toward the old stone bridge that linked Handbridge to the city.

He crossed the bridge, going back into town, took the first left, and found a vacant seat. During the week those seats would be sought after. People would hang around like hungry gulls, waiting for someone to vacate a place, giggling office girls sharing their lunches, and tales of last night's hot date, or of gossip about a new guy who had turned up in their department.

But it was Saturday, and though there were lots of people about, they were a different crowd at the weekend; they weren't stopping and eating. There was more urgency in their body language, in their movement, as there always was on a late Saturday morning, coming up lunchtime, as if they had vital shopping to find in the city, or were going on a first lunch date with a potential lover, or were in search of concert tickets, or hurrying to catch a train or bus to the evil twin sisters, as Luke thought of them, the big, hard cities of Liverpool and Manchester, an hour away.

He found a vacant seat and sat down. Pulled out his mobile. He would make a few last calls while he had the chance, for he knew better than to neglect his women friends for too long. Absence makes the heart grow fonder, too true, but one still had to keep in touch. He spent ten minutes on goodbye phone calls and then put his phone away, for he'd spotted a taxi coming. He jumped up and waved, and the old black cab rumbled to a standstill.

Luke clambered in and shouted: 'Red Rose Motel.'

'Gotcha,' said the driver, and the cab snorted and shook, and blew out black smoke and rumbled away.

In the State of Kerala, the atmosphere remained tense. Doors opened and closed. Muffled male conversation. Hushed phone calls were being made. Calls to the mosque. Long-distance calls. International calls to the real State of Kerala on the subcontinent, calls to Pakistan, calls to London. More calls back to the mosque. The phones had never been so hot.

At a quarter to twelve Wazir was still sitting in the same seat, still staring ahead, looking sad, still thinking hard on the family crisis. Ahmed and Mohammed stood before the window. They ordered Maaz to bring Sahira back to the sitting room. Mohammed glanced at his expensive wristwatch, a present from Wazir on his last birthday.

Mohammed nodded Maaz away, and he stood up and went to fetch Sahira. He was back within minutes, ushering her into the room without saying a word. Then he strode over and sat beside Wazir, and stared up at the girl, his erstwhile sister, who he now looked on as if she were a hunk of rotting fish.

'Look father, I can explain…'

'Shut up, girl!' snapped Mohammed.

'Show some respect!' yelled Maaz.

Wazir touched Maaz's wrist, and the young man fell silent.

Mohammed held up his hand. Adopted a grave face.

'As you know, Sahira, we have been seeking a suitable husband for you for some time. With the gracious help of Imam Sabir, and Imam Hujjat, at the mosque, this important work has been completed.'

Sahira shook her head and said, 'No, father. I don't want to be married.'

'Quiet, girl!' insisted Ahmed.

Mohammed continued.

'Tomorrow you will fly to Pakistan. We have obtained a standby flight. You will be married in three days to a warlord based in the city of Chitral in the north of the country, close to the Afghan border. The man is well known to people at the mosque. They speak well of him. They say he is a good man, kind and understanding. He will make you a good husband, though he is sixty-eight, and he does not speak English. You will need to learn the language, and you will need to do that fast.'

The Khan men glanced at the girl.

Her head moved slowly from side to side.

'I won't do it, father. I won't.'

'You will do it! Or face the ultimate.'

Sahira stared at the men; saw the stony looks on their faces, not a scrap of compassion to be seen.

'No, father.'

Mohammed continued.

'You may take one bag. Make sure you do not pack any western clothes, or cosmetics or technology of any kind. Maaz will check the items when you have done.'

'I won't do it, father.'

'You will do it, Sahira. Believe me, you will. Maaz, escort her back to her room. Make sure she doesn't leave it.'

Maaz jumped up. Went to grasp her arm. She pulled away and ran outside and hurried back to her room and slammed the door.

Maaz shouted through the timber, 'Make sure you say your prayers, slut!' and he grinned, and after that he slipped out of the building for ten minutes, for there was something he needed to buy.

At half-past twelve Mohammed and Maaz left the State of Kerala. Jumped in the BMW and pointed it toward the motel.

At five to one Luke strode into the motel.

207

The same dusky girl was there in her immaculate green uniform. She didn't say a word. Wouldn't look him in the eye, True deference, Luke imagined; as he picked up the room key she set on the check-in desk. Discrete or what? It was one reason he liked the Red Rose. He smirked and thanked her and turned round and headed for the internal door.

In the flat above the State of Kerala, Wazir straightened his tie and went downstairs, and wandered through the restaurant. The dreadful affair had taken the men's eyes off the principal business, the breadwinning business that he, Wazir Khan, had thought of, and pushed through, and made happen despite all the doubts and opposition of his own family. It was the restaurant that, with the grace of God, had put food into their mouths all these years.

He set that gentle smile on his face and for a moment forgot his worries and creaking bones and greeted two newcomers at the front door, nervous first-timers who had never eaten there before. There was a gentle hum of conversation through the place. He ambled around, speaking with one or two regulars who had been coming in for years, and then sat down and ordered his own lunch, as he always did, in full view of the diners, the same food, the same size portions, the same length of wait, the same dining experience, to prove to the world that only what was good enough for Wazir Khan was good enough for his valued clientele.

He had great troubles on his aging mind, though as always in the restaurant, he struggled not to show it. He wasn't feeling quite himself, but he had good cause. He was in his late eighties. After his main meal he ordered a plain ice cream, for ice cream often washes away any bad taste in the mouth.

Luke didn't return to the flat. Hector Browne and Jenny Thompson had remained there in case. They would still be waiting at 5pm when Walter relieved the pair of them, and sent down another team who secured the front door, and waited in a car across the road.

Walter went home for a change of clothing and a quick bite to eat. On the way, he'd call in at the local parade of shops he preferred to patronise, for he rarely used supermarkets.

In the end shop, Abdul sliced him four slices of boiled ham, moist and delicious, Abdul assured him, and it usually was, though Abdul would never touch a morsel himself. Next door in the old bakery, Queenie Richards had saved him a crusty loaf. She had waited on a little later in case he came in, granary, brown, and she couldn't resist the same old joke that it was a fitting colour for a man like Walter, as he forced a grin, and headed next door to the off licence owned and run by Paul Leishman.

Paul was openly gay and didn't care who knew it, as he minced up and down behind the counter, quite at home in his own private domain, two hands clasped together to the left of his heart, as he tried to sell bottles of perfumed Chianti that he knew Walter would love. Paul had bought too much of the blessed stuff and it was slow moving, but Walter wasn't a Chianti man, and grunted and shook his head.

'I'll have four cans of stout and four cans of real ale,' he said.

Paul, or Pauli, as he preferred to be called, set the beers on the counter.

'Anything else you'd like, Mr Darriteau?' minced Pauli; pursing his lips horribly, as Walter glanced away at something else.

Truth was, Paul Leishman had the hots for Walter, and Walter, being a detective of some repute, hadn't missed the signals. Couldn't imagine how Pauli had fallen under his spell, but it takes all sorts. Why couldn't he attract women in that way, he pondered?

'No, Paul, I'm fine, thanks,' he muttered, and slipped a twenty-pound note across the counter.

Paul made a big issue of slapping the change into Walter's oh-so-manly bear-like paw, and Walter bade him goodnight, and went out into the still sunny evening, clutching his provisions, laughing as he went.

Luke still hadn't returned by 10pm and Walter, who was back at his desk by then, agreed with the consensus that Luke had probably shacked up with his girlfriend. Might be staying there now, wherever that was, and they were sure they wouldn't see him again that day. At least they had his DNA, courtesy of the hairs extracted from his hairbrush, plus any number of perfect fingerprints. It was only a matter of time before they nailed him.

What was it that cyclist Colin Cresswell had said?

He was all dressed up. Hot date, I'd say.

Yeah, that made sense. All they could do was get some sleep and hope to pick him up in the morning. Walter closed his diary and left for home, where he intended making a big dent in those cans.

Chapter Thirty-Four

Iskra and Radka Kolarov were twenty-one-year-old twins. They had spent all their life in the north-eastern Bulgarian industrial town of Beloslav. They could not remember their father. He had gone into the Bulgarian army when they were nine months old and never returned.

Rumour had it many Bulgarian troops were killed during the last live firing exercises involving Warsaw Pact troops. Locals said the Bulgarians were shot dead by gloating Russians, but then they would. The official verdict was accidental death, and the Kolarovs received a modest pay-off.

The twins' mother, Nikolina, was ill, respiratory disease. They lived in a small rented house crammed in between the glass factory, the power station, and the busy, deep, and wide canal.

The quality of the air in Beloslav wasn't brilliant, but it had improved since the old communist days when production figures were everything. Back then, if the beloved workers had to suffer poor air quality to meet targets that was how it was. After all, the central politburo did not live anywhere near blighted Beloslav.

After the fall of communism prices on everything skyrocketed. Wages struggled to keep pace, and though healthcare was free for everyone in Bulgaria, even for some foreigners from within the European Union, good additional healthcare cost cold, hard money.

Nikolina Kolarov needed ample additional healthcare.

The Kolarovs held an urgent family meeting.

They agreed one of the girls would go abroad to work. Once there, she would find a job and send money home, and Nikolina would benefit. The Kolarovs had friends and distant family members working abroad, far away in a place called Chester in the north-west of England. The daughter who went to Chester would not be alone; she would be well looked after and had been assured she would soon find work.

Both of the girls wanted to go for the prospect was exciting, to see something of the world, away from industrial Beloslav, while they were still young, while they were still pretty. Both studied English hard, for who knew what might happen in a western country, and what adventures they might experience?

They quarrelled over who would go, and who should stay and look after mother, but could not decide, until Nikolina stepped in and said she was sick of the bickering, and would settle the matter with the spin of a coin.

Iskra agreed.

Radka wasn't sure, for she suspected collusion. In her eyes Iskra had always been the favourite. Both girls were strikingly pretty in a squarish, Slavic kind of way, milk white skin, jet black hair, often worn in a ponytail. It was Iskra everyone said was prettier, and sometimes, within Radka's hearing.

Radka eventually agreed, providing the coin was thrown in the air in their small kitchen and allowed to fall to the floor. She worried it could be caught by mother and flipped over in the hand to produce the desired result.

It was agreed. The toss was on.

The coin would fall to earth.

The spinning would take place at 11am on Sunday morning, tossed by Nikolina, and allowed to bounce free to the cracked terracotta tiles that lined the damp kitchen floor.

Sunday morning arrived, and the twins eyed each other hard. Nikolina produced the coin that would decide the fate of the family, a silver fifty Stotinki piece, one half of one Lev. Both sisters inspected the coin. It was a brand new piece drawn from the post office especially for the occasion.

The twins remained suspicious, but seemed satisfied, as their mother reminded them of the rules: The winner would go abroad to work hard, and send money home. The loser would stay behind, work in the glassworks, and look after mother, and the house.

'I agree,' said Iskra, keen to learn her fate.

212

The other two stared at Radka.

'Yes, I agree too,' she said, 'providing the coin falls to the floor.'

'We have already decided that!' said mother, becoming irritated. 'The coin will fall to the earth. It will be a free and fair spin. One spin, and one spin only.'

'Who's going to call?' asked Nikolina.

'I don't mind,' said Iskra.

'You call!' said Radka.

Nikolina glanced at the girls. Both twins bobbed their head, crossed their fingers, and eyed their sibling.

Nikolina flicked her thumb and tossed the coin high in the air with a fizz.

'Heads!' screamed Iskra, and she said a silent prayer to Saint John of Rila, the Patron Saint of Bulgaria.

Jimmy Mitchell sat in his five-year-old Mercedes Benz at the Thornton Hough cricket ground and opened a packet of sandwiches. They were fish. He'd bought them in the petrol station and he was beginning to wish he'd chosen chicken. They smelt like cat food, and it promised to be another hot day. He bit into the bread. It tasted better than it smelt.

He grabbed the big Sunday newspaper from the passenger seat and shook out the supplements. Through the windscreen he could see the groundsman preparing the cricket square ready for action, mowing the track, painting the lines, setting up the stumps, wiping his brow.

Jimmy's mobile burst into life.

He hoiked it from his pocket and said, 'Yeah?'

'Just letting you know I am in position, boss.'

'Good man.'

'And that action man isn't here yet.'

Jimmy glanced at the dashboard clock. It was still early. There was plenty of time.

'He'll be there soon, any sign of the main man?'

'Negative.'

213

'Keep me posted.'

'Sure thing,' and the phone went dead.

He set the newspaper down.

One more hour and both England and Liverpool City Football Club would be seeking a new centre forward. Didn't bother Jimmy. It was business, pure and simple, and lucrative business at that.

In the small kitchen in the Kolarov's house in Beloslav, the coin clattered to the floor. It landed on edge and bounced high, then landed and bounced sideways, thumping into the grey metal foot of the old gas cooker. It rolled across the centre of the kitchen, dithering over which way to lean, before settling flat on the centre tile in the room.

'Heads!' screamed Iskra, clapping her hands and doing a little jump and a dance. 'It's a head!'

'Heads it is,' confirmed Nikolina, for it was true she would prefer Iskra to go abroad, because Nikolina was more confident Iskra would send home regular funds.

'It's not fair!' whinged Radka.

'It was fair!' insisted Nikolina. 'Perfectly fair! Iskra will leave for England next Saturday.'

'When do I ever get any excitement?' moaned Radka. 'When do I get to go anywhere?'

'Don't worry, child,' said Nikolina, slipping her arm around Radka's shoulder, and patting her on the head. 'Iskra will go to England for two years, and no more, and after that, she will come home, and then you, Radka, my darling, will have your turn.'

The twins shared a knowing look, for both of them imagined that in two years their mother might not exist.

The tossing of the shiny silver fifty Stotinki coin had taken place three months before. Iskra went to England, Radka sulked for days as Iskra headed to Chester by bus, where she was met by friends and distant relations. They took her back to the big old redbrick

214

Edwardian house in a suburb called Hoole, a property they were renting close to the railway lines.

Iskra would share a room with two other Bulgarian girls.

The room was not large, and there was barely enough space for three single beds, but it didn't matter because they would be working long hours, and different shifts, so they were rarely home at the same time.

The other girls came from Sofia and considered Iskra to be a provincial no nothing. They didn't treat her bad, but neither were they friendly. Iskra didn't care. She thought them stuck up and superior, not that she had any kind of inferiority complex. She thought she was prettier than them, a fact confirmed when the menfolk in the house, and local community, were often found sniffing round the bedroom door, enquiring after Iskra's whereabouts.

That didn't help her popularity with her roommates, but that couldn't be helped, as they quizzed her and helped her with her English, and advised her of the questions she would be asked when she went for a job. Not so much out of kindness, but more because it was important she passed the interviews at the hotels. Iskra could only pay her share of the rent if she could land a job, and when she did, they would pay less.

She need not have worried.

The manager at the Red Rose Motel was tall and skinny, a Mr Heale, and he was desperate for cleaning staff. Iskra was clean, had a pleasant smile, could say please and thank you, nodded hard when asked if she was a good worker, possessed the correct documentation, and that was it, she'd passed the interview. Iskra was in. She would start the following day, and later on the same thing occurred at the Holiday Lodge Hotel. She was employed there too, and had two jobs, thirty hours a week in the mornings at the Red Rose, and the same again at the Holiday Lodge in the afternoon.

It amazed her how easy it had been.

England was a strange place.

So many people; and all rushing round everywhere, all in cars, nary a horse to be seen, and sometimes impatient too, blaring car horns,

215

screaming at passers-by, so much shouting and bad temper and pent up fury. The least thing often seemed to send them over the edge. They should all learn to relax a little, to enjoy and savour life, for they were missing so much. They seemed to have lost the knack of contentment. Perhaps they'd never had it. Why were they all so het up all the time? In Iskra's eyes their problem was that they didn't know how lucky they were.

In the morning she would rise at 6.30, eat a quick breakfast, often the remains of last night's evening meal, and then set off on the three-mile walk to the Red Rose. She would finish there at 1pm, walk home, take a quick lunch, a roll and a piece of sausage, and then undertake another three-mile hike in the opposite direction, even when it was raining, to the Holiday Lodge.

There was no point in taking public transport.

For a start, it was expensive, second, she had the time to walk, and last, she wanted to earn as much as possible, for she was always asking about her mother's condition. Iskra discovered she could afford to send home a clear thousand pounds every month, sometimes more, and in Bulgaria her mother could get a great deal of additional healthcare and medication with a thousand English pounds.

She was at the Red Rose Motel that Sunday morning, humming an old Bulgarian folk tune, as she went about cleaning and preparing the rooms. She was a quick worker and conscientious too. So much so that Mary McGrory, her supervisor, had to plead with her to slow down, for she was putting the other room maids' performance to shame.

Iskra promised she would, with a smirk and a shake of her ponytail, and they couldn't get angry with her because of the smile that rarely left her mischievous face.

She had finished in room forty-nine.

In her eyes it was just perfect.

Ready for the next guests that Iskra always imagined might be a honeymooning couple, and because of that, everything had to be just so, though honeymooners rarely troubled the Red Rose.

On to the next room with a spring in her step, and a change of record in the music in her mind. She pulled out the master key they had entrusted her with, unlocked and let herself into room fifty.

Jimmy glanced back at the clock on the dash. It was twenty minutes past ten and his spotter had still not confirmed that Luke was in place. Jimmy was getting worried. He rang his man again.

'Well? What news?'

'Nothing boss, I'd have told you if he was here.'

'Are there many there?'

'People are arriving now. Think the sunshine has brought them out.'

'No sign of the main man?'

'Nope, not yet boss. Come on, come on, you little turd.'

'He's testing my patience.'

'Mine too, boss. Loads of cars are queuing now, quite a few people about, a number of coppers as well. Maybe he's been caught in traffic.'

'I told him to get there early!'

'Well, he's not here. Eh up, I think he's here now.'

'Thank God for that!'

'No, not your man, the main man.'

'What!'

'Yep, looks like it, big black Audi, blacked-out windows, registration KEAT1, yep it's him alright.'

'Jee-zus, my client will not like this.'

'Lots of people round the car, autograph hunters, people with cameras, at least one professional photographer, I'd say, and now a copper's trying to push his way into the shot.'

'And no sign of our little weasel?'

'Nope, nada, nothing, sorry boss.'

'Don't suppose you've packed the wherewithal?'

'Geez no, boss, out of my comfort zone with that.'

'He's going to regret this.'

'The door to the car's opening. The crowd's pushing forward, not that many of them, maybe twenty odd, and the bird's got out, smiling and waving as if she's royalty. Stupid bitch, nice looking though, tumbling blonde hair, curvy body, tight flowery cotton dress.'

'All right, all right, I get the picture; this isn't a report for bloody OK magazine.'

'Sorry boss, just trying to paint the scene.'

Something in Jimmy's mind told him that Luke was there. In the past he had always been a reliable operator, and a clever one at that. He seemed to possess an almost unique ability of blending into the background, a slight, unremarkable guy who could often go unnoticed. Jimmy hoped that was the case, and that Luke had fooled everyone, including the experienced spotter he was talking to on the phone.

'JK's out of the car, grinning, waving, acting like a tosser.'

'He is a tosser!'

'If you say so, boss.'

'Now, boy, now!' whispered Jimmy to himself, sitting in the Mercedes overlooking the cricket field. He still half expected to hear four shots ring out, the sound bolting down the spotter's phone, and spilling into Jimmy's ear.

There was plenty of sound coming through the ether, but only that of a happy holiday crowd greeting their hero, the Liverpool City and England centre forward, the grinning man with magic in his toes and a price on his head.

'What a pompous arse he is. Wish you were here to see it, boss. He's loving every minute, lapping it up, I've half a mind to go over and slap him myself.'

Jimmy said nothing.

His mind was running free.

Where the hell was Luke Flowers?

What the heck would Jimmy's client say about this mess up?

And what would be a suitable punishment for Luke?

Castration would be too lenient.

Chapter Thirty-Five

Room fifty was smelly, but that wasn't unusual. It was the same design as most of the other rooms. Bathroom on the left. Ahead, a short corridor and the room opened out.

There was a king-size bed there, out of sight from the doorway, with matching light oak bedside table on either side, a big TV fitted to the opposite wall, most of them now flat screen, though there were still the occasional unliftable monster around, two small armchairs, and a long bench table fixed to the far wall where the coffee and tea and cups and saucers and glasses and menus and brochures were scattered about.

Iskra pulled the main door closed behind her and carried her box of cleaning potions and rags, hurried into the bathroom, and set it down on the tiled floor.

Most of the white towels looked as if they hadn't been used, but they would be taken out and washed again, just in case they had. She saw two or three specs of blood on the floor, and on the closed lid to the lavatory too. Maybe someone had cut themself shaving, or perhaps someone had had an accident.

The main mirror above the hand basin was clean, but Iskra took out the spray and spurted scented chemical goo over the mirrored glass, hoping it would conquer the smell. She wiped and buffed up the glass. Leant forward and huffed on a tiny mark, wiped it away, and burped, catching her mischievous face in the glass as she did so. She had indigestion all morning; it was the hurried breakfast that did it, the warmed up leftovers from last night's Bulgarian beef stew. Someone had overdone the paprika, the cayenne and the garlic. Iskra burped again and spoke to the image in the mirror as if it were her twin sister standing there with her.

220

'How is my mother, Radka? I hope you are looking after her, and getting value for money for all the cash I am sending back.'

And she laughed, and Radka in the glass laughed back.

'I'll bet you wish you were here now, have you got over it yet?' and Iskra frowned, just as she knew Radka would have frowned, and the image in the mirror frowned too, exactly as she imagined.

Iskra bent down and picked up the green squirty lavatory cleaner and opened the pan.

A young man's face stared back through blue eyes.

Iskra jumped back a pace.

Her mouth fell open.

'Jee-sus Christ!' she said, clutching hard the plastic bottle of cleaner.

She realised it was a joke.

The girls were always playing silly jokes on one another, especially on the new girls, and this had to be another. Iskra had been expecting it; and everyone knew the English had a strange sense of humour. For a moment they had her fooled. The head looked so real, so lifelike, 'cept it could not be alive, not down there, not without an attached body. Iskra grinned.

It was jammed down the pan so the back of the head was resting on the water, the face staring straight up.

She took a single pace toward the pan.

The mouth in the head was open and there was something inside the mouth, something pink, not the tongue, something else. Iskra dropped the cleaner and pointed at the face. Her forefinger approached the lavatory and closed on the head.

She touched the displayed teeth.

Nice teeth. Real teeth. Human teeth.

She touched the eye.

Nice eye. Real eye. Human eye. It didn't blink.

Her mouth fell open, and she wanted to scream, but nothing came, no sound, just flavours of garlic and cayenne and paprika and overdone fatty beef.

And then something came, flavoured vomit, a torrent of it, undigested breakfast, as it splashed down and covered the head's

221

blue eyes, filling the open mouth, burying whatever was inside, blanketing the face.

And when she had finished, she screamed.

One long, terrible exclamation from the depths of her soul.

AAAARRRRGGGGGHHHHHHHHHH!!!!!!!

Mary was busy in the room next door. Couldn't fail to hear the row through the wall.

It was Iskra, and Mary McGrory from Dungannon, an older lady with a penchant for barley wines, had taken a shine to the young and pretty Bulgarian, taken her under her wing, and by the sound of that horrendous screech, she had either fallen... or had been attacked. Maybe there was still a creepy punter in there, and he had tried it on. It happened, though never to her.

She hustled into the corridor, shouting, 'You all right, Iskra?' as Iskra opened the door and pushed past Mary without looking her in the eye, and fled down the corridor, holding her mouth, shaking her head, wanting to scream again.

'What is it, my child?' asked Mary, as she crept into room fifty, into the stinking bathroom, and saw the Technicolor mish mash that greeted her eyes when she peered down the open bowl, and the outline beyond of a young man's head.

'Jesus, Mary and Joseph!' she muttered, and crossed herself, and turned about and set off down the corridor, after Iskra, shouting, 'Mr Heale, Mr Heale, you'd better come and see this!'

Mr Heale was in reception, standing behind the counter, talking on the phone.

The dusky girl, who never said much, was sitting at the desk, busy on paperwork, every now and again glancing at her computer screen.

'Mr Heale, you must come and see this!' repeated Mary, sniffling into her handkerchief.

She didn't look well, Mr Heale thought. Bout of summer flu coming on, maybe.

He was talking to some American computer company who wanted to block book sixty rooms, but they were haggling hard on the rate.

222

'Mr Heale!'

He put his hands over the mouthpiece and whispered, mouthing it as if she were deaf, 'I am speaking to International Computers!'

'Mr Heale, there is a man's head in the lavvy!'

The dusky girl glanced up, same impassive expression.

She'd heard it all before.

There wasn't much that could surprise her.

For once Mr Heale was lost for words. Then he said, 'I am so sorry, Mrs Wendlesham, can I call you back in ten, there's just something I need to check on right now,' and he bobbed his head and said, 'Right-ho, I'll call you back,' and put the phone down.

Then he was out in the public area, pulling the door open to the corridor, muttering about how bloody busy he was, and he hoped she wasn't wasting his time, and that it was all probably some stupid student rag stunt, just like last year, don't you remember that, because it was approaching the end of term time again, rag week. That daft stunt when they dressed a whole pig in an evening suit, complete with a red silk bow tie, and placed it on the bed, sat straight up, pillows supporting its back and neck, a fat smoking cigar in its grinning mouth, and a glass of red wine somehow wedged into its front right trotter, and when Mr Heale had been called to the room, the students were outside in the car park. They'd removed the lace curtains, and were filming the event, and they put the thing up on pooptube, or whatever that time wasting trite Internet site is called, and it had received over ten million hits in forty-eight hours, and the students had done well out of it.

'It'll be a freakin' hoax again,' he said, 'sure as eggs are eggs.'

'Don't think so, Mr Heale. Don't think so, not this time.'

'Was that why Iskra came running and crying through reception?'

Mary pulled a long face and nodded twice, and by then he was opening room fifty and going inside where he hurried into the bathroom and glanced down the open lavvy bowl, and poked through the vomit, poking the head in the eye, as if he half expected the jabbing motion to wake it from its slumber.

'Mmm,' he said. 'Bugger me!' taking out his mobile and jabbing in 999.

223

'Emergency, which service do you require?'

'Police.'

A couple of seconds ticked over, no more, and then a girl said, 'Police. Emergency.'

'Someone has left their head down one of my lavatories,' said Mr Heale, straight faced, then smirking at Mary McGrory.

'Say again.'

'There is a man's head jammed down one of my lavatories.'

'Is he dead?'

'I would think so.'

'Who's calling, please?'

'My name is Mr Heale; I am the manager of the Red Rose Motel.'

'Are you being serious?'

'Of course I'm being bloody serious!'

'OK, no need to swear. We'll get somebody to you.'

'Be obliged,' and he rang off.

Mary McGrory had gone into the main part of the bedroom.

'Oh hell! I've found the rest of him.'

He ran to see.

So much blood.

Dreadful stink.

Flies too.

It was another hot day

'Look at the state of the carpet!' he said.

'Poor, poor man, what has been going on here, you think?'

'God alone knows!'

At the same moment, Jimmy was sitting in the car overlooking the cricket pitch. He shook his head and started the engine and drove home, determined to find the little weasel before nightfall, the sad little git who had failed him.

Chapter Thirty-Six

Sunday morning and Walter was standing in his kitchen, his back propped up against the worktop, eating a weighty slice of buttered toast, smothered in a generous coating of thick cut Dundee marmalade. Galina Unpronounceable was there, busy in the sink, giving it a thorough cleaning.

She'd rung to say she couldn't make Saturday, had a big job on the go, and would Sunday be all right. He was happy to see her there, and he was always more likely to be in on a Sunday.

Luke Flowers still hadn't been located. Feeling was, he'd jetted abroad again, a theory that carried some weight, after they discovered a receipt in his bedside table for a considerable amount of travellers' cheques, or checks, as they were spelt on the documentation.

She was wiping down the worktops; aggressive short right to left movements, and her neat jeaned bum was shaking in time to the swipes. Walter took another peek then glanced away, and bit into his toast.

'You catch bad man yet?' she said, as she finished what she was doing.

'Not yet, but we are close.'

'I come cook you meal when you do?'

'If you want to.'

She turned and smiled and said, 'Yes, I do that.'

'What food?' he asked, slipping the last of the sticky toast into his mouth and licking his fingers.

'You like dumplings? Meat and dumplings?'

Walter nodded, said: 'Yeah, I like meat and dumplings,' and rubbed his stomach with both hands at the thought of it. It sure as heck beat bloody chicken Kiev.

225

'I do meat and dumplings,' she said, moving over to the stained cooker top. She glanced at the mess and back at him. Walter shrugged his shoulders as if someone else was responsible.

The old phone in the hallway rang, loud tones reverberating through the Edwardian house. Ring-ring. Ring-ring.

'Phone rings,' she said, unnecessarily thought Walter, as he loped through to the hall.

'Guv?' it was Karen.

'What are you doing in today?'

'Making up lost hours, remember, I had that day off for my cousin's wedding.'

'Oh yeah. So, any news on Luke Flowers?'

'Maybe.'

'How do you mean?'

'A man's head has been found jammed down a lavvy in the Red Rose Motel.'

'That's a first, and you think it's him?'

'Might explain why we can't find him. You want me to pick you up?'

'Yeah, course, I'll get dressed.'

'See you in ten.'

Walter returned to the kitchen, where heavy scrubbing was going on.

'I've got to go out; we might have found the bad man.'

'Good – I order meat!'

'Not yet, Galina, not until we know for sure. I am going upstairs to get dressed.'

Five minutes later he was back, fiddling with his tie, setting her pay down on the draining board.

'Thank.... you,' she said, two distinct words. Almost two separate sentences.

'You can let yourself out, can't you?'

'Course, do, easy.'

Pretty much the right words, maybe not quite in the right order, thought Walter.

'I work here many times before when you not here. I not steal anything.'

'I know that, Galina,' and then they heard Karen honking from the unmarked BMW.

'Must go.'

'I see you out.'

He'd rather she didn't, but she did anyway, standing at the front door, smiling and waving a yellow duster above her head, as Walter fell into the car.

Karen smirked.

'Friend of yours?'

'No, just the cleaner.'

'Funny day for a cleaner.'

'She couldn't come yesterday.'

'Pretty, too.'

'You think? I hadn't noticed.'

'Liar!' and already they were round the corner and heading across town for the Red Rose.

Mr Heale was tall and skinny and languid, and acted as if the whole business was a minor irritant to his day. Didn't act like a man who had discovered a severed head down one of his lavvies.

Heale showed them through to room fifty, and a moment later Doc Grayling showed up.

Walter nodded a greeting, and the short, stout doc nodded back.

'Another one called in on a Sunday?' said Walter.

'No problem to me. I was on call anyway. Had a run down infant, but he was OK,' said the doc, handing out disposable latex gloves.

'So what have we here?' said Walter, as all four of them peered down at the vomit splashed head.

'Well, as you can see, it's a man,' said Heale. 'I thought it was a practical joke when they first told me.'

'Who found the body?' asked Karen, correcting herself. 'The head.'

'One of the maids, Bulgarian she is, nice kid, Iskra Kolarov, she's a bit shaken up, spewed up all over the place. The rest of him is in there,' and he nodded through toward the bedroom.

'She would be shaken up,' said Walter. 'I'd be shaken up if I discovered that in my bog! Where is she now?'

'Having a coffee in the staff room, with Mary McGrory, she's the supervisor, she's with her.'

Walter nodded at Karen, 'Go and see what they can tell you, but before that, ring SOCO and tell them to get down here straight away, and I don't care what day it is,' and Karen bobbed her head and disappeared.

There was a combination of smells in the bathroom, blood and vomit, and old dinners, and God knows what else.

Doc Grayling said: 'Goulash, methinks,' sniffing the vomit.

'Goulash is Hungarian,' said Walter. 'If the girl's Bulgarian, probably some kind of Bulgarian beef stew.'

'Well, whatever it is, there's paprika in it,' said the Doc, cleaning the face to reveal a clearer picture of Luke Flowers.

The doc saw the look of recognition in Walter's eyes.

'You know who he is?'

'Yeah, unless I am much mistaken, that is the head of Luke Edward Flowers.'

'Known to you?'

'Yes.'

'Bad egg?'

'Wanted murderer.'

'Looks like someone wanted him more than you did.'

'Seems that way.'

Mr Heale cocked his wrist and glanced at his watch.

'Look, am I OK to get away? I have so much to do.'

They had almost forgotten he was there.

'Yes, for now,' said Walter. 'But don't leave the building until we have spoken again, and DON'T tell the press.'

'I am hardly likely to do that, am I? It's not good publicity, is it? One of the guests has been decapitated; that's the place for me!'

Walter nodded the guy away, and the doc said, 'Strange fellow.'

'Yes, he is,' said Walter, peering at the head.

'There is something in his mouth,' said the doc, grabbing a pair of tweezers from his bag, getting closer, almost close enough to kiss. Peering deep into the mouth, obscuring it from Walter's view.

'What is it?'

'Just a minute. I think I have it. Yes, there you are!'

And he stood upright and displayed the foreign body.

'Soap,' said Walter.

'Pink soap,' said the doc. 'Standard motel issue, I would say,' and they both looked round, and the absence of any other soap encouraged that belief.

'And the hidden meaning is?' asked Walter.

'Wash your mouth out, mend your ways, cleanse your sins, wouldn't you think?'

'Looks that way to me.'

'We are going to have to get him out of there,' said the doc.

'Seems sensible.'

Doc Grayling retreated to his bag and brought out a large heavy duty clear plastic bag. Shook it open. Gave it to Walter.

'You hold, I'll grab.'

Walter shook the plastic bag again as the Doc slipped some implement between the head and the side of the bowl and eased it out. Filthy, bloody water dripped from the hair, and the head, and the ears, and the nose and mouth, and splashed down into the bowl, and onto the rim and the floor beyond.

'Mucky business,' whispered the doc.

Grayling lowered the head into the bag that Walter was holding open, the static blue eyes still staring out. He fastened the top and took it from Walter and through to the main bedroom. It was surprising how heavy a fresh human head could be.

Walter followed. 'Good God, what have we here?'

'Place of execution, I would say.'

229

Walter bobbed his head, couldn't speak, because he was already on the phone, ringing Karen just along the corridor.

'Find out who booked room fifty. I want to know what time they arrived, how did they pay, and did they have any visitors? Oh, and see if there is any CCTV, inside the building and out, and find out if anything in here was touched by the staff, such as the body, and we'll need fingerprints of all staff to eliminate them. We'll also need a full record of everyone employed here, and another list of all the guests from yesterday and today, no, make that the whole of last week, to be on the safe side, and the last month for this room.'

'Sure, Guv. On to it.'

'Everything else all right out there with you?' muttered Walter, as he glanced over his shoulder and watched the doc staring down at the severed neck.

'Shaken up, but they'll be OK,' said Karen.

The body was fully clothed, facing down, except there wasn't a face, lying with the shoulders at the foot of the bed, feet at the top, both arms out straight to the side, as if it had been a cross. It was a big king-size, and he was a small guy, and the hands didn't overlap the sides. At the foot of the bed where the head would have been, should have been, was a large maroon stain, turning deep brown, spreading down onto the carpet. There were flies in the room and they were all getting pretty excited, not easily put off by wafting, living humans.

The doc had set the head up on the wall table so that it could watch what was going on in the room. Walter stared at the face in the plastic bag and said to himself: What's this all about, Luke?

The doctor went to the body and was touching the severed neck with his gloved hand.

'Seems a clean cut, might even be a single blow.'

'Drugged first, you think? Or restrained?' asked Walter.

'Can't tell that yet, the PM will though.'

'Restrained means more than one person.'

230

'Yes, it would, because if it was one blow, it would have required a great deal of leverage. No one person could both hold, and sever.'

'But if the victim was drugged, that would be a different ball game.'

'You have it, Darriteau, you have it.'

Walter looked around the room, checking for a murder weapon, but he didn't expect to find one, and didn't.

'What kind of weapon are we looking at?'

'Hard to say,' said the doc, standing up straight, pursing his lips. 'But a sharp one, and a big one too. This wasn't done with some home kitchen carving knife; you are looking at something bigger, and more impressive.'

'Like an axe or a sword?'

'Yes, that would fit the bill, or a specialist implement from an abattoir maybe, or butchers.'

'And time of death?'

'You want everything, don't you, Walter?'

'Course, I am a demanding man,' and he grinned at the doc who bobbed his head and grinned back.

'Judging by the colour of that,' and he nodded at the ruined carpet, 'and the state of the remains, over twelve hours ago, and possibly more.'

'How much more?'

'Well, it wouldn't surprise me if death occurred yesterday afternoon, say in the middle of the match, around half-past three, how does that suit you?'

'OK, doc, I get it.'

'A little demo.'

The doc lifted one arm. The entire body jerked up as if it were one solid piece of timber. 'Rigor mortis speeds up in hot weather. Not to put too fine a point on it, the stiff is as stiff as a board.'

Walter sniffed a smile and said: 'Guessed as much.'

'Fly activity will support the time of death. They are industrious little buggers. Reliable as...' and he paused as if searching for the right word.

'Flies?' suggested Walter.

231

'Yes. We learn more from their activity than practically anything else.'

Walter took another look round the room. He was hoping to find a mobile or a wallet. Couldn't see either. Went closer to the bed. Took out his pen, poked in the back trouser pocket. There was a wallet in there, black, small, fold-over style, shut in by one closed trouser button. He undid the button and eased out the wallet. Took a quick peek inside. The usual thing. Plenty of cash, plenty of credit cards, all in Luke Flowers name, and not much else.

Went back and checked the other pockets.

Half a handy pack of paper handkerchiefs, a small throwaway lighter, and a crushed pack of cigarettes containing five fags, and some loose coins. Nothing else. The mobile phone was missing. The killer or killers must have taken it.

A soft knock came to the door.

SOCO arrived earlier than expected. Mob handed, two guys and a girl, already changed and ready to go, looking like operatives from the Sellafield nuclear facility.

Doc Grayling said, 'I've just about finished here,' and Walter nodded the SOCO team on, and a couple of seconds later the cameras were clicking and rolling, as everything was committed to multi-million or was it billion trillion now, pixels, digital photographs instantly available on the back of the camera, or downloaded onto a laptop in a few seconds flat, sent to anywhere in the world in a millisecond.

Every angle, every viewpoint, every spec, nothing would be left to chance, before the remains would be removed.

In due course they would call the mother to ID the body, and it would be a whole body by then. It was amazing what they could do nowadays, even when the body was in bits. Perhaps she might regret being less than helpful. Sometimes parents had to be braver and put their own children in the frame, even if they faced a heavy punishment, though it was easy to be wise after the event. But better that than the ending that befell the young man once known as Luke Edward Flowers.

Across town, in the first floor private quarters of the State of Kerala, another meeting was taking place.

Only one woman was present, Sahira Khan, dressed in her hijab, ordered to stand in the centre of the room, her face showing, no hair on view, looking like a Christian nun.

As before, Nadirah and Akleema were outside, listening at the closed door, and as before Mohammed and Ahmed were standing, Wazir and Maaz sitting together on the sofa, stern-faced, like a jury about to deliver a verdict.

Ahmed spoke first.

'You will leave for Pakistan tonight.'

'Yes, grandfather.'

'Mohammed and Maaz will take you to the airport.'

'Yes, grandfather.'

'You will leave at 9pm.'

'As you wish, grandfather,' and she glanced at her father, Mohammed, as if for comfort. He didn't look away, but stared straight through her as if she didn't exist.

'Before you go, you will say goodbye to your mother and your great grandmother. Is that clear?'

'Yes, grandfather.'

'It will be a long time before you see them again… if ever.'

'I understand, grandfather.'

'Do you have any questions?'

'None, grandfather.'

'Maaz, have you checked the sinner's bag?'

'Yes, grandfather.'

'And was it in order?'

'It was, grandfather.'

'And the passport?'

'I have it safe,' said Maaz, 'ready, with the flight details.'

Ahmed nodded his assent and slipped his hands into his tailored jacket pocket.

'Maaz, take her back to her room,' said Mohammed. 'Make sure she does not speak to the women, and that she does not leave her room.'

'Yes, father,' said Maaz, getting up and taking hold of Sahira's arm. She didn't pull away. Didn't resist. Allowed herself to be led away.

After the youngsters had gone, Wazir said, 'What a dreadful business.'

'Too terrible to imagine,' said Ahmed, sitting down.

'The girl is getting off lightly,' muttered Mohammed, still fuming.

'She's very lucky indeed,' said Ahmed, and at the other end of the landing, as Maaz shut her in her bedroom, he whispered, 'You disgust me!'

'But Maaz…'

'Don't speak to me! Don't ever speak to me again! You whore!'

Back in the sitting room, Wazir pleaded: 'When are we going to get back to normal?'

'Tomorrow, father,' said Ahmed. 'Tomorrow all will be as it should be.'

Earlier, Sahira had told her mother under no circumstances would she allow herself to be put on a plane to Pakistan. Akleema set her straight. She must go to Pakistan, she must carry out the family's wishes, and she must marry the warlord. The most important thing was, she should get out of the family home, and the family business, as quickly as possible, if she valued her life.

'You must have heard the stories of what can happen to an adulteress?' pleaded Akleema, grabbing her daughter's shoulders and staring into her dark eyes, her beautiful clear eyes. Akleema could understand how they entranced men so, but Sahira had shown herself to be weak, and she must bear the consequences.

'But he's sixty-eight, mamma, and he'll probably reek of goat.'

'Of course he will smell of goat, child, and so will you after a day or two, but after a while you won't notice. At least you will be safe. At least you will be alive, and sometime soon you might write to me, and after a while, well… who knows?'

234

'But, mamma…'

'The only thing that matters is that we keep you alive. You must show contrition. You must not argue. You must remain silent. You must do as the men say. To do otherwise is dangerous for you.'

'But, mamma…'

'No buts, child, you have no choice, you must do as they say, and pray that God will be merciful.'

Maaz came back into the sitting room and nodded at his elders. He had done his work well. Everything would proceed as they had arranged. The adulteress would go to Pakistan.

Chapter Thirty-Seven

At five to nine Mohammed brought the BMW round to the front of the State. There was still plenty of daylight; it was close to being the longest day of the year, it had seemed like it to Sahira. She was saying her goodbyes to Akleema and Nadirah, determined not to cry.

Maaz was there too, dressed in his best lightweight suit, shirt and tie, as if he had an important meet, as he glanced at his expensive watch.

'Get in the car!' he said.

'Open the boot for my bag.'

He took the bag from her and repeated, 'Get in the car!'

She kissed her mother on the cheek and pulled the rear door open and climbed inside. Maaz grabbed the open door and threw the fat bag in after her, slammed the door, ran round the front of the car and jumped in beside his father.

Sahira waved through the glass to the women standing in the doorway. They smiled and waved back, trying hard to act as normal as possible. Maaz clicked on his belt, and the car was on its way toward the inner ring road.

'What time is the flight?' asked Sahira.

'Shut up!' said her father.

'Don't you say a word!' said Maaz, as the car weaved on through the light Sunday night city traffic.

She sat back and set her cheek on her hand and stared out through the window at the bright lights of the late evening city. At the print shop, the golf shop, the electronics warehouse, the sofa shop, the

236

DIY shed, the hairdressers, as they floated by, multi coloured name signs above the display windows, lighting up the evening.

It made the place look cheerful, she thought, as did the lovers walking hand in hand and arm in arm, the old man walking the perky West Highland terrier, and the group of Christian lads in their best clothes and tight short-sleeved shirts heading down towards the Peacock pub, maybe for a night on the town, perhaps looking for a girl, maybe hoping to find a girl like Sahira, and after that she saw the young black man walking along the pavement, and making to cross the road, hand in hand with his white girl, a smile of inner satisfaction on both their faces, as if they didn't have a care in the world, and that made her jealous, as the city buses and taxis bustled to and fro, and even though it was Sunday, they all seemed busy and alive and vibrant.

It was the ancient city of Chester, full of life, her home, England on a shut down Sunday night, and it was all she had ever known. She'd been born there, never lived anywhere else, never wanted to live anywhere else. It was where her friends were. She was still in touch with most of the girls from the sixth form, and they would miss her at the next reunion, and wonder what happened to the pretty and vivacious Sahira Khan, that same girl who was always smiling and laughing, and showing an interest in everyone and everything, even in their troubles.

She had been abroad on holiday before, but not to India or Pakistan, and never into a war zone like the Pakistani-Afghani border promised to be. She wondered where Luke was, for she knew no matter how long she was away, she would never stop thinking about him, and loving him, and wondering where he was, and who he was with, and what he was doing. I love you, Luke; she whispered.

'What did you say?' snarled Maaz, turning round to gape at the girl.

'Nothing, never said a word.'

'Keep it that way!'

He'd probably be with that blonde piece, that girl he'd taken to Venice, the one he thought so much about, and that was only to be

237

expected, because Luke Flowers had a deep need for the company of women, and not just one woman either. He would never be a one-woman man, and Sahira understood that. She was happy to share him. She loved him, always had, and always would, regardless of what he did and what he said, and how he treated her.

She shivered in the back seat of the heavy saloon, though it wasn't cold, and glanced at the neatly cut hair and shaved and perfumed necks of the men sitting in the front seats. Her father Mohammed and her brother Maaz, who had both treated her so badly since her affair with Luke had come to light.

It wasn't as if they were innocent.

She had seen how her father had looked at the sixth formers coming out of school in their neat short-sleeved blouses, and short and tight skirts, how he looked at her friends with lust in his eyes, and she knew for a fact that Maaz had been out with white Christian girls, several of them, maybe more than that, slept with them too, if the street gossip was to be believed. So why in hell's name was it different for girls?

It wasn't fair. Life wasn't fair. Not at all. Not for a young British Muslim woman. She loved England, but in her world it wasn't a fair world, it wasn't a fair England. She wondered how long it would take to get to Pakistan, and how she would get from Islamabad to Chitral, wherever the heck that was.

Would there be transport?

Would she have to walk, or ride a blinking donkey, or what?

She shivered again, and tried to shut such thoughts from her mind.

And what would he be like, this sixty-eight-year-old warlord who couldn't speak a word of English, this old man from the interior who she was now betrothed to? It didn't bear thinking about. She wondered if he had any teeth. She wondered if he would stink.

Some men in their sixties were rickety wrecks, while others were passable. With her luck she knew what her future husband would be like, and the thought of him touching her, and sleeping with her, this old man who her mother had said would stink of old goat, well, it wasn't guaranteed to turn on a girl. How could she cope with that?

238

She wondered if she could buy a mobile phone and ring Luke. If she could do that there was still hope, and then she wondered why she should allow herself to be taken in that car with such opinionated men, who couldn't abide her company, and she pondered on why what she had done was so reprehensible.

She didn't want to go to Pakistan, and she didn't want to be married, unless by some miracle it was to the sweet Luke Flowers. But most of all, she didn't understand why she should do as these over-bearing men ordered.

Result? She wouldn't.

Not a chance.

She would rather kill herself than that.

Much rather kill herself.

The car had joined the motorway.

She peered between the heads of the two silent men before her and glanced at the speedometer. The German blue tints sent back their eerie message. The car was travelling at well over 70mph toward her destiny, and with a little luck they would get stopped for speeding, and maybe she could plead to the officers that she was being kidnapped, which to all intent and purposes was true, even if one of her kidnappers was her father and the other, her brother.

No, that would not happen, being stopped, she knew that well enough, and she knew too she would not go to Pakistan. That wasn't an option.

She would rather open the door and throw herself from the speeding vehicle. She would wait until they were overtaking a rumbling truck. Then she would do it, ease open the door and dive beneath the rolling wheels of the truck in the inside lane.

It would be a terrible end, but preferable to reverting to the Stone Age, and an ancient way of life, and a vile and illiterate husband who beat her and reeked of goats, living in a faraway land where the locals did not speak either of her languages.

The motorway hit an incline. It wasn't yet dark. There was a truck up ahead, travelling the same way. It was coming back into the dipped beam of the BMW. The wagon was one of Midge Ridge's, those maroon and cream trucks that haul grain and animal foods the length and breadth of the kingdom. Those famous trucks you could buy models of in most service stations and toy shops, models that guilty fathers acquire for their sons in a hurry when they have forgotten to buy anything else.

It was hauling a full load of Canadian durum wheat out of Birkenhead, bound for one of the Manchester corn mills, and it was struggling with its heavy load up the hill. It was less than forty yards away.

Sahira's left hand snaked out toward the door, low down, out of sight of the men. For a moment the BMW had to slow too. There was a caravan in front being pulled by a four by four, and Mohammed glanced in the right wing mirror, thinking he might move out and overtake, but the third lane was full of fast traffic. Nowhere to go.

He held station, eased back on the accelerator.

The truck was slowing still, and though the BMW was slowing as well, it was still overtaking the long wagon. Sahira glanced to her left. Saw the driver in the cab, seemingly going backwards, minding his own business, singing to the radio, something about Angels, if her lip reading was correct, and that seemed appropriate.

Sahira said a silent prayer, and mumbled a goodbye to her beloved mother, and a goodbye to Luke too. At least she had known him, at least she had known what life was about, and how exciting life could be, as she flipped open the door handle and threw herself to the left.

The door didn't open.

Central locking.

Wonderful invention.

Childproof locks.

Better still.

They'd saved another life.

Worth having.

'What are you doing back there?' snarled Mohammed, hearing the noise, sensing the movement, glancing back over his left shoulder.

'She tried to open the door and throw herself out!' snarled Maaz.

'Did you, Sahira? Is that what you tried to do? You stupid girl!'

'She's not only a sinner, she's a coward,' said Maaz, and he grinned at his own summation. 'Can't take her punishment, that's her trouble.'

'I want no more of it!' yelled Mohammed, glancing ahead and seeing a clear road. He took his right hand from the wheel and aimed a slap at her over his left shoulder, but missed. She felt the draught from his hand as she swayed back into her seat. Then he was facing the front, muttering to himself, and easing his right foot down on the accelerator, for he wanted the day over and done with. He wanted an end to the whole sorry business. He wanted to be rid of the girl once and for all, the stupid, selfish woman who had shamed him and his family, and had brought humiliation, disgrace, and dishonour down on them all.

The car surged forward, thrusting Sahira back in her seat.

She closed her eyes and thought of Manchester airport, and how and where and when she could make a break for it. That's what she would do; that was the new plan. She would distract them, perhaps go to the Ladies and climb out of the window and dash away. Claudia Williams, her best friend from school, who still sent her a Christmas card every year, a card her father usually found and burned in the naan bread oven, would offer Sahira sanctuary.

Claudia possessed her own car; and her own mobile too, how lucky some girls were, and if Sahira could reach a phone, she could ring her and plead for help. Sahira had no money, the over zealous Maaz had seen to that. 'You won't need money where you're going,' he said, grinning. 'You're supposed to be fasting,' but Sahira didn't need money because Claudia's phone accepted incoming calls without the caller paying.

Her concerned father had set up the tariff so that Claudia could ring home when she liked, and they could call their daughter any time of day or night without ever having to worry about credit. That's what Sahira would do. Claudia Williams would help.

241

With each passing hour Jimmy Mitchell was becoming more irritated. There had still been no word from Luke Flowers. He could not be contacted at any of his usual haunts. No one had seen the beggar.

More worryingly, when he sent a messenger to Luke's flat the guy reported back the place was swarming with the law. Luke was a wanted man. Somehow the police had twigged that it was he who had shot the Player boy and Neil Swaythling.

Perhaps Luke had gone to ground, maybe the police already had him in custody; that would explain why no one could find him, but in case he was still out there, Jimmy employed a small army of street rats to look for the weasel.

He re-employed Bunny Almond, something he swore he would never do, and for once Bunny was not living in a parallel universe. He went about his work in tracking down Mr Flowers with zeal. Bunny remembered the great payday he'd enjoyed when he found Neil Swaythling, and was still basking in that success.

He'd even taken a big bet he would be the one to find Luke Flowers, a stupid bet he could never honour, if he lost.

Jimmy Mitchell remained a worried man. It was a mystery. He imagined a scenario where Flowers was already in custody, under pressure from their best interrogator, and that probably meant that fat, black bastard with the ridiculous name, and the worry was Luke might be persuaded to point the finger at Jimmy.

If that wasn't bad enough, Jimmy had fielded three heavy phone calls from his client enquiring why the England centre forward was still living and breathing, and bragging and drinking and feeding and snorting his way through Wirral's most expensive watering holes, whorehouses, and nightclubs.

'I gave you the contract, Jimmy, not to some loser you might have employed. It's your responsibility. I expect you to complete the deal, and within seven days. Is that clear?'

Those ominous words were rattling around Jimmy's head. There would be no sleep until matters had been resolved, and the most annoying part was, he was nowhere near resolution.

242

The BMW approached Junction 5 on the M56, the Manchester Airport turnoff.

Sahira sat forward in the back seat and saw the lit-up overhead blue gantries. Get in lane. Get in Lane. Manchester Airport. But her father didn't change lane.

She thought he was leaving it till the very last moment.

Then he would cut across.

He imagined himself to be a wonderful driver, they all knew that, egotistical, quick and cute, thought of himself as a regular Lewis Hamilton, even bought the monthly F1 magazine, and annoyed everyone by sitting for ages in the bathroom reading when other people were waiting to visit.

If he didn't switch lanes in a second, he'd miss the turnoff. Both men sat in silence in the front seats. Sahira had expected Maaz to shout, 'Get in the right lane, Dad,' but he didn't. Neither man spoke. The car travelled on in silence.

Time was up. They had missed the turnoff.

They were not going to Manchester Airport.

Chapter Thirty-Eight

Sahira wondered if there was another exit a little further up the motorway, a new turnoff perhaps, an expressway in. They were always fiddling with the myriad of motorways and exits and entries around Greater Manchester, and she wouldn't have been surprised. But on reflection she thought not, and couldn't remain silent.

'Didn't you miss the turnoff?'

'Shut it!' said Mohammed.

Maaz turned around and grinned manically at her, but said nothing.

Psychological warfare, the men thought they were masters at it. But the truth was, the Khan women could play that game too, only differently. They had to be more subtle, so the men weren't aware the women were playing with them. Considering the serious handicaps the women suffered, when it came to mind games, they won hands down.

She would bide her time and wait for the right moment. She would listen and observe. Sahira would use every scrap of intelligence she possessed to outwit them. She saw them for what they were, filthy pigs, no more, no less. If they weren't going to Manchester Airport, they must be going somewhere else, and in Sahira's mind, anywhere was better than boarding that midnight flight to Islamabad, and the Stone Age that lay beyond. A place she imagined still existed up on what used to be called the North-West Frontier. It had always been a bloody place where people were being raped and murdered, and it still was, despite the billions being poured into the area by the Americans.

Some time later she said, as sweetly and as young girly as she could muster, 'Where are we going, father?'

244

'Shut up!' yelled Maaz, spitting as he spoke, depositing splashes of spittle on the glove compartment before him.

But the girly question worked on her father, to a degree, triggered some kind of long ago parental protection thing in his racing mind, and on the spur of the moment he answered the girl's question. He couldn't do anything else.

'Bradford,' he said. 'We are going to Bradford.'

She sat back in her seat and thought of Bradford. Why were they going there? Her mother, Akleema, originated from Bradford, so they must have relatives in that cosmopolitan city, though Sahira didn't know any. They hadn't kept in touch.

Perhaps they had made a UK arranged marriage for her after all, and anything was better than some old goatish man far away in the mountains. Perhaps her new fiancé would be young and handsome, and for a moment she allowed herself to daydream of the wonderful man who lay ahead, a man who would become her husband. The daydreaming didn't last.

She knew she wasn't about to be rewarded for her behaviour. That was out of the question. So if she wasn't being rewarded, why were they heading into the Pennine hills, toward Bradford?

They had switched onto the M62 and being late Sunday night the traffic was light. It wasn't at any other time, as they whizzed along at 90mph. Sahira watched for the big blue signs, ticked off the exits in her mind, past gate 20, past 21, and she noticed a clicking in the car, the regular click-click, click-click of an indicator.

She glanced behind her.

No traffic, so he wasn't pulling out to overtake. He was indicating to turn left, to leave the motorway, and they were nowhere near Bradford, as he exited at gate 22.

'Where are we going, father?' she repeated.

'Shut your mouth, bitch, or by God I'll cut your throat!' screamed Maaz, as if he was nearing the end of his tether. He had turned round and was glaring at her, and she saw the hatred and violence in his black eyes.

245

She wasn't surprised.

He had always been a weird brother.

There had been that strange incident five years earlier when he had attacked someone in the restaurant, a middle-aged man who had taken one glass of red wine too many. The guy had the temerity to glance longingly at Maaz's mother, leaving his eyes there far longer than he should, and after the confrontation that followed, a fracas that involved smashed crockery and a bleeding and damaged ear, Maaz went away for two years.

The family explained he was sick and receiving the best attention available, convalescing, they said, but one day she found a letter from some Outreach Centre that, according to the strap line beneath the name, advised: Specialising in the Treatment of Young Men with Mental Disorders.

She had started to read the letter. It said he was much better, that the medication was working, and he could soon return home, though he would remain on medication for the foreseeable future. Her frantic reading was interrupted by her father coming up the stairs, and she slipped the letter into its envelope, and back in the dressing-table drawer, in the nick of time.

There had been another incident too. On the landing upstairs, he had lobbed a full bottle of spring water at mother after she had insisted he tidy his room. Not a plastic bottle, but one of those teardrop shaped heavy, green glass bottles. It missed by a whisker because she had the foresight to duck. Sahira was always wary of Maaz after that.

It was still just light, though darkness was coming down fast. It had been a dry day, a little breezy for the time of year, but pleasant enough. The car was following a minor road, twisting and turning, rising more than falling, headlights on full beam. They had crossed the border, and were now in the white rose county, Yorkshire, as they entered the small town of Hebden Bridge.

She had never been that way before and didn't want to go that way again. Everything looked dark and doom-laden, though maybe that was just her state of mind. She again pondered on why they were there, and for a moment she imagined her father was lost, that he

246

was driving aimlessly through the hills, maybe to frighten her, maybe to bring her to her senses. It wouldn't work. She was Taurus, and Taurus's were renowned for their stubbornness.

The town was behind them and they were heading due north; then cutting left toward the last dismal light of the setting sun far away to the west. They passed another sign: The RESERVOIRS, and a minute later they were skipping by the first of many vast reservoirs that sleep in those hills, manmade lakes that quench the ever-growing thirst of the vast conurbation known as Greater Manchester.

Two more signs came and went, The PENNINE WAY, a long path and track for walkers that straddles the Pennine Hills, running south to north for a hundred miles, and then: WALSHAW DEAN RESERVOIR, a vast lake of fresh water set high in the hills to catch the frequent rains, and enable the force of gravity to deliver its precious cargo down to the city, pumps non essential. Turn a tap on down there and the goddess of gravity delivers.

Mohammed pulled the car to a standstill.

There was a small pull-in to the left of the single lane of tarmac. It was debatable if any traffic came that way, other than occasional Water Company inspection and maintenance jeeps, and bad-tempered motorised farmers seeking lost sheep. But her father seemed to know the place existed. It was as if this was the spot he had been seeking.

'Have you been here before?' she asked.

Her father sniffed a soft laugh, as if forgetting himself.

'Shut the hell up!' yelled Maaz.

'It's all right, Maaz,' father said. 'I have indeed been this way before, when I was courting your mother, we used to drive up here and picnic on this very spot, her dressed in her most expensive green robes, gold thread interwoven into the green. It was designed to impress me, and of course it did, I'll always remember that.'

'I thought you had an arranged marriage,' said an amazed Maaz, becoming interested in the strange conversation.

'Oh yes we did, through the Mosque, and I'd always recommend it. But I still had to court Akleema first. That was only right and

247

proper, and she'd expect it too. We'd sit here and talk, never touching of course, rarely daring to look into each other's eyes, because her father and his brother, big bulky men, the pair of them, sat in the gold Ford Granada behind, staring at me in the mirror every time I glanced in the glass.'

Mohammed sniffed another laugh, as if remembering those carefree days from long ago, and then he said, 'Sahira, get out of the car!'

Maaz jumped out and opened her door.

'You heard father. Get out!'

Sahira gazed at her crazy brother and did as she was told.

The men seized a wrist and walked her away from the car, down toward the glassy water. From somewhere, Mohammed produced a torch and pointed ahead.

It was grassy, but deep unkempt, windblown grass, and difficult to walk through. There were no trees to be seen anywhere and no buildings either, nothing, just thick grassland turning to heather on the moors higher up.

'What are you going to do? Throw me in the lake?'

No answer. They carried on walking, leading her away, maybe a hundred yards from the car.

The wind blew hard against their faces, whistling through the dark sky as the final jagged shards of daylight were extinguished. Not an obvious living thing about. Even the ubiquitous sheep had vanished.

It was a famous place in a quirky kind of way, not that any of them knew that. It marked the halfway spot for those individuals, crazy or hardy enough, to attempt the 875 mile Land's End to John O'Groats walk.

It often broke rainfall records, hence the proliferation of reservoirs, and not too far away, were remote buildings and Halls that had inspired some of the Bronte novels.

It was still a famous place, but that wasn't important, and fact was, everywhere in Britain is a famous place if you look hard enough.

They came to a standstill.

Maaz let go of her wrist.

Her father did not.

He stared down at her in the gloom. Shone the torch into her puzzled face.

'You have failed me, daughter. You have brought great shame on the family.'

'I am sorry, father. I was only following my heart.'

'You behaved disgracefully.'

'You're a stinking slut!' yelled Maaz, waggling his arm and pointing into her face, his poisonous words grasped by the swirling wind and whisked away into the night.

Sahira glanced at her brother. She pitied him.

The boy wasn't well. Everyone knew that.

'We could never trust you again,' Mohammed continued.

'She sleeps with filthy kaffirs! She's nothing more than a common prostitute! You are no sister of mine!'

'Oh Maaz, listen to yourself,' said Sahira.

'She's shamed the family, shamed her religion, shamed her sex, shamed her parents, shamed me!'

'Oh, and you're so pure, are you?'

'Don't you... don't you dare bring my conduct into this! It is you that has behaved blasphemously! You are an evil woman... pure evil!'

'Yes, but at least I'm not a mental case!'

The men stood before her, stunned to silence.

How could she have known about that?

How long had she known?

And how had she found out?

She glanced at Maaz's face.

Took a little comfort in knowing she had silenced him, hurt him too, by the look of him. There was spittle on the corner of his lips. The moon was out, and the spittle glistened silver in the moonlight. She thought he looked like some kind of extra from a zombie movie, or a madman from a crazy pop video.

Sahira pulled a defiant face straight at him, as she often did when they were children, a face framed in her white hijab, and then she twisted her head from side to side and glanced away. She didn't want to look at him any longer. She had seen enough.

249

Maaz scowled and stared at his father, as if for guidance; then let out a guttural noise. He pulled the short-handled ball hammer from his pocket. The gleaming tool he had slipped out to the hardware store to buy. He brandished it in the air, and crashed it down on the centre of her head, splitting her skull asunder. She fell to the ground, falling backwards, and died at their feet.

Maaz glanced across at his father.

Mohammed stared up at the black skies and yelled her name: 'Sahira!!!'

'It had to be done, father,' said Maaz, as if they had put down a rabid dog.

'I know that, son. Go back to the car and get the petrol.'

Maaz nodded and shook himself; took the proffered keys and jogged back to the vehicle. Opened the boot, took out the can of petrol, and the matches, and ran back to his father. He was kneeling down, talking to the bloody remains of his only daughter, perhaps offering one final prayer. Who knows? Who cares? Maaz thought him soft. He couldn't hear what his father was saying. Didn't want to hear either.

Mohammed stood up.

'Over the body,' he said. 'Empty it.'

Maaz splashed the stinking, oily petrol, grinning in his work, emptying the can.

'Stand back,' said Mohammed, and they moved well away.

He struck a match and tossed it forward.

It caught in an instant.

WHOOSH!

Lighting up the area, spreading warmth, destroying everything that was there, the fine cotton cloth of her best white hijab, her flat shoes, her undergarments, her hair, her flesh, everything.

'You'd better get her case,' said Mohammed.

'Yes, father,' said Maaz, and he ran back to the car.

Aromas of roasting meat floated across the moor.

Burning meat. Overdone.

250

The bones in her hands flexed and bent, as if they were still alive, as if they were in pain, contorting like a witch, as the heat burnt away the flesh, taking longer over the bones.

Maaz was back; bag in hand.

'Open it,' said Mohammed.

Maaz did so, and in the next second they were dripping her belongings onto the fire. Maaz giggled. When it was empty, Mohammed took the open bag and ripped part of it away, nicking his wrist. Set it on the fire. Twisted off the plastic handle, threw it in the flames. Black polluting smoke swirled in the wind. They wafting it away, and threw the remains of the holdall on the fire, where it burnt to nothing.

Mohammed moved closer and kicked in some remnants of cloth that had escaped the flickering flames.

He glanced across at his son.

The flames were dancing in his wide eyes.

There was nothing else there, no emotion, just coldness and total indifference. Mohammed wiped a tear from the corner of his eye. There was nothing more to be done in those inhospitable hills.

'Your trouble is, you are far too soft,' said Maaz.

Mohammed shook his head and said, 'Take the hammer, wipe it clean of prints, and using your handkerchief, throw it into the centre of the lake.'

Maaz bobbed his head.

It seemed a good plan.

Jogged across to the reservoir, and in the moonlight his father watched him wheeling around twice, like a hammer thrower at the Olympic games. Maaz hurled the ball hammer high into the sky and listened as it splashed down into the deep and black water.

If anyone ever searched there, they would find deep water, total blackness at the bottom, and a short-handled hammer sleeping in the mud. Mohammed imagined it would never be discovered, and even if it was, it couldn't be traced to their door.

The fire was burning still, though there wasn't a lot left, as Mohammed handed the empty petrol can to Maaz, and ordered him to take it to the car and stay there.

Sitting in the vehicle, Maaz watched his father crouch down and stare into the dying embers. It was true; he was too soft. Far too soft. Then his father was back on his feet, walking toward the dark outline of the BMW, the torch beam pointing the way. He never once looked back.

Sitting together in the darkness Maaz said, 'I did the right thing, father. I did the right thing.'

It wasn't a question. It was a statement, and one issued without a shred of doubt.

'Yes, son. I know.'

'It had to be done. Now we should forget all about it. About her. Get on with living our lives. Get back to normal.'

'We must never tell the others.'

'Course not! So far as anyone is concerned, we dropped the sinning bitch at the airport. The last we saw of her, she was going through the gate.'

There was a short pause and Mohammed said, 'You didn't have any qualms?'

'About killing her, you mean?'

Mohammed nodded.

'No! None! Not after you showed me the pictures.'

The blaze hadn't gone unnoticed. Two miles to the north, they were spotted by Sandy and Gerald. They were two of the hardy walkers crazy enough to attempt the great Land's End to John O'Groats walk. They were doing the trek for charity in aid of Aids awareness, and were on track to raise more than £30K. Gerald was HIV positive. They had camped there for the night. Sandy stood up and peered southwards.

'Looks like someone's having a great party.'

Gerald stood beside him and gazed south, too. Imagined a spectacular barbecue. Roasting pork sausages with lots of mustard and tomato ketchup and cans of cider. They'd made do with a tin of beans and a cold and gristly Cornish pasty.

'Why don't we scoot back and join them,' suggested Sandy.

'Oh, I don't know,' said Gerald, sitting down again, feeling his blisters. 'If it were north of us I might go, but the idea of retreating even a hundred yards is foreign to me, sorry.'

Sandy had blisters too, but would have gone. But not alone, not without Gerald, and as the flames in the distance died down, they forgot about barbecues and fires on the horizon and fresh company, and smiled at one another in the moonlight, hugged, and hunkered down together in their small two-man tent.

Chapter Thirty-Nine

Monday morning, and the Luke Flowers decapitation murder was all over the newspapers, Internet, and TV. Someone had talked, but something else important happened that morning. It was the day of the coming of the monster. Or, to give it its full name, the Hytec Corp's of San Diego, California, Constructor System.

The monster, as it had been christened the moment the team first saw it, had been trialled in the Incident Room over the previous three weeks. That day, it would go live for the first time, and everyone was there to witness it.

From the back of the room it looked like a huge white rectangle, like a half or quarter size cinema screen, but the difference was, it was alive. In the past, whenever a presentation was made, or when a case update was required, they would do what they had always done, what every police department throughout the country did. They would use the white board and felt-tip pen method, stick photos and diagrams and names up there for everyone to see, and comment on.

No longer the case, not with the monster.

The monster could handle everything.

Joan West had badgered Walter into leading the opening presentation, but he had sidestepped that date by giving the gig to Karen. Walter wasn't averse to technology; he could appreciate what it could offer, and he would use it too, but was happier still if he wasn't the driver.

She grasped the opportunity, as he always knew she would. When does a confident and striking blonde not want to be the centre of attention? Rarely, if ever, in his experience. Everyone was there. No one wanted to miss the coming of the thing.

Karen stared at the throng and seized her moment.

Stood before them, the monster to her left shoulder, smiled and said, 'Welcome to the monster.'

Ricky, the Hytec rep, who was sitting on a desk at the back, had made a big effort to get there on time, jumped up and said, 'It's the Constructor System. Can we please call it by its correct name?'

Everyone glanced back at him without comment; then back to Karen, who was gazing at the slight Ricky. He tried a smile and winked, and she began again.

'The Constructor System,' and she beckoned toward it, and did a cute little curtsey.

The crowded room applauded.

'All right,' said Walter, 'Let's be getting on with it.'

'Luke Flowers,' she said, and she touched a tiny thumbnail photo of Luke that was in the border of the screen that only she could see; then touched the centre of the white mass and an instant colour pic of Luke appeared. It was an old pic taken from when he'd been in trouble years before, flogging counterfeit software. She tapped his face twice, and the pic grew larger, left her finger on it, and the pic grew smaller until it was just as she wanted.

'Wanted for the murder of Jeffrey Player, and the attempted murder of Neil Swaythling.'

Two more touches, two more colour pics on the screen, headshots lined up together like the defence in a sports team.

'But no more,' and she made a downward sweeping motion on each of the pics, and they fell to the floor of the screen. 'Because yesterday, Luke's decapitated body was discovered rammed down a lavatory in room fifty at the Red Rose Motel.'

More touches on thumbnails, more commands, and the monster produced six enlarged full colour pics of Luke's head and his headless body. Nothing spared, some taken in the hotel, some from the prelim report. She zoomed in and out on three of them to show what she, and the monster, could do.

Karen noted the grimacing faces and soft hum of conversation as people shifted in their seats. Some of the younger ones had never seen a decapitated body before, so much blood, and some of them had never seen a murder victim, either. There was quadraphonic

255

sound too. Doctor Sara Carney's commentary as she carried out the post-mortem.

Karen again, 'The time of the killing has been estimated at between 3pm and 4pm, Saturday just gone.'

More touches and documents appeared supporting the ToD, but not big enough to make any sense to those watching, not readable. More touches and the documents were so huge even Ricky at the back could read every word.

It was going well. He liked it and grinned at Karen, as she tried hard to ignore him.

Then she was talking again. She was a good presenter, Walter wasn't alone in thinking that, and easy on the eye, and Ricky wasn't alone in thinking that.

'Luke Flowers was held down on the bed and killed by a single blow from a sword, machete, axe, or meat industry implement.'

'How do we know he was held down?' asked Gibbons.

Walter thought that a planted question because Karen gobbled it up. Brought two new pics to the audience's attention. Luke's bare shoulders, head obvious by its absence, two sets of bruises of fingers, one on the back of either shoulder, two matching heavy thumb bruises closer to the shoulder blades.

'A man's hand,' she said. 'Medium sized, strong, holding him down. One restraining the victim, one delivering the blow, a minimum of two people, busy carrying out bloody murder.'

'Don't suppose we can get any fingerprints from that?' suggested one of the younger women.

Several of the men laughed.

Hector Browne said, 'Don't be ridiculous!'

Ricky intervened.

'That is a good question, and the answer is not yet. But we are working hard on that, and by next year with the latest enhancements we should be able to reconstruct usable fingerprints from bruises.'

'They wouldn't be allowed in any court of law,' said Gibbons.

'They could still trap a killer,' muttered Walter.

'Correct,' said Chief Superintendent Joan West, not wishing to be left out, and hoping to justify the enormous expense of Hytec's Constructor System, as she would always refer to it.

Walter nodded Karen on.

'The motel room was booked in the name of Larry King – an obvious false name. He had booked the room many times before, always insisted on room fifty for reasons of his own, and always paid in cash.'

'Any luck with CCTV?' asked Walter.

Karen beamed and said, 'Glad you asked.'

More soft touches, and a picture of the scene outside the Red Rose Motel flashed up. A car pulled in and ran across the screen. The system was live in real time, showing what was happening at the Red Rose at that exact moment.

'Wowser!' said Gibbons.

Karen touched again, and the picture switched to the corridor camera.

Iskra Kolarov was walking toward the camera, carrying her red box of potions and sprays, smiled at the technology, as she always did, because she knew someone somewhere would be watching. Her mother always said that people, especially foreigners, liked pretty girls to smile.

'Brilliant,' said Walter. 'So, where are the pictures from Saturday?'

Fact was, he knew the answer.

'There aren't any,' admitted Karen. 'System down.'

'Shit!' said Gibbons, louder than he intended.

Mrs West glanced over her shoulder and stared at him as if she had stood in dog muck.

Ricky at the back butted in, 'I'd like to add that the failed software was nothing to do with the Constructor System. Nothing to do with Hytec at all.'

'We appreciate that,' said Mrs West, glancing round and smiling at Ricky, like a mother to a favourite son.

Karen again, 'The body was found by Iskra Kolarov, the Bulgarian girl, that's the girl you just saw in the corridor.'

'She legal?' asked Hector.

257

'She is,' confirmed Walter.

'It was Iskra,' continued Karen, 'who threw up over Luke's face.' Karen saw several of them grimace.

'Who else works at the Red Rose?' asked Mrs West.

'Jack Heale, the manager, Mary McGrory, room supervisor, Mary Hussein on reception, and a small army of part-timers and temps who come and go,' said Karen.

Mrs West continued. 'One of them must have seen two, maybe more, strangers entering the hotel, carrying a large and threatening looking implement.'

'It would seem not, ma'am.'

'Could have been in a case,' said Hector.

'It could. Probably was. Carry on,' said Walter.

Karen bobbed her head and moved on to the post-mortem.

'The head was decapitated by one blow.'

More gory photographs, and a brief sight of the PM report, magnified so that it was almost as tall as Karen.

Most of them scanned it, looking for clues or inspiration, but none were forthcoming.

'So,' said Karen, 'we are now investigating the murder of the murderer we were originally seeking.'

'That's about the size of it,' said Mrs West.

'More importantly,' said Walter, 'we still don't know what this is all about. We don't know why Luke was taking pot-shots at Player and Swaythling, and we don't know why Luke was killed.'

'It looks drug orientated to me,' said Hector.

'It may look like it,' said Karen, 'but there is no history of drugs or drug dealing involving Player, Swaythling, or Flowers.'

'So how did Flowers make his living?' asked Mrs West.

For the moment, the monster seemed to be out of the loop.

'It's possible that he was paid for carrying out the killing,' suggested Walter.

'A hit man,' added Gibbons.

'Don't like the term,' said Walter, 'but that seems likely.'

'Unless he was into software piracy in a big way,' suggested WPC Jenny Thompson.

'I think he'd left that gig behind long ago,' said Gibbons. 'Not enough cash in it, if you ask me.'

Ricky joined in from the back.

'Software piracy is a big problem, and some business software can cost £20,000 or £30,000 a pop.'

They turned and gawped at the systems rep who had suddenly become part of the investigation team.

'Thank you, Ricky,' said Mrs West, smiling at him. 'That's most useful. Anything else you can tell us.'

'Comes in from China usually. Worth big bucks, but it is specialised. You'd need to have contacts in big business. It's not an easy sell,' and he added a rider, aware that all eyes were on him, 'I would imagine.'

'This thing is not about software,' said Walter. 'There was none in Luke's flat. He had left that behind. It's something to do with Neil Swaythling.'

'But what?' asked Mrs West.

'I don't know,' said Walter, 'but I have closed down the Neil Swaythling protection programme and sent him home.'

Mrs West nodded, happy to have that unnecessary expense off the book.

'So if it's not drug related, and it's not software piracy, what is it about?' asked Gibbons.

'Non payment of loans?' suggested Karen, back on the monster, bringing up fresh faces, Langley Wells and his three monkeys of sons.

'That's more like it,' said Walter. 'And Neil Swaythling's father could still be involved in this somewhere.'

More monster prods and Gerry Swaythling's still picture appeared. Not a great shot, and then more video taken by Jenny and Hector from the solicitor's office opposite the Masonic Lodge, Gerry grinning and going inside.

Gibbons recognised the location and looked uncomfortable, realised his pic could be up next. Karen noted that too.

'So where do we go from here?' asked Mrs West.

'I want everyone to lean on any contacts they might have,' said Walter. 'Go round the lowlife pubs and clubs tonight. We all know which ones they are, put a bit of pressure on. All we want to know is what this is about. Discover the cause, and we'll find the killers.'

'Good,' said Mrs West, turning round and smiling at Ricky again. 'Thank you, Ricky,' she said. 'Very nice.'

'Anyone anything else they'd like to add?' asked Karen.

'What else can this thing do?' asked Gibbons.

She was happy to demonstrate, as was Ricky, grinning at the thought of her showing it off. She brought up a map of Britain, and touched on Chester. The map zoomed in. 'Give me an address,' she said.

'Percy Road, Handbridge,' said Jenny.

In seconds, the map located the road.

'It can bring up in moments any street map from any town in the UK. Works on speech recognition. It's amazing.'

'Pity it's not actual pictures,' said Hector Browne.

Karen grinned. Touched an icon and the map on the screen switched from map format to the view of Percy Road from space. Karen zoomed in until the roof tiles on an individual house were clearly visible.

'Jesus!' said an impressed Gibbons.

'Mind your language!' said Mrs West.

'You can bring up pictures of any street, any house, any pub, any factory, any river, field, bridge, forest, mountain, church, graveyard, in Britain, any time you want, you name it.'

'Can you put up the Red Rose Motel?' asked Walter.

'Sure, Guv,' said Karen, two prods, maybe three, and there it was, as she zoomed in and out.

'Leave it just there,' said Walter.

The aerial view was from an angle, the bedroom windows visible, overlooking the car park, only one way in and one way out.'

'What are you thinking?' asked Mrs West.

'Just wondering which guests might have seen the killers coming and going.'

'All along that side for sure,' said Karen, pointing at the windows.

'Only if they were looking out of the window,' said Gibbons. 'When I am in a hotel I don't spend my time gawping out of bloody windows.'

'We won't ask what you would be doing,' muttered Hector.

Gibbons grinned and muttered, 'Shaddup.'

'Let's try those visitors on that side again. Anyone who arrived before say, half-past twelve on Saturday,' said Walter. 'Someone must have seen two anxious looking men arriving together, two people we have not been able to account for. We might get a break.'

There was a short pause and Karen said, 'Anything else?'

No one had. The monster had passed its first audition, and was put into standby mode, temporarily dead, definitely alive, always there, waiting and brooding and hoping to solve dastardly crimes, as the human beings went back to their day-to-day duties, searching for food to feed it.

Ten minutes later and Walter said to Karen, 'I want to go back to the Red Rose. Something isn't right there.'

'OK, Guv, when?'

'Give me an hour.'

The phone before them burbled and Karen snatched it up.

Walter heard her say, 'Yes, he's here, just a moment.'

She held her hand over the mouthpiece and said, 'It's your girlfriend?'

He smiled; in a ridiculously optimistic moment he imagined it might be Galina the cleaner. Picked up the phone, said in as syrupy a voice as Karen had ever witnessed, 'Hello you, what can I do for you?'

'Who's been a naughty boy, then?'

Chapter Forty

It was 2am before Mohammed and Maaz arrived back at the State, plenty of time to reflect on the day, and the night, and perfect their stories. Closing in on Chester, they'd stopped at a remote spot and dumped the petrol can in the canal, and when they arrived home were surprised to find Ahmed still up.

'The old man gone to bed?' asked Maaz, acting out the everything's fine routine.

'Yeah, he gets tired, I'm worried about him,' replied Ahmed. 'Everything go all right?'

'Yes,' said Mohammed. 'The sinner should be somewhere over the Arabian Gulf by now,' and he shared a nervous look with Maaz, as Ahmed stared at his shoes.

'Just forget her,' said Maaz. 'It's finished with. She's gone for good. Let's get back to normal. We are better off without her.'

For what she had done and the shame she brought down on the family, Ahmed concurred, and he went downstairs and locked up and they all went to bed. Mohammed was the last to find sleep. He'd been wondering about Maaz's wellbeing, and whether he was taking his medication. He'd check on that in the morning. He said the last prayers of the day and lay on his back on the bed. Beside him, Akleema slumbered on, unaware her man had returned, unaware that he had witnessed the murder of their only daughter.

He couldn't sleep and got up and went to the lavatory. Sat there for a long time, thinking, replaying the horrific events of the night in his head, flicking through the pictures as he did so.

The fire in the long grass had long gone out. A black stain on the landscape, very little left, ash, fragments of human being, fragments

262

of bone, traces of woman's clothing, and part of her skull, not immediately recognisable. It could have been a sizeable chunk of charcoal from the end of a decent log, burnt in a campfire. It wasn't something most people would stop and examine, though if they did they might have given it a kick.

Inside the chunk of skull, protected from the blaze, sat a perfect set of blackened teeth.

'Who's been a naughty boy, then?'

'Who's this?' said an irritable Walter as he adjusted the phone.

'Oh Walter, have your forgotten me already?'

'Who is this!'

'Gardenia Floem of course, your favourite crime reporter.'

'It's Inspector Darriteau to you!'

'Sorry... Inspector... Darriteau, but you have been a naughty man, misleading us all with that ruse of yours that Neil Swaythling was dead. You didn't fool me, as I said before, and I don't think you fooled many others either. It was all too neat and convenient.'

'What can I do for you, Mizz Floem?'

'Who killed Luke Flowers, Inspector?'

'No idea. Who do you think?'

'Oh, don't ask me. I ask the questions, not answer them.'

'I ask questions too.'

'Yes, of course you do, but here's another one from me. Should the Cestrian public be alarmed at the outbreak of what appears to be a spate of gangland murders in their otherwise idyllic city?'

'If you know of any connection to gangland murders, Mizz Floem, perhaps you could enlighten me.'

'What else could they be?'

'I don't know, that's why I am investigating, a task you are keeping me from.'

'So sorry to delay you, Inspector, I'll be in touch.'

'Don't bother!' though by the time Walter said that, she had gone.

Karen drove them back to the Red Rose in an unmarked car. Nothing much had changed; a few different cars in the car park, not rushed off their feet, though there was plenty of time left in the day. There was no sign of any photographers or TV newshounds. They'd all been and sniffed round and click-click-clicked and had headed off somewhere else.

It was a bright day, almost no cloud, and as Walter stepped from the car he glanced into the sky to where he imagined the satellite might be stationed. Couldn't see a thing, shaded his eyes and squinted in a different direction. Same thing, not a thing.

'What are you looking for?' Karen asked, gazing across at him.

'Oh, nothing.'

'You can't see them with the naked eye, and not during the day.'

Walter bobbed his head and headed for the entrance.

'Seems strange to think we are being photographed as we go about our daily business.'

'That's the modern world for you.'

'You don't think they'd have any pics of the two guys parking the car and going inside?'

Karen laughed her neat laugh and said, 'Don't think so, Guv, and even if they did, they'd never share their images with us. They'd be too scared of litigation.'

Yeah, thought Walter, everyone was frightened of being taken to court in twenty-first century Britain, but not by the police, but by litigators and ambulance chasing solicitors. Too many people viewed the law as a potential earner, especially rogues when they were released from custody, or found not guilty, or had their convictions overturned.

There was a new girl on the counter, a temp they hadn't seen before, skinny, pale, mousy hair, bad spectacles, eminently forgettable, name of Cynthia. Mr Heale wasn't there, but she summoned him and a couple of minutes later he slipped into the reception area from the corridor.

'Just a few more quick questions,' said Walter.

Heale sighed and took them through to his tiny office, enough room for one chair on either side of a small desk, three grey metal filing cabinets away to his left. Walter sat down. Karen stood in the doorway.

'Fire away,' said Heale, glancing at his watch, giving the impression of busy-ness.

'This CCTV system you have.'

'What of it?'

'How reliable is it?'

Heale nodded his head and said, 'Pretty good, cost a lot of money, why do you ask?'

'But it didn't work on the day of the murder?'

'Seems that way.'

'How often does it fail?' asked Karen.

'Oh, let me see,' and he sat back with his hands behind his head as if thinking. He needed deodorant. 'Can't remember off the top of my head, but it will be logged.'

'Try a guess?' asked Walter.

Heale pulled a surprised face, shook his head; blew out from his closed mouth, rippling his lips, making a silly horse-like sound.

'Oh, I dunno, a month, maybe two.'

'Could it have been turned off deliberately?'

'By whom?'

Walter's turn to say, 'Dunno... you tell me.'

'I don't think so. Don't see the point.'

'How about the girl on the counter, Mary Hussein? Might she have turned it off?'

Karen added, 'Either deliberately or accidentally?'

'I wouldn't have thought so, but it's not a difficult thing to do. Throw one switch and off it goes.'

'So she could have turned it off,' said Karen, 'When the guys came in, and back on again after they had left.'

Heale smiled. 'She could have done, but she wouldn't. She's a reliable person, quiet and conscientious, a valued member of the team, and there's no way she would get mixed up in anything like that. She's hardly likely to become involved in conspiracy to murder, is she?'

Walter pulled a face. Didn't answer. Then he asked, 'How long has she worked here?'

'Five, maybe six years.'

'Where does she live?' asked Karen.

'32 Fisher Street in Hoole.'

He'd answered without hesitation, hadn't needed to look it up, Walter noted that. How many bosses would know the home addresses of their young female staff? Especially the prettier ones like Mary. Probably quite a few, and Heale certainly did. Maybe he was giving her a lift into work, maybe more. Walter would try him with another question.

'Where does the Bulgarian girl live? Iskra whatshername?'

'Kolarov, it's Kolarov, I don't know, I think she lives in Hoole too, but I'd have to look it up.'

'Do that, please,' said Karen.

Heale went to the nearest filing cabinet, screeched it open, found the address, gave it to Karen, and she noted it down, along with the other one, and after that they said thanks and drove off toward Hoole.

32 Fisher Street was a three-story Edwardian red sandstone house set in a row of similar properties. It was tall and narrow with small bay windows, long windows from top to bottom, almost no front garden, two steps through the gate and they were at the front door. Karen buzzed the bell. Mary Hussein came to the door, surprised to see them. She was dressed in some kind of paint smudged overall as if she was decorating.

'We've a few more questions about the murder at the motel,' said Karen.

'You'd better come in,' she said, though Walter imagined she wasn't thrilled at the prospect. She held the part-glazed door open and nodded them down the long and narrow hallway, toward a sizeable kitchen cum breakfast room at the rear.

To the right was a modern fitted kitchen, not top of the range, but not budget either, to the left three mismatched armchairs, small and well used, a big square grey TV pushed into the corner, open double doors to a lean-to conservatory fixed on the back. It looked hot in there too under the summer sun. In the centre of the main room was a large old- fashioned square dining table, and on the table was a canvas and a pot of paintbrushes and various oil paints.

'You paint?' asked Walter.

'I try,' she said. 'Badly,' a little embarrassed as they gazed down at her efforts. It was pretty good, maybe half finished, a picture of a man's face, not Heale, an Asian man, good head of hair, prominent nose, hard looking eyes, if the portrait was true.

'Someone you know?' asked Karen.

Mary nodded. 'Yeah, it's father, least it's supposed to be,' and she nodded across at the wall and a bank of mixed framed family photographs. Karen and Walter took a look. Several of Mary, at school, in the brownies, a leaving school pic, a growing up teenager pic, an only child, judging by the lack of anyone else, and three photos of her parents. The same Asian guy, she was a talented painter; the hard eyes were spot on, and a white woman, presumably her mother.

'Your mum and dad?' asked Walter.

She nodded, not over-keen on talking about them. Then she said, 'Take a seat,' and pointed at the armchairs.

Walter sat down. Karen stood in the hall doorway.

'It seems too much of a coincidence that the CCTV went off when the killers came into the motel, and then on again after they had left,' said Walter.

She shook her head, didn't know what to say, and said, 'That's what happened.'

'Tell me about the man who booked the room?'

'You mean the man I knew as Larry King?'

'The same.'

'Not much to tell, short bloke, unremarkable.'

'You didn't find him attractive?' asked Karen.

'Certainly not!'

267

'Lots of girls did.'

'Well, not me!'

'Why did he want the room?' asked Walter.

'How should I know?'

'Oh, come on, Miss Hussein, don't be awkward. You must wonder what your guests get up to in their rooms in the middle of the afternoon.'

'I do not! I have far too much to do to bother with silly gossip.'

'He wasn't alone, was he?' asked Karen.

'Obviously not, someone must have killed him.'

'We don't mean that,' said Walter, 'as I think you know.'

'I did not see anyone come or go from that room.'

'What about on previous visits?' asked Karen.

'I can't remember.'

'Oh, come on, Miss Hussein, try,' said Walter. 'We both know he was a regular visitor, always booking in early in the afternoons. He had a girl there, didn't he, or a woman?'

'Mr Heale says we must be a model of discretion. What goes on in the rooms is none of our business. I don't know and I don't care, I don't pay any attention to it. I just do my job.'

'Miss Hussein, a young man has been decapitated in your hotel,' said Karen. 'Aren't you in the least bit interested in that?'

She shrugged her shoulders. Drew a thin brush from the pot of paints. Walter wanted to smack it from her hand. Shifted in his seat. Gazed at Karen.

'As I said, discretion-discretion, I want to make a career in the hotel industry. If people want to get up to all sorts, that is nothing to do with me. Jack says I can go a long way in this business; says I might even land his job when he moves on to better things.'

'Mr Heale?' said Walter.

Mary nodded. Slipped the paintbrush back in the pot. Sensible girl.

'Did you ever see the woman?' asked Karen.

'No, course not... well, I must have done, but I don't remember. People come and go every minute of the day. After a while, all the faces merge into one. I just don't remember.'

'Does Mr Heale, Jack, know who the woman is?' asked Karen.

268

'Pfft! How would I know? Don't think so. You'd have to ask him.'
Walter took a card from his pocket and set it on the table.

'We are investigating a brutal murder, Miss Hussein. If you think of anything that might help, or remember anything about his visitors, call me.'

A brief pause and she said, 'OK,' but it was an unconvincing reply, and they didn't expect her to ring, and after that, she showed them out, and a minute later they were back in the car, driving back toward the station.

Chapter Forty-One

Walter changed his mind as to where they were going. 'Take me to see Langley Wells.' Karen said, 'OK, Guv,' and switched lanes in a hurry and glanced across at him and wondered what he had in mind. He was sitting back in his seat, eyes closed as if asleep.

She thought better than to disturb him, and ten minutes later they were pulling to a standstill outside Langley's house.

Walter opened his eyes. No four by fours on display. No sons home by the look of it, and that was how he wanted it. Karen buzzed the bell. Rose came to the door.

Surprised to see them.

'What do you want?'

'Hello, Rose. We'd like to see Langley.'

'What about? He's not expecting you.'

'I want to thank him.'

'That'll be a first,' she muttered, and then she said, 'wait here,' and she invited them into the hall and scuttled off to find her husband.

Karen imagined she could hear strident, muffled voices. Walter didn't pick up a thing, though his hearing was not what it once was. Rose came back, muttering, 'You'd better go through, you know where it is.'

Langley was sitting behind his desk, no sign of the boys, and both Walter and Karen gained the impression of an office hastily cleansed of records. The desk was as clean as before, just a pot of pens, and they both wondered what spreadsheets and ledgers and paperwork had been hidden in the previous minute.

'Darriteau,' said Langley, not bothering to get up. He didn't speak to Karen, just gave her the once over. 'What's this all about?'

270

'Hello, Langley,' said Walter, and not waiting to be invited, he sat in the guest chair. 'I thought I'd stop by and thank you.'

'Thank me? That's a first. Thank me for what?'

'For putting me on to Luke Flowers.'

'It won't happen again, so don't get carried away, and it didn't do the kid any good, did it?'

'That's what I wanted to explore.'

Langley let go a high-pitched, hyena-like laugh and glanced at the ceiling. Karen fought to keep a straight face and looked away.

'Explore? Explore what?'

'We need to find out who carried out this barbaric killing.'

'Don't look at me. It's nothing to do with us.'

'I'll take your word for that, Langley, but who is it to do with?'

Langley smiled and scratched his scalp.

'If I knew, I wouldn't tell ya, but I don't know, so I can't. Get my drift.'

'No hints at all?' said Karen.

He stared at the girl. Policing wasn't a woman's business. She should be home raising a family and making the dinner, and more than one of his sons had intimated they would be happy to accommodate her, except she was a rozzer, and rozzers would never be accepted in the Wells' world.

'So you've nothing more to tell us?' said Walter. 'No pointers?'

'Bugger all!' he said, smiling at Karen.

'You know where I am, if you hear anything. Barbarians like that have no place in society.'

Langley shook his head, didn't say a word, and then right on cue, Rose appeared, ready to show them out.

As Karen drove back toward the station, she said, 'Do you think they are capable of such a barbaric killing?'

'The Langley family? Oh, they are capable all right, I could imagine it too. But I don't see why Langley would tell us about Luke, and then kill him. That doesn't make much sense.'

271

'No,' said Karen. 'It doesn't. But those three sons of his give me the heebie-jeebies, and couldn't you just see it?'

Walter could, and all too clearly, that was the problem. Lawrie holding Luke down, Lenny swinging the axe, and Lewis on the door as lookout, maybe slipping Mary Hussein fifty quid to turn a blind eye, and turn off the cameras for half an hour. Yeah, the pictures were graphic, they could both envision them as clear as day. It didn't mean it had happened that way, didn't mean to say they had done it, couldn't think of a reason why they would, though it didn't make the vivid images disappear.

Back at the station, the first call Karen fielded was from Mrs Holly Swaythling. She passed the phone to Walter.

'I'd just like to thank you, Inspector.'

She sounded tired, but happy too, different to before.

'Thank me for what, Mrs Swaythling?'

'For keeping Neil safe, and for returning him to us in one piece.'

'That's what we are here for.'

'Terrible about that young boy.'

'Luke? Yes, a great pity, but play with fire and you will get burnt.'

'And there's more good news.'

'There is?'

'Yes, you'll never guess what, you remember Suzanne Knight, Gerry's er… his floozy on the side.'

'Yes, what about her?'

'Well, she was so upset about the attacks on Neil that she let slip that she was concerned about him, more than concerned, if you get my drift. To cut a long story short, her and Neil have kind of got together. I can't tell you how happy it's makes me feel. Neil practically lives here again now.'

'I see. That is a turn up. What does Gerry think about that?'

'Tell you the truth, Inspector, I'm not sure he's cottoned on. But when he does, he's in for a big surprise,' and she laughed like she hadn't laughed in months, and Walter laughed too, and then she

272

said, 'I don't really care what he thinks. Bye, Inspector, and thanks again.'

After that, the week petered out and on Saturday morning Walter waited in for Galina the cleaner. She was busy in the kitchen, up to her elbows in hot bubbly water, washing the dishes that he'd let build up in the sink.

The old portable TV was on, twelve-inch screen, set on the end of the worktop, screwed down so it couldn't move nearer the water, tuned to one of the news channels, as it always was, and there was a lot of news that morning. Walter could tell that from the excited frisson in the newscasters' voices.

Three big breaking stories, all vying for lead vocal, each trying hard to elbow the others off the screen.

Crime, Terror, and Weird Sport.

The terror was live from Moscow.

A suicide bomber had blown herself up in Moscow's largest and most modern supermarket, Saturday morning, busiest time. The early casualty figures were horrendous, and would rise as the day wore on. Ninety-two dead they were reporting, running with newsreel pictures, probably taken on someone's mobile, showing smoke and debris and human beings lying around in unnatural positions, amongst tins of meat and dead chickens, and smashed bottles of premium vodka, and frantic melons rolling every which way. Galina glanced over her shoulder and stared at the tiny screen.

'Terrible, Mr Darto,' she said. 'Bad men, bad woman, terrible.'

'Suicide bomber, by the look of it.'

'Unbelievable!' and then she said, 'Mind you Russia,' though she pronounced it Roo-si-a, 'Roo-si-a bad to Chechnya, Chechnya bad back,' and she shrugged her shoulders as if she agreed with the eye-for-an-eye philosophy.

'Terrible,' echoed Walter, pondering on what might happen if suicide bombers ever came to provincial England, to Chester. It was a thought that didn't bear thinking about, and he prayed he would never live to see it.

The robotic news gal moved on, as if she had a great deal to get through, as if she didn't have time to think about the pictures and words and the death that spewed out, as if it was nothing to do with her, somehow make believe, unreal, manufactured stories for the masses. She had a programme to complete, and was determined to do so, and time was tight. She was on to the crime story.

The remains of a body had been found on the moors north-east of Manchester, most likely a woman's body, burned beyond recognition. Dull pictures followed from the foothills of the misty Pennines, a weary-looking bloke of a reporter, squinting up the hill at a bleak and cold reservoir, and back to the police tent in the near distance, erected over the remains.

'So far the body has not been identified,' sniffed the bloke. 'In fact it may never be identified, so badly burned was it, but we believe it is the body of a young woman, though that has yet to be confirmed.'

Walter watched the pictures with interest, listened to the words, as did every off-duty police officer the length and breadth of Britain. Because that is what police officers do everywhere, because they just might learn something from pictures from afar, and anyway, bodies were often dumped by murderers miles away from the scenes of their crimes, and sometimes hundreds of miles away. You only had to recall the number of Scottish murderers arrested on the south coast of England, and vice versa, to see that was true.

The television in the State of Kerala private apartment was on, a forty-eight inch high definition 3D beast, latest top of the range model that Mohammed had insisted they acquire. What was the point in working all hours that God sent if there wasn't an occasional perk, like a magnificent new television that had cost the equivalent of six month's wages for a waiter?

Wazir had been against it from the beginning, the frittering away of hard-earned money on frippery, he said, and Ahmed too, but Maaz was all for it, as young people always are when it comes to acquiring modern technology.

Maaz was there too, watching the screen, as was his father, Mohammed. Wazir was enjoying a lie-in, for he was getting more tired with each passing month. They were eating a late breakfast. Akleema was also there, reading a woman's magazine, and Nadirah, sewing, though heaven knows why shel felt the need to sew.

Maaz glanced across at Mohammed and back at the screen. Father saw a hint of excitement in his son's eyes, and shook his head and looked away. Maaz didn't. He was glued to the pictures.

'What's that all about?' asked Akleema, looking up from her celeb gossip pages.

'Some human remains found on the moors,' said Mohammed. 'Change channel, Maaz.'

'No!' he said. 'I want to watch this,' and the men shared another hard look, and the newscast stayed on.

The broadcast switched to the red brick Manchester Police Headquarters close to Old Trafford. Walter knew the building well. He'd been there several times, knew some of the officers too, though there was no guarantee they would still be there.

A police press conference was in full swing. Two guys in their forties, one in uniform, one not, and a short-haired woman in her thirties, full uniform boasting several medal ribbons. He didn't know any of them, doubted if they were even from Manchester, judging by their accents. The woman was speaking. She had a strident voice, a little like their own Mrs West. Maybe a strident voice was a prerequisite for successful women in the force. It was an interesting theory.

'We should have more information when the body has been identified. That is proving difficult. Our main hope is a full set of good teeth, and we will be following that up in the coming hours and days.'

'Can you confirm it is a woman?' asked one reporter.

'Yes, I can.'

'Can you say what age?'

'Not for certain, but we believe between fifteen and thirty.'

There was a brief break as if for once the hacks couldn't think of anything else to ask, and then an older guy at the back announced himself from a Manchester local radio station, and asked, 'Can you comment on speculation that the death is some kind of honour killing?'

The woman officer looked shocked, thrown, as if the hack had hit a raw nerve. She went to speak but stopped and turned to her right and said, 'I think Chief Superintendent Gitts might have something to say about that.'

The grey-haired man began speaking. He was lean with a hard face, and was the senior officer the force put up to face the press.

'There is no such thing as an honour killing,' he snapped. 'The whole idea of any kind of honour being attached to cold-blooded murder is a travesty. Whoever is responsible for this death will be hunted down,' and he nodded a little nod to the press officer, a nod that Walter knew well, and one that he had used many times before himself. The "I've had enough of this nonsense, the conference is over nod", and sure enough the gathering was brought to an early end, and the TV feed reverted to the studio.

In the State, Maaz smiled to himself.

Akleema asked, 'What is an honour killing?'

'They don't know what they are talking about,' said Maaz. 'They haven't a bloody clue,' and Mohammed wanted to scream at his son and tell him to shut up, but couldn't, and then Ahmed came in and said, 'Am I the only one working here today? Have you forgotten we have a Chester Rugby Club lunch at twelve, fifty-two covers, and time is getting on.'

The phone rang, and Akleema picked up.

'The State of Kerala bespoke Indian Restaurant,' she said in her best curry house gooey voice.

Maaz squirmed in his chair and thought, what a load of bollocks.

'It's for you, Ahmed,' Akleema called through the open door. 'Imam Sabir at the mosque.'

276

Galina finished the dishes and was busy emptying and cleaning the stainless steel sink. She glanced back at the TV.

'What that all about?' she said.

Walter pulled a face. 'Dunno. Some unfortunate young woman murdered, listening to that. The body burnt. Dreadful.'

'More bad men?'

'Looks that way. Don't you have bad men in Ukraine?'

She gave him a smirk and said, 'Course, but everyone know who they are, and ignore. Just ignore.'

If only it was that easy, thought Walter, and then she said, 'They should send for you, Mr Darto. You find bad men pronto,' and she giggled and began filling the yellow plastic bowl with boiling water, God knows what for, Walter thought, but didn't say. He didn't like to interfere in such matters, and would always leave an energetic cleaning woman to get on with whatever business she was about.

Galina disappeared up the hall in a flurry of steam and chemical cleaner aroma, and Walter sipped his coffee and glanced back at the news gal. She was pressing on regardless, still more vital news to relay to the nation, and she had switched to the day's sports story, the weird sports story.

'Liverpool City Football Club has announced that Jermaine Keating will not play for the club again this year. This comes after it was announced late last night that Mr Keating, seen here at a recent appearance at the Ness Gardens fete, had failed a drugs test taken after the Cup Final, believed to be for cocaine. In the last few minutes the club has announced that this is the second time Mr Keating has failed a routine test. He has been suspended pending a full inquiry and is believed to have left the UK. There have been reports, so far unconfirmed, that he is undergoing treatment in a Swiss addiction clinic. A spokesman for the Football Association announced earlier this morning that Mr Keating would not be considered for England internationals for the foreseeable future.'

Walter pulled another knowing face. He would be a big loss. Keating's goals had been almost solely responsible for England sitting top of their qualifying group, not to mention his importance to Liverpool City FC, whose surging revival and return to the following season's Champion's League had been fired on the back of Keating's impressive strike record.

There was something else that interested him.

During his team's recent trawl through the low-life bars and clubs and snouts and grasses and bookmakers and drug addicts, a trawl that had picked up precisely zero to do with Luke Flowers' beheading, one or two of the team had picked up crazy rumours that there was a contract out for a hundred big ones on the head of a famous sportsman. No names, no pack drill, no ID, no further information available, and most of the team laughed it off and assumed, if indeed there was anything to it, it was something to do with the jockey who had failed to bring home the red hot favourite in the previous April's Grand National meeting at Aintree.

Could those threats have something to do with Jermaine Keating; pondered Walter, and more specifically, with Luke Flowers?

Could that be why Keating had fled the country?

Could there be more to this story than met the eye?

All possible, but nothing more than crazy speculation. The mind can take one to strange places on the back of a titbit of intel.

The news gal returned. She would not be denied. Smiled and said, 'And now it's straight back to Moscow for the latest casualty figures…' salivating, as if it was a sports scoreboard, and everyone must share in the updated numbers.

Walter heard Galina coming down the stairs and remembered there was something he wanted to ask her before he left her to it and went back to work.

278

Chapter Forty-Two

When Galina came down the stairs, she found Walter standing in the middle of the sitting room, hands in trouser pockets, bouncing back and forth on his toes, as if deep in thought. 'Ah, there you are,' he said. 'There's something I want to ask you.'

She lowered her head and focused on him and said, 'Yes, and what is that?'

'I am thinking of getting the room done out,' and he waved his hand around the room, in case she didn't understand. 'You know, decorated, smartened up.'

'Oh, yes,' she said, wondering where the conversation was heading.

'What do you think? What should I do? Any ideas? What needs doing?'

She glanced at his possessions, as if she had never seen them before.

'Filth!' she said.

It seemed a favourite word of hers, but she was in the filth game. Filth removal, filth relocation, filth destruction.

'What would you do?'

Another defiant look. 'Me?'

Walter nodded.

'Easy! Get rid!'

'What? Rid of everything?' he said, peering round to see if there was anything worth saving.

Galina nodded fast.

'Everything!' she said. 'Chairs, carpet, wallpaper, television, lamps, everything. Get rid, gazoom! Start again!'

'The whole lot?' said Walter, unable to resist a smirk.

'Deffo!' she said, revealing she had been mixing with, or listening to, some locals.

'Deffo!' she said again and then added, 'You want me to cook meal for you this week?'

Walter waggled his head, put on his thinking face, and said, 'All right, if you're sure.'

Galina smiled and said, 'I sure. Monday night?'

'Monday night's good.'

'Fine. I come Monday, six thirty OK?'

'Six thirty is fine. If I'm not back by then let yourself in and make yourself at home.'

'I do,' she said, as Walter took his wallet from the back pocket of his trousers. Opened it, took out a big note, and proffered it to the girl. 'For the dinner.'

'No! No!' she said. 'I buy meat, I pay meat, my idea, I pay,' and before he could say another word, she took a step toward him, took the note from his hand, took the wallet from his other hand, opened the wallet, slipped the note back inside, turned him round, jammed the wallet back in his trouser pocket, and patted it before he could say chicken bloody Kiev.

Walter sighed and shook his head and tried to remember where he had left his black shoes.

'I'll have to go to work,' he said. 'Time's getting on.'

'I not keep you,' she said, and she switched on the cleaner and frantic back and forward motion began.

Half an hour later he was sitting at his desk, eyes closed, arms locked behind his head. The place was busy, seeking murderers, Saturday morning or not. There had been a quick run on the monster, but not for long; and it hadn't revealed much, hadn't solved the crime, and the thing had been wheeled back against the wall as if it were a naughty boy, and switched off. Good job Mrs West wasn't there to witness it.

They weren't making any progress in finding Luke's killers, and neither had they solved the mystery as to why Luke had been going round taking pot-shots at various young men.

Karen came in. It was her day off, but this was a serious investigation and she had taken on the "I must never miss a thing" theory that Walter revelled in. She was wearing casual clothes, Walter noticed that. A long white tee shirt, or was it a short skirt, he couldn't tell, over the top of black cord jeans. Seemed a funny kind of garb to him, but what did he know?

His interest in fashion had stopped at the end of the seventies when his kipper ties, naturally permed hair, flared trousers flapping in time to disco music, and monster collars were the in thing. Still occasionally worn when there was nothing else clean to hand, and that provoked a laugh or two. He didn't care. Clothes were to keep you warm, and cover up your modesty, and not much else. To Walter, they served no other purpose.

She sat opposite and said, 'Can't stay long, got a girly lunch booked, five of us, going to Pierre's.'

'Lucky you.'

'Anything happening?'

'Nothing concrete. See the news this morning?'

'Yeah, terrible, death toll now 108, so they say.'

'Didn't mean that?'

'What then? The Jermaine Keating thing? Looks like our info might have been right. If there was a contract out to kill Keating, maybe Luke Flowers had something to do with that, and maybe that was why Luke was killed.'

'Just what I was thinking.'

'Keating's out of the country.'

'Yes he is, but he wasn't at the time of Luke's death.'

'You don't think it was him, do you?' she said, linking her hands together and leaning forward across the desk toward him, her eyes confirming the excitement in her voice.

'I don't think it's anyone in particular. But I'd like a general chat with Mr Keating, if only to discover why his name keeps cropping up. Find out if he's got an alibi.'

'He has, Guv. Playing football in front of 55,000 observant souls. Cast iron, I'd say,' and she grinned at him.

'Yes, well, even if he has, a bloke like that with more money than sense, he must know people, some crazy people who'd be only too pleased to serve their hero, and it would only cost the main man half a week's wages, if that, so he could afford it.'

'Do you know what? I think you could be on to something.'

'Maybe, ring the club. Find out where he is, and when he's coming back. Fix an official appointment, and when we get that, we'll turn up early and take them by surprise. Counter attack, isn't that what they are famous for?'

Karen shrugged. 'Don't ask me, Guv.'

'Give it a whirl.'

'I'll ring the club in a tick.'

'But strangely enough, Karen, it wasn't that news story that interested me either.'

'What else was there?'

'The one about the human remains on the moors.'

'Didn't see that. What was that about?'

Ahmed Khan picked up the phone and said, 'Imam Sabir, so nice to hear your voice again. What can I do for you?'

'Is that you, Ahmed?'

'Yes, Imam.'

'Are you alone?'

Ahmed paused and glanced across at Maaz.

Maaz was interested in the call. He had been expecting it. Tried to listen. The women had gone out, and so had Mohammed. Wazir was getting washed and shaved, and only Maaz remained.

'Not quite, Imam.'

'Can you be so?'

'That can be arranged.'

Ahmed held his hand over the phone and said, 'Maaz, go downstairs and help your father, and close the door behind you.'

For a moment Maaz pretended he hadn't heard.

'Go downstairs!' repeated Ahmed, pointing to the door.

Maaz pulled an insolent face and sighed and left the room, closing the door on the way out.

282

'Is there a problem, Imam?'

'It would appear that way.'

'Can you enlighten me?'

'The warlord's wife has not arrived.'

Walter scratched his chin and nodded at Karen and said, 'A body of a young woman was found burnt beyond recognition on the moors above Manchester.'

'Didn't hear about that.'

'Unrecognisable, except for a perfect set of teeth.'

'That might be enough.'

'It could well be.'

'So what about it?'

'It was something that some hack asked.'

'Like what?'

'He asked the officers if they would make a comment on the gossip going round Manchester that it was an honour killing.'

'Honour killing? Awful phrase.'

'Precisely. Terrible term that was slapped down by the senior officer.'

'Comes from India, doesn't it?'

'Yeah, there or thereabouts. It's the old, old story. Been going on since history began. Each of our tribes prefers our children to marry our own kind, and then the kids ignore their parent's thinking and advice, and as if to be awkward, they fall in love with someone from a different tribe, and a different gene pool.'

Karen was quiet for a few moments, as if thinking, and then she said, 'What did your parents say on the subject?'

Walter laughed a short, sharp laugh, and said, 'I have no idea, I haven't spoken to either of my parents for almost fifty years.'

'Sorry,' she said, forgetting for a moment they were both long dead, both died when he was a boy, indeed his mother when giving birth. Karen imagined she had touched a raw nerve.

'Don't be.'

'So what did your aunty whatsername say?'

'Mimosa. Aunt Mimosa,' and Walter smiled at her memory, and her wisdom. 'She said I should find a nice brown girl... with bumps.'

'Bumps?' smirked Karen.

'Yes, bumps, and in the right places.'

Karen grinned. 'You mean curvaceous?'

'Yes, if you prefer.'

'So what happened?'

'She wouldn't have me. The brown girl with bumps.'

'Ah, then you have a problem.'

'Yes, I did.'

'So what's your idea on this honour killing business?'

'I got round to thinking.'

'About what?'

'Luke Flowers.'

'And?'

'Could that be some kind of honour killing?'

Karen giggled. 'Don't think so, Guv. I think you'll find it's the girl who is the victim of an honour killing, or slaughtering, to give it its correct title. I haven't heard of a boy being killed, and never an English boy.'

'I don't mean that.'

'So what do you mean?'

'I mean, could he have become involved with a girl from a different tribe?'

'You mean a different colour?'

'I don't know what I mean, just different, and the elders in the tribe, whatever that tribe may be, took offence, maybe gave him a warning, a warning he didn't heed, and the next thing is they fix up a meet at a regular place, and he runs along there pretty damn quick.'

'Like the Red Rose?'

Walter bobbed his head and said, 'And the CCTV mysteriously goes on strike that same afternoon.'

'And the CCTV is controlled by another who is from a different tribe.'

'You got it.'

284

'You could be on to something. Shall we pull in Mary Hussein and put it to her?'

'Not yet. I want you to ring Manchester. Get them to email over a copy of the odontogram.'

'The tooth map, right?'

'You got it.'

'You don't think the dead girl in Manchester has something to do with Luke Flowers, do you?'

'Not especially, but I am curious.'

'Bit of a long shot.'

'Have you got anything better?'

'Only Jermaine Keating.'

'And he is out of the country.'

'So they say. I am on it, Guv.'

Ahmed buzzed the phone downstairs. The floor manager answered.

'Send up Wazir, Maaz, and Mohammed, right away. The women are not to come!'

'Yes, Mr Khan.'

A few moments later and the men drifted in. Maaz first, Mohammed behind, and Wazir a full minute later, newly shaven, but puffing and panting, after climbing those stairs he had only recently descended.

'What's this all about?' moaned Mohammed, sitting on the sofa. 'We are awfully busy.'

'I can guess,' whispered Maaz, perching on the arm.

'Close the door, father,' said Ahmed to Wazir, who did as he was asked, and then almost collapsed into his favourite armchair.

He was breathing real heavy.

'Are you all right?' asked Ahmed.

'Short of breath, those damned stairs.'

'Perhaps we should get the old man a stairlift,' suggested Maaz. 'I'd use it too.'

'Quiet, boy!' said Mohammed.

Wazir waved his hand across his face as if the idea was preposterous. An unnecessary expense he would never countenance.

285

'So what's this all about?' said Mohammed.
'I have had a call from Imam Sabir.'
'What about this time?' said Mohammed.
'Sahira, she did not arrive in Chitral.'
'What? Who says?' said Wazir.
'The Imam, he is adamant, the warlord does not have the wife he paid good money for, and he is not a happy man.'
Maaz grinned, wanted to laugh.
Wazir glanced across at Mohammed and the kid. Didn't like what he saw. He could recognise secrets and guilt when he saw it.
'What have you done with her?' Wazir asked.
Ahmed glanced at his father, not comprehending, not seeing what his father had seen, then back to the others.
'What have you done with her?' repeated Wazir, louder this time.
'Keep your voice down,' said Ahmed, glancing at the door.
'Done nothing,' grinned Maaz. 'The worthless bitch went off on the Pakistan flight as planned, didn't she, dad?'
They all stared at Mohammed for confirmation.
It wasn't forthcoming.
Mohammed shook his head from side to side and began to cry.

'You'll have the tooth fairy map within the hour,' said Karen. 'What are you going to do with it?'
'As you know there isn't a national odontological database. There isn't even a national fingerprint database for all citizens, come to that, so we have no chance with teeth, and even if there were, with so many people never visiting a dentist these days, it wouldn't be worth a great deal.'
'So what are you saying?'
'I want you to make copies of the tooth map and first thing Monday get the team round every local dentist and ask them, plead with them, order them if necessary, to check if the map matches any of their clients.'
'Do you expect it to?'
'No, not really, but it would be nice if it did.'

286

'How many dentists do you think there are in and around Chester?'

'About a hundred and fifty.'

'How do you know that?'

'Just looked it up on Yellow Pages website. There's a hundred and thirty plus listed in there, so one fifty would seem a reasonable guess.'

'I'll make two hundred copies, that should do.'

'Yeah, do that, and don't forget to speak to Liverpool City Football Club.'

'I won't, and can I get off after that?'

'Sure, have a good lunch.'

'I intend to.'

Chapter Forty-Three

Ahmed shifted in his chair. Mohammed was still snivelling. 'Can someone please tell me what is going on?' said Ahmed. 'Maaz knows,' said Wazir, 'and Mohammed too, judging by that performance.' Mohammed produced a clean handkerchief and blew hard.

Sat back in his chair and blinked and stared at the others.

Maaz grinned and said, 'Shall I tell them, or will you, father?'

'Mohammed!' yelled Ahmed, just as he did when Mohammed was a little boy. 'Explain yourself, and do it now!'

Mohammed sniffed and took a breath and began.

'We were taking her to the airport as planned.'

'And?'

'We didn't get there.'

'Why not?'

'I wanted to frighten her.'

'Don't you think we had done that already?'

'No, I mean I wanted to really frighten her.'

'You are not making much sense,' said Wazir.

Ahmed held up his hand and beckoned for his son to continue.

'She had been far more wicked than you could ever have imagined.'

'Far more wicked,' confirmed Maaz, grinning. 'Far more.'

'When? How? What do you mean? How do you know?'

'Tell them, father. Tell them or I will. Tell them about the pictures.'

'What's the boy talking about?' asked an irritated Wazir.

'What pictures?' asked Ahmed.

'On the mobile phone,' spluttered Mohammed.

'Of Sahira?' asked Ahmed.

288

Mohammed bobbed his head.

Maaz giggled.

'Shut up, boy, or by God…' said Mohammed.

'Ignore the boy!' advised Wazir.

'Compromising pictures?' asked Ahmed.

'You can say that again!' said Maaz.

'Yes,' said Mohammed. 'The very worst kind of pictures you could imagine, and she wasn't alone.'

'What do you mean?' asked Ahmed.

'There were hundreds of pictures on the phone.'

'Of women and girls?' asked Wazir.

'Older women and younger women,' said Mohammed.

'And children?' asked Wazir.

'No! None of children, just women.'

'And they were unclothed?' asked Ahmed, having difficulty getting out his words, as if those same words were too shocking to speak. 'Naked pictures?'

'Porno!' yelled Maaz.

'Does he have to be here?' asked Wazir.

Ahmed glanced at his grandson and shook his head and said, 'Now that he's here, he'd better stay.'

'Naked pictures of Sahira?' clarified Wazir.

Mohammed bobbed his head.

'Not just naked pictures,' gaped Maaz. 'Not your average page three calendar girl, girl-next-door type stuff, oh no, but hardcore, man. Hardcore!'

'What does he mean?' asked Wazir.

'Some of the pictures were…' Mohammed paused, and looked from side to side, weighing up his words, wishing he was anywhere in the world but there in the sitting room of the State. He refocused his eyes and refocused his mind. 'What shall we say… lewd, use your imagination.'

'Of Sahira?' asked Ahmed, seeking confirmation, still not believing what he was hearing, keen to nail down what they were dealing with.

Mohammed nodded.

'Hardcore porno, man!' yelled Maaz again. 'Unbelievable stuff, innit!'

'Stop using that stupid inner city lout language!' yelled Mohammed.

'Keep your voices down!' said Wazir. 'Do you want the women to hear?' and they looked at the door, imagining the women were on the other side, ears to the timber.

'It's all right,' said Ahmed. 'I told them to keep the women downstairs.' He pointed at Maaz and said, 'Are you taking your medication?'

'I don't think he is,' mumbled Mohammed.

'There's nothing wrong with me, I don't need white medicine,' said Maaz, and he jumped up and ran across the room and banged his head against the plastic window frame. 'See! No sense, no feeling, there's nowt wrong with me!'

'Sit down, boy, before you hurt yourself,' pleaded Wazir.

Maaz glanced at the old man. Nodded and whispered, 'That's cool, old man, I'll sit with you,' and he squatted on the floor beside Wazir's feet and grinned and nodded at the others.

'Where are the photographs?' asked Ahmed.

'Father's still got them,' said Maaz.

'No problem, then,' said Ahmed. 'Press the Delete All button, and they disappear. Problem solved. Job done.'

'Too late for that,' said Maaz.

'What does he mean?' said Wazir, glancing down at his great-grandson's gelled head.

Maaz answered the question.

'They're all over the Internet, innit! Hardcore, my friends, hardcore and available, featuring our very own Sahira Khan, up to her neck in sin and debauchery! Recording a huge number of hits too, and who would be surprised at that?'

'Oh God, not that,' said Ahmed.

Mohammed nodded. He'd seen them on the Internet. Free and live for anyone to look at and download. Hundreds of colour pictures of women in various stages of undress, mostly un, with the latest and hottest ones featuring his only daughter.

'She must have been drugged,' suggested Wazir. 'To do anything as vile as that. The local boy must have drugged her and taken advantage of her.'

'Doesn't look like she's drugged to me,' smirked Maaz. 'Judging by the filthy look on her face, and the sparkle in her eyes. She enjoyed every damned minute of it, but don't take my word for it. See for yourself, go on father, show them the pictures, if you dare, show them, let them all have a good look, then they'll see and know how wicked a bitch she was, how sinful and debauched, and they'll understand what we had to do. They'll understand everything.'

'You knew about these pictures before you took her to the airport?' asked Wazir.

Mohammed nodded.

'Course we did!' confirmed Maaz.

'So you had no intention of taking her to the airport?' asked Ahmed.

'Correct!' grinned Maaz. 'And quite right too.'

'Why didn't you tell us about the pictures?' asked Ahmed.

'Because we knew you old blokes wouldn't understand,' said Maaz. 'This is young man's business, and the young men should take care of it, and the young men bloody well have!'

'Don't swear!' said Ahmed.

'You killed her?' asked Wazir.

A moment's silence before Mohammed said, 'Maaz did.'

Maaz grinned and said, 'I did too, because pops here didn't have the bottle. Told you, it's young man's twenty-first century business, and the young man duly obliged. It had to be done; surely you can see that? That woman was sinful, beyond the pale, an evil sinner, walking round in a temptress's body, no doubt sent here by the devil. God alone knows how many other men there were. You don't think that little creep was the first one, or the only one, do you?'

'I believe he was the only one,' said Wazir.

'And you, old man,' said Maaz, still grinning and turning round to look up at the senile old goat, 'have long since gone cuckoo – bats, mad as a hatter. I mean for God's sake, who else would leave ten thousand pounds to Liverpool City Council in their will, but that's what he's done. How mad is that? It's not me who should be on medication. It's him! The guy should be put in a loony bin. He's gone co-co. Locked away! Should be sectioned. Spending our inheritance, he is, left, right and centre, he's gone goo goo. God alone knows who else he is giving our money to. You need to watch him, giving it to the Liverpool Council, I tell ya, it's true. He needs seeing to, and you two,' and Maaz pointed at Ahmed and Mohammed, 'should wake up and do something about it before it's too late… or I bloody will.'

Wazir turned red with fury. He struggled to get out his words.

'You have stooped so low as to read my will?'

'Just as well I did, innit. You shouldn't have left it in your bedside table, you mental case, and I'm not alone either. Bet Nadirah's read it too, Sahira as well, I shouldn't wonder. You're freakin' loopy,' and Maaz pointed to the side of his head and revolved his finger round and round and round, and nodded back up at Wazir.

'How did you kill her?' asked Ahmed.

Mohammed grimaced. Glanced at Maaz.

Maaz smirked. 'Hammer innit, thwack! One little blow to the sinner's head, sinner down, sinner dead. Amazing how easy it is, to slay a sinner.'

Wazir shared a look with Ahmed. Shared a thought, too. Maaz needed help. The boy was dangerous. Something would have to be done about him.

'You killed a girl in cold blood, your own sister,' pleaded Wazir. 'Didn't you have any qualms about what you were doing?'

Maaz turned around and smiled up at the old man. Jerked his flattened hand across the room in front of his face. 'Nah man! Easy peasy. When it's God's will, it's always so easy. I don't imagine you could understand.'

'Never mind that now,' said Ahmed. 'We'll come back to that in a moment. There are more pressing questions here.'

'Like what?' snapped Maaz.

'Like, can the police identify the body? And if they do, and I think they will, they will come here, and if they do that, what do we say? What's the story?'

'I'm not ashamed of what I have done,' grinned Maaz.

'You should be!' said Wazir.

'You might not be ashamed, Maaz, but do you want to be locked up for the rest of your life?' asked Ahmed.

Wazir wasn't the only one to think that wouldn't be the worst outcome.

'And Mohammed too, he'd get life if the police could prove he was there,' continued Ahmed.

'Father's all right,' said a cocky Maaz. 'Innocent, he is. Didn't do a freaking thing. Didn't have the bottle. I'd tell the cops that. They'll believe me. They're stupid, the cops. Father'll get off.'

'Don't think so,' said Wazir. 'He was there, he's involved. He'd be charged with murder, just as you would.'

Maaz turned around and sneered at Wazir.

'Well, just tell them he wasn't there! What the hell do I care? I'll tell them I did it by myself. I'm happy with that. It's bugger all to do with you, old man, leave it to the younger generation who understand these things.'

'There's something else we need to talk about,' said Ahmed.

'Like what?' snapped Maaz.

'The warlord hasn't taken delivery of the wife he was promised, the woman he paid the mosque for.'

'That's camel shit!' said Maaz. 'Tell the old perv to sod off!'

'We must refund the money straight away,' said Wazir.

'Good thinking,' said Ahmed. 'I'll repay it tonight.'

'I suppose we could say she was kidnapped in Pakistan,' said Mohammed. 'Gone missing, don't know where she is. She wouldn't be the first. Pretend we are distraught. Pretend we are looking for her.'

The idea of pretending anything did not appeal to Wazir, but before he could say anything Ahmed was talking again.

'That might appease the warlord. He can buy another wife anywhere, but it won't appease or convince the British police when they come snooping round. The records will show she did not board the flight.'

293

'We'll have to come up with a better story than that,' said Mohammed.

'But there is a bigger problem than that,' said Wazir, rubbing his recently shaven cheek.

'Like what, old man?' asked Maaz.

'Like for example, how did Mohammed get hold of the phone, and what happened to the owner?'

'Burn it!' yelled Maaz. 'Chuck the phone in the oven. Obliterate it!'

'I don't think we should destroy the evidence,' said Ahmed. 'Sahira was killed because of what was on that phone. Obliterate the phone and we have no reason to kill her.'

'Mad as it sounds, I agree with that,' said Mohammed.

'Whose phone were the pictures on?' asked Wazir, trying to get a clear picture in his mind.

'Wake up, old man. The kaffir's, of course!' said Maaz.

'And how did you get the phone?'

'We went to see him,' confirmed Mohammed.

'What happened?' asked Wazir.

Mohammed glanced at Maaz, as did Ahmed and Wazir.

Maaz shook his head from side to side, and started laughing.

Chapter Forty-Four

Ahmed picked up the phone on the coffee table and dialled downstairs. 'Send up coffee and biscuits for four.' 'Yes, Mr Khan.' 'And the women are not to come upstairs under any circumstances, is that clear?' 'Of course, Mr Khan.'

The coffee arrived a couple of minutes later, brought by a young Punjabi lad who hadn't been in England long. Quite legal of course. His mother and father were both doctors, and both were working at the Countess of Chester hospital. The State of Kerala never employed illegals. It was too risky. More than one competitor had been put out of business by the heavy fines. No paperwork, no job, a policy that kept the State out of trouble with the police and immigration officers.

The youth worked most weekends and some evenings during the week. He was a good boy, worked hard, a conscientious type that Wazir, Ahmed, and Mohammed had all taken a liking to from the start.

Maaz hated him for the liking his elders bestowed.

The boy set the coffee on the low table and retreated toward the door without showing his back.

'Close the door and go downstairs,' said Ahmed.

'Yes, Mr Khan,' said the young man, bowing and disappearing from view.

'Faggot!' muttered Maaz.

'Shut up!' said Mohammed.

If only Maaz could be more like that, thought Wazir, but there was never any point in wishing one human being could be like another, because it never happened that way.

'So?' said Ahmed, 'what became of Sahira's young man?'

'It had to be done!' said Maaz.

295

He was enjoying himself, thought Wazir, being the centre of attention, revelling in the notoriety of what he had done.

'And who decided that?' asked Ahmed.

'I was just so angry!' said Mohammed.

'And this was before you saw the pictures?' clarified Wazir.

Mohammed nodded and said, 'It was the shame of it, and the Imams at the mosque knowing about it. The kaffir brought it on himself. By the grace of God he deserved to die for what he did.'

'You can say that again!' said Maaz.

Mohammed shot him a look, a stare that turned into a hopeful look that pleaded with his son to learn to keep silent.

'So, to be clear, you lured him to the hotel and murdered him?' asked Ahmed.

Maaz grinned and bobbed his head. It was easy to grin. He had enjoyed it, being the deliverer of vengeance. 'Justice, it was God's justice. A Jihad.'

'And who else knows about this?'

'No one,' said Mohammed. 'Not a soul.'

'No one? I find that hard to believe!' said Ahmed.

'The girl, the one on reception, she knows,' grinned Maaz.

'And I suppose you paid for her silence?' said Wazir.

'No! We didn't,' said Mohammed. 'That's the great thing. She's a good girl. She's converting. Studying at the mosque. I've seen her there. She's with us. She'll never say a word. Turns a blind eye to everything.'

'She's a bit of a babe too,' said Maaz. 'I could get quite excited over her, know what I mean, might have a word with her father, see how the land lies.'

'You will do no such thing!' said Mohammed. 'You will stay away from that girl! You know full well you are betrothed to your cousin in Calicut.'

'What's her father's name?' asked Ahmed. 'The girl on reception.'

'Javed, he goes to the mosque all the time, a good man,' said Mohammed.

'I know him,' nodded Wazir. 'He's a decent man.'

'Her Christian name is Mary,' continued Maaz, still thinking of the babe at the Red Rose, 'but that's all about to go up in smoke. Her father now calls her Tanzeela, and she'll soon be known as that. Her Christian whore of a mother doesn't have a clue. She's in for a big surprise. Another one to us, I'd say,' and he licked his index finger and drew an imaginary figure 1 in the air.

'You're a complete idiot!' muttered Wazir.

'Don't be crass!' said Ahmed almost at the same time.

'I don't think you realise the trouble you are in,' said Wazir. 'The trouble we are all in. The police will never rest until they solve this case.'

'Let 'em try,' said Maaz.

'Oh, they'll try all right, and they will keep trying until they come for you, Maaz, until they come for all of us.'

Maaz shook his head and coughed.

'Who killed the boy?' asked Wazir.

Maaz smirked.

His eyes leapt from left to right and right to left.

It was obvious to everyone.

'How did you kill him?' asked Ahmed.

'That's the great bit!' gushed Maaz.

'What does he mean?' asked Ahmed.

Mohammed sighed hard and stared round at his elders and said, 'We used the sword.'

Wazir's mouth fell open.

'The family sword? The sacred artefact I brought from India?'

Mohammed nodded.

Maaz was still enjoying himself.

'You couldn't have done! I have never noticed it missing. Ahmed and I hold the only keys,' said Wazir. 'You're lying!'

Maaz couldn't contain himself. Idiotic laughing poured from his slim and taught body.

'I am sorry, father, but I borrowed your key,' said Mohammed to Ahmed. 'Took it when you were bathing, slipped the key back before you had noticed it had gone.'

Ahmed and Wazir shared another look.

Had things come to this? Had the family sunk so low? Their son and grandson betraying the family trust, reading wills, stealing keys, removing precious family artefacts without permission, an ancient and priceless sword demeaned by using it to carry out murder. Yes, it was true; Sahira had behaved abominably, beyond abominably. Most people would sympathise with that, and mere words could not describe the sin and shame and degradation she had committed and brought down on the family, but this? How could they ever deal with it?

Truth was, the family would never be the same again.

'So we have two murders on our hands,' said Wazir, rubbing his cold hands together, before clapping them hard. 'The blood of a local man and the blood of one of our own.'

'Stop calling them murders!' shrieked Maaz. 'No one has been murdered! We have justice! That's what it is. An eye for an eye. Start calling them by their correct name... justice!'

'Is that what you call it, justice?' asked Wazir, feeling quite ill.

'Yes, I do! It is up to the younger generation to protect our family name and maintain standards, and that is what we have done. I am proud of what I did, and I'll tell you something else: Whoever made that sword, whichever member of our family, going back deep into history, whoever held and wielded that weapon, that is a man I would like to have met. He would understand and approve, and you won't be surprised to hear it worked so well. Better than I ever imagined. One blow, that's all it took, and the kaffir's filthy head was rolling about my feet like a culled turnip in the field, as red rain came tumbling down. You should have seen the look of terror and surprise on his cocky little Christian face!'

'It's a strange way to protect the family by murdering one of our own,' muttered Wazir.

Maaz jumped to his feet and did a child-like tantrummy jump, and screamed, 'Shut the hell up, you stupid old man! What do you know? It's not murder! It's justice! I won't tell you again!'

'Don't speak to my father like that,' ordered Ahmed. 'Or I'll have you sectioned.'

Maaz turned and stared at Ahmed in silence, as if he had been shot.

He didn't say a word.

Didn't want to go there.

Didn't like Ahmed.

Didn't like the old man either.

Didn't like any of them.

They should all look out. One thing was certain: The world would belong to the young. It always did, and for Maaz, that couldn't come soon enough.

Ahmed stood up and went to the jug of coffee.

'We need a break,' he said. 'Here, take a coffee, everyone, and a sweet biscuit, and after that, we'll sit down together and make our plans.'

'Good idea,' said Mohammed. 'Do you want a coffee, granddad?'

'Our family has committed two murders and you want to sit there and drink coffee?' said Wazir.

'Might as well,' said Mohammed. 'We can't go back on what has been done. Do you want one?'

Wazir shook his head in disgust and managed a nod. 'Please, black.'

Maaz sniffed and laughed and bobbed his head and grabbed a sweet biscuit. Threw it in his mouth and crunched it like a rabid dog.

Across town, Walter was studying the idontogram. Not that there was a great deal to see. The victim had possessed a beautiful set of teeth, unlike Walter's, just the one hint of dental treatment. Small filling, bottom left molar, second from the back. Other than that, a perfect set of gnashers, teeth that would never bite or laugh or speak or eat anything again. Such a waste. Such a shame.

The young woman who had perished on the Pennines had still not been identified. The smiling teeth presented the best opportunity of doing that. It was a case of comparing the post-mortem report on the teeth with the ante-mortem reports, seeking a match. But before they could do that, they had to locate an ante-mortem report, and only the deceased victim's dentist would possess that. It wasn't like fingerprints or DNA. It wasn't a foolproof system. Two individuals could have an almost identical set of teeth.

Fact was, the less dental treatment present, the harder it would be to positively ID the teeth, and the body, what little of it remained. But it had to be followed through. It had to be tried; because there was little else the police and forensic scientists had to reach an identification.

In Walter's experience, it was more likely a family member, or friend, perhaps a boyfriend, would come forward and report the woman missing. No doubt that was what the Manchester police were hoping too, but it hadn't happened, and there was no guarantee it would.

He turned the idontogram over in his hand and in his mind tried to match the teeth with a face. Beautiful, she was, of that he was certain, though he had no evidence to back up such thinking. He wondered how old she had been, and he wondered how she had met her end.

In the meantime, Karen and her team would get on with things first thing Monday morning, paying a visit to every dentist in the area, backing the outside bet that somehow the dead woman had received her filling locally, on Walter's patch, in Walter's town, and for him, Monday morning couldn't come soon enough.

Chapter Forty-Five

The coffee jug was empty and only crumbs remained on the biscuit plate. Ahmed called the meeting to order and everyone paid attention. 'If the police cannot identify the remains on the moor, they will never come calling, and however distasteful and upsetting the whole business might be, the problem is solved.' Mohammed went to speak. Ahmed waved him away and continued.

'But if they identify the body, as I think they will, they will come calling, and we will have some explaining to do. Therefore, our plan must be based on the assumption they will come here; and sooner than we think. So what is the plan, where do we go from here?'

'Mohammed and Maaz could go to India, back to Kerala,' suggested Wazir. 'We still have relatives there. They'd be safe; they could go into the hills. No one would find them there.'

'I'm not going to some third world country, old man. You may have crawled out of some stinking hellhole out east, but I'm British Asian, born and bred, and proud of it. I'm staying here.'

'Don't be so ungrateful, Maaz,' said Ahmed. 'India is not like it used to be, it's a wonderful country, you'd enjoy it.'

'Bollocks! I'm not going. That's final. Move on granddaddy, next on the agenda.'

'So what's your plan?' asked Wazir. 'Stay here until the police come knocking on the door, drag you away in cuffs, lock you up and throw away the key?'

'The old men are right,' said Mohammed. 'The police are clever. Sooner or later they will ID the body.'

'I'll go to London,' said Maaz. 'Or Landon as they like to say, I can do cockney, innit, man. I'd be right at home, and there are plenty of bro's in the east end, innit, Brick Lane, that's where I'll go, they'll never find me there. Buy a fresh ID and papers too; you can get anything you want with ready cash.'

It was a dreadful idea but the only one on the table, and it was true, it just might work. It would get the unpredictable Maaz out of their house, and out of their hair.

'What about you, Mohammed?' asked Wazir.

'Don't know, granddad, but I don't want to go to London.'

'Do what I said before,' suggested Maaz. 'Get your head round the fact that I did the business myself. Blame me, I don't care. Father wasn't there; he might as well have missed it. I am the justice dispenser in this firm,' and he laughed at his description.

The others shared a look and glanced back at Maaz who was still grinning, though his eyes were still, as if he were miles away, visiting crazy future adventures that only he could imagine.

'The sword,' said Ahmed.

'What about it?' asked Mohammed.

'It will tie us to the killing of the boy,' said Wazir. 'Forensic tests, it'll connect us.'

'Then get rid of it,' said Mohammed.

'We can't do that!' said Ahmed.

'No, we can't, and anyway, I have a better idea,' said Wazir.

They all looked across at the old man.

'Well?' said Maaz, staring at the old fool. 'Are you going to share it or keep it to yourself? Perhaps donate it to the Liverpool City Council?' and he laughed at his train of thought.

'We'll get a copy made, put the copy in the case, and I will hide the original.'

'And where are you going to hide it, old man?'

Wazir grinned. 'I shall bury it.'

'Don't be so freakin' stupid! Who do you think you are? Long John Silver?'

'Why not? It has been buried before and it can be buried again.'

It was true; it had been buried before, all the family knew the extraordinary story of the family artefact, sleeping underground to avoid looting Hindu mobs.

'Where can you get a copy made?' asked Ahmed.

302

'I know a craftsman from Madras; he lives in Stafford. He will do a good job. No one will be able to tell the difference once it's locked in the case.'

'It's Chennai now, old man,' said Maaz. 'Madras doesn't exist anymore! Get with the programme. Geez, give me strength.'

They ignored Maaz's nonsense and Mohammed said, 'It'll cost a lot of money.'

'Money is not an issue, not where family safety is concerned,' said Ahmed.

'How long will it take?' asked Mohammed.

'Not sure, maybe a week.'

'Sooner the better,' said Ahmed. 'And make sure he makes it sharp. We don't want some feeble, impotent copy.'

Wazir nodded. 'It'll be sharp, like the original.'

'Then get it done,' said Ahmed, before turning his attention to Maaz. 'And you, young man, when are you going to London?'

'Dunno, granddad, don't think there's any hurry. We did a good job, didn't we, father? Don't think they'll be identifying the sinner's remains any time soon.'

Wazir thought different, though he didn't say.

'What about the women?' asked Ahmed.

'What about them? They are not to know!' said Mohammed. 'Not a thing.'

'Of course they are not to know, but they will wonder about our meetings. What do we tell them?'

'Tell them bugger all!' said Maaz, the silly grin back in position. 'Give them a good slap, if need be!'

It was all right for him, he didn't have a curious wife asking questions half the night.

'Tell them we are thinking of taking over a string of restaurants in Birmingham. That should do it. They'll believe that,' said Wazir, and the men agreed with that.

'What about Mohammed?' asked Ahmed. 'What is he going to do?'

Everyone looked at Mohammed.

He scratched his chin and said, 'Don't worry about me, I'll think of something.'

'It'll have to be good,' said Ahmed. 'And it will have to be quick!'

'Don't worry about me!'

There was a short pause before Wazir said, 'What is done, is done, however much I may abhor it. The important thing is we act normally, and run the business as per usual. We must not betray our worries to our customers, our family, and our friends. That could bring big trouble to our door.'

Maaz grinned and said, 'That's the ticket old man; we go on as we always have, as if nothing has happened, because nothing sodding well has!'

'Your language is getting worse,' said Ahmed.

'I don't know what to do with him,' said his father.

I know what I'd like to do with him, thought Wazir.

'After my parent's death, this has been the worst day of my life,' said Wazir. 'And no one outside this room must ever hear a word of what was said here today. Is that clear?'

Everyone agreed, even Maaz.

'Come on,' said Mohammed. 'We'd better show our faces downstairs.'

Jimmy Mitchell was also in a meeting, one that would reshape the rest of his life. The client had called him to the private home, and that was unusual. They demanded to know why the target, Jermaine Keating, had not been taken down. It was the latest in a series of cock-ups Jimmy Mitchell had presided over, and the weasel of a man had come highly recommended.

But in the days that followed, the clients were not as bitter as they might have been, not when Keating's cocaine habit caught up with him. The latest intelligence suggested Keating would never play serious football again. Liverpool City FC would cut their losses, terminate his contract, and cash in their insurance policies. No one else would touch him, and the man had outgoings, substantial bills he could not meet.

He had a gambling habit too, wagering enormous sums on the betting exchanges most afternoons, often when he was worse for wear. He'd earn a week's wages of £150,000, and would often lose twice that amount over a single session.

No, the rest of Jermaine Keating's life would be spent running from his creditors, angry people who would not take no for an answer. The girls would vanish, and the hangers on would fall away like amber leaves in October.

Before a year was out, the man would be nothing, destined to spend whatever time he had remaining wondering how it had all gone wrong. The clients got a kick out of that, of envisioning the misery that was coming Keating's way, and for that reason they didn't persist with the contract. They would take their money back and bide their time.

Sometimes a long, lingering, and miserable existence was greater punishment than a quick and clean death. For a person like Keating it would be, a man who had enjoyed the high life, but was plummeting toward the gutter.

It didn't stop them berating Jimmy Mitchell.

It didn't stop the client pointing out Jimmy Mitchell owed them, big time.

And it didn't stop the client smiling after Jimmy Mitchell had been dismissed from their custody.

Jimmy knew he would be called on to make matters good, and whatever favour was required, it would be big, difficult, and expensive. He wiped the sweat from his brow and drove home cursing the day he met Luke Edward Flowers.

Chapter Forty-Six

Sunday night. Feeding time. Walter approached the State of Kerala. Reached out and pushed open the brass and glass doors, stepped inside, wiped his feet on the copra mat. Breathed in the unmistakable aroma of the best food the subcontinent offered. There was a gentle hum of conversation, perhaps half the tables were taken, it was only just gone eight, still plenty of time.

He stepped forward onto the deep pile maroon carpet, almost disappeared into it. The half moon bar was right ahead, eight chrome stools set before it, three or four taken, people studying menus, sipping drinks, peering into a lover's eyes, maybe treating a partner to a birthday surprise.

Wazir and Ahmed were there, expensive grey suits, white shirts, colourful silk ties, polished black shoes, talking to the Punjabi kid. Nothing too strident, perhaps gentle advice dispensed, as if issued by kind mentors to someone eager to learn. The kid was wearing some kind of colourful national dress. Anywhere else he'd look ridiculous, but in the State he looked incredible.

Wazir heard the gentle clunk of the door. Knew that someone had come in. He set his best welcoming look on his handsome, if elderly face, and turned about. There was a big black guy standing there, wild grey hair, cheap looking summer jacket, standing alone; a face Wazir instantly recognised.

Walter stepped forward across the reception area. Wazir did too, only his walk betraying his eighty-eight summers, as he held out his hand.

'Walter!' he said. 'Nice to see you again. You've been away too long.'

'It's great to be back.'

The men shook hands gently, for Wazir had no wish to aggravate the arthritis, and then he said, 'Is it just you?'

'Just me, Wazir.'

'Would you like your usual table?'

'That would be nice.'

'Come then,' and he beckoned him toward the table that Walter preferred. It was set against the wall; midway between the half moon bar and the doors, from where he could see everything.

The table was square, covered in maroon linen and gleaming glasses, laid for four, and Walter took the seat on the far side with his back to the wall.

'Will you join me, Wazir?'

'Probably not. I've had plenty of food today, and I don't eat like I once did. Maybe I'll have a pancake later.'

'Join me for that, at least.'

'I may. I in the meantime, would you like company?'

'Who did you have in mind?'

'Harry Barrett's due in.'

'Harry's OK, why not, if he comes in, bring him over, but spare me Austerity Hayes.'

The men shared a look. No further words were necessary.

'I'll send the boy over in five, we'll look after you.'

'I know that, Wazir.'

Walter grasped the vast menu. He thought it the best Indian food outside London. He glanced through the dishes, though he already knew he would have lamb tikka, a particular favourite of his. Walter had been on at Wazir for years to add curried goat to the house fare, which would have been his preferred choice. But Wazir had yet to find a reliable supplier. Bought the lamb from the two-hundred-year-old butcher in Llangollen high street, and both men would swear by the quality.

The boy came over and took his order and disappeared.

Walter noted all four of the Khans were on parade, Wazir meeting and greeting, as he still insisted on doing. Mohammed working the bar, serving and chatting and flirting and smiling. Ahmed floating, as was his wont, ready to pounce on any problem in an instant, and hyperactive Maaz, who dashed around as if his life depended on it.

One man in his eighties, sixties, forties, and twenties, and Walter wasn't alone in thinking that with each passing generation the quality of the man diminished. Strange that, pondered Walter, or maybe he was getting old. He had been patronising the State for over ten years; and might have spent more cash in the place than anyone else.

In that time he'd seen half a dozen refits, including the recent one that must have cost a fortune, but one that Wazir insisted they needed to make to avoid paying trillions in tax, his expression, and if the taxman was paying the bill, it would be rude not to. The heavy brass double doors had cost over five thousand pounds, and that was before you entered the place!

Some time ago, Walter had tried the other curry houses in the city, but he'd had a bad experience in the Bengal Tiger. He'd been served by a young man in national dress, similar to the Punjabi kid, and when the guy brought the order, as he set it down, he uttered soothing words in a language that Walter did not recognise, a well-meant phrase that Walter assumed was the subcontinent equivalent of bon appetite.

An Asian lady at the next table, quite a pretty, dumpy thing, turned round and began screaming at the youth in the same tongue, and the young man looked aghast and hurried away. She leant over and said aloud, 'I don't suppose you understood what he said?'

'You're right, I didn't.'

'He said,' and she lowered her voice, 'I hope you choke on your meal and wake up with cancer, you fat, Christian cunt! - Sorry about the language.'

It put Walter clean off his meal.

'I don't care for the "fat" much,' he said, and the lady laughed and returned to her party.

Walter hadn't set foot in the Bengal Tiger since.

Never felt the need.

The State of Kerala had everything he wanted, and Wazir Khan was one of life's true gentlemen, a man Walter was proud to call his friend.

Wazir returned and lowered himself into the opposite chair. Walter thought he looked tired, but at eighty-eight, he was entitled to look tired.

'Busy as usual?' said Walter.

'Yes, sixty-six percent full tonight, not bad for a Sunday,' said Wazir, ever the businessman, always monitoring the figures. 'Over sixty percent and we make money, under sixty and I worry.'

He'd said it deadpan, and Walter wasn't sure how to take it.

'You don't know what worries are,' joked Walter.

Wazir presented his deadpan face.

He'd make an excellent poker player.

'This country has been good to us,' said Wazir. 'You and I.'

Walter grinned and said, 'It has, and to some more than others. I can't compete with an MBE.'

Wazir sniffed a laugh.

'Baubles. Tokenism. Doesn't mean a thing.'

'You can pass it to me if you don't want it.'

'Ah, now that I couldn't do.'

'Will you ever retire, Wazir?'

'Doubt it; I don't know what I'd do with myself. You?'

'I don't want to, but sooner or later they'll retire me.'

That was the benefit of working for oneself; thought Wazir, you could work for as long or as short as you wanted. Working for the government like Walter did, and you were at the mercy of politicians, and everyone knew politicians weren't up to much.

The doors clunked and Harry Barrett came in, stood in the foyer, and blinked around the room. He didn't see much, didn't have much eyesight. The clocks were responsible for that.

Walter waved his hand and said 'Harry!' and in the next moment he joined them at the table, as Wazir made his excuse and left. Harry took off his glasses and began wiping them on a maroon napkin, just as Walter's sizzling meal arrived.

'Tikka is it?' said Harry, gawping down, mouth agape.

Walter nodded.

'I'll have the same, and a jug of cold beer.'

'Good idea,' said Walter. 'One for me, too,' and the kid hurried away to fetch the beers.

Harry had been working with clocks for over fifty years. Servicing them, cleaning them, trading them, loving them, it was all the same to Harry. He was still operating out of the same small shop set halfway down one of the jiggers, opposite the cathedral.

He'd developed a tic, or more accurately a tick, as his head moved from side to side in perfect second time like a pendulum. When he was concentrating or engrossed on something, his tongue would click clock against the roof of his mouth, again in perfect time, and sometimes Walter would have to say, 'Harry, you're ticking again.'

Harry would grin and stop, for a while.

He'd lost his wife six years since, and frequented the State, the British Legion, the Connie Club, and the Masonic Lodge, ringing the changes, doing the rounds, anything to take him out of the loneliness of a chiming house at night-time. It didn't do his waistline much good, or his cholesterol count either, but he was a cheerful man, and great company.

The doors clunked again and Walter peered that way, hoping it wouldn't be, but it was, Austerity Hayes. He tried to hunker down without success. They had been spotted.

'Yoo hoo!' she screamed, and she was on her way.

'Bugger,' whispered Walter.

'Problem?' ticked Harry.

'Austerity's here.'

'You can say that again. Sales are bloody awful!' said Harry, guffawing at his little joke, as Austerity grabbed the chair between the men, whisked it out and sat down.

'That's what I like to see,' she said. 'Good company, enjoying their food. Tikka is it?'

'Yep,' said Harry, sucking sauce covered meat between his dentures.

Walter nodded and sipped his beer.

'I'll have the same,' she said, and raised her arm and yelled, 'Boy!' and the Punjabi kid came running, not portraying any offence as being addressed in that a way. In a few years he would be a specialist heart surgeon, but for now he was, in Austerity's eyes, her boy.

Walter pinched a look at her. He tried hard not to stare, but that was difficult. She was a big ruddy woman born in 1943, and with the hard food rationing on at the time her father thought it something of a jape to call her Austerity. It would remind her forever of the importance of being frugal, he said, and if she was, she didn't show it.

She was wearing a ridiculous navy blue bonnet and matching blue suit, stretching at the seams, and could have passed as a Sally Army choir-mistress.

Her father had once owned the largest independent department store in Chester and had sold it to one of the multiples in 1977 for a tidy sum. Twelve months later he was dead, and as Austerity was his only surviving relative, she had never married and never come close, Austerity copped the lot in the will.

Quite what made her put all her money into commercial property throughout the city, no one knew, but she did, and within ten years her investment had quadrupled before she sold out and banked the cash. Some called her lucky, others astute, Austerity didn't care. Looked forward to the quarterly bank statement dropping through the door.

She spent her money on eating, socialising, taking three cruises every year by herself, where she could eat and socialise her way around the globe against a different backdrop every morning. She smoked cheroots, though Walter had never seen her with one. In one of her quiet moments she calculated that at her current rate of spend, she had enough cash to last her one hundred and ninety-two years.

In her late seventies that seemed unlikely. She was trying hard to dent the cash pile, but not hard enough.

311

She was talking about an amazing meal she had enjoyed the previous night in a new Indonesian restaurant that had opened in the city centre.

'Never eaten an Indonesian before,' she said, laughing at her little joke. 'Gave me dreadful indigestion.'

Walter thought she looked capable of it, two if she was peckish, as she described the meal, course by course.

Walter's concentration wandered. He was thinking of ordering a pudding. He glanced across the bar. Something caught his tired eye. The chrome stools glistened in the gold light. There was only one couple sitting there now, a glamorous pair, if it were ever possible to describe any two people as glamorous from a rear view. The woman had an hourglass figure and was wearing a fine, flowing dress, maroon, perhaps especially chosen to match the restaurant. Who knows what extremes some people would go to make a statement. She possessed long, wavy, auburn hair that shimmered across the naked skin of her upper back, as she laughed at the stories her attentive companion dispensed.

The dress was long, halfway between knee and ankle, a classy number, imagined Walter, a show-stopper, and even though she was sitting down, it still looked elegant, so much nicer than the mini-no-dresses that many young women preferred.

The lady possessed a dainty pair of heels set in a good pair of shoes, jet black, shining like polished jade, legs tucked up, her feet perched on the lower frame of the stool, with the toes forever on the move, twitching an inch or two this way or that, restless and desperate to play footsie with her partner, and that would begin once they were sitting opposite one another.

But as her feet danced, a mini spotlight above them caught the shining surface of the shoes, and glinted across the room. But it wasn't the shoes that caught Walter's eye, or the new chrome stools; nor the chunky diamond ring on her finger she couldn't stop touching and admiring. It wasn't the polished glasses on the bar, or the lit up bottles of liquor standing to attention behind, but something higher up, further away, something more glittering, imprisoned in an impressive display case. It looked as if it should have displayed the king of salmons, but no. The item within the case, glinting in the ambient light across the restaurant, was a bejewelled sword.

Austerity was a quick eater, seemed to shovel it down as if she hadn't eaten for a week. Slammed her fork down and burped.

'Sorry,' she said, smirking, hand to mouth. 'Tikka always does that to me,' and she wafted her hand across the table over the soiled and empty dishes, and said, 'This one is on me, fellow curry lovers.'

'Oh, that's kind of you,' said Harry, who had never refused a free meal.

'Thanks, but I'll pay for my own,' said Walter, who'd given up on the pudding.

'Oh, come on, Darriteau, take my hospitality when it's offered. I need to spend my money somehow.'

'I insist,' said Walter, and he slipped a twenty from his wallet and set it on the table and bade them a good night.

'What's wrong with him?' asked Austerity.

Harry pulled a face and shrugged.

'Public servant, police inspector, maybe he imagines he'd be compromised.'

'Compromised! Oh, you are stupid, Harry. What tommyrot!'

Walter decided he would walk home. It was a lovely night, balmy, clear and still, and as he ambled along, gears crunched and banged in his head, as imaginary pieces of crazy jigsaws were being removed and retried in unlikely places. He was still doing that as he strolled up the garden path, offering those difficult pieces into the hardest part of the puzzle an hour later, before he drifted away to oblivion.

Chapter Forty-Seven

Monday morning and the team were out on the dentist round. Nothing fresh had come in from Manchester. As far as the Chester police were concerned, there was still no ID, no motive, and still no one had come forward to report the dead person missing.

As for Walter's own murder, that of Luke Flowers, the trail had fizzled out. The Hytec monster hadn't been able to help either because monsters need feeding, and nothing of any consequence had been offered for a couple of days. The monster was starving.

Karen was out with Gibbons, crawling around the dentists on the north side of the city. Hector Browne and Jenny were doing the south side. Karen wasn't alone in thinking it was a complete waste of time, and she was probably right.

While it was quiet, Walter would investigate who lived in the State of Kerala, and if they were known to the police.

The men were all well known; you could see them any time you paid a visit, but what of the women? Fact was, the women were kept away from prying eyes, as if they were the prized wives in some Arab Sheik's palace, hidden away, never to be seen by visitors and the general public, and Walter didn't have a problem with that.

If he was ever lucky enough to land a pretty wife, though that seemed unlikely, he wouldn't be that keen on other men looking at her, coveting her, and even lusting after her. Or would he?

Wouldn't it be nice to take her out and flaunt her in front of friends and workmates, take her to the State, to the theatre, or the races on Ladies' Day? Of course it would, and he would too. But therein lay one of the many differences between him and Wazir, between their differing backgrounds and cultures. They had originated from opposite sides of the planet, and who was to say which way was right, and which way was wrong? It would still be interesting though, to see how many women lived in the State.

He checked the PNC, the Police National Computer, that huge beast that began life in the same year that Walter joined the force. It was mainly a register of stolen cars back then, but now it handled almost seventy million, what they quaintly called transactions, as if it were some branch of the Stock Exchange, every year.

It was a mammoth operation, split into five sections, QUEST, VODS, ANPR, PROPERTY and CRIMELINK, and it could and would chatter into the ear of the monster every time it was switched on. Walter searched them all. Came up with a few titbits of interesting information.

Wazir held the liquor license, had done for years, no surprise there, and the police had never objected to it. Mohammed had once been caught speeding on the Wirral peninsula, three points and a seventy-pound fine, and young Maaz was recorded too. He had been in more serious trouble and that did not surprise Walter, though he hadn't been aware of it.

The younger Khan had lost his temper in the restaurant one night and had assaulted a man. Maaz had pleaded that the guy had been disrespectful to his mother, Akleema, but more than that, Maaz Khan alleged the man had made lewd comments and propositioned her. The youth, as he was then, had flipped, and the guy called the police and later left the State, bloodied and bruised.

The case was considered sufficiently serious, and Maaz's behaviour sufficiently weird, for the CPS to suggest to the family they would not prosecute, on condition Maaz attended an institution for the treatment of mental illness.

Walter called down the report.

Maaz had "gone away" for two years, had received extensive medication, drugs that appeared to have cured whatever problem there was going on inside the mixed-up mind of young Maaz Khan.

That was five years before, and Maaz was only sixteen back then. It was probably why the CPS took a lenient standpoint on the case. It wasn't unusual for teenagers, and especially boys, to suffer mental difficulty in their transforming growing-up years, and boys from minorities were more prone to that.

Walter thought back to his own teenage years. He'd struggled through them with the aid of a handful of good friends, young guys of every race, who stood by him when he needed support, came to his aid when he needed muscle, though most people would think twice about taking on the ample framed Walter. It helped that back then there was a lot more muscle and less flab. Walter weathered his teenage years unscathed, but only just, and with the help of those friends.

Maaz had been less fortunate. Perhaps he never had any real friends. They were so family orientated, very close, perhaps too close, inward looking, insular, imagined Walter. Maybe that didn't help. The last report said Maaz Khan should remain on medication indefinitely. Walter wondered if the headstrong young man agreed to that, and was acting on it.

There was nothing in the PNC relating to the women at all, or maybe that wasn't a surprise. No drivers' licenses, no licenses of any kind, no prosecutions, no reports of lost property, no filed complaints, nothing. It was as if they didn't exist. Perhaps that was how the Khan dynasty wished it to be.

Walter's next port of call was the Voters' Roll, and there he discovered a little more. Seven people listed on the Roll, the four generations of men, plus Nadirah Khan, aged eighty-four, presumably Wazir's wife, Akleema Khan, aged forty-two, possibly Mohammed's wife, or maybe even Ahmed's, and Sahira Khan, aged twenty-three, possibly Maaz's wife, though Walter doubted that, more likely a sister and daughter, could be Mohammed's, could be Ahmed's. That was how Walter saw it.

He tried to remember them, the women. He had sometimes seen them, but not recently, and he couldn't remember them, not so well as he could identify them if they walked into his office. Walter pondered on where they might be at that moment, and what they were doing, and most of all; he hoped they were safe and well.

His mind turned to food. Later on, Galina the cleaner was cooking for him, and he wondered what it might be like. He had never eaten Ukrainian before, but the thought of it made his mouth water, made him hungry, and he made his excuses and left the office and ambled over to Pierre's for a light lunch, a large portion of quiche and a pint of best. He ate alone in silence and pondered on whether he could leave early, get home on time for once, allowing plenty of time for a good wash and shave, a chance to change his shirt and lash on the deodorant, for it was another hot day, and Walter went through deodorant like water.

The team came back late afternoon. Every dentist in the area had been spoken to and a copy of the idontogram left. Most promised to get back the following day, some said it would be the day after. All had promised to help, and Walter wasn't sure he wanted to hear anything positive.

He pondered on whether he should hurry back to the State and have it out with Wazir, man to man. Just where were the womenfolk? But that kind of strident talk would only sour relationships, and he didn't want to lose his friends there.

Fact was; it was likely none of the local dentists would come up with a match, so there was no point in blundering in and making a fuss. He'd bide his time and wait. There were more pressing things on Walter's plate. Mrs West was giving him gip over why he had not brought the criminals to book for decapitating a Chester citizen, even if the deceased man was a proven murderer.

The drip drip of intelligence from the underworld had yielded nothing substantial which suggested the killers, whoever they were, were not established villains, and if they weren't known criminals, who could have done such a vile thing? So-called honour killers, that's who, and Walter shivered at the thought.

It was a little after six by the time he arrived home. He had made Pauli Leishman's day by stopping off and buying two bottles of his perfumed Chianti, a drink Walter imagined Galina might enjoy.

317

Galina the cleaner had become, for one night only, Galina the cook, and she was already in the house, and the old house felt more like a home, because of the presence of a young woman he barely knew.

Maybe it was her quiet perfume. Perhaps it was the occasional foreign song that slipped from her lips, and the aromas she brought with her, or maybe it was because of the energetic, youthful movement she brought that is always associated with vibrancy and happiness.

She was in the kitchen, still in tight jeans, ponytail alive and kicking, up to her arms in flour and pastry, and she smiled at him through her big blue eyes, as he ambled in.

'Hi, Mr Darto!'

'Hello Galina, call me Walter, how's it going?'

'All goes well. Should be ready for seven, fifteen. Seven, fifteen, OK?'

'Perfect,' he said.

There was an old-fashioned brown cane basket set on the end of the worktop, the kind of thing his Aunt Mimosa would have used forty years before. He didn't think modern women were still using such things. Maybe Ukrainian women thought they were trendy. The top was covered with a patterned red cloth. He went to lift it, to look inside.

'Ah ah!' she said. 'No! My secrets, not for you, you must wait!'

Duly admonished, he grinned and limped away and went upstairs to find hot water and a clean shirt.

It was half an hour before he returned. Exciting aromas were seeping from the kitchen and drifting into the hall and sitting room. Pastry, dumplings, meat, cheese, they were all there, Walter detected that, and all were very much on his list of must haves for dinner.

He ambled into the sitting room.

Toward the rear of the room, set in front of the window, was a drop-leaf table. He rarely used it, sat in front of the TV most nights, with his ready meal on a tray on his lap like so many others. But there was something fine about raising the leaf, fixing the table,

318

finding the white tablecloth that hadn't been unfolded for more than a year, and setting out two neat places.

There was a fat candle there too, in the tall and narrow cupboard hidden within the end of the oak table, still two-thirds remaining, and once it was lit, no one would ever know it wasn't new. Walter felt good. His nose twitched. It was driving him batty. He'd investigate.

His large pan was bubbling, maybe some kind of pasta, no, dumplings more like, and he adored spicy dumplings, and she had mentioned dumplings, he was sure of it. Another pan had meat on the go; he could detect that from two thousand yards, boiled beef maybe, tender and juicy, while oil was coming to the bubble in the frying pan and garlic going in, as he shared a smile with the pretty woman.

'Ready in ten,' she said.

'What are we having?'

'Borscht to start.'

Some kind of soup, he thought, he'd have to find soup spoons.

'Then Varenyky,' she said, 'with sauerkraut, cheese, cabbage, and meat.'

'Varenyky?'

'My special dumplings, you will love, you go, I busy,' and Walter got the message and headed back to the table to find the soup spoons and light the candle.

'Nearly ready,' he heard her call through from the kitchen. 'You sit down,' and then she was in the doorway looking in, at Mr Darto sitting, waiting, opposite the candle, opposite another empty place.

She came to the table, smiled down, glanced at the vacant place. 'You ask someone else? You expecting someone? There is enough. Your pretty friend from work, maybe?'

'No, no,' said Walter, beckoning to the empty chair. 'That's for you, your place.'

She gasped. 'Oh no, Mr Darto, I not eat! I cook, I serve, I wash, but I not eat, I eat before, I not hungry, I not eat, no, no, all for you,' and she turned and headed back to the kitchen.

Walter's shoulders slumped.

He put his right elbow on the table and his chin on his hand. He was expected to dine alone. He ate on his own every bloody night when he stayed in. He'd even prefer to eat with Austerity Hayes than dine on his own, and that was saying something.

Truth was, he hated eating on his own, and though he tried once more to persuade Galina to sit opposite, even if it was only to watch him eat the fine food she had prepared, she point blank refused, and served him his dinner in a cold atmosphere that neither of them could miss.

'What a fool I've been,' he said aloud, an hour later, after she had gone, as he opened another can.

Chapter Forty-Eight

Throughout the following day the dentists reported in, by phone, email and fax, all reporting that the teeth did not belong to one of their clients, or former clients, some adding, thank goodness for that.

The info was drip-fed into the monster and it seemed happy with that, oblivious to the fact all the data was negative. It seemed to Walter that so long as it was fed; it was happy. By the end of the day two-thirds had reported back. Mrs West told the team to remember to thank the dentists for their help and cooperation, though she didn't elaborate on how they were to do it.

It had been a dead day on every front.

Walter went home at six and re-heated what remained of the Ukrainian fare. An hour later, the phone rang. Call box by the sound of things, plenty going on in the background.

'Mr Darto! Mr Darto!'

'What is it?'

'It's Galina, the cleaner.'

'I know who it is, Galina, what's the matter?'

'Dimitri, he sick.'

'Your son?'

'Yes! Radioactivity sick, they say he better, but he much worse. He bad. I have to go. I'm at airport. I fly home to Kiev pronto. I can't clean for you anymore, Mr Darto, I so sorry.'

'Don't be. Obviously you must go home if your boy is ill.'

'I must go now, Mr Darto, plane sailing.'

'The plane's departing,' said Walter.

'Plane sailing, Mr Darto. Goodbye!' and the phone went dead.

'Damn!' said Walter aloud. He had grown used to having Galina around the place at the weekend. He'd grown used to having a clean and fresh smelling house too, and unless he found someone else, he knew it wouldn't be long before that well lived in look and aroma returned. 'Damn!' he said again, and went upstairs to run the bath.

The next day followed the same pattern, a steady stream of negatives the monster ate in a trice. At ten past five, Karen took a call. Didn't give anything away. Attracted little attention. Walter barely glanced at her. She wrote something in her diary, slipped the phone down, and looked across the desk.

'You will not believe this, but we may have a match.'

Walter sat up straight and said, 'Where?'

She glanced back at her notes.

'A dentist called Kirton & Baines; they say Mr Kirton is taking the paperwork home with him. Curzon Park. We can pick it up after seven.'

'Did they give a name?'

'Nope.'

Walter glanced at his watch. It was quarter past five.

They pulled up outside the house at five past seven. Sizeable detached property, post-war by the look of it, four, maybe five bedrooms, impressive well-tended gardens, plenty of roses competing for the bees, double garage on the right side, big driveway, two almost new cars visible.

'Fixing teeth pays well,' said Karen as they strode up the drive.

'Always has,' said Walter.

Karen rang the bell, took a step back, and peered through the wavy glass door.

Someone was coming up the hall, a young woman, slim and blonde. Opened the door and stared at the strangers on the step. She was holding a pedigree dog that looked happy at the attention.

'I am Sergeant Greenwood, and this is Inspector Darriteau,' said Karen, flashing her card.

The pretty girl nodded and said, 'It's about my poor Luke, is it? I have been expecting you.'

Walter and Karen shared a look. One of some surprise, the girl thought, and then Walter took a punt and said, 'Yes, that's right, Luke Flowers, may we come in?'

'Sure,' she said, standing to one side, 'I'll just put the mutt in the kitchen; he's been on his own all day, that's why he's so pleased to see me. Go through to the lounge, take a seat, I'll only be a sec,' and they heard her say, 'Go in, Pugsley! I won't be long,' and then she was back, taking a seat on the sofa opposite to where the coppers were sitting.

'How well did you know Luke?' asked Walter.

'We were a couple, hoped to get married later in the year.'

'What did he do for a living?' asked Karen.

'Don't know. He was cagey about that, but I think it was something to do with computers. Said it was a secret, and he'd tell me when we were married.'

'Were you surprised when he was murdered?' asked Walter.

'What do you think? Course I was, devastated, still can't get my brain around it. Still expect him to walk in the door.'

'Did you know he possessed a gun?' asked Karen.

'Course not! Never saw him with one. I still find that hard to believe. I think it might have been planted.'

'So you wouldn't know where he could have obtained such a thing?' asked Walter.

'I have no idea, Inspector. I still feel this is all one huge mistake.'

'No mistake, Miss Kirton,' said Karen. 'He murdered one man, and tried to murder another.'

Melanie shook her head, still in denial. Then she said, 'One minute he is telling me he is going to Australia and the next thing, he is all over the papers, dead, murdered. I can't believe it.'

The officers gave her a moment. She was holding herself together well. Then Walter asked 'Did you know Jeffrey Player and Neil Swaythling?'

'Not really. I'd seen Neil about, playing in the band, but the other bloke I'd never heard of.'

323

'Why would Luke want to kill either of them?'

'I have no idea; keep thinking about that, it's just so unbelievable. The kind of thing you see in movies and on TV.'

'Was he ever violent?' asked Karen.

'No. Not really. He was a bit moody, and he could be feisty, but only in play, you know what I mean?' and she glanced into Karen's eyes as if she would understand better than the big black bloke.

'How long did you know him?' asked Walter.

'About a year, I suppose.'

'How was he fixed for money?' asked Karen.

'No problem with that. We'd recently come back from Venice, he always paid for everything, very generous, he was.'

'Did he have other girlfriends?' asked Walter.

'Not that I know of, but there was always the suspicion. He was the kind of guy who had a roving eye. Know what I mean? Always looking at the girls. When we were in Italy he couldn't help himself, he was forever taking pictures of the senoritas on his mobile and flicking through them later.'

'The senoras,' said Walter.

'Yeah, them too.'

'We can't find his mobile,' said Karen. 'You wouldn't have it, would you?'

'No, that's odd, he'd never go anywhere without it. Should be in his flat somewhere.'

'It isn't.'

Melanie blew out and shrugged her shoulders.

'We want to find it because we'd like to see the pictures he took,' said Walter. 'We think it might help us find his killer.'

The girl looked puzzled and said, 'Can't think where it could be. Maybe someone stole it.'

Karen and Walter shared another look before Walter said, 'We'll need you to come in and make a statement. Can you call in at the station tomorrow?'

'Yeah, suppose so, after work OK?'

'Sure,' said Karen.

'As I said earlier, I am surprised you haven't been to see me before.'

'Until today, Melanie, we didn't know your identity. We knew he had a blonde girlfriend with a dentist for a father, but that was about it,' said Walter.

'So how did you find me?'

The police officers shared a puzzled look, before Karen said, 'Information received.'

Melanie nodded, but didn't look convinced.

'Anyway,' said Walter, 'About the other matter.'

'What other matter?'

'Your father is a dentist?' asked Karen.

'Yeah, course he is.'

'He said he'd leave something for us.'

'Did he? First I've heard of it. Just a sec, they've gone out early, Round Table do, took a taxi. I'll have a look.'

She went away and was soon back, clutching a large brown envelope. Walter took it and got up and said, 'We'll see you tomorrow?'

'Yep, OK. Bye.'

Karen drove the car round the corner and pulled up. Walter slipped the envelope to Karen and said, 'That was a crazy stroke of luck.'

'Amazing.'

'Look in the envelope, but don't tell me what it says.'

Karen opened up. There were three pieces of paper inside. A tooth map, a brief explanation from Kirton & Baines detailing their findings, and some details of the patient they thought it could be.

'Don't tell me, but is there a name?' he asked.

'There is.'

Walter sighed.

'You know who it is, don't you?' she said.

'Maybe I do.'

'Well come on, clever clogs, who do you think it is?'

'Sahira Khan, aged twenty-three.'

Karen set the papers back on her lap. Shook her head, half grinned, half sniffed, muttered, 'How could you know that?'

'Luck, and judgement. Wazir Khan is a friend of mine.'

'Oh, geez. So what now?'

'Back to the station. I want to speak to Mrs West, and after that we'll need to put a party together of ten officers, and then we are going down to the State of Kerala, and this time, not for dinner.'

Chapter Forty-Nine

Mrs West viewed the quiet day as an opportunity to go home early. She was up to her armpits in steak and kidney pie. Her husband was going out early, and she wanted him well fed before that. She shook some flour from her rubber gloves and grabbed the ringing phone off the wall in the kitchen.

'Sorry to bother you, ma'am.'

'What is it, Walter?'

'The idontogram, we may have a match.'

'Good God, that is a surprise.'

'Thing is, ma'am, I know the family concerned.'

'Who are they?'

'The Khans, they own the State of Kerala restaurant.'

'Heavens above. I think I know the guy too. Didn't he recently get an MBE?'

'That's the one, ma'am. Services to race relations and providing harmony and opportunities for under privileged kids in the inner cities, something like that.'

'You think this could be a so-called honour killing?'

'Don't know yet, ma'am, but it's not looking good.'

'So what are you proposing?'

'I am putting together a team of ten, going down there as soon as we are ready, going to scoop up all the family and bring them back here for questioning. We'll close the restaurant, it could be a crime scene, get the SOCO shift in, and take it from there.'

'Do you want me to put someone else on it, seeing as you know these people?'

'No, ma'am, I can handle it.'

327

'If you're sure, Walter. Look, I am up to my neck in something important here; I'll try to get back in later.'

'Fine, ma'am, I'll keep you posted.'

'Can't wait to tell Gitts about this.'

'Do I detect a little hostility?'

Walter guessed at the smile that came over Mrs West's face.

'Chief Superintendent Gitts, Gitt by name, git by nature. He crapped on me from on high during a course a year ago. Put me right in it, and lo-and-behold, we seem to have identified the body in his murder, and with a little luck, may have caught the ruddy killers as well! Justice, don't you think?'

'Sure, ma'am, yes,' said Walter, hoping to God they had not identified the killers.

'Well, get on with it, man, and well done. Can't imagine how you could have known the teeth belonged to that family, but something's still ticking in that old brain of yours, eh? You haven't lost it yet, have you? Keep me informed.'

'Of course, ma'am, and thank you.'

Walter returned to the Incident Room. Karen had rounded up the team and had prepared a brief presentation. The tiny green power light, bottom left, on the monster was flashing on and off like a hospital heartbeat, monsters never sleep, not completely, and it seemed to wink faster than normal, as if it had an inkling that something big was going down.

Gibbons, Hector Browne, and Jenny Thompson were there, plus two SOCO blokes, or at least one bloke and one lass; and three uniforms Karen had press-ganged into service. Not that they needed much persuading, because it was clear something exciting was about to happen.

Walter sat on the desk at the back and nodded to Karen, and she smiled and caressed the monster's face. A big colour picture appeared of the Khan menfolk, culled from the StateofKeralaRestaurant.com website.

'The Khan family,' she said, 'or at least the men. Wazir, Ahmed, Mohammed, and Maaz,' and she pointed to each in turn, and as she did so each picture magnified. 'There should be three more members of this family too, but for whatever reason, they are not pictured. But then they are women. Nadirah, an old lady, believed to be Wazir's wife, Akleema, and Sahira Khan.'

She minimised the pics and almost threw it to the bottom of the screen. Brought up a copy of the idontogram. The tooth map supplied by Manchester police.

'Late this afternoon a local dentist, Kirton & Baines, reported they had matched the idonto with one of their clients, none other than Sahira Khan. However, there are some provisos to this. Idontos are not like fingerprints. They are not foolproof, and are more likely to be compromised the less dental treatment the victim has received. With our teeth,' and she couldn't resist bringing up an enhanced picture of the perfect set of cleaned gnashers, 'there was only one small filling.'

'Lucky her,' muttered Gibbons, stroking his chin.

'She wasn't that lucky, was she?' snapped Karen.

'Yeah, no, course sarge, sorry.'

'However, the dentist has written a note to say that he would be amazed if the teeth in the body were not the ones that belonged to his client,' and Karen tapped and swiped the screen again and brought up the dentist's report, magnified it ten times so everyone could read it.

'Are we looking at some kind of honour killing?' asked Hector.

'We don't know,' said Karen. 'But we aim to find out.'

Tapped the screen again, and the monster must have liked the feel of her fingers, for it brought up a skypic of the State of Kerala, taken on a sunny day.

'This is the Indian restaurant they own in Brook Street. As far as Indian eateries go, it is very upmarket. Expensive and luxurious. Guv eats there a lot, don't you?' and she grinned and everyone turned and leered at the boss.

'I wouldn't say a lot, but quite often. I know the people there. Up to now they have been model citizens, which makes it all the more puzzling.'

'How the hell did we get on to them in the first place?' asked Hector.

Karen grinned. 'You'd have to ask Guv about that.'

'Get on with it!' said Walter.

Karen began again.

'As soon as this meeting is over, we are going down there mob handed. All family members are to be isolated in separate cars and brought back here for questioning. Jenny, have you sorted out separate rooms for them?'

'I have, sarge, yes.'

'Good, and a word of warning. Look out for the younger one, Maaz,' more screen taps and more action, and a huge colour pic of Maaz, twice life size, culled from the website publicity guff, looking devilish, beamed out across the Incident Room. 'He's been in trouble before, spent some time in a mental institution. If he needs to bring medication with him, make sure he is allowed to do that. There is a ceremonial sword we are interested in too. A family artefact, brought with them from India, generations ago, when Wazir, the old man, first came to this country. It's in a display case behind the bar. We need that for tests. No bare hand touching. Do we have the necessary bags?'

Gibbons tapped a bag of equipment on the desk before him. 'All present and correct, sarge.'

Karen nodded and continued.

'I want one uniform at the front entrance to stop anyone else entering, one uniform at the back to catch absconders, another uniform to go in with us, the senior man, to ask and tell existing diners to leave.'

The senior uniform bloke looked pleased with himself, even if he was going to be home late.

'Once we are inside, I'll make an announcement to that effect,' said Walter. 'Diners will not be charged for any food they may have eaten, but nor will they be allowed to finish their meals, and no

330

further food or drink will be served. Take all their names and addresses, with ID, and they are to be escorted off the premises as soon as possible,' and he nodded Karen back into action.

'Jenny will video everything. Hector, you are to go in from the back too. Gibbons will be at the front with us. As soon as the place has been cleared, the SOCO guys and gals can get to work.'

'Six vehicles lined up?' asked Walter.

'Sure, Guv, three marked, three un.'

'What happens if Sahira's there, too?' asked Hector.

No one had considered that possibility.

'Unlikely,' said Walter. 'We'll have a party and I'll pay for everything,' and he nodded at Karen to continue.

'The Khan family will be interviewed separately by myself and the Guv as soon as we get back, starting with the youngest. The interviews will be screened live on the monster for those that want to watch.'

'Fantastic,' said Jenny.

'Count me in,' said Hector.

'Maybe later, Hector, but first I want you to stay behind at the State and interview all the other staff. Names, addresses, how long they have worked there, how long they have been in this country, how well they know or knew Sahira, and when they last saw her, all that stuff.'

'I get all the good jobs,' sulked Hector.

Walter jumped in. 'It IS a good job! You may unearth information that we don't have. Treat it seriously!'

'Yeah, sure, sorry, Guv. Do you want me to check immigration papers as well?'

'May as well,' said Karen.

'And don't forget,' said Karen, 'we are investigating not one but two murders,' and she brought back a pic of Luke Flowers. 'We are seeking any link between Flowers and the Khans. Find out if he ever ate there, find out if he knew Sahira Khan, because that could unearth a motive, however misguided, for both murders. Go through the restaurant bookings; find out when Flowers last visited the place.'

'Got you, sarge,' said Hector.

'And while you are looking for links with Luke Flowers,' said Walter, 'See if you can find any links to Neil Swaythling as well. We still don't know what sparked this whole thing off.'

Karen saw the mention of him as something of a challenge, but a simple one, and a second later a colour pic of Neil was staring down at the evening gathering.

'This operation is top secret. No mention of it is to be leaked anywhere, no TV, press, no reporters, no nothing, until I say so. That clear?' said Walter.

Everyone nodded and muttered, 'Sure, Guv.'

'I don't want reporters trampling all over the place. Mrs West will be back in later, so stay alert and be positive. She'll be watching.'

'Questions?' asked Karen.

The team looked round and stared at one another.

Hector had a question. He always did.

'Will the Manchester boys be coming down?'

'No!' said Walter. 'Mrs West was adamant about that. There is history there. The Manchester boys know nothing about this operation, and that is the way it will stay until we are good and ready. Everyone understand?'

More knowing looks and nods, and Karen said, 'Right! Come on! Operation Korma is under way.'

'Couldn't you think of anything better than that?' teased Gibbons, grinning at his sarge.

'Belt up, Gibbons!'

Chapter Fifty

The convoy of six cars pulled into Brook Street and parked on double yellow lines, twenty yards ahead of the State. No flashing lights, no sirens, no weapons on display, no hurry, no panic. Karen sent Hector and a uniform around the back in case anyone did a runner.

Walter strode toward the doors, Jenny to his rear, videocam in hand, Karen at his side, SOCO still in the cars waiting to be summoned.

Walter eased open the brass and glass doors, conscious that it was only a short time since he had enjoyed a good dinner in the place.

Inside, the same subdued golden light, the same aromas, the same gentle hubbub of Cestrians enjoying exotic evening meals, the same expensive copra mat, the same deep pile carpet, the same discretely lit half moon bar. Walter glanced across the room toward the display case. The soft light glinted back from the sword, locked away in that expensive glass box.

The male Khans were all in the house, enjoying their evening meal, sitting at the same table Walter had used on Sunday night. Wazir with his back to the wall, perched in Walter's favourite chair, Ahmed opposite with his back to the doors.

At the next table sat Austerity Hayes and Harry Barrett, deep in conversation. It seemed they had ordered meals, but no food had yet arrived. She was wearing the same ridiculous bonnet, looked hungry, looked like she could eat everyone in the house, as she glanced up and spied people she knew.

'Yoo-ee, Walter,' she called. 'Come and join us, and bring your friends over too.'

Walter gabbled, 'Not tonight, Austerity,' and turned away and approached the Khan's table, Jenny filming the scene, Karen a pace behind.

333

Wazir stood up and wiped his mouth.

The other Khans turned and stared into the camera.

'Hello, Walter,' said Wazir, wiping his mouth and setting his napkin down. 'This doesn't look like a social call to me.'

'It isn't, Wazir. We are making enquiries into the whereabouts of Sahira Khan.'

Wazir said nothing; sat down.

'She's gone to Pakistan,' blurted Maaz, inspecting the bitches. The blonde one in the tight fitting cord trousers, he could give her something to think about, and the more curvaceous girl-next-door type, carrying the camera, filming him. What the hell was that all about? Filming him at dinner? That was a first. He smiled for the camera and stuck out and waggled his tongue, turned his eyes back to the blonde. Fit looking bitch, for a copper, for a Christian, fit looking.

'And when was that?' asked Walter.

Maaz giggled. 'Ages since, innit, man.'

'Be quiet!' said Mohammed.

Ahmed looked at Walter and said, 'Would you care to explain what is going on?'

'It's you who have some explaining to do,' said Karen. 'You are all to accompany us to the police station, right now.'

'Are you crazy?' asked Mohammed.

'Good job we've finished eating, innit,' grinned Maaz, staring down at the picked clean stainless steel serving dishes.

'What about the restaurant?' asked Ahmed.

'The restaurant is now closed,' said Walter.

'You can't do that!' protested Mohammed.

'I just have.'

'But it's never closed,' said Wazir. 'Not once since the day it opened, not even on Christmas Day, never, other than when it was being refitted.'

'There's a first time for everything,' said Karen.

Maaz gave her a hard look.

'Where are the women?' asked Walter.

334

'Where they should be!' snarled Maaz, staring at the black bloke. 'Not like your bloody lot.'

'My lot?' queried Walter.

Maaz grinned and looked round at his family, as if for support, and back at the coppers. 'Yeah you know, one third of your women are out on the streets doing tricks for twenty-five quid, another third are off their heads on coke and ganja, and the other third are at home, single mothers bringing up little brats to be just like them... and some of your women do all three,' and he giggled and grinned.

Karen glanced at Walter. She thought he was going to strike the guy and considered interrupting, but Walter was talking again.

'My lot, as you so elegantly describe us, are too busy driving the buses and trains and keeping the capital moving, too busy becoming doctors and nurses and keeping the national health service on its feet, looking after sick people, like you, too busy winning half the medals Britain wins in the Olympic Games, too busy making and influencing most of the music that pops out of your radio.... you halfwit!'

'Wow!' said Maaz, determined to come back at him. 'Fo-yi, fo-yi, innit!'

Walter and Karen glanced at the others.

'It's one of his stupid made-up words,' explained Mohammed.

'Meaning?' snapped Karen.

'Figment of your imagination, darling, know what I mean? Figment of your freaking imagination, and mine,' said Maaz leering at Karen through her clothes, as if she was standing there naked.

'Gibbons!' she said. 'Take him away!'

'Love to!' said Gibbons, seizing Maaz's wrist.

'Do you need anything, Maaz?' asked Walter.

Maaz ignored the copper and began shouting, 'I took the bitch to the airport myself. Me, Maaz Khan, took her alone. It was all down to me.'

Walter nodded at Gibbons and he slipped one end of the cuffs on Maaz's wrist, the other on his own, and led Maaz outside and back to the cars.

Walter stared around the restaurant at still, stony faces, gazing back. He clapped his hands like gunshots, and ordered everyone outside. 'What you have eaten is free, but there will be nothing else!'

Karen watched the weird Austerity making a big issue of getting her things together. Heard her say to her companion, 'We'll just have to eat an Indonesian,' followed by raucous laughter, and as the restaurant cleared, a little queue formed at the main doors as the police took the customers' details.

'Where are the women?' repeated Walter.

'Upstairs, having their evening meal,' said Wazir.

Walter nodded Karen and Jenny away to find and deal with the womenfolk.

'They're not involved,' explained Ahmed.

'We'll decide who's involved and who isn't,' snapped Hector, after making his way in through the back.

'I need the key to the display cabinet,' said Walter, nodding across toward the sword.

'It's lost,' said Mohammed.

'In that case we'll have to break it open.'

Wazir stood up and took out his keys. Removed the smallest one from a hefty clump and handed it across the table.

Walter nodded his thanks and gave it to Hector.

Within half an hour the State had closed, the remaining staff were being interviewed, while the Khan family were making themselves comfortable in six separate interview rooms on the fifth floor of the main Chester police station.

There was quite a crowd gathered round the monster as Jenny switched on the interview room live feed. There was a single table in the room with the grinning Maaz on one side and the home team opposite. The Guv, still looking grumpy, after Maaz's earlier stupid comments, and Karen who had been at her razor sharp best all day.

Karen began proceedings.

'This interview is being recorded on live sound and video.'

'It sure is,' said one of the uniforms in the Incident Room, crowding round the live colour footage beaming in from upstairs. An officer who had brought one of the Khans back from the State, and was keen to see it through, desperate to have something exciting to tell his wife over the liver and onions that would be on the table when he managed to get home. Everyone settled in for a long session.

'Are you all right, Maaz?' asked Walter.

'Never been better, fat man, black man. How did they ever let you become an Inspector?'

Walter ignored the comment and said, 'Tell us about Sahira?'

'What do you want to know, nigger?'

'Cut that out!'

Again, Karen thought Walter was about to strike Maaz. She admired his self-restraint. He was already talking again.

'She's your sister, right?'

Maaz blew out air.

'Phew! Detection gone crazy. Go to the top of the class.'

'And you took her to the airport?' asked Karen.

'Said so, didn't I?'

'Why was that?' asked Walter.

'Why do you think?'

'We don't know, Maaz. Why don't you tell us all about it?'

Maaz blew out again and looked from side to side. He seemed to be thinking of what to say, or whether to say anything at all, and for a moment it looked like he might adopt the guilty looking and unhelpful "no comment" stance. But for whatever reason, he began talking, and once he started he couldn't stop.

'She was going to Pakistan to get married, some stinking old warlord in his sixties. Can you imagine that, bitch?' he said, glaring at Karen, as if he thought that fate would be good for her too.

'Why?' asked Walter.

'Why what?'

'Why was she going to Pakistan?'

'I just told you!'

'But why Pakistan? Why not marry someone here?'

337

'She'd been a naughty girl, hadn't she, a very naughty girl, been shagging Christians. I mean, how low can you go?'

'Have you ever shagged a Christian, Maaz,' asked Karen through a deadpan face.

'None of your damn business, bitch! But if you want me to shag you, I'll do you right now across the desk, live on video. You'd get quite a thrill out of that, wouldn't ya? Just tell the black twat to leave and we can get down to business!'

'Behave yourself!' bellowed Walter.

Maaz sniffed and glanced away.

There was a brief period of silence before Walter asked, 'Who arranged the marriage?'

'The old blokes, who do ya think?'

'And you drove her to the airport?'

Maaz nodded.

'Speak your answer, please,' said Karen.

'I... drove... her... to... the... air... port.'

'When was that?' asked Walter.

Maaz gave them the date, didn't have to think about it, just spilled it out as if it were ingrained on his confused brain.

'And you saw her depart?'

'Nope! Threw her out of the car at the airport. Couldn't stand to be with the bitch for a second longer than necessary.'

'So you didn't see her on the plane?' asked Karen.

'Just said so, didn't I. Are you thick, or what?'

'The thing is, Maaz, we don't think she ever got on that plane.'

Maaz grinned and shrugged his shoulders. Then he said, 'If that's the case, the old warlord is going to be mighty angry. But maybe it was for the best, 'cos no right-minded man would want her as a wife. I mean, would you?'

'What was for the best?' asked Walter.

'What you said, if she didn't get there.'

'What happened to her, Maaz?' asked Karen.

'God alone knows, but let's hope it was something horrific.'

'Did you kill her, Maaz,' asked Walter.

'Oh yeah, strangled her with my bare hands. What do you freaking think?'

'Someone killed her,' said Karen.

'Is the bitch dead, then?'

'It's possible,' said Walter.

'Good oh, best news of the day!'

'She was your sister,' said Karen.

'Was, is the operative word, blondie. Are you a bit of a goer, by the way? You look as if there's a bit of mileage in you,' and Maaz grinned again in that odd way of his.

Karen ignored him.

'Tell me about the Christians she was involved with?' asked Walter.

'What do you want to know? Chapter and verse, old man. Bet you'd love that, wouldn't you? Get your rocks off on it, would you? The dusky wench dropping her knickers for all sorts?'

'Was she involved with one particular man?' asked Karen.

'How the hell would I know?'

'Was she involved with Luke Flowers?' asked Walter.

Maaz went to speak, reined himself back, like a pulling stallion being reined in at the last second by a tough rider.

'Luke who?'

'You heard what the Inspector said,' said Karen. 'She was involved with Luke Flowers, wasn't she?'

'I have no idea.'

In the Incident Room, the crowd was enthralled. Gibbons grinned at Hector who had joined the party.

Gibbons said, 'He's guilty as hell. We've nailed them.'

'Not yet,' said Jenny. 'There's no proof.'

'Guilty as sin!' said Hector. 'How the hell can anyone do that, murder their own sister, because they don't like who they date?'

There was a collective shrugging of shoulders as they turned back to the monster, as Walter was asking his next question.

'Tell me about the sword?'

'What sword?'

'Don't be an idiot, Maaz,' said Karen. 'The ceremonial sword that we now possess.'

'What do you want to know?'

'We think it will prove to be the weapon that killed Luke Flowers.'

Maaz let go one of his silliest, girlish, most confident giggles.

'I'll bet you anything you like it isn't!'

'Are you a gambling man?' asked Walter.

'Course not, it's against my religion.'

'But drinking alcohol and indulging in pre-marital sex are also against your religion, but it doesn't stop you doing that, does it, Maaz?' said Karen.

Maaz stood up and pointed across the table and shrieked, 'You have no idea what you are talking about! Don't you go accusing me of all sorts, you bitch!'

'Wowser!' said Gibbons sitting watching, 'It's all kicking off!'

Walter stood up and stared into the kid's face and said, 'Sit down, Maaz, we are not accusing you of anything. Not yet. We just want to know what happened to Sahira... and Luke.'

Maaz glared at the fat black guy, then his eyes changed down a gear, and he looked around as if surprised to find himself there, and sank back into his chair, and for the next few minutes he would not look at Karen at all.

Chapter Fifty-One

The sword was sent for immediate forensic examination. If they could link it to the killing of Luke Flowers, the Khan family were nailed. The police were confident it would. They couldn't wait to receive the report, and while they were waiting, the questioning of Maaz Khan continued without a break.

'How did you find out that Sahira was seeing Christians?' asked Karen.

'Wouldn't you like to know!' snarled Maaz.

'That's why we are asking,' said Walter. 'Did you see them together?'

'Nah!'

'Did you listen to her telephone calls?' asked Karen.

'What do you think I am?'

'So, how did you know?' asked Walter.

Maaz shook his head hard, leered again and said, 'It was the pictures, innit.'

'What pictures?' said Walter and Karen, almost as one.

Maaz smiled, almost charmingly, and raised his hand and arm and pointed across the desk. 'Ah, now you're interested, aren't you?'

'Of course we are interested, Maaz,' said Walter. 'We are interested in everything you have to say.'

'What pictures?' repeated Karen.

'Filthy they were; porno, of my sister.'

'Where did you see these pictures?' asked Walter.

'Where do you think?'

'On a mobile phone?' suggested Karen.

Maaz grinned at the girl, and looked at Walter. 'See! She knows. Filthy bitch, been there, done that, bet she has, she knows all about

341

it. I'll bet if you looked at her Bookface page you'd see porno pics of her, all tastefully done, it's the main use for mobile phones these days, taking filthy pictures.'

'Is that what you do, Maaz?' asked Karen.

Maaz ignored the question and said, 'Ever thought of starring in a porno pic, whore-face?'

'I don't think it would suit me,' said Walter.

'Not you, old man. Blondie here, there'd be a few quid to be made with pics of her, I can tell you.'

'Is that what you do?' repeated Karen.

'Not me! But Sahira, that's another matter. There was no low point to which she wouldn't stoop. No wonder she was struck from the earth... if indeed that's what's happened.'

'Did you strike her from this earth, Maaz?' asked Walter.

Maaz shook his head. 'Dropped her at the airport, mate. That was the last time I saw her. Why don't you check through some CCTV or summat, that'll back me up.'

'I am sure that will be done,' said Karen.

'Too true, sister, sooner the better for me, so I can get outta here and get home.'

'These mobile phone pictures,' said Walter. 'Where are they now?'

'Still on the phone, I suppose.'

'And where is the phone?' asked Karen.

'Now there I can't help you.'

'It was Luke Flowers' phone, wasn't it?' asked Walter.

'Luke who?' grinned Maaz.

Walter shrugged his shoulders.

It was time for a reassessment break.

'This interview is suspended,' said Walter. 'Terminated at 9.38pm.'

'That it then? Can I go home now?'

'No, you can't,' said Walter. 'Have him taken to the cells, and get Mohammed up here.'

Maaz was taken down to the cells by a broad red-faced twenty-five-year service man who looked way older than he was. Maaz didn't stop talking for a second. The police officer barely said a word.

There were fifteen cells in the basement, all in a line off the narrow corridor, seven feet wide, but longer than usual, to use all the available space. The building was late fifties design when cost was an issue, and early sixties build, when quality control was not much of an issue at all. There were no windows to the cells, no heating, and no air conditioning. In the winter they were freezing and in the summer it was always stifling.

Inside the cell were two items.

A metal framed bench-like bed, brown leather clad, easy to clean, hard to vandalise, welded to the floor, set parallel to the right wall of the cell. The second item was a heavy blue plastic chamber pot, unbreakable, no en suite facilities, the whole building had been earmarked for demolition and replacement, but budget restraints had delayed that, and temporary guests had to cope with nineteenth-century standards of hygiene and comfort.

There was nothing else in the cell, no table, no chair, no blanket, no radio, no knife and fork, nothing but the prisoner himself, or herself, alone with their thoughts, under the one protected ceiling light, a bulb that could be switched off at any time, plunging the visitor into total darkness, or left on all night.

Maaz Khan had been searched earlier, and before he was left alone, the custody sergeant took away his tie, checked his shoes for laces, but found the guy preferred designer gear, neat slip-on loafers; must have cost a pretty penny, maybe half a week's wages for a police officer.

Maaz was eased inside and the door slammed behind him.

He stared round and stopped talking, stopped grinning.

Licked his lips and sat on the bench, his mind a total blank.

He didn't know why he was there.

Didn't know what he had done wrong.

Didn't know where he had been.

Didn't know where he was going.

Didn't know how long it would be before he was spoken to again.

343

In the interview room, Mohammed was next up.

'Tell us about the pictures?' asked Walter.

'What pictures?'

'Don't waste our time!' snapped Karen. 'Maaz has told us all about the filthy pics on the phone.'

Mohammed shook his head.

'Where is the mobile phone now?'

'I have no idea.'

'If it's in the State, we'll find it,' said Karen.

'Of course you will,' said Mohammed.

'So, where is it?' asked Walter.

Mohammed shrugged his shoulders.

'Did you kill Luke Flowers?' asked Walter.

'Luke who?'

'You know who we are talking about!' said Karen.

'Nope, don't know anything about it. Is my solicitor coming?'

'He's been notified,' said Walter.

'He's in Birmingham for God's sake!'

Karen grinned. 'That's hardly our fault.'

'I think I'll wait until he's here.'

'Suit yourself,' said Walter. 'But fact is, he won't be here 'till tomorrow. I thought you'd prefer to get on with things, get home all the sooner.'

Mohammed twisted around in his chair, back and forth, then settled and said, 'Yeah, you're right. Let's get on with it; I have nothing to hide.'

Walter and Karen shared a look and Walter said, 'What did you think when you discovered Sahira had been sleeping with white boys?'

'I wasn't happy about it. Do you have any children? Any daughters?'

'No.'

'Well if you did, I can tell you it would burn you up inside.'

'Enough to kill the people involved?' asked Karen.

'You don't know anything, you coppers.'

'Maybe we do, maybe we don't,' said Walter. 'Here's your chance to set the record straight.'

'Look! We discovered Sahira was having this affair and for her own good we agreed she should go to Pakistan and marry there. If anything bad happened to the white guy, that's unfortunate, but don't expect me or any of our family to grieve for him.'

'She didn't get to Pakistan,' said Karen.

'So you say.'

'You don't seem particularly worried about the fact your only daughter is missing,' said Walter.

'Wherever she is, God will look after her.'

A loud rap came to the door. Karen jumped up and opened it. Jenny Thompson was there, holding a folded over note. Handed it to Karen. The women shared a silent nod, and Jenny left. Karen sat down and slipped the note to Walter. He held it up against his chest and opened the half sheet of paper.

Mohammed, sitting across the table, tried to read the words through the paper. Someone had written something heavy in ball-pen. He could see the indentations, but could not make out the message.

Walter read the five words twice and passed the note to Karen. Her eyes raced across the writing.

Sword not the murder weapon.

'What's up?' asked Mohammed.

'Nothing. This interview is suspended, timed at 10.22pm.'

Chapter Fifty-Two

Walter scratched his head and gazed through the window at the falling darkness. The last of the daylight streaks were vanishing over the Roodee. He glanced back at Mrs West sitting behind her desk and then across at Karen.

'It's not the murder weapon,' said Mrs West, leaving the thought floating in the air, and then she added, 'that's a bloody nuisance.'

'They must have had it changed,' said Walter, 'a copy made and substituted.'

'So where's the original?' asked Mrs West.

'Not in the State,' said Walter.

'How long has it been on display?' asked Karen.

'Years!' said Walter. 'For as long as I have been eating there.'

'Course they had it changed!' said Karen. 'Look at the report. It says it is newly made, less than a year old.'

'Where are we up to with the interviews?' asked Mrs West, stifling a yawn.

'About to start on Ahmed?' said Walter.

'Do you want to give it a break and come back refreshed in the morning?'

'No! Rather do it now, ma'am, if you don't mind.'

'If that's what you want, Walter. You're in charge. Get on with it and wrap it up. I want to ring Gitts and tell him we have solved his case,' and she smiled a stiff smile they hadn't seen before, and nodded them toward the door.

The interview with Ahmed Khan was brief and to the point. He refused to say a word until his solicitor was present. Fact was, his lawyer had set off from Birmingham as soon as he'd taken the call. He wouldn't have done that for just anyone, but the Khan family were one of his oldest clients, and from what had been said, they were in big trouble. But he was stuck on the M6 behind a major accident that showed no sign of being cleared. Latest forecasts predicted he wouldn't arrive in Chester for another couple of hours; and he was struggling to keep his eyes open.

Ahmed was taken away, and Wazir was brought to the interview room. Those watching on the monster hadn't lost interest. There was something about this patriarch of a man that demanded one paid attention.

Walter admired Wazir. Always had done. Everything about him. His demeanour, his principles, his conscientiousness, his hard working ethic, his achievements, his family, his sense of humour and duty, and his looks. The man was eighty-eight-years-old, and looked immaculate. Walter admired that too, for he couldn't match it.

Wazir's steel grey hair was neatly side parted, not a single strand missing, a little longer than one might expect in a man of his age. He preferred it that way. His slim and sleek moustache had been trimmed that morning, while his calm dark eyes watched the officers, never darting about. He wasn't a nervous man, never had been. It wasn't an easy moment for either of them, and they both knew it.

Karen made the formal introductions and checked the recording equipment was working. Walter glanced at the tiny camera in the topmost corner of the room, thought about how it would be portrayed on the monster downstairs. Sniffed and began again.

'Wazir?' said Walter, settling into his chair.

'Walter,' said Wazir, acknowledging the man.

'How long have we known each other?'

Wazir sucked in a half smile, a cold smile that on another day would have been warmer. He threw his head back and glanced at the false ceiling. 'Hard to remember, but it's a long time.'

'Have you ever lied to me, Wazir?'

'Of course not.'

347

'And you wouldn't lie to me now?'

'No,' yet as he said the word, Wazir wondered at the truth of his answer. Every honest man promises himself he will not tell lies. But there comes a time, maybe when one's own flesh and blood are involved, perhaps when their entire future was at stake, in those circumstances, maybe an occasional lie might be uttered, might slip from the mouth, even from the cautious and careful lips of the irreproachable Wazir Khan.

Walter too pondered on whether Wazir could make it through the interview without lying.

'Tell me about Maaz?' said Walter.

'He's not a well boy.'

'We had gathered that.'

'You will have to make allowances for him,' said Wazir. 'He needs treatment, he needs professional attention.'

'That's as maybe, but we need to know. Did he murder Sahira?'

'I wasn't there, I cannot say.'

'What happened to the sword?'

'You took it away.'

'No!' snapped Karen.

'That was a copy,' said Walter, 'as I am sure you know. We are not stupid and we want to know what happened to the original.'

Wazir opened his mouth but did not speak. Thought hard. Didn't come up with an adequate answer, and said, 'I can't help you there, Walter.'

In the cell deep down below, Maaz had taken to running from one end to the other. Seventeen feet. Longer than usual. He could get up quite a speed. He was working up a sweat. Paused for a moment. Removed all his clothes. Tossed them on the metal-framed bed. Slipped off his shoes and started running again, naked.

Walter ordered water and offered a glass to Wazir. The old man bobbed his head, thanked Walter, and accepted the drink.

'I want to go over it again,' said a refreshed Walter. 'From the beginning. Tell us again why and when it was decided Sahira should leave for Pakistan. Take your time, Wazir, but think about it, and please, don't insult our intelligence with any lies.'

Wazir sipped and thought and sipped and thought. He considered the Jamaican to be his friend. But at what point did he drop the "r" from the word friend? Despite the iced water, his mouth was dry. He possessed an MBE, the African didn't. That must mean something.

'I have told you everything I know, Walter.'

'Tell me again, Wazir, tell us again.'

The temperature in the cell was eighty-eight Fahrenheit and with the exercise, Maaz was covered in sweat. Wet footprints decorated the clammy floor. Out and back, out and back, fifty times, and pause, time for a quick break. Maaz went to the far wall. Banged his head on the grey painted plaster. Six times, ten, twenty times, gradually harder and harder. He enjoyed it. He usually did, though it was more satisfying when he performed before an audience. Maaz treasured the looks in their eyes and the puzzled masks on their faces. Obtained a real thrill through bemusing people.

He jerked away from the wall, laughed aloud, and ran down the cell. Pushed off the far wall and ran back again, pushed harder still, picking up speed, dashed down the cell, and took off, arms outstretched wide like a jet aeroplane, feet together high into the air behind like a tail-plane, straight back, a strange smile set on his face, as he crashed into the far wall, face first, head first, happy in his work, with as much pent up energy as he possessed, like a jumbo jet smashing into a skyscraper.

No one would ever know the final thoughts that swirled through his tortured brain. Split his head open. Blood gushed. Crashed to the ground in a sweaty, bloody heap. Plane down. Plane dead. Pilot error. Crew killed. No survivors. No black box. No explanation, nothing.

349

For the first time Walter thought Wazir was lying. He couldn't have told you why, just a sixth sense kicking in, as if he was playing for time. Maybe he was dragging it out until the family solicitor arrived. He was due in the building at any moment. Not that it would make any difference.

'Go over that again, Wazir, once more please.'

The custody sergeant flipped open the metal hatch on the door to Maaz's cell. Regular checkups were the norm. Couldn't believe what he saw. Maaz was naked and crumpled on the floor at the far end, his body scrunched in unnatural angles. Blood had oozed across the floor. The red river had reached almost back to the door.

'Oh, God!' and all hell broke loose as he smacked the alarm.

It was Gibbons who knocked on the interview room door and entered without waiting to be invited. Walter glanced up, irritated at being disturbed. Gibbons handed him a note. Just four words. Maaz Khan Committed Suicide. Gibbons left the room without a word.

'Oh dear!' said Walter, showing the note to Karen.

She said, 'Ouch!'

'Something the matter?' asked Wazir.

'Interview suspended at…' said Karen, as she glanced at her watch and spoke the time.

'What's happened?' asked Wazir.

'There's been a development,' said Walter. 'We'll keep you informed,' and the police officers left the room, leaving Wazir to his racing thoughts.

The suicide of Maaz Khan provided an unexpected impetus to the case. On hearing of his son's demise, coming so soon after his daughter's death, Mohammed Khan confessed to the murder of Sahira Khan and Luke Flowers. Initially, the police imagined it was a case of Mohammed taking the blame on himself. But after

350

questioning Wazir and Ahmed for a further twenty-four hours, they concluded the violent deaths had been the work of Maaz and Mohammed alone. Walter reserved judgment. The papers would go to the CPS, and they would decide if Wazir and Ahmed would face charges too.

Mrs West was understandably jubilant. Two murders cleared up in one night, and one of those was not even on her patch. It gave her great satisfaction in ringing Chief Superintendent Gitts in Manchester with the breaking news that her wonderful team had solved his murder, and had charged Mohammed Khan. Gitts bit his tongue and congratulated Mrs West, the officer he referred to behind her back as that stuck-up bitch from Chester, though inside he was seething, as the woman had always riled him for reasons only he understood,

The following morning, she called Walter into her office.

'Sit down, my man,' she said, smirking. 'Fancy a snifter?' and from her desk drawer she produced a half bottle of Irish whiskey and two tumblers.

That was a first, so far as Walter could remember, and in such circumstances, it would be rude to refuse.

Mrs West was on a high. Her face glowed as she poured two measures and slipped one across the desk.

'You did a great job, Walter, thank you,' and she raised her glass and winked at him.

Walter smiled and sipped away. It sure as hell made a change from the usual carping, and hints that maybe his retirement day was coming ever closer.

'The thing is,' she said, 'you remember that memo that came down from on high saying we should make the most of any successes we attain, through publicity. After all, our failures are always magnified a thousand times. So I thought we'd have a little party, a small cocktail effort, that kind of thing. Invite Gitts down,' she said, grinning over the top of her glass.

'If you think that's wise, ma'am, but there shouldn't be any hint of triumphalism.'

'Good God no, Walter, there will not be any triumphalism on my watch,' and she pursed her lips and smirked at him.

'Do you think Gitts will come?'

'Chief Superintendent Gitts, Walter, yes, I think he will. To not do so would be seen as sour grapes, and he wouldn't want that.'

'Whatever you say, ma'am.'

'And the press, too. Local telly, that kind of thing, and the printed press of course, and that woman as well, what's her name? Gardenia Floem, that's the one.'

'Oh no, not her.'

'Eh? Why? Don't you like her?'

'Not particularly, and the thing is, I think she might have a thing about me, ridiculous as it sounds.'

Mrs West spluttered on her drink. 'Lucky you. You could do a heck of a lot worse.'

The suggestion the local crime hack might fancy her star inspector, well, that was indeed news, and besides, it was too late, Walter's doubts aside, for she'd already invited the woman. It would make the party more interesting, and it was high time Walter found someone to look after him, though Gardenia seemed awfully young. And as Mrs West explored that fascinating train of thought, Walter said, 'The thing is, ma'am, we haven't really finished the case. There are far too many loose ends.'

'Meaning?'

'We still don't know why Luke Flowers was taking pot-shots at Neil Swaythling, and why he killed the other kid. Perhaps we should suspend any party until all the facts are known.'

She wafted her hand fast across the desk. 'Poppycock, Walter! If we waited for all loose ends to be tied up in complicated cases, we'd wait forever. The killing of Jeffrey Player was almost certainly an incidental accident, you said so yourself, and Flowers' feud with

Swaythling was probably a drugs issue. He's in a rock band, for heaven's sake. How much more proof do you need than that? And as Luke Flowers is no longer with us, that feud is dead and buried. No, I can't see too many loose ends of any consequence. The case is over, solved, lock, stock and barrel, thanks to you, so the party's on, Walter, the party's on.'

'If you say so, ma'am.'

'I do say, Walter. Anyway, you'll be pleased to know I have already invited the Floem woman. She rang before, said she wouldn't miss it for the world. I quite like her. She seems to have her finger on the pulse. You could do a lot worse. Now perhaps you could leave me to get on; I have my reports to write.'

Walter sighed and slurped what remained of his drink and bobbed his head and fled the room.

That night he sat slumped in his favourite armchair before the TV. It was on, and he was staring at the screen, but he wasn't watching. He was still working, pondering the case, thinking how lucky he had been to stumble on Sahira Khan's disappearance, because he patronised the State of Kerala.

Another unconnected thought entered his mind. The dirty dishes were piling up in the sink. He needed a new cleaner. He wondered how the much missed Galina Unpronounceable was getting on back in the Ukraine, or just Ukraine, no "the", as she insisted it should be said, and he recalled her pretty blue-eyed face admonishing him about that. You don't say "the" England, do you? Perhaps she had a point.

He glanced at his watch. 9.28pm. Pulled out his mobile and rang the office.

Gibbons answered, working the late shift, surprised to hear Walter's voice.

'Anything happening?'

'Nowt, Guv, quiet as the proverbial. You have a good rest, boss, you deserve it.'

'Could you come and pick me up?'

'What! You want to come back to work?'
'Might as well, I'm doing nothing here.'
'You sure about that?'
'Yeah, why not?'
'OK, Guv. If that's what you want. See you in twenty.'
'Thanks, Gibbons.'

Chapter Fifty-Three

The party began at 4pm. Everyone was there. Free drinks and snacks in HQ was a rare event, though the boots on the ground lot would have preferred beer to the gnats pee white wine on offer, and crisps and sausage rolls, to the fancy canapés that Mrs West's niece had rustled up at short notice. A considerable bill would be in the post before the day was out.

Chief Superintendent Gitts swallowed any chagrin he may have possessed and attended, indeed he brought two colleagues, the same pair Walter remembered had taken the original press conference in Manchester, smart uniforms, pristine medal ribbons, the look-a-like quiet man, and the forceful thirty something woman who drank juice, ate nothing, said little, and listened a lot. Ambition on legs, Walter surmised, he'd seen countless similar officers in his time. Perhaps Gitts should watch his back, maybe he already was, though Walter would be the last man to tell him.

Gitts made a beeline for Walter at the first moment, grabbing his sleeve and tugging him into a quiet corner.

'So come on, Darriteau, tell me how you got onto the Khan family?'

Walter didn't appreciate being addressed by his surname. Much preferred either Inspector or Walter, but at least he hadn't been called "Boy", something he'd often endured when he was a young uniformed bod, and sometimes until he was almost forty. But he swallowed any annoyance he possessed. Truth was, he was too tired to get annoyed.

'I had a bit of luck,' said Walter, sipping and grimacing. 'I happened to be a regular diner at the Khan's restaurant, and noticed Sahira was missing...'

355

'Thought so all along!' said Gitts, sweeping round and calling his female colleague over to share the news. 'It was pure coincidence! A fluke! No great detection at all.'

'I wouldn't have put it quite like that,' said Walter, finishing his wine. It seemed to get better the more one drank, as the Manchester officers moved away to collar someone else. Walter cast his eye across the large room filled almost to capacity. Gibbons was holding court, no doubt telling one of his mild, and sometimes not so mild, filthy jokes. Karen, Hector, Jenny, and a couple of others were gathered round. The women protesting they weren't interested in rude jokes, yet still desperate to hear the punch-line. They all burst into raucous laughter. Walter heard Karen say, still laughing, 'You are disgusting, Gibbons!'

The press were all there, too. The Liverpool Echo, Manchester Evening News, Chester Observer, Crewe Observer, and all the other little Observers, and a few other local titles too, some of the hacks relaxing, enjoying a drink and a laugh, some of them working. Even some of the London papers had sent people. There was always mileage in a good murder. Murders sold newspapers. Always had, always would, ever since Crippen. Fact was the public were as fascinated and intrigued with murders and murderers as they had ever been. Funny that, thought Walter, the general public couldn't get enough information and gossip about people who enjoyed going round killing people.

TV there too. Granada, BBC Northwest Tonight, and Sky. Several TV crews were hovering in the doorway, eager to get a better view, for it had been leaked that Mrs West would make a brief speech. Great! Walter couldn't wait. He'd enjoyed a sneak preview. He'd let himself into her office to find her practising before the glass, hand movements, eye contact, a clear, if somewhat strident voice, a winning combination in her eyes. Geez, thought Walter. Thank the Lord I'm not the senior officer.

Gardenia Floem entered the packed room. Smiled at one or two people close to the door, as if she knew them. Pushed her way through the thickening crowd to the drinks table. Helped herself to wine. Bumped into Mrs West, and the two of them enjoyed a chat, though Gardenia glanced over her shoulder a couple of times. Walter noticed that, as if she were looking for someone. Walter recalled the time he first set eyes on her. How was it? She was on the wrong side of forty, but not by much, auburn wavy hair parked on her shoulders, pretty face, nice teeth, quality dark green suit. Yep, that was about right.

He didn't go in for noting women's fashions, but his eye for detail recalled that green suit, and lo-and-behold there it was on display. It suited her, so to speak, fit her like a glove. She had a great figure, that was undeniable, as she stood with her back to him, talking to Hector. The young man probably thought he had a chance. No hope, son, Walter whispered. Find someone your own age, but then again, wasn't he hoping for the same thing, coming from the opposite end of the spectrum? It would keep Mrs West happy, if nothing else.

Gardenia glanced over her shoulder again. She wanted to be away from Hector, and that was understandable for he could be a boring twerp. He had the right name, but who was she looking for? She spotted Walter through the crowd, on the far side of the room, standing alone, hiding at the side of the monster; looking across at her. She smiled and mouthed a 'Hi', and in the next second made her apologies to Hector and began edging through the crowd and over toward where Walter was standing, holding an empty glass.

'There you are,' she said. 'For a moment I thought you'd chickened out and not come.'

'No such luck, Mizz Floem.'

'Oh Walter, call me Gardenia.'

Walter didn't answer.

'Big turn out,' she said.

'Yep, we can't miss Mrs West's big moment, can we, live on TV?'

'How exciting,' said Gardenia, glugging the drink, and noticing his glass was empty. 'Do you want another?' she said and answered her own question. 'You must have a drink, Walter. They might have a toast,' and she grabbed his bear-like paw and tugged him across the room towards the refreshment table where they loaded up on wine and canapés. Something very fishy he didn't appreciate. Mrs West, who rarely missed anything, didn't miss the pair of them crossing the room… holding hands. Just as she thought.

Mrs West stood in the centre of the room. At her request those around her backed away, leaving her alone in a clear circle, the centre of a halo from the TV lights. From somewhere she produced a metal dessert spoon and began thwacking her empty glass, Ping, Ping, Ding!!!

'Attention, everyone,' she called, smiling that well practised civil servant smile.

The crowd fell silent; her strident voice demanding it. She could stop a troop of police dogs dead with one command. Walter had witnessed her do it, and though she didn't actually say 'Sit!' to the gathered throng, Walter wouldn't have been surprised if she had.

'I'd just like to thank you all for coming today. There are a few people I would particularly like to thank. First, my super team, wonderfully led by Walter.'

'Go on, Guv!' yelled Gibbons, the wine doing its work.

Everyone stared at Walter. Gardenia beamed at him and touched his forearm. They were getting real pally, thought Karen, and not many missed that.

'And Karen too, of course,' continued Mrs West, and everyone looked at the striking blonde, including the TV crews, as she performed a silly curtsey in her beige cord jeans. 'For the wonderful way they solved the Sahira Khan murder and the Luke Flowers murder too, through sheer hard work and determination, finally bringing the perpetrators to trial. It goes without saying we were sad to hear what happened to Maaz Khan, and you can be sure there will be a full and thorough inquiry into that. I don't want to say anymore on that today. I'd also like to thank our friends and colleagues from Manchester who have taken the time and trouble to come over to be with us today,' and she bobbed her head and smirked at Gitts, and through gritted teeth he forced a smile back across the room, and raised his glass. The woman officer didn't smile, just looked plain surly, thought Walter, as if she'd endured a dreadful result.

'I would also like to thank the Chief Constable, Alan Marshall, who is with us today, and who has given me such great support in all things,' and everyone glanced at the grey-haired guy standing closest to Mrs W, a tall man who pulled a face and nodded once at the crowd, and then at the cameras, as everyone looked back at their drinks, as if to gaze upon him for too long was bad karma, 'and finally I would like to thank the local press and TV for all their help in these matters, even if, what shall we say, we don't always see eye-to-eye. But frank cooperation is the key, and especially to my new friend, Gardenia Floem, who has followed this case diligently right from the outset.'

Good God, thought Walter, whatever next?

He glanced at Gardenia's face, her white cheeks with a dash of rouge, and for a moment he imagined she was blushing. Gardenia smiled round at the throng, lifted her head and changed her profile for the TV cameras, determined to make the most of her newfound fame, as she glanced back at Mrs West and mouthed a big, 'Thank you,' and moved closer to Walter and whispered 'Well, that was a big surprise!'

'You can say that again.'

Mrs West was winding up.

'So thank you all again, and I believe those that want to, are going to The Bell afterwards, where I understand there will be a two hundred pound float behind the bar. Enjoy that while you can, and thank you again for your diligent hard work.'

'Yeah, ma'am!' yelled Gibbons, and Mrs West shot him her serious school ma'am look and Gibbons muttered back, 'Sorry, ma'am.'

It looked as if the speeches were over, but not quite.

Walter stepped into Mrs West's circle of light and muttered, 'May I say a few words, ma'am?'

Mrs West's eyebrows departed for the top of her head.

'Of course, Walter, if you feel the need, the floor's yours.'

'Go on, Guv!' yelled Gibbons.

'Shut up, Gibbons,' snapped Karen.

Walter stared at him, disgust writ large, and Gibbons snorted, looked away, and fell silent.

'I would just like to reiterate your words, ma'am, about our wonderful team who work very long hours for not too much money, who put their lives on the line every day of the week, who suffer abuse on a daily basis, and who have done such a fantastic job in bringing these matters towards their close. So please, give yourselves a good round of applause, you deserve it,' and they all did precisely that, bringing the house down, Gibbons cheering the loudest.

Walter was speaking again and the crowd hushed.

'But this case is not wrapped up, not complete or closed…'

Mrs West was heard to say, 'Oh no, Walter, not that again, not here, not today!'

But Walter was already talking again. 'I would just like to say there is still work to be done, so have a drink tonight, but not too much. There is more to do tomorrow, and lastly, I would like to say to our new-found friend, Gardenia Floem, loud and clear that… you are under arrest with regard to the murder of Jeffrey Player and the attempted murder of Neil Swaythling.'

Chapter Fifty-Four

Mouths popped open, yet no one said a word. There was a moment of stunned silence throughout the room, before Mrs West said, 'Oh Walter! Don't spoil things. You will have your little joke.'

'No joke, ma'am.'

'I know you don't like the woman, but this is ridiculous.'

Gardenia smirked. 'So you don't like me, eh, Walter? I am surprised.'

'I am only interested in facts, Mizz Floem, nothing else.'

They all stared at Gardenia's puzzled face, including the cameras.

Then she said, 'What are you talking about, Walter?'

'It's Inspector Darriteau, to you. There was always something nagging me about this case. It was only in the last couple of days that the pieces began falling into place.'

'Go on!' commanded Mrs West. 'And it had better be good.'

'I think the guy's going senile,' said Gardenia, laughing it off. 'It's time he was put out to grass.'

But everyone else wanted to hear what Walter had to say.

'I'd always been puzzled how Mizz Floem here could have arrived at the scene of the Jeff Player murder so quickly. The answer, of course, is that she knew the murder was about to happen; she was probably waiting in her car around the corner. Oh, she didn't pull the trigger, Luke Flowers did that, no one is saying she did. But she's just as responsible, more so in my view, for she commissioned the murder, either directly, or more likely through an intermediary, and she couldn't have foreseen that the wrong man had caught the bullet, and she couldn't tell who had been slain, she didn't know there had been a disastrous mistake, because by the time she arrived

361

in the bar the doctor had ordered the body covered, and Neil, the intended target, was long gone.'

'And motive?' said Gardenia, glancing around for support.

'I'm coming to that.'

'Better be good, Walter,' said Mrs West.

Walter bobbed his head and continued.

'When I visited Langley Wells office, I saw a photograph on his wall. It was taken on a jolly holly in Valletta, Malta, and there they were, Langley and all his Masonic chums.'

The Chief Constable pursed his lips and wondered what was coming next. Mrs West pulled a big lined face.

'Gerry Swaythling was in the pic too, Neil's father, the builder bloke. He had his arms around two women. This was a good few years ago, and hairstyles and fashions have changed, which is why I didn't immediately recognise that one of those women, the brunette, was none other than our Mizz Floem here, was it not?'

Everyone turned back to Gardenia. Cameramen began jostling for a better view.

'No,' she said, 'well, yes, but... that means nothing and proves nothing either.'

'There's your motive, ma'am. Gerry Swaythling changes his women like I change my shirt. It was only a matter of time before Gardenia was out, and the newer, younger model was in. How does the phrase go? Hell hath no fury like a woman scorned. Pretty apt, I'd say. Gardenia thought it would be a great idea to have Neil Swaythling blown away to get even with Gerry. That's the sum of it. Pretty good motive, I'd say.'

'You don't know what you are talking about!' yelled Gardenia.

'I think I do. Only yesterday the pieces fell into place. Mrs West told me she had invited you to this soiree, and spoilsport that I am, and I'm sorry, ma'am,' and he nodded at Mrs West, 'but something told me you didn't belong here. So I rang the Chester Observer to ask you not to come, and what am I told? They did not know who Gardenia Floem was, let alone employ a person of that name. Is there anyone here from that newspaper?'

Everyone stared around.

362

A young man in his twenties holding a tablet computer held up his hand.

'And your name is?'

'Alan McCaughey.'

'And you work for the Observer?'

'I do.'

'As what?'

'Chief crime reporter.'

'And do you know this woman?'

'No, I don't. I have never seen her before.'

Gardenia sighed in an exaggerated manner.

'You're fixing the facts to fit your case. It's nothing really. That was just a joke, about being a crime reporter. I was interested in police work, I'm writing a book about it, that's all. I found it glamorous, if you must know, still do, to be honest.'

'Yes, I'll bet you do. But let's move on. Last night I needed to use the computers, various things I wanted to check, so I asked Gibbons to come and pick me up. Interesting things, computers. What an amazing contraption the Internet is. Mine of information, if you know where to look. Floem isn't your birth name, is it?'

'Well no, what of it?'

'And your maiden name is?'

'Dennis.'

'Precisely. And you married one August Floem in Munich, possibly on the rebound from being dumped by Gerry Swaythling.'

'You don't know what you are talking about.'

'I think I do. What happened to August Floem?'

'He fell down the stairs.'

'Yes, that's what Interpol told me, fell down the stairs and broke his neck and died. Though whether he fell or was pushed is open to conjecture. Either way, you'll be delighted to know the German police, the Bundespolizei, will be re-examining the case. Married for seven months, large life insurance policy, August meets his unplanned and untimely end, and a brooding Mizz Floem arrives back in the UK, bearing funds aplenty, seeking revenge. Isn't that what happened, Gardenia?'

'You haven't a clue! I've always had money! And I have heard quite enough of this.'

'Not yet, Mizz Floem. What was Veronica Camberwell's maiden name?'

'How the hell would I know? And who is she anyway?'

'Oh, come now, Mizz Floem, this isn't a time for lies, don't be bashful. Veronica's maiden name is Dennis, the same as yours, and that's no surprise... because you are sisters.'

Karen glanced from Gardenia to Walter and back at the Floem woman, and back at her boss. Where the hell had he obtained this information, and why hadn't he shared his thoughts with her, and how come she hadn't picked up on the same things? And while she was thinking of that, Walter was talking again.

'You fell out with your sister, didn't you?'

'Did I?'

'You know full well you did, and I will tell you why. You haven't always had money at all, and when your father died he left everything to her, didn't he? Didn't leave you a bean, while Veronica did very nicely, thank you.'

'He always preferred her!'

'Yes, so it would seem, and that anger in your heart, and in your head, festered until you could stand it no longer, and when an opportunity came along to get even with Gerry Swaythling and Veronica at the same time, you couldn't resist it. Using your ill-gotten gains you thought you'd take away the one thing that Gerry and Veronica loved more than anything, the young man, Neil. Sad thing is, an innocent young man stood in the way and paid the ultimate price.'

'They deserved it! They bloody well deserved it!' she screamed, and she stared round, stunned by her own lack of self control, and realising what she had said, she bolted for the double doors. In the surreal atmosphere, no one thought to stop her. The cameramen and TV people were too busy filming the scene to intervene. It would make the best live news show since anyone could remember.

'Don't worry,' said Walter. 'She won't get far.'

And she didn't.

364

Gibbons had been forced to leave the room, not that he wanted to, but the copious amounts of wine he'd taken on board in double quick time had driven him to the Men's room, and as he came out Gardenia ran slap bang into his muscular frame, almost knocking him over.

'Where are you going, my garden girl?' he said. 'I think Guv might have a few more questions for you,' and he grabbed her wrist and tugged her back into the glare of the arc lights.

Mrs West was tapping her glass again.

'Well thank you everybody for coming, hope you enjoyed it, and I'll see any of you who are going to The Bell a little later.'

'Gibbons, take her to interview room three,' ordered Walter, nodding at Gardenia.

'Walter! My office!' shrilled Mrs West.

Walter clicked his lips like a reprimanded schoolboy and bobbed his head, something that Mrs West didn't see, as she had turned tail and was last seen opening the door to her large room. Walter grinned at Karen, and mouthed, 'See you later.'

Chapter Fifty-Five

Mrs West was standing behind her desk, arms folded across her chest. She didn't look happy at all, as Walter sauntered in. 'Sit down!' she said, and she ambled over to the large window and stared out at the green sward far below that ran down to the twisting river Dee.

She didn't say anything for a moment, just sighed heavy. Walter examined her back. She looked pretty good from the rear, he hadn't noticed that before, especially in that beige long tight skirt, or was it pink, he couldn't tell. Maybe it was time for an eye test.

'Do you mind telling me what that was all about?'

'Ma'am?'

'Don't act the innocent with me! You have embarrassed me in front of my entire team, and those buggers from Manchester, and all on live local television!'

'Sorry, ma'am, but I didn't mean to embarrass you.'

'You did, Walter, you did!'

'Sorry, ma'am.'

She snorted like an irritated sow and said, 'What was the thinking behind that performance?'

'As I said, ma'am, it was only in the last twenty-four hours it started falling into place.'

'And it didn't cross your mind to inform me of your findings?'

'I wanted to keep it until I was certain. I wanted to keep it as a surprise...'

'Well you did that, all right!'

'It was mainly circumstantial, ma'am. I was trying to trick her into confessing in front of everyone.'

'And you think you did?'

'Pretty much, yes.'

'Oh, Walter, you are such an oaf sometimes,' and she came round and slumped in her vast chair.

'I just wanted your big day to be crowned with a definite result.'

'Well you did that all right too! No one will ever forget it!'

A knock came to the door and before Mrs West could answer, the door opened and Chief Superintendent Gitts showed his head round the door and said, 'We are just on our way, Joan. Just thought I'd say a final thank you,' and he glanced down at the rebuked Walter and said, 'How's the naughty boy doing?'

'He'll live, if he's lucky! Anyway, thanks again for coming.'

'My pleasure,' he grinned, and closed the door.

'Gitts by name, git by nature,' she muttered.

'Can't argue with that, ma'am.'

'Now, where were we?'

'You said that no one would ever forget it.'

'Well that's true! In future, Walter, you discuss with me first your theories and thinking before you broadcast it to the entire world. Clear?'

'Yes, ma'am.'

'Are you going down to The Bell?'

'I will be, ma'am, it would be rude not to. But first I want a good go at Mizz Floem, so to speak, to see if she has any more gems to share with us.'

'Don't tell me there are still more loose ends to tie up?'

'Minor ones, ma'am.'

'Such as?'

'Such as, who supplied the gun, was there a middle man involved between her and Luke Flowers, and where in all this does Mr Jermaine Keating fit? Because his name keeps cropping up.'

'Well, good luck with that, but I have a feeling we have just about got to the bottom of it.'

'You're probably right, ma'am.'

'I may see you down there, don't leave it too long or the float will be exhausted.'

Walter took his cue and stood and went to the door.

'And Walter?'

'Yes, ma'am?'

'Well done, now get out of here.'

He bobbed his head and smiled and headed down to the interview room where Karen was setting up ready.

They arrived in The Bell an hour later. The place was packed, and the TV was on.

'Turn it up, Gibbons!' someone shouted, and he obliged.

The early evening news programmes were beginning.

'Here it is!' yelled Gibbons, and in the next moment Mrs West's opening speech was hurtling through the air, just as she came into the bar and stood beside Walter and Karen.

'Oh, no,' she said.

'You looked great,' said Karen, and Walter wondered if she meant it, or was saying it to make her feel better.

A moment later Walter was on the big screen and Gibbons led the cheering. Walter hid behind the big pint of stout Gibbons had thrust into his hand. On the screen Walter was talking.

They did not know who Gardenia Floem was, let alone employed a person of that name.

Mrs West rolled her eyes and sipped her gin and glanced away.

Then Gardenia herself.

They deserved it! They BLEEP BLEEP deserved it!

'Case proven, I'd say,' said Gibbons.

'Did you really not like her, Walter?' asked Mrs West.

'She irritated me.'

Karen sighed, not believing what he said.

'Just for a moment when you said, *and lastly I would just like to say to our new-found friend Gardenia Floem...* I thought you were going to propose to her, or tell us all your happy news.'

'Don't be absurd, Karen!'

'I thought that too!' said Gibbons.

'How easily led you all are,' said Walter, sinking half of his pint in one visit.

Karen and Mrs West exchanged knowing glances.

'Has she confessed?' asked Gibbons.

'Pretty much,' said Karen.

'She wants to do a deal,' said Walter. 'She'll name the fixer, the armourer, tell us everything she knows about that and other things too, providing we go easy on her.'

'We don't do deals!' said Mrs West.

'Course we don't,' said Walter, 'but I'd like to nail one or two more villains while the opportunity's there.

Thankfully the news item was over. Hector shouted, 'Turn it on the other side, it'll be on there in a sec,' and sure enough it was, and they all had to endure it all over again.

In the morning Karen looked dreadful.

'Heavy night?' asked Walter.

'Not really,' she said a bit too quickly, and Walter knew she hadn't had much sleep. She must have realised he knew that, and added, 'It was, if you must know, we all ended up going to some dance club, bobbing till dawn. I can still hear that heavy techno beat thumping in my bones.'

'The pleasures of the young,' he said, unable to keep a satisfied smile creeping over his flabby face.

'We're only young once,' she mumbled.

Too true. Thank God.

'Anyway, I have a job for you this morning. We have an arrest to make.'

'We do?'

'We certainly do.'

'Who?'

'Get a car organised and I'll show you.'

'Marked or unmarked?'

'Un!'

'OK, Guv,' and she shoved off, and as she did he said, 'I'll be down in ten.'

It was a nice Ford, pretty new, no sign of vomit on the back seat, which was always a plus, and she was standing beside it in her neat black jeans and white blouse. Hungover or not, she looked classy.

'Can I ask you something, Guv?'

'Sure.'

'Would you mind driving today?'

It wasn't what he thought she was going to say.

He pulled a face and held out his hand for the key.

'Don't make a habit of it.'

'Thanks, Guv.'

He drove across the city to the Red Rose Motel.

'Mary Hussein, right?' she said, as he pulled into the car park.

'Correct.'

'On what charge?'

'Aiding and abetting, perverting the course of justice, accessory before the fact, obstructing the police, wasting police time, take your pick.'

Karen jumped from the car, while he eased from the vehicle, and they walked toward the main entrance.

'Do you want to arrest her?' asked Walter.

'Sure, Guv.'

'Be my guest.'

It would give her arrest stats a welcome boost, and she deserved it.

'Thanks.'

Inside, they bumped into the manager, Jack Heale.

'Not more questions,' he whined, glancing at his watch.

'No questions today,' said Walter, 'just solving murders, one of which took place on these premises.'

'Yes well...'

He couldn't say anything else because the officers were at the reception desk, staring across at Mary Hussein.

'Mary Hussein?' said Karen.

'I don't recognise that name,' she said, 'My name is now Tanzeela.'

'Not under English law, love. You are under arrest for aiding and abetting murder, and perverting the course of justice,' and with that,

Karen opened the end of the counter, stepped through and asked the girl to get her things together.

'But she can't go now!' protested Heale.

Walter pulled a face, a face that said, oh, but she can.

'Who's going to do the bookings? We are short-staffed as it is!'

'Employ more people, Mr Heale, that's what the country needs. More people like you to employ more people. At the end of the day, it's all about people, there's nowt else.'

'Will she be back later?'

'No idea, but I wouldn't count on it.'

'Oh, for Pete's sake.'

'He won't help you either.'

Karen led Mary back to the car and saw her safely into the back seat. Walter fell into the front. Found the key. Located the hole. Managed to insert it. Turned the key. Looked up and ahead. A young woman was approaching, pretty girl, coming on fast, looked as if she meant business, looked as if she was late.

'Hang on a sec,' said Walter, and he turned off the engine and heaved himself out of the car.

Iskra Kolarov saw him coming. History told her to always be wary of the police, even in England. What could he want now? Her papers were in order, she had a visa, she had a work permit. She hadn't done anything wrong, that she knew of, yet she still felt uneasy. The big black man worried her, and he was standing right in front of her, obstructing her way to work where she was already one minute late.

In the car, Karen and Mary watched the conversation from thirty metres away. It began with stern faces and concern, but they soon turned to smiles and nods and thank you's, and ended with Walter giving her a card and touching her arm.

Back in the car, Karen said, 'What was that all about?'

'Need a new cleaner, Iskra's starting on Sunday. Lovely girl.'

'Iskra, is it?' teased Karen. 'She's far too young for you.'

'Don't be ridiculous,' and he started the car and pointed it toward HQ.

The following day would be the hottest day of the year. At Police HQ all the windows were wide open. The air conditioning wasn't working again, and even the monster was working slow.

Karen clasped the top of her blouse and gave it a good shake.

'So?' she said. 'Is that it, everything squared off?'

'Pretty much,' said Walter. 'Gardenia realised her only hope was to come clean and help us as much as she could. She's named the armourer cum fixer as one Jimmy Mitchell.'

'And he's known to us?'

'Oh, yes.'

'Do you want us to pick him up?'

'We'll do that later.'

'Here's his address. Get the paperwork ready, search warrants, the full McCoy.'

'Sure, Guv.'

'But better than that, she's implicating the sister, Veronica Camberwell in various misdemeanours. She knew Mitchell too, and I think that will lead us to Keating.'

'Why didn't you tell me what you knew?'

'I didn't know anything, not really, just lots of pieces that didn't fit together. Truth is, I took a bit of a punt.'

'A bit of a punt! You were damned lucky, then.'

'Mmm, maybe, but once I discovered she wasn't a reporter all the bits fell into place.'

'Not sure I would have come to the same conclusions, if you weren't here, that is.'

'Well, I am here, Karen, and I'm not going anywhere just yet. Leastways, I hope not.'

'Do you want a coffee?'

'Love one.'

The sound of sirens waved across the old city and flowed in through the open glass. Walter stood up and limped toward the window. She'd meant to ask him about that, the limp, and made a mental note not to forget. He stood in front of the glass and gazed across at the inner ring road.

'Even money it's the fire department,' said Karen, 'in this weather. Probably some bedding set alight by the sun shining in through the glass.'

'You've just lost your bet. It's our guys, two cars, heading south toward Wrexham as if their lives depend on it.'

'Wonder what's going on there. Want me to find out?'

'Too right. And why don't we know about it, anyway?'

'Probably some burglar alarm gone off in a big house in Rossett.'

'I wanna know,' he said.

But he always wanted to know. He fed on cases like a silkworm on mulberry leaves, and despite his age and build he showed no sign of slowing down. He glanced back at her. She'd given up on the coffee and was on the phone, trying to find out what was going on. Walter sighed. He hoped it would be an interesting case. Please God, not some snotty-nosed sixteen-year-old burglar with half a brain. Give us something more testing than that.

Chapter Fifty-Six

Mohammed Khan pleaded guilty to the double murder of his daughter Sahira, and Luke Flowers. The judge sympathised with the man who had acted with great dignity and honesty throughout the trial. She took into consideration his previous impeccable record, but in the end, handed down the only sentence she could.

Life imprisonment. With good behaviour it was possible that Mr Khan could be out in twelve years.

Gardenia Floem suffered a similar fate. She'd fulfilled her side of the bargain, so far as she saw it, and told Walter everything she knew, and that information proved invaluable. Walter attended every day of the trials and testified on her behalf, reiterating how helpful she had been. Before the same judge, facing charges of murder and attempted murder, she received the same sentence. Her information had been helpful, but the law's the law, and murder is murder.

'Thank you,' she mouthed across the packed courtroom to Walter, words accompanied by a warm smile.

Walter nodded back, and whether he knew he smiled, only he could tell say. Afterwards he visited her in prison. He still does, once every month. The two have become quite close, in a platonic way.

On Sunday night, just over a week after her trial, Walter remembered he hadn't done a shop. The house was bright and shiny, thanks to Iskra Kolarov, but there was nothing in for dinner. He hobbled upstairs, took a wash, shaved, and slipped on a clean shirt. Came back down, slipped on his lightweight jacket and let himself out. The bus stop was at the end of the road and his luck was in. The bus came within a minute. He hauled himself onboard and rode the handful of stops into the city.

He got off at the railway station and headed down Brook Street toward the State of Kerala. The lights were on, business as usual. Sundays were always a good night at the State because many other restaurants closed early, or didn't open at all. Walter hurried by, glanced in the windows. It was pretty busy, maybe half full. He walked to the end of the road, turned and limped back, and passed by. He couldn't bring himself to go inside. His stomach rumbled. He was getting hungrier, and limped back.

Inside, Wazir was sitting in his favourite seat. He'd finished his evening meal, and he'd eaten alone. He often did, for Ahmed was busy running things, and the others were gone. He had been reflecting on his life. People often said he had lived an eventful life, and that was true. There can't be many families with double murders at either end of their adult lives. His parents incinerated by angry Hindus, his great granddaughter, murdered by her own kind, and then that confused and angry young man, Luke Flowers, who had made his fortune by taking the lives of others, before perishing by the sword. What a senseless waste. What an incredible mess.

Despite everything, Britain had been good to him and his family. He recalled that inauspicious start, so many years before, those foul mouthed and angry dock workers, snarling, *Fuck off back to where you came from! We don't want youse lot round here!'* And that invaluable first job given to him by Jimmy Mac, and how Wazir had repaid him by stealing from the public purse, every day for several years. The thought of it made Wazir shiver, and he tried to erase the shame of it from his mind. He hoped there was still time to repair the damage done there, and one day he would set matters straight. He took out his diary to make a note, then heard the main doors open. A customer, and that was always good news. A ticking till still had the power to make him happy.

Walter returned to the outside of the Kerala. Turned left, up the single stone step. Reached out and pushed open the brass and glass doors, stepped inside, wiped his feet on the copra mat. Breathed in that unmistakable aroma of the best food the subcontinent offered.

375

There was a gentle hum of conversation, perhaps half the tables were taken; it was half-past eight, so there was plenty of time.

He stepped forward onto the deep pile maroon carpet, almost disappeared into it. The half moon bar was right ahead, eight chrome stools set before it, three or four taken, people studying menus, sipping drinks, peering into lover's eyes, perhaps treating a partner to a birthday surprise. But would Walter be made welcome? The display case on the wall was empty, the spotlights switched off. The new sword was in police custody and might never be returned, while the original was unaccounted for, sleeping out of sight of the wicked world.

Wazir glanced up from his maroon State of Kerala restaurant diary. He had finished eating and was jotting a few notes. He saw the policeman, standing alone, looking confused and forlorn. Wazir struggled to his feet and ambled across the restaurant.

'Walter,' he said, offering his hand.

'I wasn't sure I'd be made welcome.'

'Don't be absurd, you're an honourable man. You were only doing your duty. You will always be welcomed here.'

'Thank you, Wazir,' said Walter, shaking Wazir's icy hand for some time.

'Come,' said Wazir, 'come and join me, I have just finished, but you can eat with me, if you so desire.'

'I do desire, Wazir, I do.'

They sat down, the near sixty-year-old, and the near ninety-year-old, and it was debatable who possessed the most creaking bones.

They talked about everything and nothing. The Punjabi kid came and took the order, and then Walter said, 'Off the record, did you know about the murders?'

Wazir paused and thought. He could be wired, the policeman, though he thought not.

'No, Walter, I didn't.'

'I didn't think so, Wazir, and I believe you.'

'I'm glad.'

'And the sword, the original. Where's that?'

'Please don't ask me a question I cannot answer.'

'I understand.'

'And the phone? What happened to that?'

Wazir pondered the question; then answered.

'I found the phone in a can of sugar. I went to turn it on, but knew I did not wish to see pictures of our unfortunate young woman. Whatever had driven her to such a place, whatever evil might have been involved, I knew if I were to see such pictures, those images would have remained with me forever. I didn't want that, and she didn't deserve it. I took the phone to the kitchens and set it in the gas oven, and watched it burn to nothing. Did I do wrong, Walter? Am I too now a criminal?'

Walter pulled a face.

'Technically, yes. Destroying evidence is a serious offence, but that will not affect the case now. It is all over and done with, and besides, you could deny you ever said and did such a thing. It would only be your word against mine.'

'Your word is weightier than mine, Walter, but I make no bones about it, that's a relief. It has been preying on my mind, bringing me sleeplessness.'

'Forget it,' said Walter. 'It's finished.'

The old man deserved a little peace.

The main doors opened again and Austerity Hayes and Harry bustled inside.

'There!' she exclaimed. 'Darriteau's back!' and they hustled toward the table.

Walter and Wazir shared a look.

Wazir smiled and said, 'I'll leave you to your friends.'

Walter rolled his eyes, and Austerity pulled out a chair.

'Thought you'd deserted us, you old rogue,' she said. 'Glad you're back, anyhow, enjoy your company,' and she patted him on the back.

Walter and Harry exchanged glances and nods, as Austerity told them about her latest effort to spend her inheritance.

'I've booked six weeks in egg-wiped,' she said, laughing beneath that ridiculous bonnet that appeared welded to her head. 'It was the

British soldiers who first christened it that in the Great War. They couldn't say eee-jipt,' she explained, 'poor loves!'

Harry smiled at Walter, a begging smile that asked him to bear with the woman, and she was already talking again.

'And you'll never guess what?'

'What?' said Walter, right on cue, keen to humour the woman.

'They've booked us all a trek into the desert... aboard camels!'

Walter and Harry laughed, and Austerity said the thought that came to both of their heads.

'It'll have to be a big bugger to carry me!'

Walter glanced at Harry whose head was twitching in second time.

'Why don't you come with me, Darriteau?'

Walter glugged on his beer and stared at the tablecloth.

'Too busy, I'm afraid.'

Austerity snorted and said, 'Too bad. It would be fun!'

There were plenty of women Walter would like to go on holiday with, and plenty that he would not. But those he wanted to, didn't or wouldn't, and vice versa, and in a way that summed up his life in a sentence. It was a conundrum that he'd never come to terms with.

Austerity continued to tell them of her latest wheeze to spend her funds while she was still alive.

'If I don't spend it quick, the Crown will nick it!' she said.

Harry's tongue was clicking aloud, second time. Walter didn't have the heart to tell him. Austerity was rushing through her story at a rate of knots of the childcare facility in the poorest part of the city that had its funding withdrawn. She stepped in and guaranteed to cover the bill for four years.

'I read about it in the Observer,' she said. 'In the bloody paper! And Darriteau! I'm not taking no for an answer this time, I'm paying!' and she wafted her podgy hand across the table.

Walter and Harry shared a smile.

'We are living in a time of great austerity,' she said, 'and the great Austerity is alive and well and ready for anything,' she whooped, and that was that.

'If you insist,' muttered Walter.

Sometimes graciousness overtakes pride.

They sat and listened to the woman, as she made her way through most of the menu, sometimes eating and speaking at the same time, but Walter's mind drifted away. He began thinking about the case, about Wazir and Ahmed and Mohammed and Maaz, about Luke Flowers and Jermaine Keating, Gardenia Floem and Sahira Khan, because Walter was a thinking man. It was the thing he did best. It was the one attribute that made him the best detective in Chester, and beyond. Imagination, and deep thought, a potent combination.

Austerity was still eating, speaking, and talking for England. Walter half tuned in. Thought he heard her say: Tomorrow I'm going to eat an Egyptian, though he might have been mistaken. Tuned out again. He'd heard enough. Returned to his thoughts.

He valued his mind above all else, and consoled himself that it would last a year or two yet. He wasn't yet ready for the home for retired and retarded minds. Nowhere near. Thanks be to God. Walter caught the eye of the handsome Punjabi kid and ordered the biggest jug of beer they could find. The kid smiled and nodded and turned back to the bar. The world moved on. There would be another fascinating case along in a day or two. There always was.

The End

Author's Notes

Thank you for buying and reading my book and I hope you enjoyed it. Please don't write and tell me the main police station in Chester is no longer set in the city centre – I know that, but that is the joy of writing fiction. The writer can set buildings and events wherever the heck he or she desires. As far as Walter Darriteau and his team are concerned, it still looks out over the green Roodee.

When you have a few spare minutes, I would appreciate it if you placed a brief review, a single paragraph will suffice, on any of the main book sales sites. That would be kind of you.

If you would like to read more about Walter Darriteau and the gang make sure you catch the first book, "The Murder Diaries – Seven Times Over", which is out now, and there are others now ready for your eyes – "The Twelfth Apostle" which takes Walter and the team into the dark world of modern day slavery, and "Kissing a Killer" which is a whodunnit that will keep you guessing right to the end.

Next year there will be an all new full-length Walter Darriteau case released, God willing, and I am very excited about that, and so is he.

As ever, all and any mistakes in this book are mine and mine alone. You can contact me on any matter at my website www.davidcarterbooks.co.uk Thank you for supporting independent writers and publishers. Without you we would all vanish.

Have a great day wherever you may be,

David.

Made in the USA
Middletown, DE
09 August 2023

36418757R00215